PRAISE FOR HOUSE OF HYBRIDS

"In *House of Hybrids*, Savannah J. Goins delivers an exhilarating sequel to her much-beloved *Whisper of Weapons*. Reader beware: the heart-pounding action, political intrigue, swoony romance, and captivating magic system abounding in these pages will keep you reading into all hours of the night. Prepare for loved ones to ask why you look so tired by keeping a copy handy that you can then shove into their hands while ordering them to read this series!"
 —**Chelsea Bobulski, author of *The Wood* and *Remember Me***

"*House of Hybrids* is a stunning continuation in the Castors of Wrynford series. This masterful sequel features relatable and likeable POV characters that tug at your heartstrings and villains you'll love to hate. With plenty of mystery and no-spice romance, readers won't want to miss all of the feels!"
 —**Holly Davis, author of *A Diamond Bright and Broken***

"*House of Hybrids* is an adventurous new sequel to *Whisper of Weapons*! Savannah Goins artfully weaves action, heart, and a touch of romance into a fun coming-of-age story for YA readers. Get House of Hybrids for your personal library to experience a fantastic new world!"
 —**J.M. Hackman, author of *The Firebrand Chronicles***

House of Hybrids, book two of the Castors of Wrynford saga, is a high-stakes fantasy with swoony romance, thrilling adventure, and magical twists that will leave you breathless and ready for more!
—Julia Simpson, author of *Ashes Swept*

"If its predecessor was a tribute to friendship and found family, then *House of Hybrids* is its perfect sequel as a tribute to love in every form. Blossoming romance, the unbreakable bonds between friends, and the journey of self-respect forge the beating heart of this unforgettable tale. Full of personal and plot-centric twists and shocking revelations about characters we've grown to love, *House of Hybrids* will have you gasping, cheering, sobbing, and swooning until the very last page!"
—R. Dugan, author of *The Starchaser Saga* and *Tales of Wonder and Woe*

"Wholesome and heartfelt, Savannah J. Goins's vivid animal characters steal the show yet again in this fun follow-up to *Whisper of Weapons*."
—Shayla Morgansen, author of *The Elm Stone Saga* and *Shadow Kin Chronicles*

HOUSE OF HYBRIDS

HOUSE OF HYBRIDS

THE CASTORS OF WRYNFORD BOOK TWO

SAVANNAH J. GOINS

ZURRENBELG
PERLEON SEA
TERRENTHYRS
WRYNFORD
Coliseum
Emberlyn Forest
POLFRYTH CITY
copr. 2022 Jessica Khoury

THE CASTORS OF WRYNFORD
LARZANOBYL
Deadland Dunes
MORRENFAYRE
Fossil Gulley

Chapter 1

REENALYN

Being a head taller than most guys was generally a good thing. It was convenient for spotting someone in a crowd, a wonderful advantage in hand-to-hand combat, and useful for reaching things on high shelves.

But if I could change one thing about myself, I'd knock off a solid span. Maybe a few more specks for good measure.

Intimidating every guy didn't help any of them fall in love with you, after all.

Eyeing a tall dark-haired guy about my age, I considered him as he tossed sacks of wheat from one wooden cart to another.

He was already taken—I felt it as we passed him. As were the two bow hunters striding down the cobblestones toward the Emberlyn Forest. One of them was a little old for me, but the other was my age.

Also already in love.

Not a guess. Not pessimism. I could just tell when someone was in love.

And people often were. *Quite* often.

But never with me.

Not for lack of Cupid's trying, though. My five-span-long green iguana castling enjoyed sitting on my shoulders, his tail curled around my arm, pointing out possible love interests.

While I might change things about myself, I wouldn't change a thing about him. My best friend, my battle ally, and my confidant. If anyone tried to change him to fit their mold, I would end them.

No one could touch my castling.

My boots clacking against the cobblestones, I inhaled the scent of The Braided Loaf's fresh bread. *Maybe if I became a better cook...*

"What about *him*?" Cupid whispered, pointing one scaly, clawed finger across the road. A light-haired guy on the threshold of the butcher shop tied string around a bundle and handed it to a patron with a nice smile.

I considered him for a moment, not feeling very hopeful. "He's already in love."

Cupid sighed, slapping his face with his emerald lizard hand and probably rolling his eyes.

I smiled wryly. "I'm sorry, Cupid, but it is what it is."

"Reenalyn, you can't use the same skunk-dung line five times in a row and expect me to keep buying it."

I laughed, stepping over a hole in the road. "I'm not making it up, Cupid. He's already taken."

"Ah, but you can't actually know *that*." He waved a knowing finger at me. "You can only know how *he* feels. Not how someone feels about him. Maybe he's hopelessly in love with someone who doesn't return his affection. I bet he would get over her quickly if he met you."

I rolled my eyes. "You're right—I can't know every facet of a romantic feeling. But he's *happily* in love. Not frustrated. So I can guess whoever she is feels the same."

The man whistled as we passed.

I pointed my thumb over my shoulder. "See? Happy."

"What about those guys, then?" He nodded toward a group of guys laughing around a table in front of The Braided Loaf.

"Hmm...it's hard to tell height from this distance, but two of them are several specks taller than the others. By the torso at least."

Cupid perked up. "Mm-hmm..."

Laughing, I shook my head. "Nope."

"Reenalyn."

"No, really. Both are happily taken."

He grumbled. "What about the other three, then? They can't possibly *all* be in love already."

You might be surprised. Seems everyone is.

One of them met my eyes as we strolled past. I slowed a step, wondering...but his eyes drifted away, following a different girl walking in the opposite direction.

I wrinkled my nose and looked away. He was sort of infatuated with a lot of people. Like Kaido Felzane. *Not for me.*

"Come on, Reenalyn. How important is height, really? In the grand scheme of things? The female is the taller one in many animal couples. It's perfectly normal."

"It's not important to *me*. I'm not so shallow. It's important to *them*. That's the problem. Standing next to all six spans and five specks of me makes them look less manly. They seem to think so, anyway."

"Then we will find you someone whose manliness is not dependent on his stature."

I grinned. "That's a fabulous idea, Cupid. Or maybe I'll find a potion to shrink me to a normal size."

"Reenalyn Demensey, if anyone takes it upon themselves to try to change you to fit their ideals, I will have to end them."

I couldn't help giggling. "Just over shortening me a span? That seems a bit drastic."

"Anyone who thinks you're less than perfect exactly as you are doesn't deserve you. Or the ability to craft potions. Or breathe."

Emotion pricked my eyes. "Cupid, was that something heartfelt—or dare I say, *sweet*—you just said?"

"Of course not. Simply stating facts. Besides, I can see much better from here on your shoulders. I wouldn't be able to see as well if you were a span shorter. I'm speaking out of pure selfishness, here."

Though he faced away from me, I could tell from his voice he was probably smirking. But there would be warmth in his eyes.

"Well, if anyone tries to change you, rest assured I'll end them very permanently for you as well."

He harrumphed and repositioned his feet on my shoulder, curling his tail a little tighter around my arm.

I grinned, soaking up sunbeams on my skin. "Silly lizard."

CHAPTER 2

ACRES

Eyeing Trinka Seranova, I took a controlled breath, willing my exasperation away. I focused on Starstinger's soft ocher fur, laid my hand over her back, and counted how many ink-black spots I could touch at once.

"It doesn't make sense. Why?" Trinka drummed her fingers on her arms as she sat glowering on the foot of my bed.

I'd come to Wrynford a year and a half ago to *escape* floramancy, and since arriving, I'd barely done anything besides mess around with potions. And even *that* wasn't enough. *Four, five, six...*

A growl roiled in Starstinger's stomach, vibrating against my arm.

"Because, Trinka, I'm not a brilliant potion master, and I hate floramancy. That combination makes it difficult to figure out a potion for you." I sighed, stroking Starstinger behind the ears. I was glad to have been able to help defeat Narellen and restore so many peoples' memories four months ago—that was worth the endless brainstorming and frustrating experiments.

But none of those headaches had done anything so far to help Trinka with the nightmares endangering her castling's life.

She put her bald head in her hands, two sets of spiked knuckles gleaming against her dark skin.

"I'm sorry, Trinka. I want to help you remove the bad memories and protect Mauler, but I've tried everything I can think of. I can't take the memories away, and I can't turn off the nightmares they cause. And I certainly can't invent something to prevent you from needing sleep."

I'd run out of ideas more than once, but each time I considered the potential danger her nightmares posed to Mauler, I dug a little deeper and found another thing to try.

But nothing worked. Not the deecho fern, or any other leaf, stem, petal, or root. I'd managed to create a pelinary petals potion that seemed to be good for thwarting memory-altering potions, which was certainly beneficial in general.

But not for Trinka and Mauler.

Trinka crossed her arms, the thick muscles of her biceps standing out in contrast to her short stature. "Thanks for trying, Parrianther. I appreciate your effort."

Her dark eyes were weary and worried, and guilt flared once again. But what else could I do? "You're welcome. I wish I could've found something useful."

With a silent nod, she slid from the foot of the bed and vanished out the window quick as a flash.

My shoulders slumped as I lifted Starstinger from my lap and stepped away from the desk to fling myself over the bed. I set her next to me as I sprawled out with one arm by my side and one bent behind my head, closing my tired eyes.

"You're too stressed," Starstinger said. She circled a few times, then nestled in a little coal-and-ocher fluffball between my arm and ribs. "You need a break."

Since we'd both learned of my...*condition*, she'd stopped obsessing about training and started obsessing about my rest and health. It was annoying sometimes, but she was right today. My bones ached and my eyes itched.

"Yeah," I agreed, though I couldn't take time off to rest when Trinka still needed help.

We were both silent for a few moments, and then I felt a little puff of air against my wrist. And another. I knew without looking that the black tip of her long tail was flicking back and forth, and I smiled tiredly at the telltale sign she had something to say and was trying to hold back.

"What is it?" I groaned. "You might as well spit it out."

"I was wondering...since we don't know how long...how long you have...maybe a change of scenery would be good. Maybe get away from everyone for a bit." She paused, and I considered her words. She continued. "Isn't there any place you'd like to visit? Anything you'd want to do before...I mean, just, while you have the chance?"

Before I wither away and die, she meant. At an undisclosed time, after slowly losing control of my limbs.

My chest ached, and I willed my face to stay calm and dry as I opened my eyes.

The mostly untouched books on fossils caught my attention from under the dust they'd collected on the far corner of my desk. "Well, I have always wanted to visit Morrenfayre. See if fossils are as plentiful as they say. Maybe find some myself. There are probably scholars there I could talk to, maybe learn from."

It wasn't like I could visit my family. The genetic disease had surfaced from my lost memories first, then I'd had to bolt for the Tournament to help the others with the memory-restoring potion I'd finally gotten right. But later that day, when things had calmed down, I'd remembered the rest.

What happened to my family. That it had been my *grandmother*, of all people, who took my memories and the diagnosis in the first place and buried them deep in my mind. The one person I would've sworn I could trust. It made sense, though. Only she had the patience and thoroughness to erase just the right amount of everything so I didn't even wonder how she was for months.

If I could just figure out how she'd done it, I could do it for Trinka.

I'd found her grave since. In the finest cemetery in Terrenthyrs, thanks to her better-classer status. But not a relative in sight the day she'd been buried, according to the groundskeeper. I should've been there. She probably thought she was saving me—giving me a fresh start. But she shouldn't have taken her last days from me.

Goosebumps rose on my wrist where cool air bursts hit faster and faster with Starstinger's quickening tail flicks.

"That's a great idea, Acres! When can we leave?"

I smiled at her exuberance. "Uh, to Morrenfayre? I don't know. I mean, there's the flat, my belongings, transportation—lots to figure out."

"We should leave now."

I leaned up to look at her. "What? Now? Why?"

I was destined to become an old man before hitting my twenties, but I still had a couple years. Or at least several months. Gulping, I forced the looming dread down and focused on Starstinger.

"Because I know you, and if we don't leave right away, you'll talk yourself out of it."

I scoffed and rested my head on my arm. "No, I wouldn't."

"All right. Make an announcement at the bonfire tonight. Commit to it publicly so you can't back out of it, and I'll get off your case."

"I'll think about it."

Her tail paused, then started up again. What was going through her mind?

"You can give them each a portion of the antiflora powder to protect them, since it's stronger than the pelinary petals alone." She licked one paw. "Maybe leave them the recipe. That should be more than enough to take care of your perceived responsibility to be their on-call potion master."

I nodded. "That's a good idea, whether we leave or not."

She rolled her eyes.

Gradually though, my thoughts drifted from Starstinger to the possible trip. An adventure would be nice, and in reality, I may not have the luxury of putting it off until a more convenient time. A shiver ran through me at not knowing how long I had left.

I stretched my bent arm, then the one by Starstinger. They both still worked right. I wiggled my toes and flexed muscles in my legs.

No stiffness yet. No weakness. At least, I was pretty sure. Was that a little tightness in my left calf? I flexed it, rotating my ankle.

It was probably my mind playing tricks on me.

Probably.

Chapter 3

MELLA

Sitting on my bed in Bennet's little cottage, I strummed the strings lightly, enjoying the gentle melody of my new mandolin. The wood of this instrument was so smooth against my forearm—sanded by a real instrument craftsman before he tossed it out for some small imperfection.

Reenalyn had seen it in the rubbish bin and snagged it for me, which was perfect since I didn't feel right using my old one anymore. Not since I'd given it and Whisper back to Bennet. I missed the familiar feeling of the makeshift mandolin in my hands. But Whisper and Bennet belonged together, so it felt right for him to keep it.

Whisper eyed me from the foot of my bed. "You'd better leave soon, or you won't have time to pick it up before the bonfire."

Her bossy tone made me smile. Thank good fortune Queen Narellen had failed at shattering her the second time, so she was still around to be her wonderful annoying self.

Across the room, Bennet leaned forward in his chair, peering out the window of the one-room cottage the three of us had called home for the last few months.

"It is getting late," he agreed.

Behind his chair, his covers draped neatly over his bed next to the bookshelf someone had gifted us, empty but for two plates, two cups, and a couple of books from the Glenmyre library. The kitchen table stood over there too, by the door, leaving me with my own side of the one-room home for privacy.

"You're right." I laid my new mandolin on my pillow and slid off the bed, smiling at Whisper. Her crown feathers lay relaxed against her head as she perched, her hybrid coyote knees showing from under her poofy chest feathers.

The beeswax candle Bennet left burning on the table smelled of lavender and freshness—a little strong for me. But apparently it was his favorite scent, and he'd been imprisoned under false accusations for more than twice as long as I'd been alive. So he could have whatever candle he wanted.

"I'll see you two at the bonfire." I waved as I slipped out the door and headed for the blacksmith shop, sliding my housekey into my pocket.

I'd considered forging a different castling weapon this time, like a longsword or a saber. But the reality was, I knew how to fight with a scythe. I'd spent the better half of my pre-castling years training almost exclusively with scythes—a testament to my wheat farmer grandfather's skill that had inspired me as a child. So starting over with something new seemed like an unnecessary waste of the skill I'd developed.

But this time, I made the blade entirely from black metal rather than silver, and I'd given it a different name. *Magnificence* felt like something the old me would've chosen—attention-grabbing and worthy of the better-classer applause I used to crave.

Now I wanted something simpler. A bit fiercer, too. Since a saber would've been my weapon of choice if I'd chosen a different one, and since I liked how the word sounded, I'd etched it into the scythe's blade itself this time, rather than the handle.

Saber.

It sounded practical for a creature ready to fight for what's right, while *Magnificence* sounded like a peacock begging for validation of its shallow prestige.

When I reached the communal smithy where I'd left my new scythe yesterday to cool after applying the finishing touches, I couldn't help but admire it. Pitch-black blade and dark-wood handle with silver-etched stripes, it shone and glittered impressively in the sun.

I hefted it in my hand and looked it over, the heat absorbed from the sun warming my palm.

It. Was. *Gorgeous.*

With my new castling weapon in hand, I strode to my cohort's training grounds in the Emberlyn Forest to show it off.

***

"Ahh!" Reenalyn screamed when I entered the clearing, soft sunlight glinting from my new weapon. "It's *beautiful*! Let me see!"

I offered it with a grin, and she gawked, her eyes taking in every glimmer as her fingers traced one of the etched stripes.

Cupid's scaly green head appeared from the midst of Reenalyn's blonde hair, and he admired the scythe with emerald eyes.

"Wow." Reenalyn returned it reverently. "This is *unbelievable*, Mella. I love it!"

"Thank you," I said, pulling my brown hair over one shoulder and wishing I'd find my own castling there. But I didn't need to stress about that anymore. This year's Castling Ceremony was only a week away, and this time, I knew what I was doing.

There would be no forgotten bits of another castor's weapon on me, and I didn't care whether it was a tiger. It would be great if it was—and I had etched stripes on the handle—but I was a little more like Reenalyn about that now. However my castling chose to manifest, I would just be thrilled it was my castling.

Dane arrived in the clearing with Beldon, and they waved. Beaming, I held out my new scythe. Dane's jaw dropped and Beldon's eyebrows rose.

"Wow!" they both said, jogging the rest of the way.

I handed it to Beldon first so I could give Dane a hug. "Hey."

"Hey, Mella." He hugged me back and lightly kissed the side of my head before stepping away to admire the scythe.

"This is incredible!" He took it from Beldon's tanned hands and hefted it in one pale hand of his own. "Wow. Amazing work."

Beldon grinned. "I can still totally take you down, though."

I raised an eyebrow.

Dane laughed. "Don't be so sure. She bested you—what, seven times?—with a borrowed training scythe just a couple of days ago. How much more effective do you think she'll be with this?"

Dane passed it to me and wrapped an arm around my shoulders, Beldon pursing his lips at the memory.

"Let's put it to the test after dinner, Beldon," I said. "One-on-one. You down?"

His grin returned, his eyes crinkling. "You know it! I'll take it easy on you, don't worry."

"Yeah, I'm counting on that." I rolled my eyes.

A crash drew our attention to the other side of the clearing, where Brawler and Mauler wrestled their way to the bonfire, Trinka in their wake. All the castlings were nearly full-grown now, but it was especially noticeable in Beldon's gorilla castling and Trinka's grizzly bear. They were huge.

Acres and Starstinger appeared a few moments later, and the whole Wrynford cohort was together again. We were just short one adopted grandpa and his castling.

"Mella," Beldon said, "why don't you go ahead and cast tonight?"

"Ooh, yes!" Reenalyn's eyes sparkled as everyone's gaze fixed on me.

A cool evening breeze rustled the leaves as I shook my head. "I know I don't need the competition to cast, but...I still want to prove to everyone I can. To redeem myself after failing before all of Terrenthyrs last year."

Beldon sat on a log and gestured toward the group as a whole. "But you can prove it *now*, to us, without having to wait any longer!"

"I know. It's just..." I wasn't sure how to say it. I didn't care what the better classers thought of me. It wasn't that. "It's something I need to do. It's important to me."

And if I was being honest with myself, I wanted to meet my little sibling. I hadn't seen Mother and Father since Father kicked me out for failing to raise the family's social standing. Mother had already been with child for a few months. By now, my little half-brother or -sister would be eight or nine months old.

I wanted to meet him or her.

And I wanted Father to watch me cast. I wanted to see the look in his eyes when he realized he'd been wrong—that I wasn't a failure after all.

Beldon shrugged. "All right, well, if you can wait a few more days for your own castling, I guess we can, too."

Bennet and Whisper would be here any minute. My friends had taken them in as one of us right from the start, and in turn, Bennet had made room for me in his home even though there was barely room for him and Whisper.

The Wrynford cohort was by far the oddest of the last cohorts Terrenthyrs would ever see, now that Queen Narellen was in prison. Maybe we were the weirdest of all cohorts that had ever existed since she started the whole mess decades ago.

But we were by far the best, and as I watched everyone talking and laughing and helping Reenalyn chop peppers and onions for the soup and fold minced meat into little pastry envelopes, there was no place I'd rather be.

Reenalyn gushed about her little sister's piano recital, Beldon told stories of his adventures with his brothers—how he still had more to tell, I couldn't imagine, but he always did—Trinka even smiled a little at one of them.

Starstinger and Acres acted funny, though. She kept stepping on his hand with her paw every time there was a lull in the conversation, until finally he crossed his arms and gave her a pointedly annoyed look. She rolled her eyes, and he gazed over the group, his mouth open like he was about to speak.

Our eyes met and he looked away, slouching as a couple of locs fell loose from the pile on his head and into his face.

What's on his mind?

"Mella, these dumplings won't take long once I drop them in the soup," Reenalyn said over the crackling of the fire. "Do you think I should wait a little longer for Whisper and Bennet before putting them in?"

I glanced toward the cottage, which wasn't far. Odd they hadn't beaten us all here, actually. They'd been about to leave when I left, and they didn't have an errand to run in the opposite direction beforehand.

I frowned, worrying about Bennet's hip. Being old enough to be my grandfather and having spent most of his life unjustly imprisoned, his strength wasn't what it had been.

"Nah, go ahead and throw them in." I stood from the log I shared with Dane. "I'm sure they'll be here soon. I'll run over and check on them."

Dane stood. "I'll go with you."

I flashed a smile as he took my hand, and I led the way into the woods.

Kaido had never just sweetly taken my hand like Dane. He'd waltzed up and kissed me out of nowhere like I was his property to do with as he pleased, whether I liked it or not. It was too bad I *had* liked it at the time.

But any touch with Dane was a different experience.

Kaido had been quick and pushy. It had been interesting to be surprised with new things all the time, but then there was nothing left for us to explore except...except *that*. And finally his hands had become so repulsive, thank good fortune, *that* hadn't happened.

But Dane was not in a hurry to get whatever he could out of me as fast as he could demand it. He seemed to savor every moment with me and to want to make each one last. And holy skunks, could he.

"Oof." I stumbled in the dimming evening light.

"You okay?" he asked.

"Yep, tripped like an idiot."

Chuckling, he let go of my hand and wrapped his arm around my waist.

"You know, this is a rare moment of privacy for us," he whispered. "It would be a shame not to take advantage of it."

"That it would." I beamed, wrapping my arms around his neck as he leaned in and kissed me.

A sharp crack pricked my ears. Dane stiffened. As we broke apart, our eyes met for a brief moment.

"Probably a rabbit," he whispered, pulling me closer.

"Right." I kissed him again, relaxing into his warmth, breathing in his scent...

And the scent of burning.

I broke away, sniffing the air. "Do you smell smoke?"

Dane's pale eyebrows drew together as he followed my gaze. "Yeah."

We shared a worried look and took off at a sprint toward Bennet's cottage. Maybe he and Whisper misunderstood and thought they were supposed to host the bonfire?

We burst through the trees, and my heart stopped. Crimson and orange flames reached for the sky, crackling around our cottage.

"Whisper! Bennet!" I shrieked, sprinting as fast as a cheetah. "Dane, go get help!" I broke through the trees, flames licking up the sides of my home. They already reached above the roof. "Whisper!"

Dane shouted for the others, then the roaring flames drowned out everything else.

I fished out my key and struggled to unlock the door. It finally clicked just as debris crashed from the ceiling. The door wouldn't budge. I tried to kick it in with my boot, but it was blocked. *Skunks! Where are they? Please not inside...*

I couldn't see either of them through the window, but the smoke was so thick it was hard to tell for sure. And the windows were too high for me to get through.

I returned to the door and slammed my shoulder against it. "Come on, you piece of muck!" I screamed, throwing kick after kick. "Come *on!*" Another kick and it clattered to the floor. I stepped toward it, but hands wrapped around me and yanked me back as the roof fully collapsed.

Dane's grip slid to my hand, and he pulled me to the side of the house with the two windows. "I'll help you reach the window!"

He pulled his shirt off, wadded it around his hand, and punched the window, breaking jagged glass bits from the bottom. Then he laid his crumpled shirt over the edge, lacing his fingers together by my knee as if to give a leg up for a horse rider.

Understanding and appreciation flowed through me, and I shoved my boot into his hands and pulled myself through the window to tumble inside.

Smoke assailed me, and I coughed hard before pulling the neck of my tunic over my nose.

Ducking below the smoke, I peered under Bennet's bed. Nothing. I pulled off the blankets, too, for good measure. Nothing.

No one under the table—only that stupid candle on top.

Nothing around the chairs.

Debris covered my bed, but neither of them would've been over there. Empty.

I grabbed one of the chairs, burning my hand, and rushed back to the window.

"Dane?" I called, stepping on the ledge. He was there, helping me out the window and then pulling me a few feet away.

I coughed a few times, trying to catch my breath. "No one's in there," I wheezed.

"I ran around the house while you were inside but didn't see anyone, either." He patted my back. "Are you okay?"

"I'm fine." I shoved to my boots. "I just need to find them."

Now that I'd searched the house, adrenaline wore off and panic settled in. Tears welled. Bennet's cottage—my *home*—was about to be nothing but ashes.

But where was Bennet? And Whisper? And Whisper's mandolin? My new mandolin was probably already burnt to a crisp.

Beldon and Trinka rushed from the woods, followed by Reenalyn and Acres and all their castlings.

"The house is empty!" I shouted at them. "Help me search for boot prints!"

We dispersed, heads bent to the ground in search of clues.

"Over here!" Trinka shouted a few minutes later from the other side of the wall of flames. I raced around it, Dane at my side, heart pounding. What had she found?

Trinka crouched over the ground, pointing at the mud.

Boot prints? A lot of them, pointing different directions. And a wide smear like something heavy was dragged.

Could Bennet have saved something from the fire? Dragged it away on a blanket? Frowning, I realized nothing he owned would fit that description. Nothing he cared enough about to save other than Whisper, Whisper's mandolin, and me.

I thought back to the candle on the table. It was still upright. It couldn't have started the fire. So what did?

Or...or *who?*

I met Trinka's eyes, then Dane's. Beldon, Acres, and Reenalyn approached, staring at the disorganized prints and the smeared track.

Trinka flexed her fingers in her spiked bronze knuckles. "It looks like some people fought and the winners dragged the loser away."

"You don't think..." Beldon trailed off, his dark eyes on the mud.

Narellen's threat the day we put her in prison slithered through my mind. *"For the record, I wasn't really going to shatter you again. You're far too interesting a specimen to waste. You'll fall asleep soon, and when you next wake, you'll be in Morrenfayre. With the others of your kind."*

Narellen couldn't have done anything, though. Not from the dungeon. And she hadn't had time to floramance anyone into helping after the botched tournament, and no access to potion ingredients. So she couldn't have anyone working for her on the outside, could she?

Bennet and Whisper had to be around here somewhere!

I bolted for the woods, following the mud smear. *Skunk these stupid leaves and twigs!* They crunched under my boots, dry as a bone. The trail ended. I jogged around anyway, desperate for something. Any clue, any sign.

Nothing.

"Bennet!" I sobbed, hopelessness and fear weighing me down. "Whisper!"

That reminded me...I sprinted back to where the scuffle had taken place, where Beldon crouched, tracing a finger over one track and then another.

"I think there were at least two other people here," he informed me.

"No eagle tracks?"

He shook his head. I looked back to the cottage, flames already calming as their fuel ran low.

Had I missed her mandolin? I was pretty sure I'd checked everywhere, but smoke had made it hard to see, and fear made it hard to focus.

"What if...what if Whisper's mandolin *was* inside, and I missed it?" I croaked, tears welling. If a wooden castling weapon—or instrument—burned, wouldn't that be worse than shattering? Because there wouldn't be anything left to make a hybrid from.

I sat on the ground, my face in my hands. I couldn't stand the pitying looks on their faces.

What if Whisper had burned in the fire? And it was my fault?

"There's no reason to think that," Reenalyn said. "She could've been flying. She could be flying over Bennet, looking out for him..."

"But where would the mandolin be, then, Reenalyn? And if some people kidnapped Bennet, why? He doesn't have anything to give."

"Should we check if Narellen's sent any letters?" Dane wondered.

I felt the color drain from my face. "You think Narellen...made good on her threat? To send Whisper to the other hybrids?"

He shrugged, eyebrows raised.

I scrubbed my hands over my face. "Surely the king would've ordered that she couldn't send or receive post—after confessing to be loyal to Morrenfayre? The guards wouldn't be so stupid."

Dane raised an eyebrow. "Let's go find out."

CHAPTER 4

SELVERINE

Stepping off the staircase, I headed for the front door of the palace. My stomach was growling, but I sure as skunks didn't eat in this place anymore.

"Where do you think you're going?" The king's slurry voice sludged from the front room. He sat in the shadows, his scraggly white hair and beard obscuring his face further.

Striding past him, I asked, "What business is it of yours?"

"Whether we like it or not, you're next in line for the throne, young lady. You can't go traipsing about."

"What?" I turned to face him. "You've never made anything so clear as how much you *don't* want me on the throne, since I'm not your blood relation."

Steepling his fingers, he nodded. "Indeed. For a long time, your grandmother...*influenced* me to believe there was still a chance we could conceive our own child, with no regard for our ages." His bloodshot eyes clouded at the mention of her. "But removed from her floramancy, I see what a fool I've been. I'm too old to produce an heir. So you'll have to suffice."

Crossing my arms, I scowled. "How flattering." I spun on my heel and tore the door open. "I decline."

Bolting up, he shouted, "You can't *decline!*" He stumbled after me, breathing frantically. "It's your *duty!* Your *obligation!*"

Whirling on him, I scoffed, "Oh, is it now? You've spent the last seventeen years ensuring I *knew* I'd never sit on the throne. Which is fine with me. I never wanted it. So you can muck off and find someone else to fix your problems."

"No!" He grabbed my trident, forcing me to stay inside. "It *must* be you!"

Yanking my trident away, I shook him off and darted through the door. He'd have to control himself if we were in view of people. The guards posted on the front door wouldn't count for much, but anyone could be strolling by. "Why must it be me all of a sudden?"

"Because everything wrong with my life goes back to Narellen and her useless son, then later on, you." He pointed an accusing finger. "It's your destiny to atone for what your grandmother has damaged in this kingdom."

It was the first time he'd ever mentioned one of my parents. Had my father really been useless, or was there more to him?

"My destiny, is it!" I shouted. "So even though *she* floramanced *me* just as much as you, if not more, and even though she killed my parents, I'm still somehow to blame for her actions, as if I had a hand in them? As if I supported them?"

The memory of their deaths at her hand seared through my mind, clenching my heart. The potion that guy, Acres, had invented was ultimately a good thing for the kingdom, sure. But sometimes...I would've been happier without reliving that particular memory. I'd certainly choose freedom from Grandmother's manipulation even at the cost of many more painful memories. But it still stole my breath and crushed me more every time it crossed my mind.

Why had she done it? The not knowing ate at me.

Resting one hand on the doorframe, he leaned out, scowling. "You are her blood. If she cannot account for her wrongs, *it must be you.*"

Spinning, I strode toward the center of town.

"Selverine!" he raged behind me.

Bumping my pace to a run, I pumped my arms and forced my legs as fast as they could go.

Soon I was well beyond him, and he stopped, hands braced on his knees, wheezing far in the distance. *The skunking pig.*

Slowing to a walk, I crossed my arms and considered. Narellen's actions weren't my fault. She'd done most of her work before I was born. That couldn't be on me. It couldn't.

She'd been using me, like she'd used everyone else. Sometimes it seemed she was grooming me to take her place, but she also never spoke of retiring or stepping down. I wasn't sure what her plans for me had been beyond winning the Castors' Tournament, but she was gone. So it didn't matter.

And I would choose my life for myself.

Not that I had any idea what that would look like yet. But it certainly wasn't ruling Terrenthyrs.

The smell of baking bread wafted on the breeze, and I inhaled deeply. The Braided Loaf it was. King Jorros be mucked.

***

I speared another mushroom and popped it into my mouth, wondering for the thousandth time what Grandmother had been putting in my food all these years.

Even with her locked away for the past few months, I just couldn't handle eating anything from the palace. And bread was out too, even from here. How could anyone know when the last dangerous traces of her floramancy would be gone? What if there was still tainted flour or bread dough around?

Early risers and their castlings occupied several tables around me, stuffing their faces with eggs and bacon and bread. So much bread. Even though they knew now what she'd been doing.

I wouldn't take that risk. Mushrooms weren't my favorite, but they couldn't have floramantic muck baked into them.

The door opened and a tall boy with a knot of dark locs piled on his head strode inside, pulling off his spectacles to rub his eyes and yawn.

Acres Parrianther?

The Potion Composer himself. He was the reason I was finally free from Grandmother's manipulative potions. He'd worked with the king for a few weeks to produce more of the antidote. But I hadn't seen him around since they'd finished and started distribution.

And yet dark circles hung under his eyes, and the corners of his mouth turned down in a worried frown. What was his problem?

Mella with her shiny new weapon—only the worst got second chances, apparently—trudged in behind him, followed by Reenalyn with her creepy green lizard draped over her shoulder and its tail wrapped around her arm.

Ew.

They approached the counter, Dane, Beldon, and Trinka trailing after with crinkled brows and anxious frowns. After blearily ordering food, they crowded around a nearby table.

Mella dropped into a seat next to the white-haired Dane, her head in her hands. "They're nowhere in town. I'm telling you, they must've been taken." She yawned, drawing attention to the dark bags under her eyes.

Reenalyn tucked a blonde curl behind her ear, twirling the end of her lizard's tail around one finger. "To Morrenfayre? Because of Whisper being a hybrid? Nar—"

Reenalyn flinched like someone had kicked her. She glared across the table at Beldon, who nodded in my direction. I looked away, though they probably knew I was listening anyway.

Mella leaned toward the center of the table. "Even though *she's* still...*contained* and not allowed any contact with anyone, she could've ordered someone from Morrenfayre to get Whisper before she was captured."

A waiter approached with a row of plates balanced on his arm. "The braided egg and ham sandwich?"

Dane raised his hand, nodding at Mella. "Yes, but then why'd it take so long? Morrenfayre's only a few days' journey away. It's been nearly four months since we threw her in the dungeon."

The waiter distributed the plates and disappeared into the kitchen.

"Are we sure we can trust the guards?" Beldon asked, yawning and stabbing a slice of sausage. "Just because they said she's not allowed any correspondence doesn't mean that rule's been followed. She could've sent an order more recently."

They all leaned in, whispering too low for me to hear.

"But if we go to Morrenfayre now"—Reenalyn got another kick and lowered her voice—"then you'd miss the ceremony, Mella."

Inspecting another mushroom, I popped it in and stared at my plate. They were going to Morrenfayre? *How interesting.*

Since learning Grandmother had come from Morrenfayre...I couldn't shake the itch to learn more about where my family was from.

Maybe that was why I'd never wanted to be a princess. I mean, if I could stay a princess forever, maybe. All my desires at my fingertips with no responsibility was not a bad situation.

But princesses usually had to become queens.

And that was not for me.

Acres's serval castling sat on the table next to his arm, her tail flicking. He ran his hand absently down her furry, spotted back. She leaned into it like a long, lanky housecat.

They seemed to get along so well. She must've been exactly what he desired in a castling.

I wasn't sure what castling I actually wanted anymore. But I longed for Horizon now, and it had been far too many months since I'd seen her. My heart lurched every time I thought about my wolverine castling's mysterious absence.

Was she gone forever because I'd made her feel unwanted? I couldn't remember why I'd craved an avian so badly. Only that I'd hungered for it more than anything. The desire had become part of my identity for the years I spent preparing for it. But now...had that been Grandmother's floramancy, too?

Beldon yawned. "Look, we've been searching for hours. We're too exhausted to think clearly. Let's get some sleep, pack a bag, and then meet at our sparring grounds. Then we'll decide whether we should go, and if so, we'll be ready." He sent a sideways glance at me.

Mella shook her head, dark circles under her slow-blinking eyes. "I don't think we should delay that long. They've already gotten a several-hour head start..." She trailed off with a glance at me.

Who had a head start? Mella had more to say, but not in front of me. I could hardly blame her, after how I'd treated her in the arena. As far as I could remember, *that*, at least, had been all me.

She *had* deserved it.

Munching on another mushroom, I pretended not to care.

Plates scraped clean, everyone followed Mella away immediately, except Acres.

He stepped around my table to face me, his castling over his shoulders. "Do you want to pet her?" He indicated the slender yellow cat who'd finally grown into her big ears—almost.

I blinked, taken aback. "Um, she's beautiful and I'm sure she's soft, but I wouldn't presume to touch your castling, Acres."

His eyebrows rose. "It's all right. She's friendly."

"That's okay, thanks, but—"

The serval jumped down from his shoulders, slinked across the table, and rubbed her back under my chin.

"Um, hi..."

"Starstinger," she purred.

"Right. Starstinger." What a strange and beautiful name. So much better than skunking *Horizon*. And it fit her. She was lithe and lean and lanky in a teenage, not-quite-full-grown-animal way. Impossibly graceful. "That's a pretty name."

"My castor has a pretty mind."

My eyes flicked to Acres. *A pretty mind, huh? What makes someone's mind pretty?*

Smiling at Starstinger, he stepped away. "Good to see you, Selverine." With a wave, he caught up to the others on long legs. Starstinger jumped down from the table and followed.

I returned his wave and watched Starstinger slink along beside him. *Well, I don't know about his mind, but he's certainly easy on the eyes.*

I remembered his sudden personality change at the Grand Castors' Ball. He'd slipped behind a tapestry to hide—the one I was already hiding behind. He wasn't overflowing with the self-centered showing off and the obnoxious, insincere compliments I usually got from guys. But one sip of punch and he'd changed, devolving into the typical prick.

But knowing his rudeness that day was due to the influence of Narellen's floramanced punch, I didn't feel wary around him anymore.

Also, their strolling into the woods wasn't going to get rid of me. If they were going to the country I was born in, where I should've grown up with my parents and where I could now be farther away from Grandmother and her floramancy, then they could count me in whether they liked it or not.

***

The sight of the palace getting closer made a trip to Morrenfayre more and more appealing. To never see this place—or the king's stupid red face—again was exactly what I needed.

What was it like there?

Rounding the harshly groomed shrubs, I squinted in the early morning sun and strode down the stone walkway to the palace entrance.

"Selverine?"

I jumped out of my skin at the shadow lurking among the bushes, my heart racing.

"Who's there?" I brandished my trident.

"Help," the shadows whispered.

Recognizing the voice, I peered into the dimness. "Willova! What the skunk? You scared the muck out of me!"

My pulse slowed. The one person who didn't despise me for my Grandmother's actions. What was wrong?

"Selverine." She crawled forward, her crimson hair catching light. But far more than her hair was red now. Her ornate gold-and-azure dress was sliced diagonally from shoulder to hip, too much pale skin blotched in blood peeking through the rend.

My eyes widened. "Willova!" I fell to my knees. "Willova, what happened?"

"Drazdan...took Faultless." Her voice was thick with emotion, her skin paler than usual and tacky.

My fingers curled into fists. *That snake.* As much as I wished for an actual family, I was better off without it than with a brother like Willova's. Forcing my fists open, I tucked the trident under my arm and reached toward her. "Let's get you inside. Can you stand?"

She took hold of my forearms, and I stood slowly, hauling her up. She trembled, her blood smearing onto my arms as its sharp tang filled my nose.

We had to stop that bleeding.

"Princess Selverine! Are you all right?" One of the guards trotted toward me as the other peered at us from in front of the main door. "Who's with you?"

"Muck off!" I flung away the first guard's hand, daring the other to interfere with a look. "Can't you see she needs help?"

Blood slicked the key and gave me one muck of a time with the door while supporting Willova, but finally we stumbled through, and I managed to drag her upstairs and into my bathroom, where warm water had already been drawn for me.

Toeing the rug under her for some cushion, I half dropped her on the floor and leaned her against the tub.

She shivered. Which meant a hot bath was a good idea, right? She needed cleaning up, at least, and warm water was better than cold.

A servant had set out a goblet of water for me as well. Kneeling before Willova, I brushed her tangled hair off her sweaty forehead. "Willova, can you drink this? You need to replace the fluid you've lost."

She let me pour a few sips in her mouth.

"Look, I know you're the modest type, but I need to get this filthy dress off you and get you into the warm water, okay? Will you help me?"

She did a sort of wincing nod, which I took to be all the permission I was going to get.

I examined the torn, bloodied fabric and considered how best to remove it. *A castling with a sharp beak would be helpful right now.*

Instead, I sprinted to the kitchens and nicked a knife. Returning to the bathroom, I grasped the sliced fabric, careful not to touch Willova's wound, and slid the knife up to the neck of the ruined garment. Then I cut down to the bottom. The fabric fell away, and I struggled to maintain my composure at the sight.

Those strange, beautiful black marks I'd caught glimpses of before through a tear in her dress here or a shoved-up sleeve there blossomed and swirled over her legs, around her upper arms, and across her torso, strikingly dark against her pale complexion.

I'd thought they were tattoos back then, but they were drawings she created with charcoal from Emberlyn wood. Cuts and bruises healed faster when she drew over them with that stuff.

Was there an injury under each one of these?

A few of them had been sliced through by the gash running from her shoulder, over one breast, and back down to the opposite hip.

Fury roiled in my gut. So Drazdan had been doing things to her on top of controlling and judging her every breath? I'd known something was up. She'd shown me how she used Emberlyn charcoal to draw the marks over my wounds after Wager Day. She said it was for the healing properties in the charcoal. I'd thought she was naturally an artist, but these...

She was so good because she'd had a lot of practice.

I should've done something about it before now. Not that I knew what I could've done, but I'd *known* something was off and not pursued it. The weird self-deprecating things she said, the mysterious stiffness at times when we fought, her perfectly blank expression never betraying emotion.

Of course something bad had caused all that. Some friend I was.

She didn't deserve this. And she was the last friend I had. I'd have to do better.

Willova turned away, covering herself with her arms.

I ducked my head and dipped my hand into the tub to check the temperature. "I'm sorry, Willova. I was trying to assess how deep the wound is."

"How bad is it?" she moaned.

"Not great. But you're not dying."

She nodded once.

"You need to get in the tub so you can warm up and I can clean the wound, okay?"

I'd never cared for more than a scratch on my own. But it would embarrass her and draw the king's attention if I summoned the palace healer, so I'd have to do.

She shifted to her knees, grabbed hold of the tub's edge, and lifted herself into a crouch. She eased one leg in, then the other, and shrank down into the warm water without a single emotion.

I was beginning to understand how she'd gotten that stony mask.

Scooping water onto her skin, I let it run over the crusted blood, avoiding the scabbing all down her torso.

As the blood and stark black swirls and spirals washed away, purple and yellow skin showed through. The leftovers of older bruises.

Sucking in a breath, she flinched as more pinkish-red trailed down her torso from the wound.

Her brother deserved to die for this. And taking Faultless...

"Willova, what exactly happened to Faultless?"

Wincing, she closed her eyes. Then the expressionlessness mask returned, as it always did. "He caught me drawing with the Emberlyn wood, so he took my cutlass and dragged Faultless out by the scruff. He said he'd lock her up until I learned to control my imperfections"—she curled forward and looked at her legs, her sad eyes over the loss of the marks the first fleck of emotion she'd displayed—"and prove my penitence. I can't stand the thought of her locked up with him. If he gets in one of his worse moods...he might...it would be like him to...shatter..."

At last, she burst into tears. Folding over, she wrapped her arms gingerly around her wounded chest and tucked her legs in. She shook with sobs and gasping breaths. Had she ever let herself cry before? She was probably long overdue.

Sometime later, she calmed down to sniffles and I dipped my fingers into the pinkish water to check the temperature.

"We need to get you out of there. It's too cold."

I pulled a drying cloth from the rack and held it to her, turning my face to give her a little more privacy.

She stood shakily and wrapped the towel around herself. Red blotches stood out on her pale face as she focused her emerald eyes on me. "Thank you, Selverine."

Her eyes flicked away a moment later, her freckles standing out more than usual. She'd said once that she wore makeup to hide them. It must've washed away.

"You're welcome. Let's get you some clothes." I guided her through my room and sent her into my closet, hoping she'd choose pants for once, but this way it was up to her.

Feeling exhausted to the bone, I shuffled back to the bathroom to throw away her old clothes and hide the mess.

Muck it all. Morrenfayre would just have to wait. How were we going to get Faultless back?

Chapter 5

REENALYN

I stepped into our sparring grounds on my own, a rucksack over one shoulder and my spear in the other hand. Yawning, I blinked away the mid-day sleep, still feeling more tired than rested after searching for Bennet and Whisper all night. Cupid had fallen asleep after breakfast, too, and I'd let him sleep on in that mysterious space castlings disappear to while I packed and then made the trek.

Mella and Beldon were already there, deep in conversation. Their heads snapped up when my footsteps reached their ears, and they both sagged with relief.

Mella waved, and I strode toward them, stepping over her log to sit next to her and ignoring the wilted vegetables and spoiled dumplings over the cold firepit.

"So you think Bennet and Whisper were kidnapped...because Narellen wanted to force Whisper into the Avian Army?" Beldon asked.

Mella shrugged. "Why else?"

Though Mella's eyes were on Beldon as they conversed, I could sense her attention on the woods I'd just come from. Waiting for Dane. Beldon's attention was on the opposite direction, waiting for Trinka, as he responded to Mella.

If only I'd been able to sense something more useful than stupid *romantic feelings*. Why couldn't I have a mysterious ability to sense approaching danger? Then maybe I could've prevented whatever happened to Bennet and Whisper.

Mella's face broke into a huge smile, and I knew without following her gaze that Dane had arrived. His joy at finding her looking at him like that was loud. It overwhelmed my other senses like a bright flash of light.

Why did no one ever feel anything like that about me? It was always toward someone else. Of course I didn't *mind* with Dane—he and Mella were meant to be. I wasn't jealous of *him*. Just the feelings.

What would it be like to know someone felt that way about me?

I cringed, embarrassed at overhearing something so private and weary of being good for nothing else.

Cupid would've smacked me for that thought. He'd say I *was* good at plenty. Sparring and playing the violin and making delicious food...and I was.

But still. He couldn't argue with the fact that there were a lot of more useful things to be able to sense than everyone else's romance.

Acres and Trinka showed up, and Beldon's emotions grew a little brighter at the sight of Trinka. Beldon's feelings weren't deeper than Dane's, not bigger, but...I couldn't put my finger on it. There was something...older? But he'd known Trinka for less time than Dane had known Mella, so I wasn't sure.

Trinka, on the other hand—she was an interesting person. Where most people's romantic feelings were a kind of bubble around them—something projected outward—Trinka's romantic feelings were inverted. Like she had less than zero romantic feelings for anyone. Which was something I'd never seen before. *Why?*

"All right, let's get straight to the point," Mella said, her hand in Dane's as he sat next to her. "I'm confident they were taken against their will, and we need to go looking for them. And I believe Narellen's ties to the Avian Army in Morrenfayre are enough to make that our first stop. There's a good chance they're there."

"I agree," Dane said.

Trinka snorted and rolled her eyes. I almost shot her a look for snorting at my friend, but the truth was I sort of got her point. Of course Dane would do whatever Mella wanted.

What would it feel like to have that kind of support? It wasn't that I didn't have support—there was Mama and Papa and my brothers and sisters. And I was grateful for them. But there was something different about having that from a significant other.

It was hard to ignore the lack of it when I had to face everyone else's abundance of it constantly.

Beldon nodded. "I guess we're going to Morrenfayre, then."

Him too? Did everyone support anything Mella wanted to do?

Trinka threw down the stick she'd been toying with. "I'll go. I'm heading that direction soon anyway."

Beldon faced her with a furrowed brow.

"I'll go," Acres added, sounding more like he was resigning himself than agreeing.

His was an interesting romantic air to sense. He had a slight bump of feeling—not *feeling*, exactly, but openness to the chance? Not barred off like Trinka, but kind of there and not doing anything about it. So he definitely wasn't into anyone at the moment. And maybe he never had been.

I was, of course, a little taller than him. But only a smidge! With his hair piled on his head, we were about the same height. And he was a nice guy. And I truly admired how he piled his locs on top of his head in a giant bun. I wished I could do that. I hadn't done up my hair in an elaborate updo since discovering my height was the problem. Or at least, a big part of it.

But maybe, since Acres didn't have anyone else...maybe he'd fall for me. But then, why hadn't he yet?

He raised a confused eyebrow. With a start I realized I'd been staring at him, and he'd caught me. Unfortunately, everyone else was staring at me, too.

"Oh, um, what?" I asked, heat warming my cheeks.

Mella tucked a strand of dark hair behind her pale ear. "Are you in?"

"Uh...well, yes, I guess so."

She grinned at me. "Great!" Then she faced everyone else. "If everyone's packed, why don't we leave right now?"

"But your new scythe—where is it?" Dane asked.

Mella sighed and held up her dingy practice scythe. "I'm leaving my new one behind. I'm probably going to miss my chance to cast at the ceremony. If I take the scythe, I'll be tempted to cast, and I need time to decide if it's worth waiting another year. I don't want to make that decision under pressure. Besides, I need to focus on finding Bennet and Whisper. A new castling—which would be a baby animal—would be a huge distraction. Once Bennet and Whisper are safe, I can cast when the castling will be safe while it grows."

Dane laid an understanding hand on her shoulder. "All right, then. Let's go!"

A wave of shrugs and glances to the side went around the group, and then everyone was standing and stretching, hauling packs over their shoulders.

And that was that. We were leaving. Good thing I'd left my violin at home.

Annoyance flared at everyone just doing whatever Mella wanted, but then a thought crossed my mind.

There would be lots of new people in Morrenfayre. *Maybe...one of them...*

I smiled to myself as I slung my own pack over my shoulder. Maybe I'd finally find someone to love me like Dane loved Mella.

Revived by the thought, I fell into line with the others as we began the long trek to Morrenfayre.

Chapter 6
SELVERINE

Late afternoon light streamed through the windows in my room.

I blinked and sat up, then remembered Willova. She slept on the other side of the bed, her bandages tinged brown. Hopefully she'd feel a little better after getting a few hours of sleep.

I should've paid more attention—should have done something sooner. How could I have ignored the signs? Was that something Grandmother had done to me, or was it something truly wrong with who I was?

And who was that, anyway?

Willova stirred and opened her eyes. Confusion flitted over her face, then fear widened her eyes as she shoved herself up and winced, cradling her chest. "I shouldn't have fallen asleep." She lifted the covers and examined her bruised legs, no longer covered in inky flourishes. "I should've gone home. I'll be in so much trouble, and Faultless..."

"Willova, you can't go back there. He'll keep doing this to you."

"But Faultless is still there. I have to rescue her." She slid over the side of the bed, turning away gingerly as her feet hit the floor.

"But Willova—"

"You wouldn't understand," she said. "You never loved your castling. But I love mine, and I won't leave her. Not with him."

Her words stung. It was true, I hadn't loved my castling. I hadn't even *liked* her. But now that it had been a few months...I missed her. I barely knew her, but I wanted to know her more. I worried about her.

Had my dislike and resentment toward Horizon been Grandmother's doing? I remembered admiring Grandmother's sea eagle, Selvenair, as a child. But I didn't remember deciding I wanted an avian. It was just something about me.

But what if it wasn't? How much of my identity was Grandmother's making? That thought had been rising to the surface these last months. It terrified me. Did I know myself at all? Could I trust anything I thought I knew?

"I'm sorry. That was harsh." Willova stood a few spans away, her arms hanging at her sides.

"Yeah, it was." I sighed, sliding out of bed. "But you're not completely wrong."

I crossed the room to my closet.

"What are you doing?" she asked.

"Looking for clothes you can borrow, since there's no salvaging your dress." And packing. A plan had been forming in my mind earlier. Why not satisfy my curiosity for Morrenfayre and protect Willova at the same time by taking her and Faultless with me?

"Thank you."

"Could we return for Faultless when he isn't there, at least?" I stepped out of the closet with an empty bag over my shoulder and armloads of garments and held a couple of pretty but practical dresses out to her.

She took the top one and held it up. "We?"

I dumped the rest at her feet. "Yes, we."

Her eyebrows drew together. "You don't have to—"

"I know I don't. But I am."

She nodded. "Then yes, we should wait till he's away from the house."

I dropped the bag and shoved the other clothes in. "Okay. When should he be away next?" Facing her, I crossed my arms.

"Um..." Willova considered the last dress and took it with her into the closest, cracking the door behind her. "Probably this afternoon."

"Then let's watch your house and wait for him to leave. I'll help you free Faultless, then we're getting out of town."

She stepped out of the closet in the borrowed dress.

"That fits you well, Wil..." My voice trailed off at the terror in her eyes. "What's wrong?"

"I can't leave," she whispered, eyes wide and glassy. "He'd catch me and...he'd murder me for such disobedience. He's probably considering murdering me now for being gone so long."

I rolled my eyes. "That skunk's not going to get the chance. Look at me, Willova. It just so happens *I'm* leaving town today. You're coming with me. You may see him from a distance today, while we wait for him to leave, but from the moment you retrieve Faultless, you'll never have to see him again. Let that sink in."

Why not? I could keep my plans and keep my friend safe at the same time. Win-win.

She shakily sat on the floor, staring into space.

I grinned. "Right? Wouldn't that be nice? And you'll have Faultless and me with you. So you won't be with him, and you won't be alone, either."

She blinked slowly, her eyes lifting to meet my gaze. "That sounds impossible."

"But it's not." I scooped up my bag and tossed it to the bed, then headed past her toward the closet. "And you won't need to waste time packing anything there. Here's a sack for you." I threw another bag from the closet. "And you're welcome to go through my clothes and take anything else you need. The others that are too small for me are on that rack at the bottom left. But you're welcome to any of it—I won't be returning either."

I stepped in front of her and sat, annoyed and a little amused by her silence. "Willova? Are you in?"

Sunlight shone over a peppering of freckles I'd never seen before this morning. They added depth and uniqueness to her face. A definite improvement over the pasty makeup. Away from Drazdan, she wouldn't have to hide behind excessive makeup or hideous, opulent dresses ever again.

She stared at me. "But, I don't deserve...to live without him."

Taken aback, I frowned. "What the muck are you talking about?"

"Everything wrong with our lives—it's all my fault. If I leave him to bear it alone, I'm even more worthless. I couldn't handle so much guilt. Besides, maintaining an appearance of pleasing aesthetics and symmetry worthy of the family Calentine shouldn't be that hard. I'm weak. I need to try harder."

I frowned. *Again with the family Calentine mantra.* We couldn't go a single sparring session without it, and now it would be stuck in my head. *"I must maintain an appearance of pleasing aesthetics and symmetry worthy of the family Calentine."* Or, *"Oh no, I failed to maintain an appearance of pleasing aesthetics and symmetry worthy of the family Calentine."* Basically, *"My life's purpose is to do nothing but maintain an appearance of pleasing aesthetics and symmetry worthy of the family Calentine."*

It was ridiculous she hadn't run away from him and his obscene, unattainable perfectionism well before now.

"Uh-huh. Well. Firstly, I don't believe for a second any of it was your fault, much less that it *all* was. And more importantly, forget what you deserve. Doesn't Faultless deserve a good life free of abuse? What does it do to her to see you being treated like that? Does she deserve to deal with that every day for the rest of forever?"

Resolve hardened her slight features. "No."

Was that a little righteous indignation finally coloring her cheeks?

"Right. So let's get you packed and go get Faultless so we can get the skunk out of this place."

A knock sounded faintly at the front door below. I wished it could be lunch from The Braided Loaf, but it would be foolish to think I was safe with food prepared elsewhere and then *delivered through the palace.*

I'd tried it once but hadn't been able to bring myself to eat any, despite how much the delicious aroma made my stomach growl.

"Are you sure it's okay to take so much?" Willova held out a small armload of dresses, worry creasing her brow.

"That's hardly anything, and those are too small for me anyway. Help yourself. Like I said, I won't be using anything in here that's not already in my pack. Take tunics and pants, too. If you're free from Drazdan, there's no need to train in those elaborate dresses anymore."

Her brow crumpled like she didn't believe me as she carefully rolled up two dresses and stuffed them into the bag, then hung the others in the closet.

I rolled my eyes and shrugged. What else could I do? If she wanted to waste time and energy sparring in dresses, then fine. But it wouldn't be because I'd been stingy about my old stuff.

Someone knocked on *my* door then. Who'd been at the front door?

"Just a moment!" I glanced at Willova, who'd gone paler. "Don't worry. No one would let Drazdan into the palace. Seriously, you're safe. But go hide in the closet if you'd feel better."

I opened the door, expecting one of the maids, or at worst, the king to rail at me about his expectations for my *destiny*.

But before I could see who it was, a fist slammed into my face, knocking me back.

"Skunking muck!" I stumbled, catching myself on the bed and blinking rapidly, trying to focus through the haze over my vision.

"Where is she?" A man bellowed, taking hold of my nightgown and shaking me.

Still reeling from the punch to the face, I struggled to regain control.

"I propose to you, and you *reject* and *humiliate* me in front of the entire Grand Castors' Ball!" he screamed.

Who the muck let *Drazdan* up to *my room*?

"And *then* you assist Willova in defying me. Just *what* do you *think* you're doing!"

I finally had enough sense to drive my knee into his conveniently placed crotch. He stiffened, taking a step back, and I balanced as best as I could to slam a kick into his chest.

But I was still too shaky, and he caught my leg mid-kick and shoved it to the side, throwing me hard to the ground.

My ears rang and the haze still refused to clear. Where was Willova? Shouldn't she be able to knock him out from behind?

He was on his feet, glaring daggers, and I couldn't shift fast enough before he landed a kick to my stomach.

The wind whooshed from me as he leaned forward, readying another kick. I managed to catch his incoming boot and threw all my weight into hauling it to the side. He launched over me, but not far enough. His torso landed on my head. I blindly swiped at his face with my nails, struggling to get out from under him.

Where the muck is Willova!

Howling curses, he shifted and threw punch after punch, and I floundered for anything to hit him back with. Finding the vanity stool, I yanked it over by the leg and slammed it into his head, then shoved away and staggered toward the other side of the room.

But of course, that skunk caught my foot and tripped me. I chanced a flailing kick and earned the satisfying crunch of a nose breaking. He screamed and I finally got to my feet, staring at the spray of blood on my floor and bedcover. *Ew.*

"How *dare* you!" he shouted, holding one hand over his streaming nose and struggling to get to his feet.

"How dare *you* propose to someone you don't know, and then attack her for refusing you?" I shot back, groping my vanity stand for anything I could use as a weapon. My trident was by my nightstand on his other side. "And how dare *you* steal your sister's castling weapon and slice her down the middle with it! You skunking *monster!*"

"So you *have* seen her!" His eyes shone with crazed brilliance. "Where is she?" He was up and stumbling toward me too fast, and I didn't want him to think of checking the closet, so I threw the door open and ran for the stairs.

The skunk chased after me and tripped. Pivoting, I rerouted my momentum into a kick to his legs.

With great satisfaction I watched him tumble head over boots down two flights of stairs. When he finally reached ground level, he didn't rise.

Please be mucking dead already.

I watched for a few more seconds, then whirled. "Willova!" I snarled at my bedroom door.

Nothing.

Scowling, I slammed and locked the bedroom door, marched through the room, and ripped open the closet. A wild strand of scarlet gave away her hiding place among the hanging clothes, and I shoved everything on the bottom rack out of the way. "What the muck, Willova? Why'd you leave me to fight him myself?"

Blood dripped from my nose onto her shoulder, where she lay curled in a ball, nearly hyperventilating.

I could haul her up, but I'd never seen her like this before. Was she having a panic attack? A breakdown? I lowered my voice and tried to reduce my annoyance. For the moment. Whatever state she was in, shouting wasn't going to do either of us any good, no matter how mucky of her it was to abandon me in a fight with her brother.

"Look, Willova, he's knocked out. Now's our chance to get Faultless. But we need to hurry. Okay?"

She finally met my eyes. "Faultless—right." Her voice shook.

Swiping a tunic off the floor, I tripped out of the closet, tore off my nightgown, and stepped into a pair of sparring leggings. She got herself up and followed me.

My eyes narrowed at her pinking bandage. I was pissed she hadn't helped, but maybe there was more to it than I could see. I'd have to tell her what I thought of that later.

Grabbing the rucksack I'd chucked at her, I scooped garments from the pile she'd made and stuffed them in. "Here." I dropped it at her feet and went for my own pack.

Flecks of Drazdan's nasty nose blood speckled the top garment. I pulled it out and threw it on the floor, then reached under the bed for my stash of Wager Day winnings.

With one last glance around the room, I stuffed in the money, flipped the flap closed, and lifted the strap over my neck and shoulder. "Let's go."

More Drazdan blood had dripped on the carpet between my door and the stairs. Splotches painted every few steps. *That had to hurt. Hopefully a lot.*

Thank good fortune he was still face down. "Come on, Willova. He's still out. But we don't know how long that'll last. I could finish him off..."

Hefting my trident, I considered the merits and risks.

"No!" Willova hissed.

I scowled at her. "Why the muck not?"

"It would break our parents' hearts."

"I thought your parents had both passed?"

She shook her head. "Yes, they're gone. But even so, I couldn't do something so horrible."

"Whatever." I stepped down the stairs, avoiding the blood as much as possible, partially hoping Willova was behind me, but also getting tired of her lack of action. "I'm leaving whether you are or not."

Tiptoeing around Drazdan's limp form, I noticed with disappointment he was still breathing. Willova lurked halfway up the stairs, staring at her brother's body.

"He's still out," I repeated. "Come *on!*"

I rolled my eyes and tore open the front door, breaking into a jog past the knocked-out guards. Let her come with me or not—I wasn't going to keep doing all the work for both of us.

She caught up with me before I was out of sight of the palace, already breathing heavily. Sweat darkened her underarms and shone on her forehead. I slowed a bit, remembering her injuries despite my frustration. "So what was that? Why'd you abandon me?"

Staring down at the road, she said, "I'm sorry. I'm not sure—I hid in the closet because I didn't want you to be punished for letting me in. I thought it would be the king, or someone else from the palace."

She panted, swiping sweat from her forehead. "I was shocked it was him. I didn't mean to abandon you. I just—you told me to hide in the closet, and it would've been worse for both of us if he knew for sure I was there. I'm sorry."

I frowned. "Great. Super confident I can count on you in a real fight now."

Pumping my arms as I ran, I asked, "Why haven't you killed him, if he's this horrible all the time?"

She gasped, and then kept silent.

"You said you were afraid he was going to murder you. Is it so bizarre to consider murdering him first so he wouldn't get the chance?"

She struggled on, avoiding my eyes. "I'd never do such a thing."

"Why the muck not?"

"It's not my place."

I stared at her. "You really believe that?"

She frowned. "Of course."

Shaking my head, I realized I couldn't count on her to have my back. At least not against him.

But for some reason, it didn't change my plans to get Faultless back and take them both with me.

***

By the time we reached her house, we'd slowed to a walk and were both checking over our shoulders. Was Drazdan still face down? Or already coming after us?

My boots clacked on the stones leading to the vast front door of their manor when Willova finally spoke. "Back door."

Shrugging, I followed her lead and avoided her eyes. I'd begun to regret inviting her along, and that regret only grew as we got closer to her house. There was something ominous about the...*perfection* of it. Could I handle whatever I'd gotten myself into?

Pushing open a servants' door, she led the way inside.

Even the servants' hallway felt expensive, if stark. The candlestands in the stone walls were more elaborate than those at the palace, but there wasn't a single painting on the wall or a side table or anything. Not a speck of dust, either.

She rounded a corner into a kitchen and knelt in front of a cabinet. "He could've hidden her anywhere. Maybe we could start in here and work our way around the other basement rooms? The basement seems more likely..." She trailed off, busy with pulling tins and baskets from the cabinet. "Be sure you put it all back the right way."

"He won't get the chance to punish *me* for anything being out of place." I, at least, would be heading to Morrenfayre before seeing that skunk-ass again.

Ages later, we'd searched the entire basement and climbed the stairs as quietly as we could.

After so much time had passed—well over an hour at least—he could arrive any minute. I kept my ears pricked for the door and wished we would've started upstairs since that was where we were most likely to run into him. If he recovered.

Which hopefully he wouldn't.

"Isn't there a good chance he would've stashed her in his room?" I asked.

"I'm not allowed in there."

I rolled my eyes. "Fine. Point it out, and *I'll* go."

With a worried look, she led me down another short hall on the first floor and pointed to a sturdy-looking, dark wooden door at the end.

Nodding, I stepped toward it.

I reached for the door handle, and to my surprise, the knob turned before I touched it. Willova gasped, and Drazdan appeared in the open doorway, bruised and scabbed, but wearing clean clothes and bandages.

"Willova? I'm disappointed in you," he said, crossing his arms and frowning down at her. "Your behavior the past two days, and your appearance. Filthy, sweaty..." He shook his head. "You're not maintaining an appearance of pleasing aesthetics and symmetry worthy of the family Calentine."

I cringed. "*You* invented that skunking mantra yourself, did you? *Please.*"

His condescending gaze fell on me. "And you, Princess Selverine. You should be ashamed."

I raised an eyebrow. "Who the *muck* do you think you are to tell me I should be ashamed?" I hefted my trident, aiming at him. "Where's Faultless?"

His frown deepened, and he drew his broadsword. "You dare raise your weapon against me, your elder?" He brandished the sword, two razor-sharp edges glinting.

"I don't give a muck who you are. You have no right to conceal a castling weapon from its castor. So where is she?"

A dark grin spread across his face. "How can you be sure I haven't already shattered her?"

A gasp escaped Willova's otherwise perfectly stoic expression.

"You know he hasn't, Willova." She'd better not pick this moment for an emotional breakdown. "You'd feel it if she was shattered, so she's still in one piece."

Glaring at Drazdan, I added, "You wouldn't shatter her yet because you're a skunk who likes holding things over peoples' heads. You're keeping her around so you can manipulate Willova further."

His grin faltered slightly. "You are indeed disappointing."

I squinted at him. "Once again, why the muck would I care—"

He swung the sword with a grunt, catching it on my trident as he spun, and cutting me off with a kick to the throat.

Oh, muck it all. Staggering, I blinked blearily, relieved I'd kept my hold on my trident at least.

"Willova, front door!" I wheezed, my voice barely projecting after the blow to my windpipe. If she wasn't any good in a fight against Drazdan, maybe she'd be worth something running from him.

Or not.

"Willova, *please*!" I shouted at her stock-still form, blocking another blow from Drazdan and catching one to my calf.

"You think you'll get off easier if you don't fight back?" Drazdan shouted at Willova as he dropped and spun his legs around, knocking my feet out from under me.

My breath whooshed away as I hit the cold stone.

Willova quailed at the threat in his eye, and I was so over it.

I lifted the handle of my trident at just the right moment to catch Drazdan full in the gut when he launched at me, knocking the breath from him. I got to my feet and raced toward the door.

Which was, of course, locked. A frantic inspection proved there was no latch to turn and no key present. I spun to face Willova, who watched me with bright eyes. She flicked a glance farther up the door, and following her gaze, I found another knob I'd missed in the fray.

Drazdan bellowed behind me as I twisted the second knob, wrenched open the door, and bolted. "Come on, Willova! We have to go!"

CHAPTER 7

MELLA

Leaving an assortment of boot and paw prints in our wake, the lowly Wrynford castors and their castlings trudged toward Morrenfayre. Only a few hours in, and the two-day journey was already wearing on me.

"I'm bored," Beldon whined.

Apparently I'm not the only one.

Darting to the front of the group, Beldon spun and walked backward, facing us. "We need a story to pass the time!"

"Ooh yes!" Brawler and Mauler said together, giggling as they raced to catch up to Beldon.

"Okay, what do you have in mind?" Reenalyn asked, Cupid curled around her shoulders.

Beldon wagged a finger. "No, no, no. I'm always regaling you all with fascinating stories from my life with too many brothers. It's someone else's turn." He eyed me.

"Uh...I don't know any stories."

Beldon rolled his eyes with mock annoyance. "Dane? Got anything for us?"

Smiling, Dane waved Beldon away. "Pass."

"You guys are killing me! Okay, how about this. A simple prompt. Favorite scar—where is it, and how'd you get it? And"—he pointed at Reenalyn with both hands—"go!"

"Oh, um…" She inspected her hands and arms. "Well, this was a cut from when my papa taught me to use a whetstone to sharpen metal weapons." She raised her palm, pointing to the space between her thumb and first finger. "I felt so bad that I couldn't do it right, but my papa was so encouraging and comforting that, after he bandaged my wound, I tried again. So this scar is a reminder of my parents' love and support."

Must be nice. I shoved away my irritation. I was happy for Reenalyn to have such a supportive family. I didn't want her to have been replaced by a better child and kicked out of the house. But still. The next story couldn't come fast enough.

Clapping, Beldon grinned. "Nice! Who's next? No one? All right, then. Trinka! If I can make a request, I'm dying to know the story behind the half-burned wrist tattoo."

He did not!

There was almost a *whoosh* sound as we all spun for Trinka's reaction.

I was honestly surprised she'd come. She restricted herself to the edge of the group so much—I'd always thought she didn't like us much. But she'd still hung around after the tournament and prize money fell through. And she'd seemed in favor of the decision to go to Morrenfayre. Her shoulders had lifted a little. And her gaze was more determined and purposeful.

I wonder why she'd already been planning to head that direction?

"No chance, Berroman. Pick someone else."

"Uh, uh, uh!" he wagged his finger. "Everyone gets a turn. Come on, don't you have any good scar stories?"

Her face hardened and twitched. "No."

"Please?" Beldon begged, dragging out the word.

He was asking for it. If he didn't let up soon, she'd resort to a more physical means of communication.

"You got a theory? Share that for my turn."

Beldon sighed dramatically, still grinning. "Okay, fine. If I were to guess, I'd say you were apprenticed to a candlestick maker, where you burned your wrist with hot wax. You also caught your long hair on fire, which is why you keep your head shaved and glare at flames."

She shrugged. "Sure. I'll take it."

He chuckled. "All right. I took your turn. Now you make up a story for me."

She blinked. "Why? You already like your story."

A beat late, he said, "Because I gave you one. It's only fair."

"Nope. Can't."

"Why not?"

"Because I already know a ton about you. There's nothing left to invent."

"Like what?"

She ticked off one finger at a time. "You grew up in Wrynford with a bunch of older brothers. Your parents like you. You smile at your scars for some reason I can't imagine. And every time you talk, you give too much away."

He tilted his head and crossed his arms, smiling more softly. "I didn't know you were listening."

Reenalyn met my eyes with an amused smile. Acres focused on the ground, seemingly oblivious to the turn Beldon's game had taken.

I glanced at Dane. He raised his eyebrows, grinning slightly.

"Yeah, but see," Trinka went on, "someone could use any of that against you."

"But you won't."

"No. But anyone could."

"Is that why you never tell me"—Beldon looked up, suddenly remembering his audience—"*any* of us stuff about you? Because you're afraid we'll use it against you?"

"You might."

"I wouldn't."

"Maybe not."

"Okay then. We'll come back to scar stories in a minute. Is there anything about you that's completely ridiculous and doesn't matter at all and so could never be used against you?"

"Can't think of anything."

"You didn't try," Beldon protested.

"Like what, Berroman? I don't waste my time thinking about anything ridiculous."

"What's your favorite color?"

"Favorites could be used against you."

He threw his hands up and then ran them through his hair. "Right. Silly me. Most wretchedly *despised* color, then?"

She glared at him.

"Oh, come on, Trinka! How could I ever hurt you with your least favorite color? Wear it as an anti-Trinka charm next time you're in a bad mood and I want to avoid you?"

"Orange."

"Orange?"

"Orange."

"Okay. Can I ask what you have against the color orange, or is that going too far?"

"It's...the color of things I don't like."

"So between red and yellow, which are parts of orange, which do you have a stronger feeling about?"

I couldn't believe she hadn't punched him yet. I'd never heard her carry on a conversation for this long before, not even to analyze someone's fighting style or weapon choice.

"I don't give a muck about red. But yellow...is nicer," she said.

"Ah! Have I stumbled upon your favorite color, then?"

"Yellow is the color of sunlight and warmth and good things."

"I've never seen you wear yellow before."

"Of course not. Do I look like I wanna die?"

Reenalyn burst in. "I wear yellow and am perfectly safe! You should totally try it!"

"So wait," Beldon said, tripping over a stone and regaining his balance. "Yellow's not your favorite color?"

"It's too bright, too obvious," Trinka said. "Too attention-grabbing. Black is the best color to wear."

"Mm. I've never thought much about yellow," he said, squinting at the sunbeams shining through the leaves.

"Don't you ever think about the sun on your skin?"

He glanced down to where the sunlight filtered through the leaves and dappled his skin. "I will now."

Holy skunks. Were Beldon and Trinka of all people having a moment?

"Hey, Mella?"

I turned as Acres caught up. "Yeah?"

He held out a little pouch.

Straining to eavesdrop on Beldon and Trinka, I reached for it, Dane sniffing a similar pouch a few steps behind. "What's this?"

"It's an antiflora powder that counteracts magical elements in food. If you sprinkle a little on your meal before you eat it, it will neutralize any potions."

I raised my eyebrows, impressed and fully focused on Acres's gift. "Wow, Acres! That's amazing! Did you make this one up, too?"

I tucked the dingy handle of my practice scythe under my elbow, freeing both hands to pull apart the pouch's ties. It smelled faintly of pelinary petals and another scent I couldn't place.

Looking away, he rubbed the back of his neck as a loose loc bounced against his forehead. "Um, yeah. After pelinary petals weren't enough for the potion the queen used on you during the tournament, I put time into making a combination stronger than the petals alone."

I cinched the pouch, kicking myself for not having thought of anything like this before leaving. Good thing we had Acres. "Wow. Amazing. Thank you."

Acres nodded and handed another pouch to Dane. Then he slowed, another pouch in hand, heading for Reenalyn next.

To my disappointment, Beldon was walking normally, Trinka many paces ahead of the group. *Skunks.* I'd missed the end, and it looked like it hadn't gone well. *Bummer.*

Sliding the pouch into my pocket, my fingers brushed something cold and sharp. I smiled.

A moment later the key shone dully in the dappled light. Thank good fortune I hadn't lost it.

My favorite memory of Bennet and Whisper together was when they'd almost finished repairing the old cottage. Whisper had strained her wing flying heavy beams up to reinforce the roof, and Bennet was sweaty and needing a haircut—his scraggly gray hair kept hanging in his eyes as he hammered one nail after another into his new-to-him home.

I'd brought them water, and they invited me inside to sit at their kitchen table—one of Beldon's brothers had built a bigger one for his expanding family and gifted that one to Bennet.

On the table sat two keys. I laughed and asked Whisper how she was going to keep a key with her since castlings can't bring anything when they come or go.

When she didn't laugh, I worried I'd offended her, but she and Bennet shared a smile and then faced me.

"That key is for you, if you want it, Mella," Bennet said. "You're welcome to come live here with us."

Whisper had leaned forward, rested her beak against it, and slid it closer to me. "We'd love to share this home with you."

I'd cried—of course. And then traded my pad of fallen leaves next to a downed tree trunk for a real bed, the first bed I'd slept in since Father kicked me out.

And that key became my most precious possession. It was a symbol of somewhere I was wanted. A place I was welcome. Where I was good enough.

Now it sat in my hand, a worthless piece of metal with no home to open.

But no, it wasn't worthless. It couldn't open locks anymore, but it *still* meant there were people who wanted me around.

That was worth more than anything.

And I had to bring them back.

I had no possessions anymore—even my new mandolin was gone. Burned in the fire. Now it was just the key, the clothes on my back, and my practice scythe. And my new castling weapon, which I'd left at the smithy for safekeeping.

"This will be good to have on hand," Dane said, sniffing the pouch.

I nodded. "I wish someone would've invented it a few decades ago."

"Yeah. Do you think the Castling Ceremony would still have started, just without Narellen's Wager Day and the 'winning just to be lazy for the rest of your life' garbage?"

"Maybe." It was a huge bummer not to get the Wager Day winnings Whisper and I had earned, but he was right. Those winnings were meant to support a lifestyle of laziness to keep the fittest, most driven people in Terrenthyrs from being effective fighters in the event of a war. Which she would've started any time.

This year, the Castling Ceremony would still take place, thanks to a popular vote. The Castling Tournament would, too, to encourage everyone to train hard with their castlings.

But Wager Day was out. No more competing for the right never to work hard again. The tournament winners would get bragging rights, and maybe a fancy dinner, and then go about their lives. Probably they would all join the military, but it would be their choice.

Like it should've been ours.

Would Bennet and Whisper be there to see me cast my true castling for the first time? Would we even get back in time for me to cast, or catch a glimpse of my little sibling?

I hoped we would find them quickly.

Chapter 8

SELVERINE

"What the muck are you doing?" I shouted at Willova. We'd hit a fork in the road, and she'd stepped on the path toward Wrynford and the Emberlyn Forest. "We need a *crowd* to slow Drazdan down, not an empty, quiet place where he can safely murder us with no witnesses!"

She paused, heaving for breath with one hand over her sliced chest. That had to hurt. But we'd both be in more pain soon if we didn't get into the city before Drazdan reached us.

"Come *on!*" Grabbing her wrist, I hauled her in the right direction.

Our shoes clapped against the cobblestones as we raced through Polfryth City, the heart of Terrenthyrs, passing buildings and beggars and jumping over puddles. Finally, we shot through an alley opening onto the square.

Slowing to a stop, we both panted, mixing in with the crowd in the shadow of the huge coliseum.

"Tell me...you don't usually run...to the *woods*...to escape him," I wheezed, eyeing Willova.

She shook her head. "I don't usually get the chance. But it seemed better to hide in the woods than show myself to everyone here." Hugging her chest wound, she glanced furtively at the locals inspecting produce and other goods at the market stands.

"No one's looking at us, Willova. They're busy. We're simply another pair of strangers. The benefit of hiding among other people instead of trees is Drazdan can't do whatever he wants to you if he finds us here. Don't you see?"

"I just want Faultless. Maybe we can search again—"

"We tried that already. We looked everywhere. And he knows you'll return for her, so if he's not already waiting to ambush you, he will be as soon as he gives up searching."

"But I can't go with you to Morrenfayre without getting Faultless first, Selverine. What if he hurts her while I'm gone?" Her pale hands fisted at her sides.

Too bad she was more bark than bite. And barely any bark at that.

"You're coming with me, Willova. I've seen what Drazdan does to you when he's angry, and I'm not leaving you to face it again."

"Exactly, which is why—"

I cut her off. "Which is why you have to come with me, for Faultless's sake as well as your own. Think about it." Dropping two coins in the hand of an apple merchant, I nabbed a couple golden deliciouses and tossed one to Willova. Further blending in.

"If Drazdan kills you, Faultless won't have her castor anymore. She'll be writhing in pain at the loss until she crumbles to nothing. Is that what you want for her?"

I bit into the apple, wiping away excess juice and eyeing a vendor with strips of dried meat and fruit.

Willova stuffed the apple in her pack. I couldn't blame her. I didn't have much of an appetite either, and I'd had months of separation from my castling to get used to the discomfort.

"No, of course not. But what if I leave and he shatters her?" A tear shimmered down her cheek for a moment before she swiped it away.

I shook my head. "He won't. Just think about it."

I stopped in front of the stall, dropped several coins into the man's hands, and scooped fistfuls of dried meat, fruit, and an assortment of nuts into my bag. No one could've known I'd be coming through here today, so this food was most likely safe.

"She's the only leverage he has on you. As long as he has her, there's a reason for you to return to him. Which is what he wants, because he's a conniving control freak with tiny man syndrome and you let him take it out on you."

She made a face. "I can't *let* him do anything. He's my older brother, so I have to put up with whatever he chooses."

My skin crawled at her words. "There are so many problems with that sentence. For starters—"

Someone crashed into me, throwing me to the ground.

Kicking like a wild horse, I shoved the scoundrel off me, leaped to my feet and brandished my trident. *What the muck? I didn't think he'd attack us here—*

"Oh, hey! Sorry. Didn't see you there." Kaido Felzane flashed his winning smile, but his cut lip, swollen cheek, and black eye diminished the effect.

"Skunk you, Kaido!" Glancing around, I found Willova peeking out from behind a barrel. "And thanks for the help! So glad I can count on you!" *That girl has issues.*

Inspecting the stinging scrapes on my elbows, I scowled at Kaido. "What the muck happened to your face?"

He smirked. "You should see the other guy."

"Oh yeah? What was it about? A girl?"

"Wouldn't you like to know." He grinned like he thought I actually cared.

I rolled my eyes, glaring at Willova as she emerged from her hiding place, now that it was safe. "Willova, are you going to let him kill me for helping you?"

"I told you, I can't *let* him do anything. He just *does*. There's nothing I can do about it."

"Whoa, I'm not here to kill anyone," Kaido informed us, raising his hands.

"Not you, idiot. You can run along. We're busy."

"Someone's coming to kill you?" he asked, raising an eyebrow.

"If he is, it's none of your business."

"I mean, being the honorable man I am, I could hardly allow two young ladies to scamper around town without protection if they're being pursued by a vicious killer."

"Scamper? Young ladies? What are you, a hundred-year-old man? And *honorable?* Ha! I think your opponent knocked some brains out of your ear when he gave you that black eye. We can handle it ourselves. Muck. Off."

He nodded at Willova. "She looks scared."

I gestured to myself. "Do *I?*"

"No, but you *sounded* scared when you asked Willova if she was going to let someone kill you. A reasonable fear, I'd say. And where the muck are your castlings? Shouldn't they be here to help you fight this guy?"

"It might be good to have another person on our side," Willova whispered, "if he finds us."

Or maybe I would ditch *both* their asses. "We're mucking fine, all right? You"—I pointed at Kaido—"get lost. You"—I pointed at Willova—"you and I are not scampering young ladies. We're skilled castors, and we're going to get out of here so you can heal, then come back to deal with this when you're in one piece. Got it? On that note, you're going to need a temporary cutlass."

Willova's face crumpled as I grabbed her hand and hauled her toward a vendor stall with lots of metal on display.

"I said temporary, Willova." We stopped by the stall, Kaido on our heels. "Don't you think you'd be better off with a weapon? What if Kaido had been trying to attack you? You can't rely on making a run for it every time."

She cupped her elbow in one hand, staring at the cobblestones. "It does make sense..."

I raised an eyebrow, then focused on the available weapons, impatient for her to finish. "But...?"

"I...I'm not allowed to carry money with me. So I can't buy one."

I threw up my hands. *Unbelievable.* Apparently I would have to do absolutely everything myself. Spotting a silver cutlass with a loop guard on the hilt similar to Willova's castling cutlass, I pointed to it. "How much for that one?"

The scruffy man named a price and I scoffed, preparing to haggle.

"Who is this guy we're outrunning, by the way?" Kaido asked, craning his neck to peer over the crowd.

A commotion caught my attention, and I scowled at it. Someone tore through the crowd, pushing people down and shouting for everyone to get out of his way.

"Oh, muck it all! We'll take it." Throwing the exorbitant number of coins at the weapon crafter, I helped myself to the cutlass and sheath, then shoved them in Willova's face. "There. You're armed. Now *run!*"

Dragging Willova, I darted through the square. A glance behind me confirmed my suspicion that Kaido had bailed like the coward he was. *Of course.*

And Drazdan was gaining, his sheathed sword swinging at his side.

We ran though crowds, past produce stands, and in between wagons.

Ducking into another shadowed alley, I peered out to see if Drazdan noticed, hoping he'd run past.

Willova and Kaido piled in behind me.

"The muck are you still doing here?" I hissed at Kaido.

"The real question," he panted, "is why are *you* running for your life from a guy with a double-edged broadsword to help a girl who doesn't help you and would crawl back to him in a heartbeat?"

I blinked. It was a good question. But I'd die before I'd admit Kaido Felzane had a point.

I'd befriended Willova at first because she was elegant and richly-dressed—the kind of person I wanted to be associated with. When she'd cast a gorgeous tiger, she was even more valuable. Had befriending her for those reasons been my idea, or Grandmother's?

But then I'd realized she was...different. A little off. Drazdan had done a number on her, and now she didn't know what was fair and what wasn't. I wasn't here to fight her battles for her. Not for the long run, anyway. But I couldn't leave her thinking that muck was all right. I hadn't helped before when I should have, so I would make it up to her now.

"Because my grandmother got away with mistreating and manipulating me for so long..." He didn't deserve the details. "Because I can't stand seeing someone else get away with that kind of behavior, and worse. Drazdan should be imprisoned for what he's done. I can't make that happen, but I can get Willova away from him and muck up his plans.

He's been grooming her to marry well to help his lost fortune. Without her, his plan falls through."

I *could* have him imprisoned if I accepted King Jorros's demands and became the next ruler of Terrenthyrs.

But I would not be doing that.

"So it's to stick it to Drazdan, then? Not because you and Willova are friends?"

I thought we were friends. Weren't we? I fisted my hands, fury squeezing my heart. With Grandmother's influence, I didn't know.

"It's my personal mission to get it through her head that she doesn't have to let people treat her like that, just because they want to. She needs to grow a backbone and learn to fight back."

"So what, are you going to hide her at the palace?"

"Skunks, no. I'm never going back to that place. The king can go die in a hole, too."

His dark eyebrows rose. "Then where the muck are you going to live?"

"I guess we'll find out."

CHAPTER 9

REENALYN

A day on the road proved to be a bit more challenging than I expect-ed. I was used to standing and walking a lot—and sparring. But constant walking for hours carrying a pack had turned out to be....pretty tiring.

"This looks like a good spot to make camp," Beldon said from behind me and Mella. He pointed at a bit of weedy grass between trees that looked like every other section of roadside we'd seen today.

So I wasn't the only one, then. "Sounds good to me," I said, throwing down my pack and stretching my arms over my head.

I scanned the ground for my campfire pot, then remembered, of course, we'd left it behind. It would've been too heavy and not worth getting a cart for since it was only a few days' journey to Morrenfayre, where we would then eat in town.

So my job was easier than usual tonight.

I picked a bit of grass and plopped down, then opened my pack and pulled out a braided loaf and a few berries I'd nabbed on the way. Spotting the pouch Acres gave me earlier, I examined it in the fading light.

And pondered his romantic potential once more.

No one else in Wrynford's sixteen years or older population could be found without at least a smidgeon of romance going on.

Besides Trinka. And sort-of Acres.

Maybe he's in love with his studies.

Which we appreciated. If anyone could come up with useful potions, it was Acres.

And Trinka didn't care about anything but her castling, which she reminded us of often.

Beldon sat a little ways away. Next to him sat Dane with Sprinter, Sprinter's pink tongue lolling from one side of his mouth as he panted. Trinka perched on her own log, undoing the ties on her pack. I'd never seen her pack before. She always slept away from the rest of us. Somewhere deeper in the Emberlyn Forest.

Branches cracked nearby, followed by shrieks and shouts that were beginning to morph more into roars and bellows with Brawler's and Mauler's rapid growth. They were both taller than Trinka now, even when sitting, and they'd probably pass Beldon standing any time.

Beldon joined the fray, wrestling with the castlings and cackling like he was one of them.

I glanced at Trinka. *Is that...*

A little hint of something flickered from her, so faint it had taken me longer than usual to notice it.

She had a *feeling*. A *romantic* feeling? It had to be, if I sensed it. But then it must be the faintest one I'd ever sensed.

I grinned. So Trinka wasn't as cold and hard as I thought. Whatever she'd gone through...maybe she'd give Beldon a chance, after all.

Mella sat nearby, dropping her scythe and pack as I popped a berry into my mouth. I offered one to her.

"Thanks." She smiled, taking it and then glancing around for Dane.

I eyed her with a suspicious smile, my eyes narrowed. "So...how's Dane?"

She grinned and turned away from me. "Fantastic, as usual." She eyed Acres and Dane, who were apparently trying to evenly divide the various types of dried meat they and Beldon had brought.

"Mm-hmm." I popped another berry in my mouth and savored the sweet tartness as Trinka lifted an enormous boulder and headed deeper into the trees. "It's crazy how much he cares about you. I mean, of course he should, because you deserve it and you're awesome"—I grinned at her—"but I know other people who are also awesome and don't have that."

"What do you mean?"

"I mean, he's always liked you a lot—and been much better of a person about it than Kaido—but he also...keeps liking you more. Like, his feelings get deeper and more intense."

She raised an eyebrow at me. "More intense?"

"I'm talking about *love*. Real, true, actual love."

She scoffed. "Oh, I know that. We've already told each other we love each other."

Her response stung. Didn't she appreciate what that meant? "Oh, so it's no big deal, then?" I snapped.

Mella faced me as I avoided her gaze. "Of course it's a big deal. I just meant I already knew."

"Oh. I see." I made a show of selecting the perfect bite of bread and pinching it off the loaf to nibble on.

"Are you okay?" she asked.

"Yeah. Tired."

"I've seen you tired plenty of times, and you've never snapped at me before. What's wrong?"

"Nothing's wrong, Mella." I sighed. "I'm sorry I snapped."

"It's fine." I could hear her narrowed eyes in her slow reply. "But—"

"Hey, Mella!" Dane called.

I felt like rolling my eyes, but I didn't. "Better go see what he wants." I hoped she'd go so I could be alone for a few minutes.

"Yeah. Well, when you wanna talk, I'm here. Okay?"

"Sounds good." I tried to smile at her, and she finally left.

How could she brush that off like it was nothing? I'd give *anything* to have someone look at me like that and feel so much love for me. She didn't know what she had. And *I* couldn't escape knowing about it *constantly*.

Even more constantly than usual over the next...however long this trip took.

Maybe I shouldn't have come.

CHAPTER 10

MELLA

I sat in the grass next to Dane and accepted the piece of dried meat he offered. "Thanks."

"I have to warn you, it's pretty spicy."

I grinned and took a bite. "I can handle it." Chewing, I appreciated the flavors.

"What do you think?" he asked. "The Braided Loaf is about to start offering it, but they're still perfecting the recipe. So I get the rejects, but this is the best one so far."

I winced as the cracked pepper got spicier. "You were right about the spice. What's in that?"

"Aged habanero seeds."

"Wow. Yeah. I get that." I coughed and reached for my canteen.

His face fell. "Sorry—is it too spicy? Here—take some of this barley cheese. It's creamy and it'll cut the spice a little."

I pinched off a bit, and it definitely helped cool the heat. "Thanks."

"Hey!" Beldon leaned around Acres, who he'd been discussing routes in Morrenfayre with, and frowned at Dane. "How come you didn't offer us any of that when our mouths were on fire?"

Beldon eyed the cheese with disdain as Acres swung around to face us, the ends of his tied-up locs swaying.

"Because neither of you is my girlfriend." Dane laughed.

I grinned down at the cheese and took another bite. Reenalyn was right—it was nice being Dane's girlfriend.

Beldon grinned and shrugged. "Well, you have me there."

"So," Dane said as he rolled up the rest of his food and stuffed it into his pack. "How do you think we'll go about finding Bennet and Whisper when we get to Morrenfayre?"

My cheerfulness faded. "I have no idea. I...I hope I haven't dragged everyone away for nothing. I have a strong feeling they're there against their wills, and I can't stand it." Lying in the grass, I covered my face with my hands.

"It's all right, Mella." He took my hand, and my face warmed as our fingers intertwined. "You didn't force anyone to come. We each decided on our own."

"Right—I know. I hope it doesn't become a wild goose chase. Maybe we should've separated and tried different places—"

He shrugged. "We're already here. Don't stress about it. If we need to split up later, we can, but for now, we're making progress toward hopefully finding them. Which brings me back to my original question: how do we find them when we get there? We don't know the lay of the land well enough to be much good at sneaking around."

"Yeah, probably not."

"Okay." He leaned back and stretched out his legs, thinking. "Then maybe we should start by seeking an audience with the king. Or the regent? Narellen must have left someone in charge. But then there's the risk of him being behind it, or working with the one behind it, so that's not foolproof. It would be nice if we happened across some old traveler with a walking stick and the exact information we needed, plus some extra food. Like they do in stories. Maybe there will be a sign to the kidnappers' weekly meeting place."

I laughed. "If only it were that easy. We probably couldn't run into that conveniently, but maybe we could search it out."

He shifted his weight in the grass. "What do you mean?"

"Well, we discovered vital information about Whisper from travelers in The Braided Loaf, didn't we? We could go into a tavern in Morrenfayre and listen for a while. Drunk people say useful things sometimes. And if that doesn't work, then we can buy food and drinks for everyone—which would make them open up to us—and then ask what they've heard about hybrid castlings. Or if they've seen any."

He smiled. "That could work. Good thinking."

"Thanks. We might have to pool our resources to accomplish that, though. I managed to find the coins I was saving in the rubble of the cottage, but they're not much."

"I'll share what I have," he whispered, stroking his thumb over the back of my hand. Was he thinking about the first time we met, when I'd shared what I'd had with him when he'd been in need?

"Dane?"

"Hmm?"

"Do you think we would've ended up together if I hadn't bought you and Sprinter a sandwich that day?"

"If I had somehow survived without your help, then I sure hope so."

"But what would you have thought if your first glimpse of me had been something other than me being generous? What if it had been when I was sparring with Yulroe, or judging jewelry and gown choices with Selverine?"

He chuckled. "I probably would've been afraid of you."

"*Afraid* of me? What?"

"If my first impression was of you sparring, I'd have been intimidated. If it was of you in a ballgown discussing fashion with the princess, I would've been even more intimidated. Lucky for me you're the kindest, nicest, prettiest girl—" His eyes flew open and he paused, then glanced at me with a quirky half smile. "Sorry, I didn't mean to be so..."

"So...what?"

He shifted uncomfortably. "I don't know. Coming on too strong or something. Saying mushy stuff too much."

I giggled. "Mushy stuff?"

He smiled wryly and faced the sky, where the first stars had just started sparkling. "Yeah, I guess."

"I thought it was nice."

He faced me, his white-blond bangs falling into his eyes. "So not too over-the-top, then?"

"No, Dane. Sweet. Thank you."

His smile widened. "Well then. You're welcome." After a moment, he said, "What would you have thought if you'd remembered me when we met in the woods after the Castling Ceremony? That I was a degenerate bum to avoid at all costs?"

"No, of course not!" I playfully smacked him. "I think I would've been impressed by how far you'd come."

"I have a lot farther to go."

"What do you mean?"

"I, well...I've been hanging out with Beldon."

I raised an eyebrow. "Yeah, I noticed. He's a fun person. But what does that have to do with this?"

"He's been giving me a few pointers."

"Pointers? On what?" I asked.

"If you haven't noticed yet, then it's a surprise."

"I have no idea what you're talking about."

He laughed, brushing his bangs from his face. "Thanks. You will eventually."

"Can't you at least give me a hint?"

He shook his head. "Nope."

"It's going to drive me crazy."

"Best not to dwell on it, then." He smirked.

"You're a pain, Dane Velowinzinger."

He chuckled.

"Then you have to distract me with something interesting," I said.

"Of course. Like what?"

"Tell me something about your family."

He was silent for a moment, then, "What do you want to know?"

"You've told me a little about your parents. What about your siblings? What are their names?"

"Tyro, Maylee, and Milrah."

"And Tyro—that's your brother, right?—has the long hair?"

"Yeah. He does. He can't help it. But it is a nice dark brown color, like yours. Sometimes he teases me about being an old man with how white my hair is."

"I don't think it makes you look old. It looks good on you. I'm trying to picture you with any other hair color, and it just doesn't work." I considered, tugging on a strand of my hair. "I'm kind of jealous of Reenalyn's blonde hair. It's such a warm and free color. Maybe I could ask Acres if there are any hair-color-changing potions."

Dane grimaced.

I braced myself on one arm. "What's with that face?"

He chuckled and closed his eyes. "Sorry. It's just—I like it how it is. I mean, it's your hair and you should do whatever you want with it. But I wouldn't be opposed to leaving it exactly like this."

After a moment he winced and peeked from one eye. "Sorry, was that too much? I'm not trying to tell you what to do with your own hair or anything—I meant it as a compliment, but it came out wrong."

I laughed. "I knew what you meant, Dane. You worry too much."

He opened the other eye and grinned at me, the breeze blowing his hair around and catching bits of moonlight.

"I just love you, Dane."

His eyes brightened as his expression tilted from warm and funny to warmer and something else. "I love you, too." He shifted to one elbow like I was. I smiled up at him, leaning into his warmth as he wrapped his other arm around me and pulled me closer.

Smiling, I closed my eyes and waited for him to kiss me.

Then Beldon shouted, "Hey! Who's out there?" and everyone scrambled to grab their weapons.

CHAPTER 11

ACRES

Beldon shouted the warning, and I leaped up, drawing my throwing stars from their pouch at my hip and squinting through the dimming evening.

I did a double take when Selverine Merrandil's face caught the moonlight, Willova Calentine right behind her. Did Selverine have a black eye?

"It's just us. Relax." Selverine swept to the middle of our camp and dropped a pack at her feet. "Fancy meeting you here."

Mella glowered, brandishing her scythe. "What the muck are you doing here?"

"We're visiting Morrenfayre. We don't need anyone's permission." Selverine crossed her arms as Willova inched in behind her, a pack on her shoulder as well and a long, slanted pink stain on the front of her dress. It looked almost like blood, but it couldn't be. Had to be the dimming light.

Surely Selverine didn't use floramantic punch on Willova to make her join her on her trip?

"No, you don't need permission to travel to Morrenfayre. But you *do* need permission to travel *with us*, and you don't have it," Mella said. "So find your own campsite. There's plenty of roadside...especially about a mile east or west of here."

Selverine scoffed. "But, Mella, I brought you a present."

Mella made a face. "I don't want any presents from you."

"Are you sure? You used to like this one. Maybe you still do."

"What the muck are you talking about, Selverine?"

"Hey, guys!" came a male voice from the road.

Everyone was instantly on alert again, weapons raised, as Kaido Felzane sauntered into camp. Also with a black eye. He threw a careless wave in our general direction. "So where can I sleep?"

"What the skunking muck is this?" Mella gestured at Kaido, scowling at Selverine.

Selverine held up two hands. "Hey, I didn't ask him to come. He started following us and wouldn't muck off. What was I supposed to do?"

"Camp. Somewhere. Else!" Mella shouted.

Selverine shrugged. "This seems as good a place as any, don't you think, Willova?"

Willova half-nodded and half-glanced around uncomfortably at the rest of us. Were those freckles on her face? How had I never noticed them before?

"Great." Selverine sat on the ground, pulled a robe from her pack, and laid it over herself like a blanket. Then she fluffed her pack like a pillow and rested her head on it, rolling to the side to face away from everyone. Everyone but me, who she must not have realized was on this side.

Our eyes met, then she closed hers and kept them shut.

Now that I could see her better, she looked pretty rough, too. Dried blood crusted her hairline and one ear, and her nose looked different. Had she and Kaido thrown fists?

Willova finally laid down on the other side of Selverine, using her pack as a pillow, too. She curled into a ball with no covering and stared at nothing. After a moment, Selverine rolled halfway over to peek at Willova, and then threw her blanket over Willova and pulled a tunic out of her pack to cover her top half.

Something seemed off about that. It was...uncharacteristically *nice* of Selverine.

Movement caught my eye behind them—Dane's whiteish hair reflecting the moonlight. He and Mella were in a deep discussion, both frowning. Trinka was still gone, and Reenalyn and Beldon were getting out their own bedrolls.

"So..." Kaido stepped toward Mella. "This looks like a good spot."

She whirled on him, her spare scythe raised and fire in her eyes. "That spot is not available, Kaido Felzane. Muck off and pick somewhere on the other side of camp. I don't want you over here."

Kaido rubbed the back of his neck, a sheepish grin on his face. "Right. Okay."

Surprise flashed on Mella's face as Kaido spun without another word and strode to the outside of our makeshift circle.

Mella resumed talking to Dane, who glared at Kaido's retreating form.

I pulled out my bedroll and blanket, conscious of Selverine having sacrificed hers for Willova.

I spread it over myself and tried to get comfortable. Facing Selverine, I realized she looked prettier when she was asleep, despite the evidence of a fight—not stressed, not angry, just relaxed. Staring at her was a dumb thing to do though, so I turned away.

Now, not only was my entire cohort along for the ride, three extra stragglers had invited themselves.

Apparently staying in Terrenthyrs would've been the best way to get time to myself.

***

"You'll have to set boundaries for yourself and enforce them." Starstinger's long, lanky body wrapped around my neck, her whiskers tickling my chin as her tail flicked on the edge of my vision.

I plucked another dark purple berry and dropped it in the makeshift basket that was the bottom of my tunic held up partway. "How do you even know what that means?"

She shrugged her tiny cat shoulders against my chest. "Just do. And you'll have to listen to me if you want personal time to study fossils and get a break from people needing potions."

"Hmm." I considered taking a few of the berry leaves to learn what I could about their floramantic properties, but Starstinger was right. I wasn't here to mess around with potions. I was here to enjoy however much life I had left.

Which stress and exhaustion from floramantic experimentation would likely shorten.

"Seriously, Acres, I can support you and encourage you, but I can't make you enforce your own boundaries. Only you can do that. So you should start getting used to the idea."

"I'll work on it." I turned and headed for camp with a load of berries, hoping everyone else had scavenged other items to share.

When I arrived, Selverine and Willova sat side by side, a cloth full of the same purple berries between them. Selverine had tied her dark amber hair up, and the ponytail barely brushed her shoulder blades. Willova's red waves streamed down her back in a frizzy array. She wiped sweat from her forehead. Why not tie it like Selverine, if she was so warm?

Selverine tossed a berry in her mouth, then spun, probably hearing my approach.

"Hi..." I said.

"You found berries, too? Looks like that's what everyone found. So cheers for breakfast."

"Uh, yeah."

The crusted blood was gone, but a black eye more impressive than Kaido's stood out starkly on her delicate features. "Uh, did you and Kaido have an argument?"

She spit out the berry, laughing harshly. "Ha! You think that prick could lay a hand on me?"

"Oh, sorry..."

Selecting another berry, she nodded sharply at Willova. "Her brother caught me off guard. But I knocked him down two flights of stairs, so he probably looks worse than I do. Though I'll thank good fortune to let us live in mystery on that one."

"Oh." *Willova's brother did that to her face? What?*

She popped another berry in her mouth, and a little curve of puncture scars shone on her hand when the sun hit just right. An animal bite?

The green avian earrings she always wore glittered in the sunlight.

Her eyes were on me. "What? Want a closer look at it or something?"

"Oh, no. No, sorry." Pivoting, I strode back to the bushes—an easy way out of whatever that was. Must've been wrong about her last night.

"Scared of Selverine?" Starstinger purred from my shoulder.

"What? No, of course not. She made it clear I was annoying her, so I moved on."

"Uh-huh."

"Well, I wasn't going to keep making a nuisance of myself."

"This is the second time you've talked to the princess in as many days, isn't it?"

"So?"

"So you, Acres Parrianther, who vastly prefers books to people in every possible instance and hates crowds even more than a dog-eared page, both sought out and spoke to Selverine Merrandil on two different occasions a mere few hours apart."

"I did not seek her out either time, actually. I ran into her unexpectedly."

"Hmm."

Tearing a fistful of berries from a bush, I frowned. "And your point is?"

Starstinger's tail flicked faster, and I raised a brow. She made a face and whispered, "Your heart just sped up. Like, a lot."

"Oh, please." I rolled my eyes, scooped her off my shoulders, and set her on the ground.

"Oh, the ground, is it? Must've touched a nerve," she said as I poured more berries into a pocket on my pack next to the dapplemint leaves.

Whatever. Selverine was entirely beyond my class, and I didn't know how long I had anyway. There was no chance I'd be wasting any time on that kind of muck. I just wanted to get to Morrenfayre and find a few fossils.

CHAPTER 12

MELLA

I squinted at the sun, more visible now that the thick forest trees thinned into varieties that grew nearer to the desert. There was still shade, but it was sparser. Did Acres know any potions to prevent sunburns?

"So, Mella." Kaido appeared out of nowhere and slung an arm around my shoulder. "What are you gonna do with your time in Morrenfayre?"

I ducked out from under his arm and stepped away. "I'll be busy."

"Not too busy for any fun, I hope." He fell into step with me.

"*Far* too busy for any fun with *you*." I crossed my arms and watched the back of Dane's head. He was talking to Beldon and hadn't noticed Kaido yet. I shouldn't have been surprised. Of course Kaido was too much of a coward to act like this in front of Dane. He was just being a skunk behind his back.

"I bet I can change your mind."

I glared at him from the corner of my eye. A dark shiner over one eye stood out against his light-brown skin, and scabs covered his nose and jaw. "What the muck happened to your face?"

He grinned. "You should see the other guy."

I faced away from him. "Right."

"No, really. I'm a badass."

"I think the term you're searching for is ass*hole*."

"Aw, come on, Mella. Don't you miss me at least a little?"

"Nope. I could really do without you."

"But don't you think about it? About us?"

"Hmm..." I pretended to deliberate. "Also no."

He laughed and bounced ahead a few steps. "I don't believe you," he sang.

Dane turned and frowned at him, then glanced my way. I smiled and rolled my eyes, and he must've taken that as me handling Kaido well enough on my own. He continued talking to Beldon.

"Seriously, Mella." Kaido paused, glancing between Dane and me. "What the muck do you see in that pale, skinny freak?" He strolled ahead of me and grinned, gesturing to himself. "I mean, look at what you're missing."

Rolling my eyes, I said, "All I see is the skunk who ditched me without warning because I turned him down on a trip to his bed."

"Harsh, Mella. You know you would've had a good time."

This was getting old. How could I escape this conversation without begging someone else to rescue me? "Clearly I *don't* think that, since there's the part where I *turned you down*. Will you *please* go irritate someone else? I've put up with more than my fair share of your muck for the day." *For the week. For the year!*

I marched in front of him and caught up with Reenalyn. "Apparently the scar you gave him still hasn't put a damper on his confidence, the piece of skunk dung."

"I'm sorry the scar didn't change his personality, Mella," she said, staring straight ahead. "I don't know what else you want me to do."

So it was still the cold shoulder from her, was it? "Reenalyn, I wasn't criticizing you. Just commenting on Kaido's behavior."

"Oh. Okay."

I sighed. "Reenalyn, why are you mad at me? You've never had a problem with Dane and me before, so why now? You don't ...do you have...*feelings* for him?"

I didn't know what I'd do if she did. But why else would she be like this?

She made a face. "No, Mella." She sighed, too, and ran a pale hand through her blonde hair. "I'm not going to try to steal Dane from you or anything, okay? I don't want to talk about it, but there's nothing like that to worry about. All right?"

"Okay. If you say so." But something clearly still bothered her.

Not having a boyfriend wasn't some kind of personal failing. It was a situation you could change if you wanted to. Not having a castling—that was my fault. It made sense now that I understood how Whisper's bowstrings had affected my first Castling Ceremony, but there was still a part of me that was terrified to stand on that stage and risk failing in front of all Terrenthyrs a second time.

What if I couldn't do it? What if there was some other reason I didn't know about yet? For all I knew, I was less than Reenalyn and everybody else. Maybe I was a coward, too, and that was the biggest reason for leaving my new scythe behind.

***

As the sun faded on the second evening of our journey, I caught sight of Trinka's head snapping up, her dark eyes skimming the view before us. I followed her gaze, and a few moments later I heard something. It sounded like...music. And laughing.

"What's that sound?" Beldon asked.

Dane abandoned Acres and Beldon to stand closer to me. "Maybe that's the tavern you were hoping for?" he whispered.

Beldon sniffed the air loudly. "Do you guys smell that? I smell meat! And potatoes! Hot dinner tonight!" He hooted and took off at a sprint.

The music and aromas came from an old building, two stories tall with two peaks in the roof and candles in the windows. Judging by the front porch, it could've been a house once.

I laced my fingers through Dane's and led the way through the dark double doors into the dimly lit tavern. Several tables were strewn around the room, some with chairs and others with benches. Most were occupied.

The nine of us strode in, trying to be inconspicuous. At least, as inconspicuous as a group of nine unbathed, ravenous teenagers could be.

A few pairs of eyes flicked toward us—to be expected when a door opens, especially when a crowd comes through. They'd surely return to their food and conversations any moment.

But they kept staring. And more joined them.

By the time we'd crossed the room and reached the bar, every eye in the place was on us.

Many of which belonged to animals. A sheep lay curled under a bench, pretending to sleep. At the next table, three black goats stood on chairs and one on the table, their castors reaching around them for their food.

A shrill squeak pulled my attention to where a squirrel ran up and down her castor's tunic, then ran out of slack in its string. Why did it have string tied around it?

The goats and sheep had strings too. So did every other castling in the place.

My skin crawled.

And the sheep was *still* sleeping without disappearing.

But they had to be castlings, didn't they? No one brought regular sheep and goats into a tavern. Did they?

What kind of place tied up their castlings? And how did they keep them manifested while sleeping?

Something was definitely off. I went from wondering if we were in danger to wondering how much danger we were in.

Beldon approached the bar first, leaned on the counter with one elbow, and grinned at the elderly woman who'd paused in polishing a glass to stare at us with wide dark eyes. "Hello, ma'am. We're looking to get some dinner. What's the special today?"

"You should leave," she whispered, glancing around furtively. "Turn around and go right back where you came from before it's too late."

CHAPTER 13
SELVERINE

From where I stood near Beldon's side, I watched his smile melt into a frown at the tavern master's words. "Uh...why do you say—"

"Oh, don't listen to her." A scruffy old man with a smokey beard and thinning, cottony hair strode through a pair of swinging saloon doors and lightly patted the woman on the shoulder, grinning. "She's just tired and doesn't want to serve any more customers today." Facing her, he said, "Why don't you go rest a bit, hmm?"

Without another glance at us, she set the glass and rag on the wooden counter and left through the same swinging doors.

My eyes narrowed. No way that was all it was. We should leave now while we still could.

He stretched his long arms out, gripping the counter's edge, and leaned toward us with a welcoming smile. "I'm sorry. What can I get you?"

"Um..." Beldon seemed to be struggling with what to say.

A salty, meaty aroma drifted from the kitchen, making my stomach rumble.

Beldon must've noticed it, too. "We want dinner. What do you have?"

He nodded with a welcoming smile. "Well, we've got hearty lamb chops today, and the usual sausage and rice. And plenty of potatoes."

A much less varied selection than The Braided Loaf, but I wouldn't be eating a bit of it anyway. No matter that we were far away from Grandmother and her floramancy. Something was off about this place.

Beldon ordered the lamb and a potato and slid a couple of coins over the counter.

I searched for a table big enough for all of us while the rest placed their orders. Many patrons still stared, though more furtively than before. Those whose gaze I met flicked away instantly.

My eyes narrowed more. What was the deal? Had we walked into a literal den of thieves? I thought of the Wager Day winnings weighing down my pack and hoped not.

Spotting two empty tables near each other, I crossed the room, passed a goat tied to a table and a small dog tied to a chair, and moved chairs around to slide the tables together. Beldon must've caught on. He appeared a moment later, helping me slide one of the heavy round tables over to the other. "Thanks."

"No problem." He pulled out a chair and dropped into it, glancing around. "Is this place creepy or what?"

I sat across from him, keeping my pack slung over one shoulder and in my lap rather than hanging it off the chair or putting it under the table. "Yeah. I was afraid we might get a reaction like this if we came in with castlings, but maybe we would've blended in better with them."

The others approached and took their seats.

Mella leaned her ugly practice scythe against the table and sat next to me and across from the bald one—Trinka, was it?

"Trinka," Mella whispered, "why do you look so relaxed? This place is creepy as skunks, but you look less tense than usual."

Trinka crossed her arms and placed her elbows on the table. "Look around. Didn't you notice anything weird about this place—besides the staring and animals?"

I followed Mella's gaze, searching the tavern for anything else unusual. "Holy skunks," I said, finally noticing what had felt off before. "They're all...*old*."

Trinka's dark eyes flicked to mine, and she nodded, reclining. "I could take any of them. Even a strong sixty-year-old man has weak joints. If you kick him in the knees just right, you've got him."

"Weird," Mella said.

I eyed Trinka. "So your mood is dependent on whether you feel like you could take anyone in the immediate vicinity down in a fight?"

Her dark eyes met mine for only a moment before flitting around the room again. "Yours isn't?"

Before I could answer, the ominous lady from behind the bar brought out food for Reenalyn and Acres. The man followed closely behind with Kaido and Beldon's orders. Soon everyone from the Wrynford cohort was sprinkling something over their food and then digging in, too interested in the first hot meal they'd had in days to keep a conversation going.

What were they doing? Adding some kind of Wrynford seasoning?

Kaido didn't seem to think his food needed seasoning. He shoveled it in with abandon. And Willova took another delicate bite from her fork, her eyes downcast as usual.

Acres hesitated on the other side of the table, looking for a seat. Starstinger gestured to the seat next to me, and the two proceeded to have a silent argument of scowls and gestures.

What was that about? I probably smelled mucky, but so did everyone else after a day and a night on the road.

Rounding the table, Acres drew out the chair and sat. "Aren't you going to eat?" he asked, taller than I remembered.

"Would you eat anything prepared by someone else ever again if you'd spent the last several years being magically manipulated by floramancy in your food?"

Retrieving a little pouch from beside his plate, he shrugged. "I have this, so, yes."

I took it from him and inspected it, sniffing the contents. "Ew. That's no spice I've ever smelled before." I held it out. "You're way off if you think *more* floramancy is the answer."

He held up both hands, refusing to take it back. "It's a dry potion like what I gave all of Terrenthyrs to combat Narellen's manipulation. It will neutralize any potions in your food. Hold on to it, just in case."

Rolling my eyes, I shoved it in my pack and pulled out a strip of meat from the preserved food I'd bought in Terrenthyrs. As I nibbled on it, I strained to hear the conversations around me to see if I could learn anything useful.

I caught snippets about crops this year and weather. A lot of boring muck. One lady got loud enough for me to hear everything she said rather than just snatches, but she was only fretting about her granddaughter getting older. *Almost of age* or something.

"She's already eleven?" the other woman at her table asked in a low voice.

Eleven? That's not of age for anything. I must've misunderstood.

"She has been...for a while."

I unstoppered my water flask and sipped.

"But she's getting too old to claim that age, if you know what I mean."

"Boobs?" the other woman asked knowingly.

I nearly spewed water in Beldon's face. *What the muck?*

There was silence from their table, and I wondered if the first woman had nodded.

The other woman tsked. "I never thought I'd say I missed the regent, but his son—unbelievable."

"I still say the son killed him. He's crazy enough to do it."

"Hmm," the other replied.

"How about those travelers, though? Not a single one could pass for less than seventeen, and that's a stretch for some."

She must've noticed Beldon's stature and biceps.

"Do you reckon they know...?"

The first woman harrumphed. "If they did, would they be here?"

Shoving my chair from the table, I turned in my seat and found the two women, one with dark-gray hair in a braid over one shoulder, the other with her white hair knotted into a low bun. Two cats sat curled on their table, the black one grooming itself and the tabby sleeping.

The two women looked at me with surprise, though their castlings ignored me.

"I couldn't help overhearing that we're getting into something we apparently don't fully understand. Would you mind explaining what the muck that is?" I asked.

The white-haired one glanced around furtively while the other held my gaze. "We don't know what you're talking about. You must've misheard."

I raised an eyebrow. "Uh-huh."

They glanced at each other, then slid from their chairs, plates only half-finished, each scooping up a cat. The black one meowed as the tabby startled and hissed. But it couldn't have actually been *asleep*. Why was it acting like it was? They couldn't be floramancing them, surely. Or could they?

"Hey! We deserve an explanation!" I shouted as they headed for the door without a backward glance.

"What was that about?" Kaido asked.

I shrugged, scooting my chair to the table. "Apparently Morrenfayre is mysteriously dangerous, and we should go home. According to them."

Kaido glanced around the table covered in mostly empty plates. "Aren't we going to consider their advice?"

"Consider whatever you want, Kaido," Mella spat, "but we're still going after Bennet and Whisper. At least *I* am." She scowled at the rest of us with one eyebrow raised.

Well, I certainly wasn't returning to Grandmother or Jorros. And Willova wasn't going back to Drazdan.

"I'm still in," Dane and Acres said at the same time. Beldon shrugged and Reenalyn nodded at Mella.

"Okay then," Kaido said, sounding unsure. "Well, I guess I'm in, too."

"All right. How about we get out of this creepy tavern, then?" I suggested.

"That's a plan." Beldon shoved his chair back and stretched, not even a drop of sauce left on his plate.

Something bugged me about those castlings. The tabby looked like it was sleeping, which castlings couldn't do for more than a second without disappearing. But they also just...didn't act like castlings. Or look like them, either. But why bring regular animals into a tavern?

I slid out of my chair, my pack still on my shoulder, and took one last glance around the room. The old people still watched us furtively, but many of them also looked kind of...concerned for us? Definitely worried, but not so much afraid of us like many had seemed when we first arrived.

Why were there only old people here, and why did they look so fearful?

Chapter 14

REENALYN

E yeing the odd animals seeming less and less like castlings, I shoveled herbed lamb and potatoes into my mouth as quickly as possible. We needed to leave, but with Acres's potion to make the food floramancy-free, I wasn't interested in wasting any of it.

A glimmer of light caught my eye from a dark corner of the tavern. Chewing another bite of lamb, I glanced that way.

A guy about my age—the youngest stranger I'd seen since leaving Wrynford—with dirty blond hair sat, his face shaded by a cloak, twirling something between his fingers that reflected flickers of light. I couldn't see him behind the two ladies before, but since they'd left, he stood out.

Nudging Beldon, I nodded toward the guy. "There's someone our age. Think we should ask him what's up before we go?"

"Maybe." Beldon stood, eyeing the guy. "But he had to have noticed us. If he wanted to help, he probably would've. I don't know if we can trust him."

He had a good point. Deciding against it, I reached under the table for my pack.

Doors slammed open with a clang.

The room went silent as a gust of air blew through the tavern.

"Prepare to submit to searches, by order of the regent!" A man's voice rang through the room.

Oh no!

Still leaning over, I glimpsed the young stranger dart under the table the two ladies had left. And something slipped from his fingers as he dove. It clinked and shimmered as it bounced toward me, just out of reach.

A key?

Our eyes met, and his were wide with terror.

Making a split-second decision, I tossed my pack so that it covered the key and rose slowly, finding the owner of the voice. And his friends.

Five soldiers stood in the doorway. The shortest one, a dark-skinned man with a wavy sword partially drawn from the wooden scabbard at his side and a scowl cold enough to cause frostbite, led the others into the tavern, searching our fellow diners' faces.

He was the only one without a castling. But the others...

Oh my goodness...

Next to the tallest, darkest man behind the scowler, a pale lion with a mane of cream and beige feathers growled and showed his fangs, ready to pounce. On the shoulders of the tan woman in the back sat a possum with a tangerine beak and feather-tipped tail.

A pale, red-haired man with arms thick as Brawler's rested his huge hand on the head of a kangaroo with a set of talons sticking out of its tail. A broad brunette woman stood with her arms crossed. Her feathered fox growled and showed its teeth through its fox muzzle and an avian beak protruding next to it.

So there are *hybrids here!*

The sixth person, a slight, pale woman with cropped black hair and angular eyes, crouched next to what looked like a red hog castling with a white face and long ear tufts. I couldn't tell whether that one was a hybrid or not.

And something huge, gray, and wrinkly moved outside the tavern, barely visible through the open doors. The scowling man's castling? Was it too big to get through the door?

The tan woman stepped out from behind the others, and to my shock, *more* castlings followed her. A badger with feather tufts sprouting from various parts of its body, a black-and-white monitor lizard with a red beak and tiny black wings that couldn't possibly work sprouting from its shoulders, and more besides.

An ebony leopard with owlish talons instead of paws and what looked like bare white wing bones protruding from its rippling shoulders stepped in front of the others and sniffed the air, its eyes narrowed.

"Marken Drother, we know you're in here. Show yourself," the scowling man said.

I was beginning to feel I'd made the right choice to hide the key from these people.

"I'm sure you've not forgotten what happens when you harbor criminals." The leopard addressed the room in a threatening, fierce female voice. "We just went through this."

Spreading around the room, the other soldiers and their castlings peered into peoples' faces and under tables and chairs. Except for the red-haired guard with the hybrid kangaroo. He stood at the door, looking longingly at the others as they inspected patrons.

The scowling man came around our table, pausing when he caught sight of us.

"Hello," I said brightly with my best smile. The others looked at me like I'd lost my mind. But I had to do something to distract this horrible man before he could capture the guy who must be Marken. "I'm Reenalyn. It's nice to meet you. What's your name?"

Ignoring me with a frown, the scowler continued his search.

I held my breath, hoping the key was completely covered.

He moved on to the next table, and my heart sank. He hadn't found the key, but there was no way he'd miss Marken.

"It's clear over here," he said, shocking me as he strode toward the counter, peering behind it. Did he *look* under the table? Maybe Marken would get away yet!

The monitor with the little wings skittered over the floor, flicking its pink tongue to taste the air. Its eyes narrowed, and it slunk toward Marken's table.

Oh no! He was almost home free!

The lizard dove under the table, and Marken screamed.

My stomach dropped, icy fear spreading through my veins. *No, no, no! What's going to happen to him now?*

The solders and hybrids converged in our corner as the monitor dragged the guy out by a bloody ankle, shaking him relentlessly. Blood oozed from around the lizard's avian beak.

"Stay on the ground!" the scowling man yelled, running back over.

He was on Marken in an instant, rolling him onto his stomach and shoving a knee in his back.

With Marken restrained, the monitor let go, and the scowler pulled a length of rope from his pocket. "I told you we'd catch you eventually, Drother. You shouldn't have wasted your time here."

Marken faced our table, his cheek pressed into the floor, and his eyes met mine, wide with urgency.

Was there anything I could do to help?

The scowler patted him down, his hand disappearing from view as he shook out Marken's sleeve.

Which was out of view because our table was in the way.

Marken might be able to grab the key with the hand they'd just searched and cleared! Was it a good idea to have it on him even while captured? He must think so, if I was reading his meaning correctly.

The black leopard loomed over the kneeling scowler, her teeth bared as she observed the search. "Be thorough," she growled.

The scowler bristled.

Wasn't he in charge? Why was she butting in with orders?

Pressing the toe of my boot against my pack, I gently slid it toward Marken's hand. I hit something—probably Selverine's chair—and rotated around it.

His arm strained toward it as the scowler finished his inspection by yanking off his boots and examining the soles.

He couldn't reach it. But I couldn't push it any further.

I had to do something!

But all I had within reach was my spoon.

Actually, I could do some damage with a spoon.

With a flick of my wrist, I sent it clamoring over the plates and cutlery the old ladies had left on their table when they ran for it.

The soldiers' heads whipped toward the clamor, and I ducked under the table.

Folded in half, I struggled to breathe silently. Yet another reason my height was getting on my nerves.

Pressing a hand to the pack, I slid it slowly toward Marken so the metal wouldn't scrape against the floor.

His hand disappeared, yanked out of view.

What!

"Get on your feet. Boots on," the scowler ordered. "You're coming with us."

No! I missed my chance!

Someone hauled Marken to his feet, kicking his boots in front of him so he could put them on.

Which brought them closer to my table.

Did I dare?

Yep. I did.

Snatching the key from under the bag, I aimed at an empty boot.

Marken stuck his stupid foot into it before I could throw.

My fingers slid over a thickness in the key, as if it had been broken and welded together. But there was no time to investigate.

Flinging it at the second boot, I overshot, but managed to bounce the key off his ankle and into the boot as he shoved his foot in.

My jaw dropped.

There's no way that just worked.

"Come on. Let's get out of here," the scowler said, shuffling Marken past our table.

I covered my mouth. *It did!*

"Wait," growled the jaguar. "Who are all of you?"

Oh no.

Silence reigned for a long moment.

"I'm traveling to Morrenfayre on behalf of Queen Narellen," Selverine cut in. "I need to see the regent."

What was she doing?

"Oh, is that so? Presumptuous of you," the jaguar drawled, raising a brow.

"Hardly," Mella said. "She's the q—"

But Selverine stopped her. "I'm a servant of the queen's, and she demanded I speak directly with the regent."

The jaguar mock-bowed and gestured with one paw toward the door. "By all means. Let us escort you to the regent."

The smile in her tone set me on edge. Going with them was a bad idea. But if people our age were such a rare thing, they were probably going to take us in anyway. At least this way they led us to the regent as human beings rather than dragging us as prisoners like Marken. Though how long they'd leave us untied…

The immediate question for me was how to get out from under the table without drawing attention to the fact that I'd been up to something under here.

Beldon bent down and grabbed my pack, dragging me out with it. "Oh, thanks for reminding me of my pack, Reenalyn."

His pack was already slung over his shoulder. The jaguar squinted at me as I got to my feet.

"Eclipse, are these bindings suitable?" the scowler asked her, presenting Marken's bound hands just in time.

Whew. I was standing with the others. Out of the frying pan, but still sizzling right in the center of the fire.

The jaguar—Eclipse, apparently—inspected the bindings closely, looking pleased to have been asked for her opinion. "Yes, they'll do." Turning around, she stalked toward the door, her owlish taloned feet scraping on stone.

Mella and Selverine followed Eclipse and the scowler as they pushed Marken ahead of them through the door. The rest of us followed, leaving the staring elderly people and their odd castlings behind.

"I'm sure you're up-to-date on everything?" Eclipse asked Selverine, squinting in the sunlight.

"I'm sure I am, but tell me what you know anyway," Selverine replied with haughtiness equal to the jaguar's.

"Why don't you tell me what you know, so I can avoid wasting your time with unnecessary information?" Eclipse countered.

"Because I surely know more than you," Selverine snapped indignantly, "and the queen will want to know what the common knowledge is here."

Eclipse paused, peering at Selverine with dark feline eyes.

I hid a smile. I didn't care much for Selverine, but her quick wit was useful today.

The scowler ignored us, dragging Marken behind him to the giant gray animal. It was a rhinoceros, larger than Mauler and Brawler put together, and a comical contrast to the short stature of the scowling man. Two enormous horns the same grayish hue as its skin grew on its face, one between its eyes and one on the end of its nose.

He mounted it, making it look easier than it must surely be, and said, "To the manor, Rumble."

The rhino lumbered onto the road, Marken walking sullenly at his side.

Marken hadn't said a word of protest. Was he mute? Or shy or scared, maybe?

Odd that he walked next to the rhino rather than behind it.

The two women and the dark-skinned guard with the lion hybrid herded us after the scowler, the red-haired guard bringing up the rear.

Dane fell into step with Mella in front of me as the remaining soldiers and castlings encircled us and herded us after Rumble onto the main road. Beldon eased toward Trinka over the course of several steps. Kaido and Acres were near the back with Willova.

I was in the middle. Alone.

Why did no one glance at me to make sure *I* was okay? Even Kaido eyed Willova for a moment, and of course Dane held Mella's hand.

Maybe it was because I should be able to fend for myself—as skilled as I was.

Or maybe it was because I was still too tall.

Here I am worrying about this, when we've been captured by Morrenfayre and have no idea what we're walking into. I've got bigger problems.

The dirt road grew redder and harder to walk on. Was this sand? It must be.

We hadn't seen a tree since the ones around the tavern. Instead, huge boulders rose from the sand, casting long shadows in the evening light.

Acres stooped to snatch something from the ground more than once as we trekked. What was he finding? The red-haired guard—the closest one to him—raised an eyebrow each time but never tried to stop him.

Voices clamored from around the corner, and we reached a marketplace. If you could call it that.

A row of dilapidated stands and carts spread out along either side of the road. Vendors, some with white fabric tied around their heads, noticed us and our escorts and took a seat on the hot sandy ground instantly, averting their eyes.

Not a good sign.

One old woman held a squirming toddler in her lap, shielding him from the sun with her body as best she could. I glanced over the people we'd passed. Wrinkly skin. Gray or white beards. Many bone thin.

I'd missed it before due to the head coverings, but just like in the tavern, everyone here was at least sixty years old. Unless they were under ten.

Where are the teenagers and middle-age people?

One of the guards tapped my shoulder and I flinched, tripping sideways to avoid being trodden on.

"Sorry, but we do need to keep going," whispered the red-haired guard with the hybrid kangaroo castling.

They steered our whole group down a side road.

When we rounded another bend, a huge stone building loomed into view. I stared over Marken's head, past the scowling guard still mounted on the rhino, at the enormous building. The rows of windows across the front made it look more like a sprawling manor house than the palace I had been expecting to find a regent in.

We neared the stone steps leading to a set of enormous double front doors. Dozens of windows glinted in bright sunlight—except for one window on the bottom floor, where I could barely make out a man with longish wavy hair watching us.

My heart lurched, but it was different this time. I felt a flicker of emotion from that direction—was it the blond guy? But it felt like...like a feeling toward *me*.

He disappeared and shut the window, and the feeling vanished. I shook my head. I was being ridiculous. Of course this random guy wouldn't know who I was, much less have any feelings for me. Not when I was a total stranger surrounded by prettier girls.

But that's okay. I'm here to find Bennet and Whisper. That's all.

Foolishly I'd kept my eye on the window with the blond man as we approached, but the glare from the sun at this angle made it too bright to see through. He was probably gone anyway.

Dismounting, the scowler dragged Marken up the stairs and through the huge wooden door.

The guards guided the rest of us through the same door, then shut it behind us.

Our footsteps echoed through the two-story entryway. Further in, a beautiful balcony stretched from one wing to the other with a wrought-iron railing overlooking the spacious room. The stone wall rounded out a little on one side of the balcony, maybe housing a staircase?

"Xerrome!" A booming voice echoed. "You found him!" A tall man with long, dark blondish hair appeared under the balcony, striding toward us with one arm resting over a jeweled dagger on his hip. "Thank goodness we can finally put a stop to his conniving."

The scowler, *Xerrome*, apparently, crossed the stone floor and held a whispered conversation with the man, then strode out of sight with Marken. Where was he taking him? Why was he in trouble, and would the key be safe?

The long-haired man returned his attention to us, beaming with an attractive smile.

He really was quite tall. Maybe even taller than *me*.

Oh, my.

I straightened, eyeing him with interest.

"Now." He eyed the leopard, her white wing bones standing out against her ebony fur. "Eclipse, who are our guests?"

Eclipse prowled before us, her strange taloned feet clacking on the stone. "Travelers from Terrenthyrs. Or so they claim."

"Ah." His eyes darted over each of us, and they might have lingered on me for a beat longer than the others. "It's wonderful to meet you. What brings you to Morrenfayre?"

Acres's knee must've buckled because he fell forward before catching himself and straightening. "Sorry!"

Shaking his head, the man said, "No, I must apologize. You've been out in the desert sun for who knows how long. Please come in and take a seat. Wallen? Water."

The red-haired guard with the kangaroo castling opened a door in the wall and strode through, his castling hopping behind him.

Gesturing for us to follow, the tall man spun and strode deeper into the manor, behind the rounded-out wall.

Someone—Trinka, probably—said something about only idiots following a stranger farther away from the exit of an unknown place, but I was too curious to listen.

Following him, I found that there was a staircase, but it wasn't a regular one. This one went around in a spiral as it rose to the second floor.

Fascinating!

Striding through an archway, he led us past a huge dining room to a beautiful sitting room with chaise lounges and settees.

The man seated himself on a chaise as the rest of us and the remaining guards caught up.

He welcomed us in, shooing the soldiers away. "Let them breathe! It's hot enough in here." Glancing at us, he said with a smile, "Please, take a seat."

His voice was rich and warm.

And it seemed like his smiling eyes lingered on me again as he gestured to the seat next to him.

Intrigued, I stepped around Willova and Acres to sit on his other side. I focused on what romantic feeling he might have toward anyone, and something was there, dimly. Was I a fluttering fool, or was it directed at *me?*

Was that admiration aimed in my direction? Had I finally found the one man who wouldn't shy away from me?

No, of course not. I just met him. I won't get my hopes up. Though…it wouldn't hurt to keep an eye on him.

"Please, make yourselves comfortable," he said.

The tan woman with too many castlings stood guard at the door as the ebony-headed lion castor brushed past her and took a seat at the far end of the room, his castling sitting on the floor at his side.

"I'm curious to learn what brings you all here today, but first, introductions." The long-haired man faced me. "My name is Zaylan, the regent of Morrenfayre. Tell me, miss"—he beamed at me—"what's your name?"

Oh wow. This is the regent? He can't be much older than us.

"Reenalyn Demensey." I blushed, appreciating his hazel eyes.

What if I'd been wrong about Marken? Surely someone as kind and welcoming as Zaylan couldn't be *bad*. Should I tell him about the key?

No, not yet. I'd wait on that just in case.

"Lovely to meet you, Reenalyn." He placed his huge hand over mine where it rested on the table, only for an instant, and sparks flew up my arm and through my stomach.

Oh. My. Goodness.

The red-haired guard returned with goblets of water. With a welcoming smile, he set one before me, then offered one to everyone else.

I longed for a sip, but I couldn't drink any without adding a sprinkle of Acres's antiflora potion. How to manage that with so many eyes on us…

"So you're from Terrenthyrs? Xerrome mentioned you're here on behalf of the queen?"

Mella sat opposite Zaylan, Dane and Kaido seating themselves on either side of her, and interrupted me. "She is." Mella pointed at Selverine. "But the rest of us—we're concerned friends of ours have been captured and brought and held here against their will."

"Oh no. What led you to that conclusion?" Zaylan's eyebrows drew together.

Grateful I'd put the antiflora powder packet in my pocket, I slowly pulled it out and pinched a bit from the top.

Eclipse, sitting on her haunches next to Zaylan, frowned. "You left out that only one of you were here on behalf of the queen."

Selverine shrugged. "We traveled together since we were going in the same direction."

Zaylan nodded. "I'll speak to you about the queen right away. But first, tell me about these friends, and why you believe them to be here." He steepled his fingers, giving Mella his full attention.

Passing my hand slowly over the goblet, I released the sprinkle and then pulled the cup toward me. Heart racing, I swirled it a few times and then took a sip. It was divine. A bit of a funny aftertaste from the potion, but well worth it.

"We heard from travelers in our village that castlings manifesting as hybrids have been spotted in the area." Her eyes skimmed over Eclipse and the tan woman's collection of hybrid castlings. "Which appears to be true. Since our friend Bennet's castling is a hybrid, we're worried someone may have thought she belonged here, even if she wanted to be in Terrenthyrs."

Zaylan scratched his fine jawline. "Hmm. This is troubling. As you've seen, we do have a few castors with hybrid castlings, but we wouldn't have reason to go search for more. Especially not from another country. But please, rest assured I will conduct a full inquiry into the matter for you."

Wow. How generous! A bit odd that a regent would care so much about a missing castor and castling from another country. But maybe Zaylan was just that kind of person.

"Oh." Mella blinked. "Thank you."

"Xerrome?" Zaylan called.

The scowler entered, no Marken with him this time. Was he in a dungeon now? Xerrome approached Zaylan, glowering at the rest of us.

Goodness, what could've put him in such a bad mood?

"Yes, sir?"

"Please let Jathe and the others know I have an errand for them first thing in the morning. I'll send detailed instructions before they depart."

He nodded to Xerrome, who bowed and left the room, still scowling. What was his problem? *Maybe he's jealous of Zaylan's good looks.*

"Oh, um...thank you. For the help. What errand, exactly?" Mella asked.

Zaylan smiled at me as he replied, "There are a few places a hybrid would likely hide. I'm going to send some people to check them out."

Another flair of feeling bloomed from his direction. It brought on a rush of my own.

Oh my goodness. This guy likes me!

CHAPTER 15

ACRES

This Zaylan guy was too nice. His eagerness to help didn't make sense.

"It's getting late. Please feel free to make yourselves at home in the guests' wing," Zaylan offered, his pine marten castling's pink nose twitching on his shoulder. It appeared to be only one type of animal.

So now he was offering us a place to stay in the manor? Definitely too nice.

"No. Thank you, but I think we'll be all right outside," Selverine objected.

I raised an eyebrow. Interesting that the palace girl protested when her only other option was sleeping in the sand on the side of the dirt road.

"Oh, I insist! There's no place to rent sleeping quarters nearby, and we have plenty of guest rooms in the north wing." Zaylan stood, gesturing toward the arched entryway. "Come, I'll show you."

Reenalyn was the first to stand and follow, looking more trusting and appreciative than this situation called for. Everyone else followed suit, so I did the same, my hand on my throwing star pouch just in case.

Zaylan led us from the dining room and into the huge receiving room we'd entered earlier toward a spiral staircase. Zaylan and Reenalyn climbed around the staircase toward the second-floor balcony, Reenalyn hitting her head with a *thunk* on the bottom of the stairs above.

"Oops! Clumsy me." She blushed deeply and slouched the rest of the way up the stairs.

An iron railing ran along the edge of the balcony, overlooking the front entry room. The setting sun shone through a giant window in the front wall at the balcony's level. A window that would probably let in enough moonlight for reading on a clear night.

I rested a hand on the railing, bearing my weight on one leg. Was my knee hurting, or was that my imagination? Everything as simple as soreness from sleeping on the ground made me nervous lately.

Would I recognize when it started, or would it slowly take over my body before I realized what was going on? And once it started, how long would I have left?

Zaylan led us to the right and strode down a hallway. Gesturing toward the doors on either side, he grinned and said, "Please, help yourselves to any of these rooms. We keep them in good order to receive guests, should the opportunity arise, so you'll find fresh linens on the beds and oil in the lamps."

"Thank you, Zaylan." Reenalyn beamed up at him, which made a point of how tall he was.

"You're welcome, Reenalyn." He beamed at her, too. "Well, I'll leave you to get settled. Tomorrow there will be breakfast in the dining room, and once we've eaten, I'll have a few more questions about your friends, and then we'll form a plan to look for them. Goodnight!"

He strode back up the hall and across the balcony. It was too dark to see where he went, but a door closed a few moments later.

I glanced at the rest of the Wrynford castors. Selverine was waving everyone into one of the rooms. I followed the others inside. The room had a large four-poster bed, a chest of drawers, and flowy curtains over the windows.

"I don't trust him." Selverine closed the door. "Anyone else?"

Trinka crossed her arms and leaned against the wall by the door. "Not a bit."

"Probably not," said Beldon, scratching the back of his neck with a yawn.

"Nope," Kaido said, crossing his arms.

Mella and Dane shook their heads, and Willova stepped into the shadows behind Selverine, her face expressionless.

"Well, what other choice do we have?" Reenalyn asked, standing by the window. "He's been kind to us, and he said he'd help us find Bennet and Whisper tomorrow. What's wrong with that?"

"Firstly, the fact you seem to believe him." Selverine tapped one finger, then another as she rattled off a list. "Also, the fact that he's being *too* nice. And that he said he'll *try* to help. It's easy to back out of a *try*."

"Hang on," I interrupted. Did anyone else notice the guards' hybrid castlings are all part avian? Shouldn't they be different kinds of combinations? Perhaps a jaguar and a kangaroo or a possum and a monitor lizard. Why are they all half avian?"

"Yeah." Trinka pushed off from the wall, her arms still crossed. "And where are the full avian castlings? Narellen said she'd built an army of castors with avian castlings, but we haven't seen a single one yet."

"That's a good point," I agreed. "However we only just arrived, and it is nearly nighttime. Maybe we'll see them in the morning."

Trinka flicked her cold gaze around the room.

"And where's everyone else our age?" Dane added. "And everyone between ten and sixty?"

Selverine gestured around the room. "*Which* brings me back to my point that something is definitely sketchy."

"While I agree we should be cautious," Mella said from the foot of the bed next to Dane, "this is also our best chance for finding them. I mean, anyone else have a better lead? We've made it to Morrenfayre, but we don't have any other clues. Maybe Zaylan can find them faster than we could."

Reenalyn nodded. "That's right! And where have we seen hybrids so far? Just with the soldiers! Who are all here, working under Zaylan. Who better to help us find our missing hybrid?"

Nodding, Kaido said, "I agree with Mella."

"Good to know you three—well, two of you, anyway—clearly rate your curiosity about Bennet and Whisper above our safety," Selverine snapped. "Kaido, your motivations are always questionable, so no surprise there."

With his eyes wide in mock hurt, he laid a hand dramatically over his chest. "You wound me, madame."

Selverine ignored him as Mella scowled and said, "I question the mo-tivations of all three of you. You still haven't told us why the muck you showed up and crashed our expedition. It's not because you give a muck about Bennet or Whisper. So what is it?" Crossing her arms, she raised an expectant eyebrow.

"Not that it's any of your business," Selverine spat, "but I'm here because I want to be. Willova's here because I brought her."

Mella nodded at Kaido. "And him?"

"I have no idea what his deal is. Like I told you, we couldn't shake him off."

"You're lucky to have run into me! Without my help, you—" Kaido started.

"Oh, muck off Kaido!" Selverine scowled. "You haven't helped with anything."

He put on a face of mock hurt once again. "But—"

"Okay, ladies." Beldon slid between them. "How about we sleep on this? For now, we all get a good night's sleep in a comfortable bed."

Selverine tried to interrupt him, but he spoke over her. "And we can set someone on watch. I'll take the first shift and keep an eye on the hallway. I'll wake everyone if anything funny happens."

I nodded. "I'll relieve you in a few hours so you can sleep, too."

"Great." Beldon nodded. "Thanks, Acres. We can all take turns over the next few nights. No matter where we sleep, we'll need to post a watch just in case."

"That's the first sensible thing anyone's said today." Selverine sighed. "All right, well, I'll take this room. Night."

Mella scoffed at the clear dismissal and strode from the room, followed by the rest of us. Willova left right before me and walked into the room across the hall, while I headed for a door at the far end of the hallway and breathed a sigh of relief.

Finally, my own space.

Movement from the balcony by the spiral staircase caught my eye. The female soldier with cropped black hair and the hog castling stood against the back wall, facing the giant window. Light from the moon poured in, highlighting her face and reflecting on the hilt of a longsword at her side.

Something about the handle was funny—something whitish that didn't shine like the metal around it—but she turned away from the moonlight before I could make it out.

Zaylan put someone on watch, too. Not surprising.

Opening the door with a soft knock, I found the room empty. Wonderfully, beautifully empty, and with windows on two sides, since it was on a corner of the manor.

Closing the door, I dropped onto the bed and absorbed the first bit of peace and quiet I'd had in days. *Days.* I wasn't sure who snored worse between Kaido and Beldon, but it was *bad*.

Finally, space to myself. It was a little bigger than the room Selverine had taken—maybe because it was a corner room. I couldn't care less how spacious it was. I wanted a room without people on either side of me.

A chest of drawers stood against one wall, too, and a vanity with a plush stool, and the same four-poster bed and flowy curtains.

No desk, though.

But the vanity was sort of like a desk. It would do.

Falling on the bed, I pulled out a throwing star to cast Starstinger. Her presence never tired me like everyone else's did, and I needed to update her on the day.

Holding the star out, I spoke my castling call.

"Spring forth, my Starstinger,
Lithe and quick,
Run, jump, climb,
But never be hit!"

Dust and coal swirled from the throwing star, morphing into my castling.

"Acres!" She jumped into my arms. "How are you feeling?" With a glance around the room, she asked, "And where are we?"

I filled her in on finding Morrenfayre, running into the guy who was our age after only seeing elderly people and kids, the guards bringing us here and Zaylan being too nice.

"And look at these!" I whispered, pulling the fossil bits from my pocket. "I found them on the way in. Just sitting along the road. Didn't even have to work to find them. Aren't they fascinating?"

Eying them with interest, she gently brushed one fossil with a paw. It made a soft *chink* as her claws scraped it. "What's this one?"

"It's a fossilized claw. If it's from a foreleg, it might be from something as big as an Allosaurus. But if it's from a toe, it would have to be from something smaller. I think these bones are phalanges—fingerbones. But I don't know about the others. But I will after I look them up!"

I flipped open my fossil guide with a flourish, grinning like a fool over having actual fossils I'd found myself to research.

"Hmm. Well, maybe you should sleep first."

"I need to read for a few minutes to relax a little. Could you wake me in three hours, no matter when I actually fall asleep?"

She raised a disapproving eyebrow. "Why?"

"It'll be my turn to take the watch."

Sighing dramatically, she relented. "Fine. Goodnight, Acres."

"Goodnight, Starstinger," I said with a grin as I settled into the vanity chair and buried my nose in the book.

I shivered with excitement—a new book about fossils in the place most fossils originated from.

Maybe it was worth it to have come after all. No matter what everyone else did when they were done here, I hoped I could find a place to stay. It would be a good way to spend my last days.

Chapter 16

REENALYN

I woke delighted and energized the next morning, despite lying awake most of the night thinking about Zaylan. I'd see him again today, alone, for the interview. I wanted to squeal about it with Mella, and to tell her how it went after. But she was still pissed at me.

Maybe I could fix things between us. Besides wanting her to be excited with me, I didn't like being mad at Mella. Sure, it annoyed me that she took what she had with Dane completely for granted, but that wasn't worth losing a friend.

I would talk to Mella today. Crossing my room, I shoved the curtains aside to take in the view.

My window overlooked the front of the grounds. Reddish sand covered everything, with large boulders looming all around. The ramshackle huts of the town were barely visible at a distance.

Were Bennet and Whisper out there somewhere?

Returning to the bed, I cast Cupid.

"Join me, my Cupid,
Brave and true,
Surefooted and witty,
I already love you!"

Emerald flecks spun from my spear's point and swirled over the bed. Cupid materialized on the duvet and I held out my arm.

"Good morning," he said as he rounded my shoulders and emerged from my hair on the other side.

I pulled my hair over the other shoulder to keep it from his eyes and stooped to pull on my boots. "Good morning."

"Going to talk to Mella, then?"

I frowned. "What gave me away?"

"You're lollygagging."

"What? I am not!" I glanced down and found my hands had been untying and retying the laces on one boot. I sighed and chuckled. "Okay, maybe I am. A little."

"It'll be fine. And better to get it over."

"Stop sounding so old and wise."

He shook his head. "Can't."

Smiling, I scratched next to his neck spikes. "You're a silly lizard."

"The best kind, then."

"Absolutely."

Entering the hall, I approached Mella's door. It stood ajar, and footsteps sounded inside. Knocking lightly, I leaned in and waved, trying to smile like normal. But she turned away. Did she not see me? My eyes narrowed. Or was she giving me the cold shoulder?

"Who's ready for breakfast?" Kaido called from behind me.

I jumped at the sudden noise.

He strode down the hall toward the balcony. "I smell meat. Let's get down there!"

I glared at him. That scar over his lips from our fight on Wager Day had faded. I should've made it deeper. If he pissed me off enough this trip, I just might.

But not wanting to start any other fights today, I ignored him and stepped through Mella's open door.

"Hey, Mella," I said.

She flipped her pack, shaking out the contents on the bed.

Reorganizing her things? "Do you, um, need any help?"

"No, Reenalyn," she ground out. "Just because I don't have a castling like you doesn't mean I can't do stuff myself, you know."

"I didn't think it did."

She paused, finally facing me. "Then what the muck *do* you think, Reenalyn?"

I bristled at her tone. She *cussed* at me! We'd never cussed at each other unless it was jokingly. "I thought I'd see if I could help you with anything, since everyone else is ready to go downstairs."

Shaking out a tunic, Mella flung it away and went through the pockets on a pair of pants. "Great. Go ahead without me—I don't want to slow everyone down. I'll catch up in a minute."

Maybe if I could get my good news out, she'd care more about that than being upset. Maybe she'd still be excited for me. "I don't mind waiting. Why don't we walk down together once you're ready? Because I wanted to tell—"

She paused, one hand in one of the pant pockets, her frown deepening. "Why? Because I'm a castlingless weakling? Because I can't handle myself?"

"What? Mella, no." I stepped back, surprised at the depth of her anger and how she assumed I meant something worse than I did. "That's not what I'm saying. I just think, with everything that's happened—"

"That it's sad I don't have a castling to talk about it with? Yeah, I thought so, too. But my new scythe is ready, and it will cast just as well as anyone else's. So stop rubbing it in my face, okay? I see you and Cupid being all happy and perfect. You know, I'm not the only person who takes things for granted."

I staggered back. "Are you seriously comparing your *boyfriend* to my castling?"

"No! I'm just sick of you being a skunk to me because I have a boyfriend and you don't!"

My face heated with the sting of her words. I realized we were shouting, and the light conversation coming from the balcony before had gone silent.

Embarrassed and furious, I pivoted from the room and strode to the spiral staircase, fighting tears. Passing the others, I avoided their eyes.

Cupid laid a small, green hand on my shoulder. "I'm sorry, Reenalyn. I didn't know she was upset about the castling thing, too. But she shouldn't have said that."

I nodded, then pain seared the top of my head. "Ow! Not again!"

Slouching as far from the ceiling as I could, I gingerly felt the swelling goose egg.

Usually anything Cupid said made me feel better, but right now, it didn't. I was too consumed by the fact I couldn't keep my closest friendship intact. Or walk downstairs without messing that up, too. If I wasn't so abominably tall, I'd already have a boyfriend, Mella and I would be fine, and I wouldn't keep headbutting the stupid staircase ceiling.

"Cupid, sometimes I hate my body." My voice shook as I struggled to hold in the emotion and speak too low for anyone but him to hear. "I hate to admit it, but I do. It's the cause of all my problems. Everything that's wrong with me is because I'm too tall."

"Hey, now," Cupid whispered. "You know that's a bunch of skunk muck."

"No, Cupid. It's just the facts. And there's no way to fix it. I will *always* be tall. Even if I get old and hunched, I'll still be taller than all the other old, hunched people."

I swiped away a tear and sucked in a sob. "And you know what? It might not be that bad if I didn't also have to constantly sense everyone's happy romantic feelings. If I could only be oblivious to that, maybe it wouldn't bother me so much that no one feels that way about me. So I guess I hate my mind, too. Or whatever part of me forces me to sense that muck all the time. I wish I could turn it off! Even for a little while. You know, Mella can still get a castling. She'll cast as soon as we get home. But I'll never get shorter, and I'll never get a break from everyone else's constant emotions. So she's completely wrong about us being even."

"Oh. So...it's a competition for who has it hardest, then?"

"No! I don't know. I'm sick of her attitude and her acting like she doesn't have an easier time of it."

There was a silent pause, then, "Isn't that what I just said?"

I ignored him, too busy fuming at Mella. Why did she get to fall in love so easily, and be on her way to getting a castling, while I couldn't find anyone to give me a chance?

"I wish I could turn it off." I sighed.

But if it were off, I wouldn't have sensed that little hint of a feeling from Zaylan yesterday. Maybe...maybe it could be something. But what if I saw him this morning and the feeling was gone? What if I'd imagined the whole thing?

But maybe it would still be there. Maybe. I'd just have to check. And reel myself in enough to keep it together.

Taking a deep breath, I headed for the stairs.

"Well, good morning, Reenalyn!" Zaylan emerged from the dining room as I hunched down the spiral staircase. "You're looking lovely today."

I blinked. "Oh, wow, um...thank you." I struggled to push my frustration with Mella aside as I swiped away another tear and ran my fingers through my hair.

He'd just said I was *lovely*. Could he mean it?

I smiled at him. "You look great as well."

That sounded much better in my head.

Stepping aside, he gestured to the dining room. "Please, help yourself to a hearty Morrenfayre breakfast. If it's all right with you, I'll return to interview you after you've satisfied your hunger."

Smiling, he bowed, his pine marten eyeing me from his shoulders.

"Oh, of course. I won't be long." With a little luck, I'd eat and leave before Mella even came down.

Sitting across from Kaido, I ignored him and served myself a plate of prickly pear wedges and toast with a pomegranate spread. I sprinkled a bit of antiflora powder over everything, and into the crystal goblet of water.

He said I was lovely.

I dug in, determined to finish in record time and be the first ready for an interview.

Chapter 17

SELVERINE

S unlight streamed through the gauzy curtains, and I stared at the ceiling of a room I would've been more familiar with if Grandmother hadn't waltzed into Terrenthyrs to play her manipulative games decades ago.

As the princess, I likely would've had a larger room in a different wing, away from the guest rooms.

But I might've played hide-and-seek with my parents in this room.

Or hidden in it for real, if I'd needed to.

Or known a guest staying in it.

The whole manor and grounds would've been familiar. Like home, rather than a strange, foreign place.

What would my life have been like if it had started here instead?

I was almost an actual princess. No one had known where Grandmother came from with her young son, just that she'd married the prince of Terrenthyrs who later became the king. And who'd never liked me because I wasn't his descendant.

Ugh. Thank good fortune *that* hadn't worked out. Having to solve everyone else's problems all the time was not for me. I had enough of my own, and I'd taken Willova's on to some degree, too. No more.

But the other parts—my parents, the friends I might've had, the healthier state this country would surely be in if Grandmother hadn't neglected it—what would it have felt like to experience those things?

I pulled the soft pillow over my eyes, shielding them from the morning light, and appreciated the fact that one good thing had come from my grandmother's running off to Terrenthyrs—the fact that I did *not* have to be a princess destined to rule.

Throwing my legs over the side of the bed, I stretched, yawned, and pulled a fresh tunic and pants from my pack.

Voices wafted up the spiral staircase, growing louder as I crossed the hall.

The huge dark-skinned guard stood by the balcony, his arms crossed and the beautiful beige lion with a feathered mane sitting at his side.

They were both gorgeous.

He nodded curtly, and I returned the gesture, rolling my eyes at how half-dead I probably looked after the journey, and I didn't know how much of Drazdan's damage still showed on my face.

Padding sleepily down the spiral staircase, I reached the bottom floor and found the others around the dining room table.

Zaylan's long hair and suspicious-looking pine marten greeted me at the foot of the stairs.

"Good morning!" he said. "How did you sleep? I hope you were comfortable."

Blinking slowly, I glared. "Fine, thanks."

His enthusiasm was far too much this early in the morning.

I stalked past him toward the dining room and the others' voices.

If Zaylan was the regent, he had to know my grandmother, right? They must've written, if she'd been ruling from a distance. He wasn't old enough to have been the regent the whole time. He was barely older than us. So maybe his mother or father was the first regent, and he inherited the role?

Who would he be now if my grandmother hadn't run off to Terrenthyrs? I would've been a princess, and if he was regent, he must be from an important family I would've grown up around. Would we have been friends? Forced to get married? He wasn't hard on the eyes...just *weirdly* too helpful.

Another thing I was glad to have avoided in spite of the things I missed out on.

Breakfast smelled delicious as I yanked out a chair between Beldon and Willova and dropped into it.

Beldon shoveled toast and what looked like cactus into his face, the spicy scent of Acres's antiflora powder mixing with other aromas. Willova cut tiny, polite bites and slowly chewed one at a time, her eyes never leaving her plate.

The same spicy scent came from Willova's food. Good thing he'd given her some as well, and that she had the sense to use it.

I was a little tempted. I had a pouch from Acres, too, still sitting in my pocket. But the nuts and cheese from my pack were less likely to be tampered with, and I couldn't quite bring myself to risk it.

"Sent some castors out this morning," Zaylan said, pulling out a chair at the head of the table. "However, I believe if I was able to learn more details about this missing castor and castling, I'd be more helpful."

"We want to find them as soon as possible," Mella agreed, "so whatever you need."

"Wonderful." He steepled his fingers on the table before him.

"Now, have you noticed if someone tells you not to think about something, it's all you can think about?" His gaze passed among each of us. "It's the same concept here. If you hear what one person says about your friends, you'll only think those same things and may not think of other details that could be key in their recovery. So I'd like to interview each of you separately, if you agree. It's our best plan for finding them as quickly as possible."

He folded his hands, eyeing us one by one. "Will that be agreeable to you? Interviews will take place here, in the manor. No one will be far from the rest of you."

That sounded sketchy as skunks.

Trinka glowered. Beldon glanced at her, his forehead creased. Acres raised a wary eyebrow.

Reenalyn, who'd been beaming at Zaylan all along, did an awkward combination of raising her hand and waving. "I'm happy to do an interview."

"Wonderful! Thank you for agreeing to help, Reenalyn." He actually kissed her hand before addressing the rest of us. "And will you join Reenalyn in helping your friends?"

Dane found Mella's gaze and raised his eyebrows, Kaido frowning at their interaction.

Mella shrugged and smiled. "I'll do it."

Trinka shot her a horrified look. No surprise there. Trinka seemed to be the most sensible of us—except for me when it came to food.

"I will, too," Dane said.

Of course.

"And me," Kaido added, not to be outdone by Dane. The idiot.

I rolled my eyes.

Zaylan beamed. "Wonderful! Thank you, Mella, Dane, and Kaido."

He pushed his chair aside and stood, bowing to Reenalyn. "Reenalyn, would you care to go first?"

She glowed as he took her hand and kissed it again, waiting for her answer.

"I would be delighted."

"Wonderful!"

Get a new vocabulary.

"Please, right this way." Without releasing her hand, he led her from the table.

Trinka leaned back and crossed her arms, glowering after them.

Well, I for one didn't plan to talk to the guy alone. I didn't know anything about Bennet or Whisper, so there wouldn't be a point.

Though there was the whole thing about how I was on a mission from the queen...I'd better give that story some thought. Skunks.

A cook walked in carrying a tray covered with a napkin. Pausing before the table, she pulled off the napkin and set the steaming meat on the table.

Right in front of me.

It smelled absolutely divine.

Shoving my chair away, I stormed out. They could risk who knows what kind of floramancy on themselves if they wanted to. But not me.

I would never be under someone else's control again.

***

Munching on a piece of cheese from my pack, I marched up the spiral staircase.

I didn't want to sit around in my room. Overstuffed chairs and assorted chaise lounges sat near the balcony window. On the opposite side, another long hallway stretched in that direction.

I took another furtive peek around the balcony. The guard had vanished. This manor was basically mine anyway, right? My family's, at least. And I wasn't going to take anything. Just have a look around. Maybe learn something about my parents, if I was lucky. Or at least some other relative.

The more I could learn about my ancestors, the more I'd understand who I really was.

I strode down the hallway, noticing a few doors that needed investigating.

The first one, wider than the bedroom doors and with a worn knob, didn't budge.

The next few were also locked. But finally I found one that gave. Twisting the handle, I yanked the door open.

Shelves and shelves of dusty books filled my view.

Now we're talking. There had to be something about my family in there.

I stepped inside, pulling the door closed behind me.

More books stuck out from wobbly piles leaning in all different directions, and more still were scattered over the floor.

Now, where would royal family history be?

I walked between the first few rows of shelves, trailing my fingers over the spines. These shelves led to a much larger spiral staircase lined with bookshelf walls.

Following the staircase down and around, I found the exit blocked with dusty rubble. Had there been a collapse in the next room? If there was, it had happened a while ago. Why, though?

Interesting. But this was going to take a lot longer than I thought. Maybe I could ask Willova to help me look. It would only be fair after I helped her get away from Drazdan.

I climbed the stairs and faced the tall shelves. Picking a random book off the closest shelf, I opened the faded cover. It was a novel.

Not what I'm looking for.

Shelving it, I backtracked to another bookcase.

Pulling a faded red tome from a spiderwebby corner, I checked that one. Something about cooking with ingredients from the desert.

Flicking a spider off my hand, I shoved that one back and stepped to the other side.

A few worn covers stood out from the rest. I picked up the first one. "Laws of Morrenfayre."

Raising an eyebrow, I returned to the stairs, reading the first page.

"Herein rest the laws of the country of Morrenfayre, agreed upon and endorsed by a majority of its citizens."

Brushing dust away, I found a date. Over two hundred years ago.

Surely many of these laws had changed. But maybe a distant Merrandil ancestor would be mentioned? It was certainly worth a look.

I sat on the second stair and leaned against the first, flipping to the next page. It wasn't exactly what I'd had in mind, but it sounded interesting enough to spend a few minutes with.

"If a royal marries someone who already has children, those children are eligible for the throne regardless of their lack of royal family blood. This is to necessitate the royal to invest in the children's education and wellbeing, and to force the royal to be sure that not only the adult, but also the children, will be a good fit to care for our people."

Huh. That would be why it seemed so normal to Grandmother while it was so odd to King Jorros. Maybe laws as old as these did still apply.

Why didn't Grandmother make the king like me if she was already going to floramance him anyway? Why let him dislike me all that time?

Well, he'd just have to find someone else to take the throne after him. If he wanted me to, he should've trained me from childhood and let me get used to the idea. And not being an absolute skunk to me all the time would've helped, too. It was too late now. I didn't want that responsibility.

Focusing on the words in front of me, I read on, hoping it would take my mind off Jorros and Grandmother. I'd never been anything more than a pawn to be used by either of them, and that was a load of muck. Surely there had to be something more interesting in this book.

CHAPTER 18

REENALYN

Zaylan's hand was warm around mine, and actually bigger, too, as he led me to an adjacent sitting room. Having my hand dwarfed by his felt so wonderfully feminine. Something I'd been missing out on.

This was just like Dane and Mella.

But *my* size.

He led me into a study and offered me a seat on a bright-green chaise lounge. "Would you care for a drink, Reenalyn?"

"No, thank you. I had plenty with breakfast." As intrigued as I was by him, it would be foolish to let him see we were taking precautions with his food and even more foolish to drink something without it.

I beamed, hoping I hadn't offended him.

"Very well." He poured himself a goblet full of tea-colored liquid and took a sip.

Sitting opposite me on a beige settee, he planted his elbows on his thighs and leaned toward me with a pen and book in one hand and his chin in the other, as if enraptured.

It felt good to be seen, but also a bit embarrassing. I felt bare before that gaze of his, drinking me in. But also a little daring.

"Now Reenalyn and Cupid, please tell me what happened with Bennet and his castling that brought you and your friends here."

I thought back. Had it only been three days? "When Whisper and Bennet were late to meet with us, Mella and Dane went to check on them and found their cottage burning down. They searched, but they weren't there. Then we found tracks like something had been dragged away. When we still couldn't find them in Terrenthyrs, we decided to look here."

If he asked why, could I tell him about what the queen said about hybrids being here, or should I keep that to myself?

"I see." He frowned. "That must've been terribly disturbing."

I nodded, glancing down at Cupid. "We're worried about them."

"Indeed. Now, what else can you tell me about Bennet and Whisper?" He cracked the book and held the pen at the ready.

"Well, I know they're old."

He smiled encouragement. "Yes? How old?"

"I think Bennet is in his seventies?" I wasn't sure of Whisper's age, given the circumstances.

"I see." He scribbled a note. "What else?" His eyes flicked back to mine.

"And they were framed for a crime they didn't commit several decades ago."

His eyebrows rose. "Is that so? Were they acquitted quickly, then?"

I shook my head. "No. Whisper was sentenced to death by shattering, and Bennet was locked in prison for decades and forgotten about."

"You say Whisper was shattered? How did she survive?" The quill zipped across the pages.

I checked again for feelings of attraction coming from Zaylan's direction.

They were there. He was definitely attracted to me.

Barely holding in my giddy, girlish smile, I said, "I'm not sure. Mella knows more. She was there when Whisper returned in a different form."

His eyes flicked to mine as his hand paused. "Her hybrid form."

I nodded. "Whisper used to manifest differently, before Mella."

"And what was her first form?"

"Something canine...I think a coyote."

He laid the notebook down and crossed one ankle over the opposite knee, stroking his chin with his pointer finger. "How interesting. So Mella cast Whisper, someone else's castling who'd been shattered, and she not only survived, but manifested into an avian hybrid."

I nodded, a little confused by this line of questioning. Cupid eyed me with one brow raised, apparently also confused. "Will that help you find them?"

"I think it will. Once I've heard everyone's versions of the story and can piece together a whole account. Thank you, Reenalyn." His warm smile lit his eyes. "And Cupid, as well. So kind of you to share this information."

"Of course. But how will that help, if you don't mind my asking?"

Taking another sip, he smiled. "You met castors with hybrid castlings yesterday."

I nodded, running a finger over Cupid's comfortingly familiar neck spikes.

"Yes," he said. "There are many different kinds of hybrids, depending on animal combination, what was used to cast them, and how old they are. I've been keeping notes on the behaviors of various types for years and can usually predict future behaviors with enough background information."

"What kind of behavior?"

Closing his notebook, he set it and the quill pen on a side table, clasping his hands in his lap. "There are a lot of places to look for a missing castor and castling. But we may be able to narrow our search if we can determine, for example, if they are seeking a last adventure before old age slows them down too much. Then we could assume they'd likely gone on to Larzanobyl to experience what life has to offer there. Or perhaps they fled due to fear, which would indicate they're likely hiding in the forest you traveled through to get here, or the canyon behind the manor. Lots of rocks and caves there. There are also other things to consider—especially the castling's age—that could indicate other possibilities."

Wow. He knows so much about hybrids. "Oh. I see. Fascinating! Thank you."

He rose, bowed, took my hand, and kissed it again, sending a spark through me. Looking up at me, he slowly released my hand with a searching gaze that made me feel all melty inside. "Of course, Reenalyn. It is a pleasure to spend time with you."

I hoped my smile was pretty and not ridiculous. "Oh, Zaylan, I had one other question…"

He raised one eyebrow and looked so good doing it. "Yes?"

"Since we've been here, we've mostly seen older people and a few little kids. Where are the people in between?"

Zaylan sighed. "A few decades ago, the queen drafted many people into the Morrenfayre army, a force she was building to stand against opposition rumored to be building in Larzanobyl. Our neighboring country was supposedly after our land to expand their crowded kingdom. But some time after the queen abandoned us, the army fell apart. Many of them sought refuge in Larzanobyl rather than remaining here, where there was sure to be a war soon. With that generation gone, we didn't have many children born here. The few who were are wards of the manor, as it turns out. You'll likely see them from time to time."

"Oh, thank you for explaining." So that's what happened to the Avian Army? But surely the queen must've found out? Unless…could Zaylan be lying to her about the army for some reason? Maybe to protect the kids who are wards of the manor?

Maybe, but then why risk telling me?

I continued. "And…they seemed to keep their castlings tied up. Only I'm not sure they really were castlings…"

Zaylan sighed. "That's a leftover fear from when my father was regent, I'm afraid. There was a time when he was pressured into swelling the Avian Army ranks, so anyone without a castling was deemed eligible and pressed into joining. Some people who don't wish to be castors still attempt to keep up the farce."

"And they think they're getting away with it?" I asked, incredulous.

He shrugged. "We let them think so. They've been through enough."

Well, that was considerate.

He leaned out the door behind him, tossing me a wink just before disappearing into the hallway. "Xerrome! Please escort Miss Reenalyn to her friends and bring Mella next," he called, his rich voice echoing. Then, to me, "I'll return shortly."

His pine marten blinked at me as Zaylan walked away. It was pretty cute, sitting on his shoulder like Cupid sat on mine.

Xerrome scowled into the room, his enormous rhino peering through one of the windows.

It must be hard to have a castling so large that it couldn't fit inside the building you work in.

"Please follow me." Xerrome bowed slightly at the neck without meeting my eyes.

What was his problem?

I ignored his grouchiness and followed him down the hall. Refusing to let his mood affect mine, I snickered to myself as I stared well over this short man's head, thinking how delightfully tall Zaylan was.

He's taller than me and he...loves me? Of course not that. Not yet. But he has feelings for me for sure. He thought I was attractive. And his feelings will grow if I have anything to do with it!

Xerrome's odd wooden sheath tapped against his leg with every stride, and he strode quickly.

"Why are you in such a hurry?" I asked, barely keeping up.

He jumped like my question surprised him. "What?" he asked, marching on toward the spiral staircase.

"Why are we rushing to get Mella? Do you have somewhere else to be?"

Pausing, he faced me. "Why would you ask that?"

I'd guessed he was in his mid twenties yesterday, with the way he scowled and ordered everyone around. But the concerned expression made him look younger. Maybe even my age, or at least between mine and Zaylan's.

"Just making conversation."

"I don't have time for conversation." He harumphed, taking the stairs two at a time.

Okay then. Hurrying after him, I banged my head on the bottom of the upper stairs again. "Ow."

"Watch your step."

"It's not my feet I have to worry about."

He glanced back as we climbed the stairs, but I couldn't read his expression.

The balcony came into view over his head. Mella sat next to Dane in one of the chairs. Right next to him. Holding hands. Staring into each other's eyes.

She wouldn't be happy for me. Not until we resolved our fight. If we could. But I had to tell someone, and Cupid would be excited with me.

Xerrome eyed Mella and said, "Would you please follow me to give Zaylan your account of your friends going missing?" He gestured toward the stairs.

Clearly dismissed, I waltzed down the hall to my room.

Closing the door, I fell back onto the bed and kicked off my shoes, wondering if Zaylan was still thinking about me.

Cupid crawled out from under my blonde tangles and regarded me from the foot of the bed. "Well? What am I missing? You seem...giddy."

"You'll never believe it!" I squealed, covering my face with a pillow to hide my giddiness.

"Uh, what?"

"Zaylan..." I stifled another out-of-control giggle. "Zaylan definitely likes me!"

The pillow vanished from over my face, and Cupid's green lizard eyes appeared in its place.

"You sensed his feelings?" he asked, eyes wide.

"Yes! And he has feelings *for me*!" I squealed.

"I *knew* it!" He did a fist pump with his little green hand. "What did I tell you? That it would just take time to find the right person—I was suspicious of him at first, but his answers to your questions made sense."

"I know! You were right! Ahh! I still can't believe it."

Cupid grinned from ear to ear, beaming with self-satisfaction. "*I* can! Like I've said from the beginning, you're amazing and beautiful. Someone admiring you is no surprise to me."

CHAPTER 19

MELLA

Following the rhino castling guard—Xerrome, was it?—down the spiral staircase, I wondered where else Bennet and Whisper could've gone. I had such a strong gut feeling they'd be here. That they'd been forced here against their wills and were in danger. Dread gnawed at me.

Poor Bennet. Whisper was sort of a fraction his age in a way, since she'd been shattered in his thirties when she was only in her teen years of castlinghood, and had only been around about a year now, and he was in his seventies.

But still.

Being a hybrid—I had no idea what all went into that. Could it affect her health? Especially in the presence of a stressful event like traveling long distances with kidnappers?

Xerrome faced me by an open door next to the dining room and gestured for me to enter. He avoided my eyes, focusing just past me.

Light streamed in through vast windows with silky curtains framing their edges. A few seats filled the middle of the room, and Zaylan stood from the green chaise and bowed. "Miss Mella, it is a pleasure to see you again so soon! Thank you for agreeing to answer some questions."

"Uh, you're welcome." *Of course I came. This is one step toward finding Bennet and Whisper. Let's get on with it.*

He offered me a drink, which I politely declined, and gestured to a seat before returning to his. "So Mella, Reenalyn tells me Whisper was shattered many years ago, but then you managed to cast her in a different form. Is that correct?"

I nodded, my eyebrows drawing together. "Yes, but how is that relevant to the search?"

He laced his fingers together in front of him, his jeweled dagger glinting from his belt. "As I told Reenalyn, I've spent a great deal of time studying hybrid behavior, and with more information, I should be able to understand their intentions and predict their upcoming behavior."

"What if they were kidnapped, though? How would that figure into your predictions?"

He nodded, steepling his fingers in front of his chin. "An excellent question. That would be another piece of information to factor into my assessment. Depending on how Whisper's temperament changes over time as her hybridity becomes more apparent, she will react in a specific way to something such as being taken against her will. With a little more background, I'll be able to tell you how she would likely react, and where that would put her now. We'll be able to search strategically rather than haphazardly, which should drastically improve our odds."

"Oh." That seemed reasonable. "All right, then. What other questions do you have for me?"

His face brightened as he leaned further toward me. "How did you manage to cast Whisper after she'd been shattered?" He swiped a thin notebook from the table along with a quill and paused, quill over parchment, his eyes on me.

I would've been annoyed with Reenalyn for divulging so much, but if Zaylan was right and it could help us find them...

Nodding, I crossed one leg over the other and laced my fingers around it. "Sure. I took an old bowstring from a trash heap and used it to string my mandolin. I was completely shocked when Whisper came out of it."

He laughed good-naturedly. "I can imagine what a shock that must've been. So it was an accident? You weren't trying to produce a hybrid?"

"No, I had no idea hybrids existed. I didn't find out she was a hybrid until several months later. She hid it well."

He nodded, tapping his chin with his index finger. "And what did you think about casting an avian?"

"Honestly, at first I was disappointed because it wasn't the creature I'd been hoping for. But as I got to know her, I came to appreciate her. She's an awesome castling."

"She sounds like it." His smile morphed to concern. "I hope we'll be able to help you find them, Mella."

My bottom lip trembled, and I willed it still. "Thank you. When do you expect to start?"

"By this afternoon. Once I've heard everyone's version of the story, I'll combine the information and compare it to my notes on hybrid behavior. Then I'll report my findings, and we'll decide together how to proceed."

"That sounds great." How did the regent have enough time on his hands to spend a whole day on some foreigners' problem? Maybe it was the lack of citizens needing to be ruled. Or an obsession with hybrids?

He leaned forward, fixing his eyes on me as though he were about to ask something terribly important. "Mella...I know you didn't know Whisper before—when Bennet first cast her. But, after meeting Bennet and seeing them interact, did you notice anything different, mentally or emotionally? I mean, did her personality change between manifestations?"

"Hmm. Not that I know of. She was pretty grouchy at first, but that was a mood, not her whole personality. She definitely relaxed once Bennet was around, but it was just who she was no matter her manifestation. Why?"

He sighed and glanced away. "You've seen a few hybrids here, yes?"

I nodded, worried by his hesitation.

"Well, sometimes things...go a bit wrong with hybrids. You see, they're a little different in the head than pure castlings. I saw one lose its mind once. About a year after it was cast in its new form, something went very wrong. It ran around screaming like a madwoman, throwing things and breaking windows and setting things on fire."

I gulped. *Setting things on fire?*

"I hope I was right to tell you. I don't want to worry you, but I thought you should be aware of the facts."

I nodded. "Yeah, I'd rather know. Thanks."

"Do you know how long it's been since the first time you cast her as a hybrid?" he asked gently.

I barely held in my emotion. "Um, almost exactly a year."

His lips pursed as his eyebrows drew together. He tapped his knee, nodding seriously. "And...forgive me, but it seemed you were holding something back when I mentioned fire...?"

I took a slow breath. "Bennet's cottage burned down when they disappeared."

"Oh, I see. That is...alarming."

So it was concern for what few citizens he had, then. Because a wild, flammable castling running through his country was a threat to their safety.

"Then why do some of the manor guards have hybrids? If they're so dangerous."

"Someone...forced them to make their castling hybrids. They didn't want to, and besides, it's forbidden, due to the possible consequences. But since they were under duress, I allowed them to continue working normally. As they reached their one-year marks, some remained unchanged, while some exhibited concerning behaviors. Even so, most came through after a few weeks."

Glancing at the ground, he sighed. "Though there was one that was too dangerous. We had to eliminate it. To protect everyone else."

"Oh." I covered my mouth. "That's so sad. Who forced them to create hybrids?"

"Do you remember the person my guards captured the night they found you?"

I nodded.

He inclined his head.

Really? "Wow. Where is he now?"

"In the dungeons," said a deep voice behind me. Xerrome returning to swap me out for the next interviewee. "Where people who harm another's castling belong."

***

Xerrome led me to the balcony and left immediately in search of Selver-ine. I filled the others in on what I'd learned. "According to Zaylan, some hybrids get messed up after a while—I guess because being a hybrid affects their head. So he's saying it's possible Whisper went crazy and burned Bennet's house down."

Dane wrapped a comforting arm around me.

Leaning forward in my chair with my elbows on my knees, I dropped my head into my hands. "I can't imagine she would do that. But Zaylan's had experience with hybrids, and apparently, it's happened before."

"Only some hybrids?" Dane asked. "Why only some?"

I shook my head. "I don't think anyone knows."

"Wow." Beldon rubbed the back of his neck, staring at the floor. "So do we still think they could be here? Or did we come all this way for nothing?"

I shot him a glare. "Zaylan said he has a lot of notes on hybrid behavior, and he's going to compare our information on Bennet and Whisper to those. Then he'll be able to predict what they're most likely to do next, and that will narrow our search. He said he'll have a plan for us by this afternoon. He also offered for us to continue using this entire wing of the manor as long as we need to."

"How long will that be?" Trinka snapped.

I threw my hands up, frowning at her. "I have no idea, Trinka. Until they're found or Zaylan tells us nothing they've tried has worked, so we have no choice but to keep looking on our own."

I scrubbed the heels of my hands over my eyes. "I know we're exhaust-ed and cranky after a long trip here. Why don't we accept his offer to help, at least for a few more days? He's going to involve us in the search, and if it takes a while, we could use warm beds and food. He has experience with hybrids, so he has more knowledge than us and might be better at finding clues."

Dane stood. "I think we should take him up on his offer."

I nodded, grateful for his support.

Grunts of various stages of agreement filled the balcony.

"I don't like it," Trinka announced as Reenalyn and Cupid joined us.

I rolled my eyes. "What do you propose we do instead?"

"Live outside on our own while he searches. Maybe he'll find something, maybe not. But we shouldn't live in his manor and eat his food while he does it. We'll be in debt to him enough for finding Bennet and Whisper if he can. We don't want to owe him for food and lodgings, too." She crossed her arms, daring anyone to contest what she said. "And I have a bad feeling about this place. I don't think we're safe here."

I sighed. "Why not?"

"Because he wants us here so bad, Mella. Doesn't that seem weird to you?"

Reenalyn twirled a blonde strand around her finger nervously. "I don't know, he seems pretty nice to me."

Trinka whirled on her. "*Everyone* seems nice to you, Reenalyn."

Reenalyn met her gaze. "And that's something to scoff at because...?"

"Because it's *naïve* and could get us *killed!*"

Dane sighed. "Okay, Trinka, lay off Reenalyn. We get your point."

I pushed myself to my feet. "Let's vote on it, then. On whether we stay—either in the manor or on the grounds—for a few days to hear Zaylan's plan and use his knowledge to guide our search."

Each of us raised one hand.

"Okay. So we're staying. Who votes to live inside the manor with shade, water, comfy beds, and free access outside whenever we want?"

Everyone but Trinka and Beldon raised their hands.

"Overruled, guys. Sorry," I said.

Trinka crossed her arms more tightly than ever. Beldon looked relieved.

Only voting with her cause she was watching, huh?

That didn't exactly endear Beldon to me. But for now, we needed to get to our rooms and get baths. I could barely remember the last time I'd had a real bath with soap and heated water.

Xerrome strode back down the hallway toward the stairs, Selverine following him.

"Whatever you just voted on," Selverine said, "we're revoting when I get back."

I scowled after her as she descended the stairs, Willova standing awkwardly on the balcony. "That vote was for us lowly castors from Wrynford. So no, actually, we're not."

Selverine shot a rude hand gesture at me as she rounded the staircase. I rolled my eyes, and Willova disappeared into her room. I didn't mean to hurt her. She seemed all right. But she was with *them*—they all thought they were better than us.

Hoping Selverine would have something useful and not idiotic to say to Zaylan, I headed to my room to search for the key. I couldn't believe I'd lost the one symbol of belonging and being wanted I had. It had to be in my room...maybe I'd just missed it when Reenalyn had interrupted me.

"Mella?" Reenalyn followed me down the hall.

I paused, facing her. "Yes?"

"I just wanted to say I'm sorry for our fight, and I'd like to be friends again. Wouldn't you?"

Crossing my arms, I raised an eyebrow at her choice of words. "You're sorry for our fight? But not for taking your castling for granted and making me feel like I'd wronged you for having a happy relationship?"

Her face fell. "I mean, I'm sorry for that, too, but I didn't mean to make you feel bad for being happy. And I don't take Cupid for granted..."

I whirled and headed for my room. "I want to be friends again, too, Reenalyn. But a fake apology isn't going to get us there."

CHAPTER 20
SELVERINE

Xerrome might have a decent face if he wasn't constantly scowling. But it was hard to be sure, since that seemed to be his only expression.

He was shorter than me by a smidge, but the rippling arm muscles and broad chest more than made up for that.

Not that he was the approachable type. But he hadn't been upset about finding me in the library, and that was a good sign. It would be harder to find what I was looking for if someone tried to keep me from the books.

With a stern nod, he gestured to a room with several comfy-looking seats.

Nodding, I entered, finding Zaylan already seated with a book and quill in hand.

Now *Zaylan* knew how to smile. He had it all. Gorgeous eyes, attractive form, impressive height, and even nice hair.

But something about him was *slimy*.

It was a struggle not to narrow my eyes right away.

"Sit, please." He nodded at the other seat with his typical smile.

I wanted to tell him I'd rather stand, but maybe it would be better not to come off too combative yet. He thought I was only here to give him information. But I was also hunting for some myself.

"Thank you."

"And a drink for you as well, if you'd like some refreshment." He nodded at a tumbler on the table.

"Thank you," I repeated, though there was zero chance I'd be touching that.

"So you're a servant of Queen Narellen's, but you're also on a mission to discover the missing castor and hybrid castling?"

I was prepared for this question. "Yes. The queen sent me to check on Morrenfayre on her behalf. I ran into the others on the way and traveled with them."

His eyebrows rose. "And how do you find the kingdom?"

I had to be as broad and vague as possible here, because I had no idea what answer would make sense. Turning it back on him would be even better if it worked. "How do you think I've found it?"

He shuffled his feet, crossing one ankle over the opposite knee. "It would be in better condition if our queen hadn't neglected us for so long, I'm sure."

"So I should report to the queen that her regent isn't handling the country well in her absence, and blames her for his shortcoming?"

He frowned. Had I gone too far? Maybe if I could get him uncomfortable, but not *too* uncomfortable, I could convince him to agree to a bargain for me to keep quiet.

Which I would do anyway since I didn't speak to the queen anymore. But no reason for him to know that.

"Her Majesty is aware of the toll the Avian Army debacle has taken on the kingdom. I cannot be blamed for that."

Debacle? It would probably give me away to ask what that meant.

"How about this, Zaylan." I scrambled to invent a reasonable deal that would get me the information I needed. "You'd rather I didn't tell the queen how dismal Morrenfayre has become in your care. I'm willing to...*embellish* my report, if you help me with something."

Zaylan raised one eyebrow. "Oh? How interesting. What would you like help with?"

"The queen's granddaughter asked me to find out any information I could on her parents and ancestors. The queen refuses to speak about them, and she's curious. I looked in the library, but I haven't found anything helpful yet. Could you point me in the right direction?"

Slowly, Zaylan's heart-stopping smile returned.

Oh no. What did I mess up?

My pulse increased as I waited for him to explain his expression. It couldn't be good.

"You're not a very loyal servant if you're eager to lie to the queen while supplying her own granddaughter with secrets the queen doesn't want her to know."

Sweat dripping down my back, I struggled for a salvageable response. "The queen's granddaughter has my loyalty. The queen only has it to the extent that it doesn't hurt her."

"A true friend, to take such a risk."

There wasn't a soul I would actually risk Grandmother's wrath for. Not while she could still use floramancy to make me forget who I was.

"And the information?"

Zaylan stood, pocketing the little book and holding the quill between two fingers. "Right this way."

I stood and followed him from the room and up the staircase. He could easily end me in the library without a soul to overhear. *Skunks.* But I had left my trident there. I could at least have something to defend myself with. If I could reach it in time.

When we reached the top of the stairs, he headed toward the library.

We crossed the balcony in silence. Then he paused in front of the first door.

Taking a key from his pocket, he unlocked the door and opened it, revealing more shelves of books. The room was a study, with bookshelves cut into the top half of the two long walls. These were neat and clean—no dust to be found. And a huge dark wooden desk stood in front of the floor-to-ceiling windows at the far end.

It was a study. The regent's study?

"You'll find the genealogies of the royal family there." He pointed to a spot on one shelf. "Will that take care of our deal, then?"

Crossing the room to the shelf, I said, "If I find information the queen's granddaughter will want, then yes."

"Wonderful. I'll leave you to your research."

I spun, worried for a heartbeat he might lock me in. But he walked out, leaving the door open.

Breathing a sigh of relief, I pulled a book from the shelf and flipped it open to the first page.

"Oh, and by the way." Zaylan's voice drifted from the doorway. "What did the queen tell you to say about why she hasn't answered my letters in the last few months?"

Skunks.

"The queen's been busy," I hissed, pretending to be too interested in the book to meet his eyes. "I assume she'll reply as soon as she has time, but that isn't up to me."

"I thought so. Good luck with your search."

Had he believed all that?

I waited several heartbeats, then peeked around the doorframe. He was gone.

Had I gotten away with it?

Whatever he thought of the load of muck I'd just shoved down his throat, I now had access to my genealogy. I wouldn't waste time worrying about him when I didn't know how long I'd have to search and how hard it would be to find.

Shoving the unhelpful first book back into its place, I pulled down the next one. Several books later, I finally found it.

The genealogy of the Merrandil family.

I skipped to the last entry, about three quarters through the book.

King Tarolon married Lady Shrilana, who gave birth to Narellen and a few other children.

What happened to my great aunts and uncles?

Narellen mothered Greshen, the first son of that generation.

Staring at his name, I traced a finger over it.

My father's name. Greshen Merrandil. No mention of my mother, Feylie. But that made sense. She came after they moved to Terrenthyrs.

Hang on, who'd Grandmother marry?

Glancing back over the last few lines, I found nothing. No mention of my grandfather. Not even a hint.

Dropping to the floor, I let it sink in. Grandmother had had a son. An illegitimate son?

What had my father done to make her hate him? And who had he grown up to be? Who had he loved?

Returning to the book, I hoped for more information. But all that remained was the date of the king's death. And the deaths of Grandmother's siblings. Had she murdered them as well?

Movement at the door drew my eye, and a little dark something darted out of view on the floor.

For half a moment I thought it might've been Horizon. But of course it wasn't.

It was probably Zaylan's pine marten spying on me.

If having his castling tail me was the worst he was going to do, I could live with that. Pushing myself up, I set the book on a table and pulled out the next one. If there was any more information about who my parents were and why Grandmother wanted them dead, I was going to find it.

CHAPTER 21

REENALYN

Mella and I were apparently still in a fight and Cupid needed a rest, so I decided to stroll down the hall to the balcony with an antifloraed water goblet. I needed to try out the pretty furniture.

I started with the tan poof chair, but it was too low. The purple silk chaise lounge was more my style. I waited alone for the plan Zaylan was going to present soon and wondered about him. How old was he? What went into being regent?

Through the huge windows, I glimpsed the garden outside. Green shrubs and manicured archways and all sorts of flowers grew and bloomed in full sun. A few stone paths wound through the greenery, converging on a stone fountain in the middle.

How did they grow such a gorgeous garden out in the desert? Some of the plants were unfamiliar, but I also recognized several from home. And the water fountain—a water source must be nearby.

What would it be like to stroll through the garden with Zaylan under the moonlight?

Would I make a good...*regentess*? Is that what you call the wife of a regent?

I am getting so ahead of myself. Calm down.

"Reenalyn?"

I jumped and spun, spotting Beldon.

"Oh, hi, Beldon." Blushing, I tried to hide my disappointment that it wasn't Zaylan. "Done with your interview?"

His gaze roved over the hardwood floor as he nervously scratched the back of his neck. "Yeah, and I, well, had a question for you."

I smiled encouragingly. "Sure. What?"

"Well, you have a thing about being extra sensitive to romantic feelings, right? Or something like that." He laced his fingers before him. "And so I was wondering if maybe you could help me...in that area." His light-brown eyes finally met mine, and he lowered his voice. "With Trinka."

I winced, hating to disappoint him but also afraid of interfering and making anything worse. "Oh, Beldon, I don't know...I don't want to get in the middle of anything."

"Come on, Reenalyn, please?" He sat next to me, eyes pleading. "You don't have to actually *do* anything, just give me some tips on what to say. I always say the wrong thing."

"I'm not sure..."

"Look, I'd rather talk to my brother about this. But he's gone." He sighed, turning the puppy-dog eyes on full blast. "He helped me through a lot, and I really miss that. So could you please help me? Just a little?"

"Hmm." I set my goblet on the glass side table and considered him. It wasn't my place to interfere. Even so, he'd been pining after her for over a year, and she'd remained as stoic and inverted as ever.

Except for that teeny tiny feeling she'd had on the way here. So maybe it wouldn't hurt to help just a smidge.

"Oh, fine. How about this: I'm not going to tell you what to say, but I'll listen to whatever you think up yourself and tell you whether it's likely to get through to her or not."

That was the most I'd do. Trinka surely wouldn't want me interfering even that much.

I held up one finger. "And just this once."

He cocked his head and squinted like he might counteroffer.

I shook my head. "No, Beldon, that's my final offer. Take it or leave it." I sipped from the goblet once more, hoping to avoid any further puppy-dog eyes.

Sighing, he leaned forward. "Fine. Thank you." He cleared his throat. "Trinka, your muscles are incredible."

I stifled a cackle, nearly spewing my drink. "Beldon. Please."

He threw his hands up, scowling at me. "It was a *compliment*! What's so terrible about that? She doesn't appreciate normal compliments about being pretty or anything—I found *that* out." He winced, rubbing his thigh.

"Oh." I winced with him. "I can imagine."

"Yeah. So why not a compliment about her muscles, which she invests more time in than I do mine? Clearly she takes a lot of pride in them."

I scratched my forehead, looking away to decide how to word this. "Trinka works hard on maintaining her body, but doesn't she strike you as the type who might knock you over if you walk up and say you've been checking her out? I mean, it sounds like you know this from experience."

"Hmm." He stared at the ground, eyebrows scrunched, and rubbed his chin. "Trinka, I think your shaved head looks cool. Don't worry about what anyone else says." He stretched out his arms in some kind of victory move and met my gaze. "Ah?"

I took a deep breath through my nose.

"What the skunk is wrong with that?" His arms dropped. "You don't have to check her out to know she shaves her head! You don't actually need to check her out to know she's stronger and more dedicated than any other girl—sorry." He scrubbed both hands over his face. "I don't mean to be a skunk to you. I'm just frustrated. What did I do wrong that time?"

"Well, for starters, don't make it sound like you've heard anyone talk negatively about her shaved head—that's incredibly rude. Don't draw attention to anything negative."

He nodded. "Okay. Nothing negative."

"And...Beldon, I can sense you have growing feelings for her, but isn't there more to it than just physical attraction? Obviously she's a beautiful girl, but aren't you falling in love with who she is, and not only what she looks like?"

His face went serious. "Falling in love, huh? Is that what I'm doing?"

Oops. I needed to watch my words. I shook my head. "I'm not here to tell you what you're feeling, Beldon. I can only see vague impressions, and it's not perfect. It's just…I want it to work out for you. You two could be wonderful together. But she might not be ready for a relationship."

He eyed me. "Well, to answer your question, of course I'm falling in love with who she is and not just what she looks like. She's fierce but so kind to Mauler and Brawler, and she's so…always far away. Hard to reach. But I want to reach for her. She…"

He sighed. "The evening after the Castling Ceremony, when I was having a rough day, I met Trinka. Before I met any other castors from the Wrynford cohort. And it felt like…I don't know. Kind of like she was reaching for me, in a way. I keep wondering if I misunderstood, but then I remember what she said and how she looked, and I just don't think I imagined that. I know it'll be hard, but it's worth it to try. Who she is, is worth it. Surely there's a chance that would matter to her eventually."

He breathed deeply a couple of times. "Now, if you can sense my feelings, you must be able to sense hers, too." He closed his eyes and took a deep breath. "Does…does she have any feelings for me?" Wincing, he opened just one eye.

I scrubbed the tear off my cheek the moment I felt it trickling down—hopefully before Beldon noticed it. Sniffling, I struggled for the right answer.

"Reenalyn, I'm so sorry, what did I say?"

Shoot. My face was probably red. Whoops. "Nothing wrong, Beldon," I whispered, trying to smile and not wipe at my eyes. "That was a beautiful thing to say."

I sighed, wondering when Zaylan's feelings would progress to that point…*if* they would.

"Oh, um…" He looked around the room awkwardly. "Okay. So about Trinka's feelings…?"

I shook my head. "I can't tell you her feelings. It's not fair to share her private feelings, and I'm not going to do it."

"But Reenalyn—"

I held up my hand. "No, Beldon. I won't budge on this. But." I lowered my voice, "I will tell you this. If I knew there was *no* hope for you, I would save you the embarrassment. And I'm not trying to stop you, so." I crossed my arms. "Take that as you will."

A grin stretched across his face as my words sank in.

Maybe that sounded a little more encouraging than I meant it to.

"Now don't ask me anything else! I'm not giving away a single other thing, Beldon, okay? Try again. Say something better. More meaning-ful."

He thought for a few seconds, then said, "You train harder than anyone else I know, and I admire that and would like to develop better training habits like yours. I was wondering if we could train together sometime? Maybe today?"

I clapped. "Yes!"

Grinning, he shrugged. "And I'll leave out the part about how incredibly beautiful and fantastic you are, since apparently that's not okay to say. But I'll be saying it in my head the whole time!"

I laughed. "You should definitely leave those last bits out for now, but the first half is perfect. There's a good chance she'll respond well to it." I winked at him.

He jumped up. "Okay, I'm gonna do this." Bolting for the stairs, he waved. "Thank you!"

CHAPTER 22

SELVERINE

Fed up with the noise Reenalyn and Beldon were making on the balcony, I slammed the book full of indecipherable handwriting closed and threw it on a stack. Heaving the pile of books in my arms, I marched from the study, down the hall, and into the library.

"You couldn't just talk with your inside voices, you obnoxious Wrynfordian peasants—"

Someone cleared his throat a few rows farther down.

"Who's there?" I spat, my face warming.

"Only me." Acres Parrianther's loc bun leaned out two shelves down. "One of those obnoxious Wrynfordian peasants."

Turning away, I set the books on a dusty table. "I wasn't talking about you. Reenalyn and Beldon were being noisy, and I couldn't focus." Crossing my arms, I faced him with a glare. "You like to read, don't you?"

He spread his arms and glanced at the books surrounding him with a small smile.

Duh. Obviously. I could've smacked myself. "Right. Then I'm sure you appreciate quiet when you're trying to focus on what you're reading."

He shrugged. "Yeah, I do."

"Well, then."

Nodding at my stack, he asked, "So what are you reading?"

I bristled at the question. It wasn't any of his business. "Why do you care?"

Shrugging again, he ducked behind his shelf. "No reason. Just making conversation."

"Oh. Well. Then since we're not appreciating the quiet, what are *you* reading? More floramancy?"

"No. I've had enough of floramancy. I'm...researching fossils, actually. Did you notice there were a lot around here?"

"Fossils? Instead of floramancy? But what good are fossils?"

Peeking out, he grinned. "That's what's nice about them. They're merely interesting. There's no pressure to solve problems with them."

"Then what's the point?"

"Don't you ever read anything just because you enjoy it?"

"Sure. Novels for entertainment or distraction. But I don't see how *fossils* could be entertaining or distracting. They're dead bones."

"Of creatures that don't exist anymore! The only way to learn about them is to study their fossils. How could another subject be more fascinating?"

Rolling my eyes, I swiped the top book off the pile and found my place. "You're crazy, Acres Parrianther."

***

Somewhere behind my eyes, my head throbbed. I needed a break from dimly lit words on pages. Leaving the library, I strode down the hall. The aroma wafting from the dining room smelled absolutely divine. It was a mucking shame I wouldn't get to eat any of it.

Fishing a handful of nuts from my pack, I discovered my store was nearly spent. No more jerky, or dried fruit. Only a few nuts. And the antiflora potion Acres gave me. I glared at it, suspicious. Could it work?

I shoved it into my pocket, undecided. Nibbling on a nut, I descended the spiral stairs and entered the dining room, where everyone else was already eating lunch.

Spotting an empty chair next to Zaylan, I darted for it. Maybe I could learn something useful while I watched everyone else eat.

I pulled the chair from the table, and my heart leaped at the little brown furball curled up in it.

Horizon?

A moment later, the pointy nose and beady eyes of Zaylan's pine marten peered up from the pile of floof.

Ah. No. Of course not.

The creature stretched, shook itself out, and popped onto the table. It then darted up Zaylan's chest, scurrying to rest on his shoulder.

Shaky with disappointment, I took a deep breath to steady my pulse and sat.

Little white eggs speckled with brown filled two bowls to overflowing. Quail eggs?

The others scooped eggs and strange-looking desert vegetables onto their plates, pouring what could be creamed tomato sauce from silver tureens.

Reenalyn was the last to join us. With Cupid draped over her shoulder and his tail wrapped around her arm, she headed for the empty chair next to Mella. Dane, of course, was already on her other side.

Mella glanced up, and their eyes locked for a moment before she went right back to smiling at Dane without acknowledging Reenalyn.

The tall blonde paused, then pivoted for the empty chair next to Acres instead.

What was going on with them?

I didn't care. But what I did care about was what I could learn from Zaylan to make this dining room torture worth it. Not that I wanted everyone to hear my business. But Zaylan was hard to come by outside of meals.

I cleared my throat. "So, Zaylan, does any of the royal family still live in Morrenfayre?"

He chewed what looked like a piece of cactus. I wasn't sure I'd eat that even if I wasn't taking precautions against floramancy.

But the peppered meat with creamy sauce...my stomach growled. I struggled not to admit to myself the nuts simply weren't enough. I'd have to eat sooner or later. Starving myself wasn't an option—weakness could be just as risky as floramancy. And I wasn't familiar enough with the plants and creatures here to forage safely.

He swallowed the bite and wiped his mouth with a cream-colored napkin. "No, I don't believe so. What family the queen had died many years ago."

Muck. "The queen's granddaughter will be disappointed. Do you know what happened to the queen's son?" I pushed the meat on my plate around with my fork.

He shook his head. "That was well before my time. I believe the queen took him with her when she vanished to Terrenthyrs, where he eventually died of an illness. But surely the queen's granddaughter knows what happened to her own father?"

I shook my head. "The queen is disappointingly silent on the subject."

My fist closed around the antiflora powder potion in my pocket.

"Interesting." His blue eyes bored into mine, as if he knew who I really was and was only amusing himself by humoring my story.

His eyes narrowing, he opened his mouth, and I had to interrupt him before he asked a question I couldn't answer.

"Why is the mano so empty? Only a handful of guards, no royals, none of your family. Why is that?"

Sweat dripped down my back as I realized too late that was probably a bad choice. If I'd caught on to something he didn't want noticed, I would've been better off keeping it to myself.

Zaylan smiled his gorgeous smile and said, "Most of the guards are out looking for your friends, as I told you."

"Oh. Right. Good to know."

There had to be more to it. But I'd leave it alone for now.

"And, tell me." He speared a slimy bit of okra with his fork. "How did you come to serve the queen in Terrenthyrs, hmm? She's selective about the people she lets into her inner circle. How did you secure a place for yourself?"

My pulse quickened. This was a bit of false history I hadn't prepared. "Um..."

Willova leaned forward for a bite, and a strand of long crimson hair landed in her plate, soaking up the juice around the meat.

Kaido frowned. "You know, if you tied your hair back it wouldn't be soaking up your food right now."

Leaping on the opportunity for interruption, I glared at him as Willova blanched and tried to dry her hair with her napkin. "Kaido Felzane, leave her alone! Nobody wants your opinions. Her hair is fine."

She'd had someone telling her how to breathe and blink for too long as it was. I wouldn't let Kaido keep that kind of crap going.

Avoiding Zaylan's eyes and hoping he'd drop it, I glanced around the dining table for anyone else to engage in conversation.

Acres read a book under the table as he ate without looking at his food. I rolled my eyes. Probably a book about fossils. *Why?*

Mella and Dane whispered to each other, laughing about something—the idiots. Reenalyn picked at her food while frequently peeking at Zaylan. Beldon glanced at Trinka every few moments while she scowled at her untouched plate.

"You know," Beldon said to her, "I admire how hard you've been training lately. It would do me good to have some of that discipline rub off on me..."

She stuffed a bite of potato in her mouth and chewed, raising an eyebrow at him.

His face fell, but he struggled on. "So I was wondering if, maybe, I could train with you sometime—maybe today? Or tomorrow?"

She swallowed, still staring.

"Would that be...okay?" he asked, sounding less and less confident.

"You're just as disciplined as me."

"Yes, well, then, we can be good influences on each other," he stammered.

"Don't we already spar together most days?" she asked.

"Well—yes."

Trinka shrugged. "Okay. Then sure. We can continue to do exactly what we've been doing all along. No problem."

"Great! Thank you." Beldon ran a hand over his hair, glancing nervously at Reenalyn as sweat beaded down his forehead.

Trinka's eyebrows drew together as she considered him.

I lost interest.

Zaylan's attention was on his plate, so I took the opportunity to dump the potion on mine. As the powder soaked into the sauce on the meat and the oil on the roasted vegetables, the food became...transparent? I blinked, shoving the empty packet back into my pocket. Where had the food gone? Did Acres forget to tell me the potion also transported the food straight to your stomach?

Mine growled audibly, so that couldn't be it.

"Has there been any progress in the search for our friends?" Mella stopped fawning over Dane long enough to ask Zaylan.

How about some progress in the search for my food? My plate was spotless, as if there'd never been food on it at all. *What the muck?*

Lifting it to look under it, even though I knew that was silly, I felt something slide against my thumb. And the plate was heavier than an empty plate should be. Had the food gone...invisible?

Zaylan wiped his mouth and fixed a smile on Mella. "Not yet, but it's only been a day. Now that I've interviewed you all, I'm reviewing my notes and comparing them to what I've learned about hybrids to make a well-informed search plan. If you can spare me another hour or two, I'll have something for you."

I retrieved my fork and stabbed at my plate. It hit something where the meat had been. Lifting the forkful of invisible food to my mouth, I took a bite. And winced. It felt like meat and sauce. But it tasted like nothing.

My stomach turned, and I struggled to get it down. What the muck did Acres do to my food? I hadn't noticed anyone else's food disappearing, and I'd seen them using his stuff. Swallowing with great effort, I struggled not to gag.

Mella nodded, then grinned at Dane. He put his arm around her, and I'd had enough of the relationship drama and invisible food in this room. I excused myself and headed around the table, pausing by Kaido's seat.

"Uh, hey?" he said, raising an eyebrow.

"What the skunk did you say that muck to Willova for?" I hissed, glowering at his stupid face. I'd shouted at him to distract Zaylan, but I needed to be sure I'd put a permanent stop to that.

"What? I just shared some friendly advice. It's not *my* fault she got weird about it and quit eating. Move along."

My arm shot out, blocking the path from his plate to his mouth and knocking the visible meat off his fork.

"Hey!" He sighed dramatically. "What do you want me to do? Apologize?"

"No, definitely don't do that. *Don't* talk to her. Leave her alone. Stuff affects her more than other people." I leaned in and spoke softly enough that I hoped Willova couldn't hear me. "Don't. Talk. To. Her. Do we understand each other?"

"Sure, sure, whatever suits your fancy. Can I finish eating now?"

I shoved away from him and left. Time to return to the library and discover what I could about the royal family I was unfortunately a part of.

***

I was a handful of paragraphs into another handwritten mess I couldn't make heads or tails of when someone knocked on the door.

Scowling, I opened my mouth to tell them to muck off, but waves of red hair surrounded the pale freckled face leaning in.

"Oh. Hi, Willova. What's up?"

Silently, she closed the door and sat in a dusty chair on the other side of my table. "Why'd you tell Kaido to leave me alone?"

I raised an eyebrow. "Did it bother you that I did?"

"No, it's just confusing. I *should've* managed my hair better. It was wrong of me to let it fall into my plate and get dirty. So why'd you reprimand him for pointing out my fault?"

"Because it was a skunk move. And your hair's none of his business."

"But he was still right, and I was wrong."

"So what? You sure weren't going to put him in his place. Do you want me to just stand by and let him be a skunk to you next time?"

My stomach roiled from the one bite of overly antifloramanced food, and I took a deep breath. Acres's muck better not make me vomit.

She shook her head. "No. It felt...good, I think. You were defending me, right?"

"Obviously."

"Thank you. I just don't understand. He *was* right. I was sloppy."

"Look, everyone's sloppy sometimes. It's not a big deal. Don't be so hard on yourself."

"I don't understand when you say that, either. If I'm not hard on myself, that much more will be wrong with me. And it's worse if Drazdan has to correct my mistakes."

Setting down the book, I met her eyes. How could I make this make sense to someone who'd been abused and brainwashed for so long? "Look, Willova, how critical Drazdan was of you—that's not normal. And it's not normal to be so critical of yourself, either."

She stared at me, her delicate brows pinching together.

"I don't know what else to tell you, Willova. Maybe it'll make sense after more time away from Drazdan."

"I must return to him soon."

My jaw dropped. "Excuse me?"

"For Faultless. I ran away and left her there. With him. I have to get her out."

"Oh. I thought you were saying you wanted to go back to Drazdan."

She shook her head. "No. I like being away from him. Things are confusing, but...nicer. I just need Faultless, and everything will be okay. My wound is nearly healed enough. So I can return for her soon."

I swiped the top book off the stack, knowing I'd be going to help her and dreading it. If only we could've found Faultless before.

But I knew how it felt to be away from your castling for far too long without knowing if you'd ever see her again. And with a brother like Drazdan...hopefully Faultless was still in one piece. Willova was right. We couldn't delay much longer.

But I couldn't leave empty-handed. I had to find out *something* about my family.

"Yeah, well, until we can leave, how about you distract yourself with a little reading?" I handed her the book. "See if you can decipher this handwriting."

Taking it from me, she opened it and said, "I think it's an expense ledger."

I stared at her.

Her green eyes glanced up. "What?"

"What the muck makes you think that?"

Laying the book flat on the table, she pointed to the gibberish. "These are coin symbols. And this is a list of items." She squinted, running her finger down the page. "A custom bracelet, an expensive hand fan, a pair of shoes, another pair of shoes, another custom bracelet—I'm not sure what that says next to it...dump cake? That doesn't make sense. There's also a set of dresses—"

"Thanks, Willova. That's not the book I'm looking for. But more importantly, how can you read this drivel?"

She shrugged. "It's bad manners not to be able to read rough handwriting. I learned to do it perfectly."

Sighing, I wondered just how bad Drazdan's handwriting was and how many punishments it had taken for Willova to develop the ability to read it. "Okay. Well, thanks for deciphering that for me."

She smiled a little, looking like a whole different person. Maybe one day she'd do it more often.

"You're welcome. Are there any others?"

Chuckling darkly, I slid the next one off the stack and set it in front of her. "You're going to regret that."

"I think it's interesting, reading what people wrote long ago. Even when nothing else is left of them, their words live on."

"You and Acres are both crazy."

"Acres?"

"Never mind."

"Acres isn't like Drazdan."

I looked at her. What brought that on? "No, I don't think he is."

I watched her, waiting for her to elaborate. But she focused on a page of scrawled ink, running a finger over the lines.

What *was* Acres like? Definitely not like Drazdan...not important. Finding a printed book I could read, I focused on the first page.

Fossils and floramancy...

Focus.

Was he actually from Wrynford? He was in their cohort, but didn't I hear he lived near Glenmeyer?

Why do you care? Read about your own family.

Who was his family? As far as I knew, I didn't know anyone related to him.

What the muck? Focus!

Chapter 23

MELLA

S itting in the same chaise lounge I'd used during the interview, I scooted over to make room for Dane. He sat next to me, entwining our fingers.

Zaylan stood in the entryway waiting for everyone else to sit down, his hands clasped as he smiled encouragingly.

"Thank you for your patience. As I mentioned this morning, hybrids tend to become...not themselves, either temporarily or permanently, around the one-year mark from when they became a hybrid. This can result in accidents such as fires"—he nodded at me—"which Mella mentioned took place around the time your friends disappeared."

He paced, gesturing as he spoke. "Now this is only speculation, but it is likely close to what happened given the information we have. Whisper experienced a state of confusion and accidentally set the cottage on fire. Bennet saw it and, after a traumatic life spent in prison, may have assumed his past imprisoners or a fellow inmate with a grudge was to blame. He grabbed the most important part of his life—his precious castling and her castling instrument—and ran for it. Whisper, not aware of her actions or embarrassed by them, ran with him."

His eyes met mine.

"Okay, so," I said, annoyed at his pause, "where does that put them now?"

"Of course, yes." Pacing, he continued. "Assuming this is correct, they've gone into hiding, not in search of entertainment or accomplishment. The best places to hide from crowds are the forest you traversed on your way here and the canyons all around us on this side of Morrenfayre. So we're going to separate into search parties."

I'd been expecting something more climactic. And separating us...that sounded suspicious. "What exactly is that going to look like?"

"Great question, Mella." He smiled and nodded, his jeweled dagger bouncing against his hip with each step. "I'm sure the idea of separating is an uncomfortable one, so as a show of good faith, I would keep you together in groups of four—three of you with one local guide. Would you be comfortable with that?"

There were nine of us, so three groups with three of us in each. "We'll decide together once we're done here. Will three groups be able to cover enough ground?" I asked.

"Another excellent point. Your three groups will search the areas around the manor. I sent castors to Terrenthyrs who will search the forest. It should only delay them a day or two."

I glanced at Dane. He nodded encouragingly.

"All right. Thanks for the recommendation. Can we have a few minutes to discuss it?"

"Of course." With a smile and a bow, he strode from the room, closing the doors behind himself.

"It's clearly a complete waste of time," Selverine spat. "Come on. Does no one else see what a wild goose chase this is?"

"Then what alternative do you suggest, Selverine?" I rolled my eyes. "Because there's not a chance we're going to just hope Whisper and Bennet are okay wherever they are."

"Oh, I'm allowed to suggest alternatives now? I thought I didn't get a vote."

"If you're going to whine about the plan we've got, I assume you've got a better offer. Which I'd love to hear."

"I think we should give Zaylan's plan a try," Reenalyn said.

"Of course you do." Selverine snickered.

Dane shifted. "Reenalyn has just as much right to an opinion as you, Selverine."

"I didn't know you were capable of defending anyone besides Mella," Selverine shot back.

Dane ignored the jab. "Trinka? What do you think?"

"I think we should leave while we still can. But Bennet and Whisper do deserve more effort from us, despite the risk. And if it really is one of them to three of us"—she shrugged—"I can live with those odds."

Selverine rolled her eyes.

Nodding at Trinka, Dane turned to Acres. "Your thoughts?"

Acres swept a loose loc from his face. "It's worth trying for a day. Then if we don't find them, we can reevaluate whether to stay any longer."

Dane faced Beldon. "Beldon?"

"I'm down. Let's explore!"

I smiled at his exuberance.

"Willova?" he asked gently.

Her eyes widened as if she were shocked he'd asked for her opinion. "I...uh...will do whatever is decided."

Selverine rolled her eyes, and Dane grudgingly faced Kaido. "You?"

"Ooh, I get a vote, too?" Kaido grinned.

"More like you're going to share your opinion whether we want you to or not, so let's get it over with."

"Then I say we look for them. Like Trinka said, if one of them comes after three of us..." He held out his arms in a gesture of invincibility.

Dane faced me. "Well, Mella, there you go."

"All right. Thank you." Shoving to my feet, I reached for the door. "I'll let Zaylan know."

Opening the door, I leaned out to tell Zaylan. He was gone, but some of the hybrid castor guards from the tavern waited outside with their arms crossed.

"Uh, where's Zaylan?" I asked.

The red-haired castor rolled his shoulders, laying a hand on the falchion sheathed on his hip. "He has regent responsibilities to take care of. What did you decide?"

I *had* been surprised Zaylan had so much time to spend on finding Bennet and Whisper. "We're going to look for them. You three are our guides, I'm guessing?"

"That's right," the slender tan woman with straight black hair declared, striding past me into the room. "Listen up. We're looking for evidence of a human and a castor living on the run in the desert. That means fire pits, ashes, cooking utensils, animal skins or bones, dropped pieces of clothing, and the like."

"And boot prints!" the red-haired guard added exuberantly.

The woman frowned. "How long do you think boot prints last in the desert, Wallen?"

He scratched his head, smiling sheepishly. "Well, they'd have to be pretty recent."

She rolled her eyes. "And *recent* boot prints." Pointing around the room, she continued, "You, you, and you—you're with me. I'm Famita. Let's go!"

Acres leaped up, limped once, and stumbled across the room to stand awkwardly next to her. Kaido stretched and stood to join them. Trinka looked the woman up and down, then stood with a chuckle and joined the boys. She was probably thinking how easily she could take her on her own.

Probably the only thing that could make Trinka laugh.

"We've got the boulders on the west side," she spat at the remaining guards. "Come on, you three. Let's go!"

The two guys leaned in and eyed us.

The hybrid lion castor motioned with his quarterstaff to the red-headed guard, gesturing for him to choose next.

Wallen rubbed his hands together with a Beldon-esque grin. "Thanks, Gomund. Hi. I'm Wallen. You"—he pointed at Willova—"fellow ginger. Join me. And you"—he pointed at Beldon—"you seem like fun. Get over here! And—"

Selverine stood before he could call another name, nodding at Willova. "Where she goes, I go."

Wallen held out his arms and grinned. "It's a party! We've got the caverns in the north beyond the ravine." He smirked. "It's a bit of a hike, but definitely the most interesting place to search. So let's get going!"

As the four of them left, the remaining guard, the one with the feathered lion, nodded at Dane, Reenalyn, and I. "We have the scrubland between here and the ravine. Let's go."

Taking Dane's hand, I was glad to have him on my search team. But catching sight of Reenalyn's furrowed brow and downcast eyes, I wished she had a different group.

And I hated feeling that way. We'd been best friends a few days ago. I wanted to get that back, but I didn't know how.

I tried to send her a half-hearted smile as we followed— "What's your name?"

"Gomund."

Dane and I followed Gomund from the room, Reenalyn avoiding my eyes.

Fine, then.

Gomund led us through a hallway, past a couple of ballrooms, and out a door in the back.

Into a garden that had no business being so lush and green in a desert. They'd mentioned a ravine—maybe it fed the garden from below somehow.

Using his quarterstaff as a walking stick, he led us over a flat stone pathway lined with everything from familiar shrubs to flowering cacti I'd never seen before. I only recognized those because Acres had read about them and mentioned them to me while brainstorming potion ingredients once.

Latticework archways stood here and there in the garden, joined above our heads by thin wood runners covered in vining plants. Odd trumpet-shaped flowers with petals ranging from sunset-orange to blood-red spouted every few specks down the vines.

"Is that...a brook I hear?" Dane asked.

"There's a water fountain ahead." Gomund nodded forward.

I heard it too. Then we rounded a tall shrub, and there it was. A small stone pool filled with crystal-clear water had a tall structure in the middle. Water poured from the top in several arching streams, splashing in the pool below.

"Wow!" Reenalyn gushed, her eyes shining. "It's beautiful!"

Gomund didn't seem to think it was worth wasting time on. He strode past it down the stone path ahead, and we hurried to keep up.

CHAPTER 24

SELVERINE

Sweat poured down my face and soaked into my tunic as we trudged under the relentless desert sun. My stomach finally stopped roiling from the horrible lunch and resorted to merely growling painfully. And worse, Beldon and Wallen appeared completely unaffected by the heat. They laughed and joked as if we strolled under the shady leaves of the Emberlyn Forest rather than evaporated in this heat.

I had to give that to Terrenthyrs. Its weather was certainly more my style.

Willova trudged at my side, her pale skin already red from too much sun. That would hurt later. But despite her keeping her gaze on the sandy ground, she appeared to be less annoyed by the heat. Whether because of the big lunch she'd had or her unshakable ability to keep emotions off her face.

"You know, Willova," I panted, "you *are* allowed to have opinions. It's not even a matter of being allowed. You just get to have them. As a person. What did you *actually* want?"

Her green eyes focused on me, wide with confusion. "What?"

"Dane asked whether you wanted to search or not, and you said you'd do whatever everyone else wanted."

"Yes."

"Well, what did you want?"

"What I said. Whatever everyone else wanted."

I rolled my eyes. "You have realized by now Drazdan's not here, right?"

"Of course."

"Then you're free to express your opinion. No one's going to mistreat you for having a thought."

"But Selverine, I really didn't. Have a thought, I mean. I told the truth. I would've been fine with what everyone else chose."

"Really? You didn't have any preference?"

She shook her head. "No. It's easier not to."

I frowned. "What do you mean?"

"If I think too much about something and develop a preference, then it's worse when I don't get it. And if Drazdan can tell I'm upset or disappointed...well, you know. It's better not to have a feeling than to work to hide it and potentially fail. So I try not to have an opinion and let whoever is in charge decide."

She eyed me, her eyebrows bent in confusion. "I guess that's not how you do it."

"Nope. If you don't express what you want, you can't be upset when you don't get it."

"Right. Which...if you don't want anything, then it's the same result. Isn't it? Not having to be upset, or having anyone else upset with you."

"So you seriously don't want anything?"

She shook her head. "I want Faultless to be safe. With me."

I nodded. "And once you're reunited?"

"I'm not sure. What do you think?"

"Doesn't matter what I think. Or more importantly, it doesn't matter what Drazdan thinks."

"My leaving will upset him. I want Faultless to be safe, and I want to continue to have the freedom I've had here. But Drazdan is my older brother. I'm supposed to do whatever he says. The oldest knows best. Right?" Her green eyes looked younger than her seventeen years, so full of insecurity and fear. And...trust? Yes. She trusted me.

I might be the only person in the world she could trust.

"Look, Willova, it might be true the oldest knows best when the people in question are children. But you're an adult now. You produced a castling and entered society, same as me. Drazdan doesn't have the right to dictate your life." Not that he ever had. But especially not now.

"But I live in his house."

"Then move out."

"He'd never give his permission."

I gestured to the red sands and looming caverns before us. "Look around, Willova. You didn't need his permission to come here."

"But he will punish me severely for leaving without it."

"Which is further evidence he's a skunkass who doesn't deserve to be in your life."

She was silent for a while, sand crunching under our boots. "I see what you're saying, Selverine. And it kind of makes sense. But...I don't know. It's just...is that how most people live?"

"By making their own decisions and not submitting to abusive assholes? Yeah, it is. And it's disturbing that you have to ask."

"That makes more sense. I guess I have seen other people do that. But it's just not something I do."

"Yeah?" I blinked as we followed Beldon and Wallen into a cavern. "And why's that?" My voice echoed slightly as I shivered in the sudden shady cool.

"I just never get it right. I make so many mistakes. No matter how hard I try, how much attention I devote to detail...I always mess up. I don't understand how I can fail to be perfect so often, despite all my effort. I never see anyone else fail as much as I do. That's the difference. Something's wrong with me."

"Willova. Listen to yourself. There's another common denominator here."

She turned questioning eyes on me, her fists clenched nervously at her sides. "What?"

"Your piece-of-muck brother."

Her eyebrows drew together as she turned away. "I don't know..."

"Echooo!" Beldon shouted from the back of the cave.

"Can't you think of anything more original?" Wallen yelled, cackling.

"Dooon't echooo!" Beldon hooted.

Rolling my eyes, I stepped toward the entrance for as much distance from their obnoxious noise as I could get while remaining in the shade.

Bennet and Whisper probably weren't here. But if they were, one of them would find them.

I leaned against the rock face just inside the cavern, as far as I could get from Beldon and Wallen without being in direct sunlight.

I'd thought Grandmother had done a number on me—manipulating me and what I thought I wanted with floramancy. At least floramancy could be undone. What Drazdan had done to Willova...would she ever recover? I could try to force her to see things the way they really were, but then I'd be as bad as Drazdan. I would have to approach this delicately.

I was not good at approaching things delicately.

A gust of wind blew sand in my face, and I spun toward the cavern. Something on the wall caught my eye. I stepped away, and light instantly filled in the carved names.

Greshen Merrandil and Soryna...something I couldn't make out.

My father's name.

And another name I didn't know.

Enclosed together in a heart.

My pulse pounded in my head.

What was this? Who was this Soryna woman?

But Narellen had taken him away to Terrenthyrs when he was a baby, hadn't she?

They must've returned occasionally for her to check up on the regent. Whoever the previous regent had been.

And maybe he'd fallen in love with someone here, in his home country.

But it hadn't worked out.

Or Grandmother had stepped in.

But she hadn't liked my mother or my father. She didn't choose my mother and force my father to marry her just to murder her a few years later, did she?

Heart racing, I stormed from the cavern, shielding my eyes from the blinding sun. The manipulation was too much. I couldn't stand any more lies. Any more mysteries about my family. About who I was.

Willova would be safe with Beldon and Wallen, however obnoxious they were. I'd return to help with the search in a few minutes. I needed to stomp off some frustration.

Just when I thought I'd uncovered the last lie, the last manipulative maneuver...

"Ugh!" I shrieked at the boulders and sky and blistering heat.

My stomach ached, both with hunger and discomfort over whatever Acres had put in his stupid powder potion.

I needed water. And shade without company.

Squinting at the horizon, I spotted the biggest dark spot and headed toward it. The more shade, the better. I would lay down and stretch out and breathe for a few minutes.

The closer I got, the more it looked like the manor. Had I found my way back on my own? Good. Water and a bed.

But no, it wasn't the manor. It was a similar structure—almost its twin. But smaller. More the size of the manor houses Willova and Mella lived in back home.

What was another manor house doing in the middle of the desert? *Why not find out?*

I marched on, cursing the miles of sand I'd already traveled today. Was that someone in the window?

On high alert, I hefted my trident, glaring at the building.

There was a silhouette, someone remarkably good at standing still for a long time. Were they watching me, too?

I finally got bored and approached the house. The silhouette remained in place.

Barge in, or knock on the door?

They already know I'm here, so no element of surprise. Might as well err on the side of politeness, then.

I rapped my knuckles against the dusty wooden door three times, then stepped back and waited.

After a minute of silence, I tried once more.

But still, nothing. Not even the sound of feet running away from the door.

I twisted the handle, and to my shock, the door opened. I pushed it inward, brandishing my trident for an attack.

But nothing happened.

Despite the crowd of people and...castlings? Yes, *winged* castlings—pure avians and avian hybrids—in the front room.

The Avian Army.

I stared, heart racing.

But they didn't move.

Wind rustled hair and feathers and threadbare clothes.

But they stayed still.

Were they elaborately life-like statues? They stood in normal positions, as if they'd been carved to set onlookers at rest by their leisurely stances.

Stepping into the doorway, I poked the nearest human with the edge of my trident. It slid over his granite bicep with a scraping sound.

Jabbing toward a ferocious-looking blue-feathered bird, I ducked away quickly, just in case. But it remained still, its big eyes moist-looking, but stuck open as it peered down at something that wasn't there.

What the muck?

Was this...floramancy? Or something worse?

Craning my neck around the entryway wall, I found more rooms crammed wall-to-wall with these things. Humans with enormous avians. Castlings I would've died with envy for last year. A few hybrids as well. A warthog with enormous tusks and little hawk wings. A deer whose fur transitioned to pink feathers up its neck, where a huge black bill like a flamingo's took the place of a deer head. A swan-like neck mounted on the body of a huge turtle.

Could they hear me, despite being immobilized? "Hello?"

Nothing. Of course.

Had Zaylan done this? Or was this another of the queen's evil doings?

Would it happen to us?

Would I be petrified like this, unable to fight for freedom from manipulation anymore?

Slamming the door shut, I rushed back to Willova, the sickness in my stomach having nothing to do with Acres's potion this time.

***

"There you are!" Beldon shouted when I finally found them.

Willova's pinched eyebrows relaxed, and she dropped her wringing hands to her sides.

Wallen scratched the back of his neck, a carefree smile on his face. "So glad we found each other! I was worried we'd lost you."

He looked pointedly at me, and I frowned. Why would he care?

"So now that we're all together and it's the end of the day," Beldon said, "should we return to the manor for dinner?"

Wallen nodded. "Definitely. Selverine, a word?"

Lifting an eyebrow, I fell into step with Wallen as he led the way to the manor a few paces ahead of the others. "What?"

"Did you find what you were looking for?" he whispered.

"You mean, a sign of Bennet and Whisper? Obviously not."

"I mean what you were sent to find."

My eyebrows pushed together. Best to be vague. "I haven't found anything satisfactory, if that's what you mean."

"Oh. Understood."

He surged ahead, and I frowned after him. What was that about?

Chapter 25

REENALYN

Hours after trudging behind the two most in-love people in the world, I was struggling. I just wanted to focus on the search. But I couldn't ignore them, as much as I wished I could.

Was this how Acres felt when he needed to be alone? I usually hated being alone. But now nothing sounded better.

Were we close enough that I could find my way back on my own?

But I couldn't stop looking. I'd have to keep at it a little longer. For Whisper and Bennet.

Was that...? Instantly on alert, I leaned around a nearby boulder. It was definitely Zaylan's feelings. But just barely. Either he was far away, or they were only in the back of his mind while he focused on something else.

And they were fading.

Turning toward the sound of my retreating companions, I made an easy choice. Ditch them and chase Zaylan down? Yes, please. I'd look for Whisper and Bennet, too, while I was at it.

Following the essence of his emotions, I hurried over rocks and sand, rounding boulder after boulder.

I almost lost him once, then picked up the sense.

If I got lost and he found me, that would be so romantic.

Where was he?

I lost it again for a moment and paused, trying to focus.

A sob came from one side, and my head whipped toward that direction. Echoing over the boulders, the whimpers continued. And they were definitely too soft and feminine to be Zaylan.

Stepping toward the sound, I tiptoed around another boulder and found a young girl sitting on top of it. Her arms were wrapped around her knees, her head resting on them as she cried. Long dark hair obscured her face.

"Hello," I said softly.

She started, scrambling away with wide eyes.

"It's okay, I just want to make sure you're all right." I crouched, cursing my height for making me scarier to this poor girl.

She stared, breathing rapidly.

"Are you stuck? I can help you down." Stepping closer, I reached slowly toward her, waiting to see if she'd let me.

Hesitantly, she approached me and let me lift her down. The moment her shoes touched the sand though, she bolted.

"Can you tell me what's wrong? Maybe I can help."

"Trissa!" a deep voice barked.

The girl jumped, and Xerrome the scowler appeared behind her, a grey stuffed grey sack in his arms.

Trissa leaped up, and I held out my arms to protect her from the grouch.

But she darted around him, fisted both hands in his shirt, then leaned out from behind him to stare me down.

Letting my arms drop, I straightened with a frown. She...knew him? And he wasn't a complete skunk to her, apparently.

"Why aren't you with your search group?" Xerrome asked briskly, shifting the sack to one arm and laying a protective hand on Trissa's head.

"I got separated. I heard her—Trissa—crying, and came to make sure she was okay."

A familiar feeling sparked from behind Xerrome. I stood on my tiptoes to peer over the boulders. "Is Zaylan with you?"

His scowl faltered as his eyes widened. Following my gaze, he said, "I need to get her home. You should return to the main manor." He nodded to the side. "It's that way."

With a hand on Trissa's shoulder, he hurried her away.

Well that was...weird.

Facing the direction Xerrome had indicated, I veered toward where I thought I'd sensed Zaylan.

"Zaylan? Is that you?"

No answer.

Hurrying around nearby boulders, I found a climbable one and hoisted myself up for a better look. No Zaylan.

But a ramshackle manor house was in the distance. Faded and dusty looking. What was it doing out here?

I was still too far from the main manor to find it on the horizon. And I wasn't in any hurry to hang out with Dane and Mella. As far as I knew, no one had checked this building for Bennet and Whisper.

Crouching, I slid off the boulder and headed for this other manor. Dilapidated as it was, it would be an excellent hiding place for someone on the run.

Sweat dripped into my eyes and slid down my back as I trekked to the house. Finally nearing it, I leaned against the shaded side of a boulder to catch my breath and observe the building.

Its stone walls rose two stories high, and more than a few windows were broken. But it looked a lot like the main manor.

Something moved behind one of the windows. What if Bennet and Whisper had found this place? What if they were inside right now?

Stepping out from the shade, I hefted my spear and crossed the distance toward the house.

The door opened, and Xerrome strode out. With a *smile* on his face, of all things. The shock of it halted me in my tracks. The scowler had a nice smile, actually.

He caught sight of me and froze, the usual glower slipping into place as he pulled the door closed. "What are you doing here?"

"I got turned around looking for the manor."

Rolling his eyes, he strode past me. "Come on. I'll take you."

With one last glance at the old manor, I followed him. "What happened to Trissa? And your bag of stuff?"

"They're safe."

"Safe where? In that place?"

"It's none of your concern."

I bristled. "Why wasn't she afraid of you?"

He stepped over a small rock and strode over the sand as if it wasn't any harder to walk on than solid dirt. "Because she knows me."

"You didn't leave her in that old building, did you?"

He sighed, dragging a hand over his face as if I was being a lot of trouble on purpose. He faced me with an unreadable expression. "Why so many questions?"

Something pricked my senses, and I caught a sense of Zaylan. I should insist he explain where Trissa was, but I had to check...I stood on my tiptoes to peer over Xerrome. "Are you supposed to meet Zaylan?"

His eyes narrowed as he whipped around to follow my gaze. "Did you see him?"

"No, I just...thought I heard him." It would've been too hard to explain how I'd sensed him.

"Come on." He strode ahead. "Let's go."

He headed in the same direction I thought I'd sensed Zaylan from. I glanced back at the house. What if Trissa needed help?

"She'll be safest if you stay out of it. Please."

Well fine then. Maybe I'd come back tomorrow and check on her. With a shrug, I followed Xerrome toward Zaylan. But he never appeared. He must've come out to check on our progress and given up when he couldn't find anyone.

"Xerrome," I asked, trudging over the hot sand, "how long has Zaylan been regent?"

"A few years," he grumbled.

"And does he like being regent?"

"Why don't you ask him?"

He had a point. "What's it like working for him?"

"It's a job. It's fine."

Maybe he'd be happier answering questions about himself instead of his boss.

"What's it like having a castling that's so big you can't cast him indoors?"

He actually chuckled once. "Inconvenient. But nice when I need to get somewhere faster than I can run. He's a good castling."

"My castling is small enough to ride on my shoulders. He wishes he was bigger sometimes, but he's perfect just as he is. It's nice always having him around. He's a good castling, too. And a good friend." He liked the hot sun in Morrenfayre and had fallen asleep basking in it a few hours ago. "Oh, are we catching up to Zaylan? Is he nearby?"

Once again, he tensed and searched the path ahead, but he must not have seen anything. "I don't think so. You may be seeing mirages if you keep thinking you see him. We should hurry to the fountain."

It wasn't a mirage. The feelings I could sense weren't visible. Extreme heat and dehydration though...maybe that could affect their accuracy.

The manor loomed ahead, and we plodded on in silence. Xerrome led the way over the garden path to the fountain, taking a cup from a pouch on his belt. He dipped it into the pool and offered it to me.

"Here. You should drink."

My eyes narrowed as I accepted the cup with one hand, fishing Acres's powdered potion from my pocket with the other. I didn't want to be rude, but I couldn't just drink it. Especially if he didn't drink it first. And even then.

"Thanks for this, and for walking me back. It must've been"—I turned as if to look how far we'd come, shielding the cup with my body as I sprinkled some powder in it—"several hundred spans."

Facing him again, I sipped and lifted my eyebrows, waiting for him to confirm or correct the distance.

"Quite a ways, yes. You should find ointment for sun exposure as well. You're probably burned after such a long search this afternoon."

Downing the rest of the cupful, I nodded. "What if no one found Whisper or Bennet? What will we do?"

Accepting the cup, he dipped it in the fountain again and gulped water. Wiping his mouth, he caught my glance with his dark brown eyes for a moment, then looked away. "Zaylan's got castors searching the forest on their way to Terrenthyrs. If your friends aren't here, they're probably there. We'll wait for the castors' report."

He slid the cup into its pouch, rattling a set of keys hanging next to it.

"How's Marken?"

Xerrome paused, then spun toward the manor. "He's in the dungeons."

I followed after him. "Didn't Zaylan say he forced people to cast hybrids?"

Xerrome shook his head. "It was some version of extreme idiocy."

That brought me up short. "What? What does that mean?"

We reached the edge of the path, and the black jaguar, Eclipse, appeared out of nowhere, staring us down with a frown, her owl talons scraping over the stones. "The rest of your group returned two hours ago. Where have you been?"

"She got lost. I found her and brought her back," Xerrome said, opening a door to the manor.

"Fortunate you were so nearby," she said, watching us as she headed down the path. She faced ahead and then disappeared.

"Well that wasn't creepy at all." I peeked at the path as I slid through the door, Xerrome closing it behind me.

"I'm glad you're safe. I think I hear your friends upstairs. I'll leave you now." He bowed slightly, then strode away without another word.

Watching him go, I raised an eyebrow. Did the scowler just say he was glad I was safe?

CHAPTER 26

MELLA

A whole day of searching, and no one found a single clue. Waking up on the fifth day since Whisper and Bennet's disappearance felt horrible. Had I made the wrong choice in bringing everyone here?

With no guides available today and nothing to do until Zaylan's castors returned from their search, the others had headed out to spar behind the garden. I joined them half-heartedly.

Eyeing the reddish sand under my boots, I wondered how it would impact sparring. My feet were skilled at keeping me upright and out of danger on every kind of grass, uneven cobblestones, dusty dirt, and slippery leaf litter.

Sand was new.

Stretching one arm overhead, I leaned the other way to stretch my side muscle. My boots sank a speck into the sand as I shifted my weight. Would I ever get used to the feeling of *sand* under my boots instead of grass or crunchy leaves or twigs from home?

Bending the other way, I glanced at the manor for Dane. I frowned at the grinning dark-haired Kaido, who was unfortunately waving at me as he strode from the manor, where Dane should've been. Dane and Sprinter had taken the second shift of night watch duty, so they'd earned a rest after breakfast.

I didn't want to spar with Kaido, though.

Turning away, I looked for someone else to start training with before he reached me.

Acres and Reenalyn were sparring, their castlings wrestling a few paces away. Mauler and Brawler were play-fighting, too, as Trinka did pushups in the sand—how did she do that?—and several spans farther, Beldon stretched, facing the opposite direction.

Everyone and their castlings.

Selverine and Willova fought as well. Two close friends.

I felt empty and lonely and annoyed that Bennet and Whisper had to go missing right before I was supposed to cast from my new scythe. I'd be more effective if I had a mucking castling.

But it was my choice to wait for the next ceremony.

Maybe I'd made the wrong one.

Waiting to prove myself to all of Terrenthyrs wouldn't be worth much if I died before I could pull it off.

More annoying, though, was waiting for the castors Zaylan sent out to complete their search. Maybe we should wait for them, like Zaylan suggested, or maybe we should go back across Morrenfayre and search ourselves. Could we trust them to be thorough?

What if they didn't find them either?

"Hey." Kaido beamed, spinning the handle of his whip. "Looks like it's your lucky day—I don't have a sparring partner yet."

Striker's black-and-green snake body wound around Kaido's biceps and shoulders, his tail dragging in the sand. Was it just me, or was Striker still growing? It was harder to tell with him than other castlings, since he was usually curled several times around Kaido.

Avoiding Kaido's eyes, I said, "I'd call that an *unlucky* day, actually."

I caught a glimpse of Dane emerging from the desert garden behind Kaido.

Grinning, I saw a chance to show off a little for Dane. I'd only have to spar with Kaido for a few moments. "But you know what? It just so happens to be *your* lucky day, because I'm in the mood to hit something, and you happen to be the closest target."

Glowering, I squared up and dug my boots into the skunking sand.

"No weapons, then? If you can land a punch, I'll be impressed." Kaido stretched an arm toward the ground for his castling to slither down.

Striker slid to the sand and slithered away—probably to find another castling to train with. I almost grinned as he gave Cupid a wide berth and headed toward Brawler and Mauler instead.

Pulling the whip from his belt, Kaido set it in the sand a few paces away and then squared up with me. "In fact, I could *reward* you for such an impressive feat. You may even be able to convince me to *let* you win…"

The sun shone over his tan skin, a light sweat already glistening on his forehead and his scarred upper lip as he grinned.

Being this close to him pissed me off more. I hadn't been this physically near him since the night I turned him down on sleeping together, which resulted in him dumping me at the ball after I arrived in an expensive dress I'd sacrificed so much for to impress him.

All that remembered embarrassment and rage boiled over. With a shout, I threw the first punch.

He blocked me with one arm and struck with the other. I barely ducked in time and threw a kick at his legs, then rolled to the side so he couldn't catch me. The kick hadn't done a thing—his legs were too muscular.

He leaped at me, and I dove under him. Catching my boot, he pulled me back. With a shout I kicked him in the face with the other foot, and he let go of the first one. That finally knocked the smile off his face.

A small victory, but still a victory.

He struck out at me again, and I ducked and blocked, but missed his other arm coming from the opposite direction. *Skunks!*

His fist caught me right in the jaw, throwing me back. I stumbled to keep my footing, then overcorrected and felt a *pop* in one ankle.

I dropped to the ground and grunted, reaching down. "Skunking muck!"

"You okay?" Kaido asked, his fists falling to his sides as he straightened.

I shifted that leg so I could pull off my boot and take a look, but a tearing pain screamed though me before I even touched the ties. "Skuuunks! That hurts!"

I rocked back and forth in the sand, trying to blink away the moisture pooling in my eyes.

Dane sprinted the rest of the way to us and skidded on his knees to my side. "What happened?" He glared at Kaido.

Kaido held up both hands. "We were just sparring, man. She fell on her ankle."

"Monkey's teeth, Felzane! Mella doesn't just topple over in the middle of a spar. What did you do?"

"If you mean, 'did I try to make her fall,' then no, I didn't. And honestly I'm insulted you asked." He crossed his arms and tilted his head toward the sky. "Also falling is kind of a hazard of sparring, so..."

Dane's eyes flared with fury, then focused on mine. "Mella, do you want me to carry you inside?"

The concern in his eyes was sweet.

I grimaced. "That's okay. I think I can walk, if you could help me up?"

He stood and offered his hand. I grabbed it, and he hoisted me off the ground.

I fell into him a bit, trying to catch my balance. "Oops, sorry."

"You never have to apologize for getting closer to me," he whispered, blushing and avoiding my eyes.

I smiled and took a step, but then stumbled.

Dane straightened me. "I don't think you should walk on it, Mella. You'll damage it more."

"Well...I'm not sure how to keep all my weight off it."

"What about..." Dane swung me into his arms, an arm behind my back and the other under my knees.

"Dane, you don't have to."

He smiled. "If it will make you feel better, I'm happy to."

He took a step forward and grunted, shifting my weight in his arms. Pausing, he repositioned and took another step, leaning back awkwardly.

"Dane, really. It's fine if you just help me. You don't need to carry me."

"I'm so sorry, Mella." Letting my legs down, he kept his other arm around my back but avoided my eyes again. "Remember that surprise I mentioned? I pulled something in my shoulder working on it yesterday."

I frowned. What surprise could he be working on in Terrenthyrs and Morrenfayre that caused a pulled muscle?

"Holy skunking muck." Kaido marched over to us. "Simple solution." He took hold of my free arm and wrapped it over his shoulders before I could stop him, then shoved his other arm around my waist. "It'll take both of us to get her to her room. Think of all those stairs, Dane."

Dane scowled daggers at Kaido's sunny face.

"Do you want her to damage it further?" Kaido asked, trying to look innocent and not pulling it off.

"It's up to you, Mella. What do you want?" Dane asked.

"I want to go back in time and not spar with Kaido. But since I can't do that...neither of us has time for long-term wounds. Trying to hobble all the way inside and up the stairs on our own would strain both injuries and potentially cause them to take longer to heal."

I winced at Dane, hating that I'd gotten us into this.

"All right, then." Dane nodded.

Kaido beamed.

"Save it," I hissed. "Let's go, okay?"

Skunks. This'll be fun.

I realized I'd left my practice scythe in the sand. It would just have to wait. Maybe I could use it as a walking stick later.

We hobbled toward the manor and through the garden door, Kaido opening it and hauling me through roughly enough to dislodge Dane.

"Muck off, Kaido!" I smacked him with my free hand, then reached for Dane. "Anyone seen a healer around here?"

A door opened and Zaylan walked through, followed by his scampering pine marten.

"Hey, Zaylan!" Kaido shouted and waved.

Zaylan looked up from the book he'd been scribbling in, snapped it shut, and smiled at us. "Hello!" His eyes landed on the leg I held bent behind me, and he frowned. "Was there an accident?"

"I think I sprained my ankle sparring. Is there a healer in the manor?"

"Oh no! Unfortunately I sent our healer out with the search party for your friends, in case they should have any injuries when we find them. But"—he held up one finger with a smile—"you can find his supplies downstairs through that door."

Pointing to the door closing behind him, he added, "There should be bandaging materials, potions, the like. You're welcome to help yourself."

"Thank you." Dane nodded and supported me forward, more gently than Kaido.

"Thanks, Zaylan." I grunted as we awkwardly headed for the door. How would we handle the stairs?

"All right, Dane, you've gotten your chance to help. Now get out of the way and let me carry her down." Kaido's thick arm snaked between Dane and me as he tried to lift me.

"Skunk you, Kaido," I growled, shoving his arm away. "That's not happening. It's disgusting enough to have you around. Dane's staying to dilute your obnoxiousness."

Dane scowled at the stairs as he wrapped his arm around me, looking ready to murder Kaido. Who wasn't much more muscular than he was. He probably couldn't carry me either. Maybe I should insist Kaido muck off. But if I did damage it more, it would take that much longer to heal before I could be useful in the search...*muck*.

I never should've sparred with Kaido. Now look at the mess I'd gotten us into. Who would've ever thought Dane and I would need Kaido's help? I squirmed at the irritating thought.

"Let's just get this over with." I sighed, bearing my weight on both their shoulders as I hopped on one foot down the next stair.

By the time we reached the next level down, my good ankle ached from doing the work for two. Kaido grinned as hugely as ever, Dane still unusually sullen.

It was ridiculous. And honestly, kind of funny. I would've laughed if I wasn't so busy trying not to cry from the pain.

"Kaido, go figure out where the medical supplies are so you don't have to drag me around any more than necessary."

"Sure thing." His arm slid away, and he stalked off to the closest door.

"Dane?" I asked, examining his face. "Are you okay?"

"I'm fine." He met my eyes, still sullen. "How's your ankle feeling?"

"Pretty mucky."

"I'm sorry. I wish I could do more to help."

"You're doing great, Dane. Thank you. I'm sorry I got us into this mess."

He smiled half-heartedly at me, then looked away.

Kaido was getting to him.

"Here it is!" Kaido shouted from the far end of the hallway, pointing to an open door.

Dane and I started toward it, and Kaido sprinted back to pushily help.

"Maybe you could find a candle, Kaido, so we can see what we're working with?" I suggested, giving him another reason to leave us alone.

Slipping into the dim room, he fumbled around, muttering to himself.

I reached for Dane's hand and kissed it, wishing we didn't need Kaido's help.

"Here we go." A flickering light illuminated Kaido's face as he lit a candle, then set it on a table in the middle of the room.

Two chairs sat next to one wall, one of them on wheels with handles on the back. Dane eased me into the stationary one. Both legs ached now. It felt good to get off them.

The table took up the middle of the room. Wooden shelves and drawers covered the wall across from me.

Without a word, Dane crossed the room and opened a drawer, searching for supplies.

Kaido joined him a few shelves away. "So bandaging materials and a splint to wrap it, right? Anything else we need?"

"Something for the pain should come first," Dane said. In a whisper, he added, "Since you can't be near her without causing pain."

Kaido slammed a cabinet shut, facing Dane with a scowl. "You wanna say that to my face, man?"

Kaido stepped into Dane's space, glowering at him.

With a cutting scowl, Dane turned away from Kaido and yanked open another drawer. "Ah! Here we go." He reached into the drawer and glass clinked as he sifted through the contents. He removed two vials and held them up to the light. Brownish liquid sloshed inside and a little parchment tag fluttered with it. Dane read the tag. "Soothing potion. One dose. Good for eight hours."

Kaido snatched them from him. "I'll give it to her."

"The muck you will without trying some first."

Kaido whirled around. "What?"

"You think it's a good idea to just give her some random potion we found in a foreign kingdom? We don't know how old it is, or *what* it is for sure. It could've been mislabeled or spoiled over time. It could be deadly poison."

Kaido squinted at the vial as if he could tell what it was with a closer look.

Dane crossed his arms. "You going to test it for her? Make sure it's safe?"

"Uh..." Kaido looked at the vial. "I don't think..."

Rolling his eyes, Dane snatched the vial from Kaido and sat in the chair next to me. It rocked forward a speck on its wheels. Silently, he worked out the cork.

"Maybe we should skip the soothing potion," I said. "It doesn't hurt bad enough for you to risk—"

But he downed one vial before I could finish. "It's probably fine. Let's just give it a minute to see."

Silently, Kaido continued searching the cabinet wall.

I watched Dane intently. "Do you feel okay?"

"Yeah. The cut I got earlier doesn't burn anymore, and my shoulder aches less. I feel a little tired, though."

"Drowsiness side effect, I bet."

Dane yawned. "Probably."

"Thanks for testing it for me. You didn't have to."

He shrugged. "At least I'm good for something."

I rolled my eyes. "Dane—"

He interrupted me. "Do you want to try the soothing potion?"

Relief from the screaming in both ankles was too tempting. Taking the second vial from Dane, I unstoppered it and drank the dose.

"I knew it would be fine," Kaido mumbled, shuffling through the contents of another cubby. "I wanted to give it to her faster so she'd feel better sooner. No point wasting time taking some yourself so your stupid cut would feel better."

I glared at Kaido. He knew Dane had done a good thing, and he was floundering for a way to outdo him. Or at least what he viewed as outdoing. He couldn't get much lower in my opinion.

Pulling out a long piece of smooth flat wood, he said, "I'm not sure what this is, but it looks like we could use it as a splint. And here are bandages we can wrap it with."

Carrying the items to us, Kaido knelt in front of me and reached for my sore ankle.

Dane's boot shot out, blocking his way. "You think you're going to touch her again in any way beyond helping her get upstairs?"

"I'd like to see you stop me."

With a snap of his boot, Dane kicked Kaido in the chest, knocking him onto his butt.

"The skunking muck!" Kaido roared, shoving to his feet.

Dane stood in front of me, arms bent, ready for whatever Kaido would do next. "You might get away with helping her up and down stairs, but I've got this." He held out one hand. "Hand over the stuff."

"Yeah right! Muck you, Velowinzinger!"

"Kaido, just give him the stuff. If you'd actually touched my ankle, I would've kicked you even harder than Dane did."

"Oh yeah?"

"Yeah, so come on."

"Come on, you say?" Tucking the splint and unrolling bandages under one arm, he held his chin and grinned. "I'd be only too happy to—"

Dane's fist shot out and into Kaido's face, striking him squarely on the nose.

Kaido flew back into the cabinets and drawers with a resounding crash, leaving a few cabinet doors hanging loose.

"Oh, you're gonna regret that!" he shouted, stumbling to his feet and fisting his fingers.

"All right!" I hopped around Dane, blocking Kaido with my whole body. "I'm over this. Kaido, drop the supplies. You can stay while Dane wraps my ankle and shut up, or get the muck out and leave us alone. Those are your only two options."

Breathing hard, he deliberated.

"You know what Reenalyn did to you last time you were a skunk to me," I reminded him. "I'd love to see what she'd do with you if your skunkery left a mark this time."

With a vein pulsing on his forehead, Kaido dropped the supplies and strode from the room, shooting a glare at Dane.

I wobbled, catching hold of Dane to stay on my one foot.

"Here." Dane gripped my arm with one hand and slid the other around my waist, sending chills over my back. He gently set me in the chair and retrieved the supplies.

"I'm sorry you had to do that." He sighed, taking Kaido's place in front of me, and carefully propped my boot on his knee.

"Stop you and Kaido from fighting?" I shrugged. "I'll never understand why guys are so quick to solve everything with blows when words work just fine."

His nimble fingers made short work of my bootlaces. "If there are words for that piece of..." He let out a harsh laugh. "Well, I don't know what they are."

With one hand supporting my calf, he took great care to pull the boot off without causing so much as a twinge in my ankle.

"That didn't hurt, did it?" His heart-stopping blue eyes met mine with concern as he set the boot on the floor.

"No."

"Good." He rolled my pant leg up to my knee and swallowed.

"Dane"—I squinted with a grin—"are you *blushing*?"

"Of course not. It's the light in here." But he didn't meet my eyes.

"Uh-huh."

Without another word, he placed the makeshift splint against my ankle and started wrapping it. "It's pretty swollen. We should prop it up when we get you back upstairs."

"Sure."

Why was my leg making him blush? He'd seen my legs before. We'd been swimming together several times. It was only a leg. But he was *definitely* blushing. There was something undeniably sweet about his response. And a little flattering, too.

Bandaging finished, he unrolled the pant leg and glanced at the boot. "Probably we should leave the boot off, don't you think?"

I nodded, dreading the long hobble up two flights of stairs and across two hallways to my room. *Great. A lot of good I'll be when we do find out anything about Bennet and Whisper.*

He gently set my foot down and stood. "Are you ready?"

I nodded, and he held out a hand.

Taking it, I said, "You know, Dane, this reminds me of the first time we danced. At the Grand Castors' Ball."

Helping me up to my good leg, he grinned. Stepping to my side and wrapping an arm around me, he whispered, "I could never forget. It's one of my favorite memories of you."

"Oh yeah?" I took a hobbling step forward, and Dane moved with me. "What's another of your favorites?"

"Huh." He helped me forward. "There are so many."

"Pick your top three," I suggested as he reached into a drawer and pulled out two more vials of soothing potion. We didn't have much left. Might have to bother Acres after all.

We reached the door, and Dane helped me through. "Okay. Well, besides that dance, when you walked into The Braided Loaf looking for me and then smiled when you found me."

"For our first date?"

"Yeah." He grinned, lowering his voice to a whisper. "I couldn't believe you were there for *me*. And how happy you looked when you found me. It's one of the *good* things there are no words for."

"What's the next one?"

"When you—"

"Are you about finished yet?" Kaido appeared from one of the darkened doorways, striding toward us like he owned the place. "Mucking skunks, how long does it take to wrap an ankle? Let's go."

Dane's tender demeanor vanished, replaced with the deadly scowl he reserved for Kaido. Positively stiff with fury, Dane blocked Kaido's arm from snaking under his around my back.

Kaido gave up and settled for squishing me as closely against him as he could. "I could carry you to your room, Mella, to make it easier on everyone."

Dane's face reddened, but he glanced at me rather than shouting at Kaido. He seemed to think it was more important for me to choose what made me more comfortable than for him to prove to anyone he was the manliest or that I was his. I appreciated his consideration and respect.

"I'll need as much exercise as I can get, and it looks like I won't be getting as much as usual for a while, so I'd appreciate it if you both could help me walk up the stairs."

Dane nodded, and Kaido shrugged. "Whatever you want, girl."

Rolling his eyes, Dane wrapped his fingers around my waist reassuringly.

Sparks scattered from his touch, and I considered again how much nicer and nicer-looking his hands were than Kaido's. I'd have to tell him later.

Kaido gestured toward the stairs with a flourish. "On we go, madame."

Dane scoffed out loud.

"Come on, guys. Let's get this over with so you don't have to keep being around each other."

"I'm perfectly fine, Mella. I don't know what you're talking about." Kaido grinned at Dane.

What a day.

We started back down the long hallway, the steps of our five boots echoing. A cheerful voice rang up ahead, and soon we reached the door Wallen was guarding. It had been silent before, but voices came from inside. Young voices. Were these the kids Zaylan said were wards of the manor? I strained toward the sound, curious.

Dane leaned us toward it so I could get a peek through the crack.

The doorway opened in the side of a classroom full of teenagers sitting at wooden desks, looking unhappy. Some had their heads buried in the crooks of their arms, some laid miserably on their hands, others leaned back in their chairs with their arms crossed, looking murderous.

Not little kids or old people. Teenagers just a few years younger than us.

One of them sighed aloud, like he was annoyed.

What could they be learning that was so horrible?

I glanced toward the front of the room where a girl faced an easel with her back to the others and made dramatic motions with a paintbrush, her blonde ponytail bobbing and swaying. "And *that's* how you use negative space to help when you're having trouble getting the shapes you want on the page. Any questions?"

She twirled around to face the others and saw us at the door. "Oh. Hey. Are they chucking you in here, too?" She looked the same age as the others.

The red-haired guard, Wallen, appeared in the doorway with a raised eyebrow. "Need something?"

"Oh, um, no. I was just curious what was going on," I stuttered, my good ankle shaking again.

The girl gestured to those in their seats. "Passing the time. I'm trying to teach them about art." She shrugged. "If you're hurt and need something to do while you heal, I can teach you, too. Most of them don't care."

"Oh, well, thank you. I appreciate the offer," I said, doubting Wallen would let me in. I eyed him.

He shrugged. "Doesn't matter who goes in. Just can't take anything out with you."

Huh. Interesting.

If they were so bored they moaned through taking art classes in their spare time, they must not be too bad off.

"Um, thanks. I might come back later then," I said.

The girl nodded, then pointed at the easel and addressed the others. "Any questions on negative space?"

Wallen nodded and closed the door.

"What a weird kid." Kaido snickered as we continued stumbling toward the stairs.

"I thought she was nice," I said, "if a bit odd."

"What, you actually going to take her art class or something?"

"Do you have to have an attitude about this, too, Kaido? Yeah, I think I might." Though hopefully not for long, if we could find Bennet and Whisper soon.

We finally reached the staircase.

"Oh. Well, in that case...maybe I will, too. It could be fun. I guess."

I rolled my eyes. He'd better not try. He didn't give a muck about art. He'd bug me the whole time. But saying anything about it now would only make him more determined. I'd leave it and hope he'd forget.

Kaido and Dane helped me upstairs, then across the main floor to the spiral staircase. That would be fun.

"Mella, I've *generously* allowed Dane to help so he can feel useful even though he isn't. But this staircase is going to be more challenging. I vote you let me carry you and save us the trouble."

Dane stiffened, but once again, he held back, letting me choose what I needed rather than asserting himself at my ankle's expense.

"Kaido, give it up. You know I'm with Dane, and that's not going to change. What's the point of being so obnoxious?"

I leaned toward the stairs and hopped up the first one. They squished into the staircase around me, and I hopped up the next one.

"Obnoxious?" Kaido dramatically pressed his free hand against his chest, pretending to be offended. "I was under the impression I was being sacrificially helpful, since your little boyfriend can't lift you himself."

Would this stupid peacock stop preening? "Shut up, Kaido. Dane has literally jumped out of a tree with me in his arms. He's just got an injury right now."

Finally we reached the top of the stairs. I was winded and so ready for Kaido to go.

"In fact," Kaido said with an evil grin, "I bet that's *not all* he can't do himself."

Dane's body jerked like he was about to knock Kaido down again, but he kept his arm around me instead. His self-control was admirable. And it was about time I made myself clear.

"Kaido, let me tell you something." I shoved his arm away and leaned into Dane.

Kaido raised an eyebrow and crossed his arms, still grinning. "What's that?"

"Dane holds more attraction for me in one little finger than you have in your whole body. Many times over. Besides being a genuinely good person, he makes me feel things you never could."

Kaido frowned, dropping his arms to his sides.

His eyebrow rose for a moment before he pasted on a fake grin and rocked back on his heels. "Whatever you need to tell yourself to cope, poor girl. Let me know when you change your mind."

Rolling my eyes, I faced the hallway. "Come on, Dane."

Kaido followed us the few steps to my door. *Take a hint!*

Dane pushed his door open and cleared his throat. "We can take it from here, Felzane."

"Actually, I feel a chaperone is needed, don't you, Mella? The two of you shouldn't be *alone* in your room. People might talk."

Hypocrite.

I swung my other arm around Dane's neck. "Thanks for your non-hypocritical consideration, Kaido, but we're good. You can leave."

Dane backed into the room, and I hobbled with him.

Kaido stepped after us. "Mella, seriously, you'll be bored to tears with that skinny, pale—"

I slammed the door in his face and turned the lock with a sharp snap. "Good*bye*, Kaido!"

Facing Dane, I looped both arms around his neck and raised my eyebrows, unable to stop my yawn. "You'd think he'd get the hint already."

He didn't meet my eyes. "Come on." His voice shook. "Let's sit you down." He helped me hop to the bed and gently lifted my legs. "Do you want to prop that one on one of these pillows?"

"Sure. If you'll come sit here and talk to me."

Silently, and still avoiding my eyes, he pulled one of the pillows from the head of the bed, gently lifted my bandaged foot, and rested it on the pillow.

He hesitated, glancing furtively at me.

"Are you sure—"

"Yes, Dane, please. Come here." I patted the plush covers next to me.

He sat as far away from me as he could get, leaned back on the remaining pillows, and laid an arm over his eyes.

I eyed the gap between us. *Oh, we'll be fixing that.*

"So what's up?"

"Kaido…" He trailed off and sighed.

"Yeah, what about him?"

He heaved another sigh and then was silent.

I reached for the arm covering his face and pulled it down, sliding my hand over the lean muscles of his forearm until I reached his fingers and laced ours together.

He looked at our hands and glowered.

I raised a brow. "Do you not want to hold my hand?"

"Are you sure you wouldn't rather be holding Kaido's hand, Mella? Or someone more like him? He's so much…I mean, he's tan. Stronger. Taller. And he's right, you know. He could've carried you across the yard and up and down those stairs without you having to hobble. Including me only made the whole thing harder for you. You defended me, but you had to lie to do it."

"First of all, Kaido's hands are ugly as skunks. Haven't you seen them? They're…really the most unattractive hands I've ever seen, actually. And I'm not just saying that to make you feel better." I yawned, laying my head on the pillow but still facing Dane.

He lifted an eyebrow.

"Second, you didn't insist on helping me yourself or being included even though that meant I could've chosen to have Kaido carry me. You put me and my pain above your need to assert yourself. Kaido only volunteered to help to annoy you. He doesn't give a muck about anyone but himself. You left the choice up to me. Kaido wouldn't have. He's too much of a pompous peacock. And he probably couldn't actually have carried me all that way either."

Dane's glower dimmed to a frown.

Progress.

"Thirdly, I only went after Kaido last year because I thought it was what I was supposed to do to get what I thought I wanted. It was supposed to make me more popular with Selverine and her crowd. I was shallow and vain and wanted to do whatever it took to be liked by high society."

"You're just saying that to be nice, Mella."

"Oh, am I? So now you're deciding what my type is, huh?" I crossed my arms and pretended to look angry. "Okay then, I take back my appreciation for you not trying to make my decisions for me."

He stared sullenly ahead.

"Fourthly, it was you who came to my rescue at the ball after Kaido dumped and humiliated me. And I've loved you for that and much more ever since."

His frown melted away a little more. "Mella..."

I patted the space next to me again, and he shifted closer. I scooted toward him to fill in the rest of the gap and slung his arm around my shoulders.

"Yes, Dane," I whispered. "I love *you*."

He already knew it, but it wasn't something I could over say.

He leaned toward me, looking afraid to believe me and completely adorable.

"Mella..." He laid his other perfect hand against my cheek. "You know I've been in love with you for almost two years."

"I know," I whispered, "but hearing it is still nice."

He stroked my cheek with his thumb, sending delightful chills all over me. "Mella Yarinelle, I love you. I am so desperately in love with you there aren't even any real words for it." The light in his eyes dimmed. "But I wish you wouldn't have had to lie to Kaido to defend me."

I frowned. "What do you mean? I didn't lie to him."

He raised an eyebrow. "The part about..." His face reddened. "How I make you feel things he never could...?" He cleared his throat. "We haven't..."

I grinned. "Let him take it however he wants. It wasn't a lie, even if it had other implications."

"What do you mean?"

I laid my hand over his on my cheek. "I mean the sparks you send through me every time you touch me. How your whispers make me shiver and feel loved and safe and happy. The goosebumps you send over my skin when you brush against me. That's what I mean."

"Oh."

"You look surprised."

"I didn't realize…that was something I did."

"Well, you do."

Slowly, my favorite smile of his appeared. "You mean, like this?" He slid the hand on my cheek down to brush my neck, then over my shoulder and down my arm.

Closing my eyes, I whispered, "Yes, like that."

"Wow."

I opened my eyes, grinning at him. "Wow what?"

"It's good to know you meant what you said to Kaido. That I can make you feel so good just with this."

I closed my eyes and leaned into his hand. I opened my mouth to say something witty, and then forgot it. Sleep overtook me as I succumbed to the pain-relief potion.

Stay with me, Dane. Forever.

CHAPTER 27

ACRES

Leaning on the balcony railing, I psyched myself up for what it would take to check whether Zaylan had actually sent people to search for Bennet and Whisper, or was lying and up to something.

The first time I'd used this potion, I'd accidentally made Trinka throw up. Hopefully that wouldn't happen again.

It was supposed to remove dangerous memories so her castling would be safe, but instead it had brought the worst memories into focus, while allowing me to see what she was seeing.

Starstinger met my eyes from the floor, her black-tipped tail whipping at top speed. With a sigh, I pushed off from the railing and headed for the stairs.

With Trinka, she'd taken most of the potion, and I'd accidentally provided the other ingredient when I'd reached out to stop her from falling. That connection was how we'd both seen into each other's minds. But when I'd seen Mella's memories, I'd had all the ingredients myself and she'd had none, so she didn't see what I saw. Which meant as long as I contained the whole potion, the other person involved wouldn't see anything in my head.

But they had both felt when it happened. That was a complication I hadn't been able to work out yet.

I had to try, though. Even if Zaylan's explanations made some sense, there was still too much at stake to trust his word. And I had to test it on someone slightly less dangerous than him first.

Taking a deep breath, I downed the vial of potion and prepared myself for what I had to do.

It was so awkward. Why couldn't it just be a proximity thing?

Steeling myself, I opened the door and stepped out.

"Oh, hello! I'm glad I found you. Gomund, right?" Hiding a wince, I laid my hand on the guard's uniformed shoulder, hoping he wouldn't throw me down the front stairs for it.

"Uh, can I help you?" he asked with a raised eyebrow, shifting away from me, his striking feathered lion castling eyeing me lazily.

"Yes! Um…"

There was nothing. My hand was definitely touching his shoulder. Was it the clothes? Did I need direct contact with his skin? I was afraid of that. I had touched Trinka's forearm to steady her, and I'd gripped Mella's hand for her to pull me up after a spar.

Unable to restrain a wince, I stepped closer and reached for his hand. "You see, I'm trying to find…" My fingers brushed his, and he pulled away, frowning darkly.

Skunks. If I couldn't touch his skin, I couldn't test the perception potion, and the experiment would be a flop. How else would I confirm whether it would work without the other person taking one of the ingredients? The only other option was experimenting on my friends, and this was already questionable enough.

"What are you trying to find?" he growled.

"Uh, ingredients. Yes! Ingredients for a potion."

Not that I intended to waste time working on any other potions. As long as I could prove this perception potion worked and that the energy-draining feeling wasn't too noticeable since the ingredients had now had more time to integrate, I'd be done for a good long while. I would use it on Zaylan to find out what he was really up to. Once that was settled, I'd be on my own again.

I was here for fossils, and once I was sure everyone was safe, I'd focus on that.

"There are some medical potions in the basement." Nodding down the road, he said, "And an apothecary a few hundred spans that direction." Stepping away, he straightened and faced the road.

I glanced toward the apothecary's place. Hopefully this potion would work like it was supposed to and I wouldn't need an apothecary. But I still had to touch his skin to be sure.

Maybe it would be less weird if I could get *him* to touch *me*.

"Perfect. Thank you. I need a potion to help with, um…" My leg tremored and buckled under me. My knees hit the ground hard, and I fell over.

The worst symptom I'd experienced yet. My arms shook as I pushed myself up to kneel on the ground, waiting for the pain in my knee to subside. The side of my leg hurt now, too, like I'd landed on something sharp.

No! Not now! How am I going to explain this?

"I'm sure she has a potion to help with…whatever that was." Gomund watched me warily. "Can you stand?"

"I'm fi—" I started to say out of habit, then changed tactics. "Feeling dizzy. Can you give me a hand so I can go inside and get out of the sun?" *If only the sun was the actual problem.*

I reached one hand toward him.

Hesitantly, he gripped my hand and hauled me up.

Images flashed through my mind—fear. Fear of being frozen.

In this heat?

Not frozen exactly, but *stilled*. Like the others.

Which others?

That would be the cost of failing to follow orders.

Guilt over a stolen castling. It belonged to a child.

A child with a castling?

He shoved me away, brandishing his quarterstaff. "What did you do to me?"

Holding up my hands, I pretended innocence. "What? What do you mean?"

"I…it felt like you drained energy from me." His scowl deepened. "What did you do?"

He shoved the quarterstaff closer, nearly touching the point to my chest.

"I didn't do that." I swallowed. I'd hoped it wouldn't be as noticeable for him as it has been for Mella and Trinka. But that had been a miscalculation. And a huge downside to this potion. Could I alter the recipe to dilute that side effect without weakening the mind reading?

"Maybe the sun's getting to you, too," I added, pulling the excuse from thin air. "Maybe you need to get in the shade and rest."

Straightening, he glowered down at me. "I don't need rest." Gesturing to the door with his head, he growled, "You go inside and don't come back out. I'm working, and I don't have time for this."

"Right. Ah, sorry for bothering you."

Stepping through the door, I closed it behind me, barely restraining a victory fist pump.

Starstinger flicked the black tip of her tail over the stone entryway. "It worked?" she asked eagerly.

"Yes! Not perfectly, though." *I'd have to tweak it before using it on Zaylan. But how?*

"But it *does* work. So now you're taking a break. As you agreed. Right, Acres?"

I hesitated. The side effect made it too risky to use on Zaylan. I'd have to eliminate that. Which would take some more experimenting.

But Starstinger had begged me to promise I'd take a break from floramancy after this experiment, regardless of the outcome, and I'd agreed.

Sighing, I nodded. "Yes. I think I'll return to the library and see if I can find the second volume to that one on fossils I found yesterday."

That would be enough to get her off my back about it, and then I'd make a plan for adjusting the ingredients to get rid of that side effect.

With a satisfied smile, Starstinger nodded, getting to her feet. "Acres, what's that discoloration on your pocket?"

Glancing down, I saw a dark stain spreading over the pocket. Right where I'd felt something cut my leg when I fell.

"Oh no!" I peered inside at the shattered glass vials. What an idiot. The last of my perception potion, gone.

Wait, was that one intact vial?

Careful to avoid the glass shards, I pulled out the one remaining dose. Skunks.

"Hey, Acres." Dane waved down from the other side of the balcony railing.

"Oh, hey, Dane." Why was he half-whispering?

"Mella sprained her ankle earlier, and we found this soothing potion, but it's got a major sleepiness side effect. Any chance you could take a look and see if you can reduce it? I don't want her to have to choose between being awake and in pain or being out of it for some relief. Especially when we find out where Whisper and Bennet are, if they need our help."

"Oh, sure. I'll see what I can do," I agreed automatically. I couldn't put fossils over Mella's health. Besides, it was only a soothing potion. It couldn't take that long to figure out.

I avoided Starstinger's sparking eyes as Dane held the potion vial over the railing and I stepped closer to catch it.

"Thanks, Acres!" he hissed. "I appreciate it!" With a nod, he spun away from the railing and strode out of sight.

I couldn't hide from Starstinger any longer.

Wincing, I faced her.

She scowled, her tail whipping back and forth at top speed. "Next time, Acres, I'll speak up for you if you won't do it yourself. And you can pocket that thing, because you're still taking a break."

"But Mella—"

"Is resting and not in pain. She doesn't need a better potion *this second*. You need rest, too, and to do something for yourself for once. That was the whole reason we came out here in the first place."

"Well, okay. I'll spend an hour on fossil reading and then go to the apothecary for ingredients for Mella and to make more perception potion since I busted most of mine."

"One hour? No way! At least three."

"Fine. Two. And then more tonight after I've done what I can with the potions and everyone else is asleep."

She threw a paw over her face and dragged it down dramatically. "Acres, you also need sleep! You were just on watch, after staying up to read for hours, so you really should give your mind a break tonight."

"Ugh, come on!" I headed for the stairs. "How am I supposed to do stuff for myself and help other people and still sleep a normal amount? You're being unreasonable."

"*I'm* being unreasonable!" She trotted behind me, tail flicking. "Acres Parrianther, you listen here—"

I crashed into someone on the stairs. "Sorry! Are you okay?"

A slender girl with cropped black hair stood before I could offer a hand to help her up, her hog castling jumping between us with narrowed eyes and tusks brandished.

The guard from our first night, the one with the weird sword hilt, smiled at me. "All good. My bad. I was running down the stairs, which was stupid since they're curved and it's impossible to see far ahead. You okay?"

She lifted her hand from the hilt at her hip to brush her bangs away, and a white bone stood out against the dark metal of the weapon. What looked like a fossilized tusk was set into the grip.

What a cool feature!

"Uh, yeah. Thanks. By the way, I heard there's an apothecary nearby. Do you know how to get there?"

"Oh, sure." She patted her hog's head, and it snorted. Running through a few instructions, she finished with, "If you hit the village market, you've gone too far."

"Thank you." Smiling and sweating, I held out my hand, hoping I could shake hers in a gesture of thanks and maybe pick up something useful about Zaylan or Morrenfayre in general.

"No problem." She grasped my hand and shook it twice.

Avian castlings. Hybrids suspended in time.

Stilled?

The grouchy guard. A key.

A key to what?

Stress. Something hadn't gone to plan. Someone always saw her coming.

Who? How? What does she need to do?

"I'd make a run for it if I were you, though," she said, pulling her hand back and shaking it out. Frowning at me, she rested her hand on her sword hilt again.

I struggled to force myself back to our conversation. "Uh, why?"

"Because she closes in half an hour."

"Oh. Good to know. Thank you...what's your name, by the way?"

"Erisole. And this is Tusker." She smiled, gesturing to the hog.

"Nice to meet you, Erisole and Tusker. I'm Acres, and this is Starstinger."

"Ooh! I love that name." Erisole grinned at my castling, who only glared in return. "Well, I'll let you get going, then. You'd better hurry if you want to reach the apothecary's shop before she closes."

Shimmying around me, she breezed down the rest of the stairs, Tusker on her heels.

How had she gotten the fossil in her sword? That was cool. Was that why she cast an animal with tusks?

I'd think about that later. Right now...

I hesitantly met Starstinger's eyes. She'd leaped silently up several stairs so she was on my eye level. "Acres, I know what you're thinking—"

"We've got to go, Starstinger. I'll take a break later. I promise."

Rolling her eyes, she sighed dramatically and tripped lightly down the stairs. "Fine. Let's get this over with."

Chapter 28

SELVERINE

I slammed the cover closed and coughed at the poof of dust exploding around it. Stupid old books. There wasn't a useful bit of information in the last three enormous volumes I'd trudged through, and now I was thirsty and needed to stretch my legs before continuing this monotonous chore.

Standing from the dusty wooden desk, I strode from the library and down the hall, considering my options for safe drinking water. It wasn't possible to get water I could be completely sure wasn't floramanced, but the fountain was less likely to be contaminated than anything in the kitchen. If only Acres's antiflora powder would've worked! Then I wouldn't have to worry about it.

With a stretch and a yawn, I headed across the balcony for the spiral staircase.

"You'd better hurry if you want to reach the apothecary's shop before she closes," a girl's voice said on the stairs.

Apothecary? Was Acres getting ingredients to make more antiflora powder? Maybe an improved version that would work better? I wasn't a huge fan of any floramancy. But if it was the only way I could eat while in Morrenfayre...

I jogged downstairs and spotted Acres and Starstinger. "Were you just talking to someone about an apothecary?"

His eyebrows drew together. "Yes...I was. Why?"

"Because I used all the antiflora powder you gave me, and I need more. But do you have anything better? Because it had a weird side effect."

His eyes bugged. "You already used it all? That was a several-week supply, even if you used it on every meal! And I've only seen you eating from your pack. How did you use it so fast?"

I glared at him. Who did he think he was to lecture me? "I ran out of packed food and had to eat something. So I doused it in your potion to be safe."

"You used the *whole packet* on one meal?"

I nodded, crossing my arms in anticipation of more lecturing. Why didn't I walk away? I didn't need to listen to him fuss.

"What was the weird side effect?"

I raised an eyebrow. "You give out potions to people without knowing their side effects?"

"There *aren't* any side effects for taking a *normal* amount!"

"Whatever. Look, if you don't have anything better, then I need to speak to an apothecary. Are you going now?"

He nodded. "Apparently she's about to close."

"Great. Let's go." Passing him, I headed for the front door.

"Okay, sure," he mumbled. "Better go out the garden door, though," he called. "I pissed off the guard out front."

Pivoting to follow him to the garden door, I grinned. "What the muck did you do to piss off the guard?" I'd never heard of Acres pissing off anyone.

"I was experimenting. On a potion. It didn't go to plan."

"You experiment on people without their consent?" I stopped in my tracks. Had he ever experimented on me?

"No, of course not. *I* took a potion—didn't give any to the guard—and it needed another person to work."

"Hmm." Catching up, I waited for him to start another conversation, but he was silent, his hands in his pockets and his gorgeous castling slinking at his side.

Starstinger was enviable. Even back when I'd wanted an avian castling so bad, I'd always thought I'd want a castling like her if I had to have something else. I would've taken her over Horizon any day.

Though if I'd arrived here with the avian castling I'd always wanted, would we be taxidermy now?

He and his castling were so...*happy*. They got along. They fought well, conversed about his nerdy fossil stuff, and went everywhere together.

It was annoying to see a castor and castling getting along so abominably well when mine still refused to appear.

The few people we passed on the road avoided eye contact. And it was like in that tavern—everyone was either younger than ten or older than sixty.

What was with that? And why did they look so...shifty?

Most wore either hoods or some other fabric around their heads, and grandparents kept their young grandchildren or greatgrandchildren close with a tight hand around theirs.

Hopefully some less furtive people would be near the shops. Maybe in a more cheerful mood.

"Wondering why everyone's either a kid or an old person?" Acres asked.

I started. Did he know the answer? "Yeah, I am. It's weird. So what happened to everyone in between?"

Acres squinted at the sun. "I think something bad."

"Why?"

"Zaylan's not as nice as he seems," Starstinger offered. "He's up to something."

"Well, yeah, anyone could guess that." I rolled my eyes.

She sent me a haughty look, which I ignored.

"You know, Selverine," Starstinger sighed, "if you want your castling to return, it might be helpful to practice being nice to other castlings in the meantime."

That hit hard. "How dare you—"

"Come on, we're almost there," Acres interrupted, lagging behind a step to come between Starstinger and me.

I fought to keep my arms at my side rather than crossing them angrily, and I marched on, furious she was right and clueless how to make it work and get Horizon back. Would she even want to return? I'd been so terrible to her.

"So what ingredients do you need from the apothecary?" I asked.

He held up a hand and ticked off one finger at a time. "I need ingredients for the potion that didn't work on the guard, Mella needs a better pain medicine, and you need more antiflora powder. So all those things." He pulled a crumpled piece of parchment and a quill from his pocket. "I should write it all down so I don't forget any."

He had a lot of projects going. But hadn't he just said he wanted to study fossils rather than potions?

"I'm curious about the recipe for the remedy for Mella. So far in my studies, anything that has a useful result often has a non-useful side effect, as you apparently found out with the antiflora powder. But if I can use multiple things that produce the desired result, I can minimize the negative effects significantly with every additional plant. Isn't that fascinating?"

I tried not to roll my eyes. But I didn't succeed. "Quite."

We reached a tiny shop with a sign identifying it as The Apothecary's Hut, and Acres held the faded wooden door for Starstinger and me.

The shop had a thick, humid, earthy smell, which was unexpected in this desert. And it was dimly lit.

As my eyes adjusted, someone appeared behind the counter.

"How can I...how can I help you?" an elderly woman asked.

I could just make out the shine of her eyes and the flash of silver on her arm. Her voice shook on the second phrase. Was she surprised to see people our age?

"You sell potion ingredients, right?"

My eyes grew accustomed enough to the dark to see her rolling her sleeves down, covering pale arms and a silver bracelet. "Yes, I do, young man. What do you need?"

"Everything on this list." He handed her the scrap of parchment.

She peered at it, apparently able to read even in the dim light. "Oh. Very well. I have everything but the ground thyka thorns. Luckily for you, thyka plants grow in the royal gardens. You should be able to harvest some yourself. Look for poison-purple flowers that only open at night. They can be hard to see in the dark, but if you can spot moonbeam moths, you're in the right place. They like the flower nectar. For the rest, just a moment."

She disappeared deeper into the dim shop, glass clinking as she prepared Acres's order. She returned to the counter with several little sacks and vials of ingredients.

Acres laid a few coins on the counter. "Will these cover it?"

She eyed them, then swept them into her pocket. "You traveled a long way for a few ingredients. I would suggest you return to Terrenthyrs as quickly as you can. And it would be wise not to return here."

She'd noticed the coins were foreign. Acres was spending his *own* money on potion ingredients for everyone else?

"Thank you for the advice. There's one more thing we need before we leave," Acres said, gathering the pouches. "Could you please share your recipe for that pain-relief potion, and supply the ingredients? For studying purposes. I mean to find out if I can produce the same properties without the drowsiness." He held up two more coins.

She put her hands on her hips, her grandmotherly manner replaced with a fierce defensive expression. Something about the same size of Starstinger whizzed around the room and landed on her shoulder, staring us down with sharp, bright eyes.

Wings spread for a moment before it folded them against its back.

My heart skipped a beat. Was this woman the only avian castor not turned into a statue? "Is that an avian castling?"

"Of course not," the woman spat at me. "No one with avian castlings goes free."

"What? Why not?"

"Well are you here for Avian Army theories, or for my private potion recipes? It doesn't matter either way, cause you'll not get either out of me. There's the door."

She pointed behind us, and a small guttural growling noise came from her direction. Probably the castling, but I wasn't sure.

Disappointment slumped my shoulders. Once again, answers wouldn't come easily.

Acres glared at me. I'd skunked his whole mission. Shoot.

"Actually, if Acres has no intention to sell the recipe or to use it to make a duplicate product to sell, you have a legal obligation to share what you know for the benefit of everyone in Morrenfayre."

She huffed and leaned toward me, looking me over. "What are you on about, girl?"

"According to law four-hundred-seventy-three section D part iii, if you have intelligence that could be used to improve the lives of citizens of the kingdom, and can share that information without it resulting in a loss of business, then you're legally required to do so. And Acres here doesn't want to sell the recipe or make his own duplicate product. He wants to study your method and learn from it to create a different product. And not to sell, either. Just to help a friend."

"But how can I be sure it won't result in a loss of business? If he takes my years of research and refining and creates something better, no one will be coming to me to buy the outdated version."

I finally crossed my arms and looked down my nose at her. "Would you rather your fellow citizens be condemned to an outdated product just so you get money in your pocket?"

She remained silent.

"I thought not. And besides, people like to rest when they're injured. Your product will still be needed. But sometimes an injured person needs to stay awake and focused. And Acres has no intention of selling in this region anyway. So your sales will not be affected."

She regarded us for a long moment, drumming her fingers on her own crossed arms. "A trade then."

Acres piped up. "What do you have in mind?"

I shot him a look. *Shut up! Let me handle this!*

"I want your improved recipe as soon as you've developed it. To distribute it from here. For the betterment of the kingdom." She eyed me.

"Done." He held out his hand, and she shook it.

"Very well. A moment to write it all down." She hobbled farther into the depths of the shop.

"I'd like to know why it's so dark in here," I said.

"Sunlight can damage potion ingredients," a rusty voice cooed from the darkness over the woman's shoulder. "We store potions and ingredients in here to preserve them."

"Oh. And you are?" I finally caught that tiny, sharp pair of eyes glowing from a shelf or something a few feet away.

"Barronell, bat castling of the apothecary. It's a pleasure to meet you."

"And you as well," Acres said sunnily.

Apparently he was so excited about getting this recipe that his mood had lifted.

The woman came shuffling back into the room. "It took me decades to get it this good. If you can make it better—well, it'll be a blow to my pride, boy, but good for my kingdom. So I wish the best of luck to you."

She reached out for Acres's hand, closed his fingers over the humid parchment, and patted them.

"Thank you, ma'am. I appreciate you trusting me with your work, and I look forward to sharing mine with you. I'm sorry, but I didn't catch your name earlier."

She reached out to shake his other hand. "My name is Narellen Merrandil."

CHAPTER 29

ACRES

"**N**arellen Merrandil?" My voice rose octaves as if I was nine years old as I stepped back involuntarily, her unfamiliar voice warring with the fear her name inspired. She couldn't be the Narellen Merrandil we knew, could she?

"Yes...?" Her voice rose in question, too.

It took a few tugs to realize she was trying to pull her hand away.

"Oh, sorry." I released her hand. The last of the perception potion had worn off, so I had nothing from her mind to go on.

"You've heard of another by that name, have you?" she accused. "She stole it from me. It was never hers, like so many other things. So I finally took it back."

Why would the queen have *stolen* an apothecary's name?

"But, why—oof!"

Selverine stepped on my foot, and I tried not to cry out. Starstinger hissed, and Baronell hissed back.

"Thanks for your help." Selverine grabbed my arm and yanked me toward the door. "Acres will bring you his version of the recipe when he finishes."

Selverine groped for the door, found it, and pushed me through.

The bright midday light blinded me, but I spun for a last look at the apothecary. What light shone through illuminated a totally different face than that of the Narellen we knew. This woman was pale, with graying wispy blonde hair, and wider features.

Mucking skunks.

Selverine pulled me from the shop and back down the stairs to the main road. "Come on, Acres. Let's go."

"Selverine, did you hear—"

"Of course I heard her claim my grandmother's name, Acres!" she snapped.

"But why—"

"If I knew, I'd skunking tell you!"

"I only saw her face for a moment, but she doesn't look anything like the queen. Did you notice any similarities?"

"I couldn't see well either," she said. "Weird that two people with the same name are potion pros. They're probably close in age…but they couldn't be sisters. The apothecary is as pale as Dane and has wider features than Grandmother and me. Maybe they had the same potions teacher? Maybe student rivals."

"Skunks. Do you think she knows about the queen's manipulation potions?" I glanced down at Starstinger, draped over my shoulders. "Do I seem weird to you?"

She slid to the ground. "No, you're not under the influence of anything, Acres. I think I would be able to tell now that I know to look for it."

I sighed, reaching down to scratch between her shoulder blades. "That's a relief. Thanks."

Selverine crossed her arms, kicking up sand as she marched alongside us with her eyebrows slanted down. "If they were student rivals, would she know about the manipulation potion? What if she invented it and my grandmother stole it from her? I wouldn't put it past her."

Starstinger stretched, arching into my scratch. "Okay, so how do we know we can trust this recipe? What if she put something weird in it?"

I pulled out the recipe to look it over in the light. The plants I recognized made sense. But some were unfamiliar. "We'll have to do a lot of experimenting on me again."

Starstinger growled.

"I know. I'm not a fan of it either, but I can't ask anyone else to take the risk."

She growled again, staring straight ahead.

Selverine eyed me. "But what if she *did* put something horrible in there?"

"Well...we'll have to test it to know for sure. But she had a different castling. And if she knew of a plant that could change your appearance—which wouldn't surprise me—she couldn't change her *castling's species*...I don't think...so she's got to be a different Narellen. So she doesn't have a reason to try to poison me. Unless she wasn't as convinced as she let on by your promise that I wouldn't sell it. But if that was the case, why give it to us?"

"Because we could've taken her. Two against one." Selverine laughed. "Trinka's rubbing off on me."

My leg twinged, and I tried not to limp as I struggled to block how much it hurt. Was it going to give out on me? *Not in front of Selverine!*

"And she's obviously not my grandmother in disguise! If it was her and she went to all that trouble to change her appearance and found a way to alter her castling, she would've used a different name. There's no reason for her to look like someone else and then still use the same name in front of people who would know her."

"Excellent point." I should've thought of that.

And since I had some perception potion left back at the manor, I could just use some on her. Though she'd know I was up to something with its current unfortunate side effect.

Good thing it was out of my system from earlier, because I did shake her hand.

"She would've had to be an incredible actress to pull that off without manipulating us," Selverine said. "And since she was used to influencing us all the time, she never needed to develop good acting or lying skills."

"So maybe your student rivals theory, then?"

She nodded. "Yeah." Her voice was softer, and the look on her face was more sad than disturbed or angry.

"Selverine? What are you thinking?"

She shrugged. "It's just...Grandmother is the only relative I've ever known. What if...what if this person, the only other person I know of with the same last name, is the only remaining relative I have in the whole world? And what if she's as evil and self-serving as my grandmother? What if…what if everyone in my family is horrible? And I'm destined to be exactly like them."

She winced and shrugged, as if she wished she wouldn't have said so much.

I stood still, waiting for her eyes to meet mine. After a couple of steps she noticed I'd stopped and faced me.

"Selverine, you can't let anything your relatives do define you. Their successes and failures are theirs alone, not yours."

"That's a nice sentiment, Acres, but when everyone else associates me with what my grandmother did…it doesn't matter what I think about myself, does it?"

"Yeah, it does." It *had* to.

Her eyes focused on mine, and she looked surprised by my seriousness.

"You can't control what others think of you, only what you think about yourself. If you aren't who you want to be, then start changing that and eventually you'll be proud of yourself, even if no one else knows it."

It was the same thing my Gram had told my sister and me when our mother couldn't let go of the bottle and our father couldn't stop misusing potions. I remembered now how ashamed and grieved we'd felt.

But Gram said we could choose a different path. My sister might have, if she'd lived long enough. And I was determined to, for however much life I had left.

"Otherwise, if you choose to let yourself become what everyone thinks you are, you'll waste your life."

I had to look away, hoping she couldn't see my own fears.

"Don't waste your life, Selverine. No one ever knows how long they have. So don't let someone else tell you how to spend whatever life you have to live. No matter anyone else's choices, the choice of who you become is yours."

I hoped she couldn't see the weight of my own mortality in my eyes.

Her wide eyes met mine for a long moment before she broke the gaze and shrugged it off. "That's the biggest speech I've ever heard from you.

At least, the biggest one not involving plants or fossils. What brought that on?"

She spun away and walked a little ahead of us. I hung back in case she didn't want me to see her face, and Starstinger weaved around my boots.

"I know how hopeless the weight of someone else's negative expectations can be because of decisions someone close to you made. I don't want you to be stuck under that."

She eyed me with a guarded expression. "Why do you care?"

"I just don't judge anyone else based on the actions of their family members. I don't know you well, but I'm choosing to assume you're not like Queen Narellen. And it looks like I'm right. Narellen wouldn't have helped me back there. Was that an actual law, or did you pull it out of thin air?"

She relaxed a little, letting her arms swing at her sides and slowing to keep pace with us. "It *was* a real law—at least, at some point. I read about it while searching for information on Grandmother in the library. It might not legally apply anymore. I don't know. But neither did the apothecary. And it's to help us find Whisper and Bennet, and to help other people too. Everything I said about not stealing her business was true. Or at least, it better be." She glared at me.

I held my hands up. "I don't intend to sell her recipe or my discoveries, if that's what you mean. I still want out of this. I'm not a floramancer. I'm just trying to help out a friend." *Again.*

"Good. But why are you so determined not to do something you're so good at?"

I straightened. *She thinks I'm good at floramancy?* "Remember when you asked me at the tavern if I'd ever eat again if I'd spent the last several years manipulated by floramancy in my food?"

She nodded, meeting my gaze.

"I actually have spent a lot of time being manipulated with floramancy. And I've seen other people treated that way, too, on a closer-to-home level than everything we discovered about the queen at the tournament. And I'm not going to be someone who does that to people."

"Oh."

"I wouldn't have touched it again if a friend didn't need help. Since then, I've had to use it a few times. But still, I'm not a floramancer. I'll help friends out when I can, but that's not what I want to do with my life. That's my choice."

Selverine's stomach growled, and she stared straight ahead, possibly embarrassed. How long had it been since she'd last eaten?

I pulled some peppered jerky from my pocket and unwrapped it. "Here. This is from Morrenfayre, but..." I took my packet of antiflora powder and grabbed a pinch. "You can have some of my antiflora powder. *This* is how much to use." I sprinkled the pinch over the jerky. "There. You could use a little more for a full plate, but you don't need much." I held out the jerky.

She eyed it suspiciously. "How am I supposed to know whether you actually put antiflora potion on it or something else?"

"Oh." I pulled it back, stung. "Sorry. I thought—I guess you'd have to trust me."

I waited a moment then started wrapping it back up.

Her stomach growled again. "Ugh, fine," she spat, snatching it from my hand.

I nodded, hiding a smile.

She'd decided to trust me.

I straightened, grinned at Starstinger.

Starstinger winked at me, but I ignored it, a new spring in my step.

We walked on in silence. I enjoyed the feel of the breeze on my skin and Starstinger's fur brushing against my leg.

Selverine mumbled something.

"What? Sorry, didn't hear you."

"Do you really think I'm nothing like Queen Narellen?"

"I think you helped me do something to help a lot of people. Narellen wouldn't have done that—unless maybe she had a secret agenda. Do you have a secret agenda?"

She laughed a little. "No. I came with you for more antiflora powder. I definitely didn't expect to find anyone using my grandmother's name. What am I supposed to do with that?"

"I don't know the answer to that question, but to answer the previous one, everything I know about you points to you being a different person than Narellen. But I won't know for sure who you are unless I get to know you better."

Crossing her arms, she gave me a look. "Are you asking me out, Acres?"

I stopped in my tracks. "What?"

I hadn't meant that. How had I given her that impression? My face heated. Was that sweat beading on my forehead?

"No, Selverine, I just meant I literally can't know who you are without spending time with you. Not dating, just like, sparring or talking during dinner or something. Skunks, that also sounds like a date, doesn't it?" Wincing sheepishly, I looked everywhere but at her face. "Sorry, I know you're way beyond my class. I wasn't hitting on you, I promise."

Her emerald avian earrings shimmered as I paused for her response, and then stupidly kept talking. "And that time I did at the ball—that was an accident too. I mean, not me. It was the punch. Really, I was being literal...in a way I guess didn't work. I'm sorry."

What an idiot. Was that rude? Ugh. I didn't want her to think I was being annoying when I was trying to be encouraging.

I was way too busy with floramantic research to date, and if I was ever able to find anything out about the fossils here, that would take up the rest of my time, and I didn't know how much I had left. Which also wouldn't be fair to someone. No dating.

Besides, like I said, way beyond my class. If I'd said I *was* asking her out, she probably would've punched me and never spoken to me again. I'd seen her do that to other guys.

"Oh. Okay." She spun away. "Well, sure, we can spar. Prepare to have your ass handed to you."

"Great. Sure, I'm prepared." I searched for something—anything—else to say to move past my blunder, but I was too distracted thinking through my words and finding ways I could've said them better.

Starstinger chuckled softly and rubbed against my leg.

I frowned down at her, but she kept her eyes fixed on the road ahead. I could tell by her smile, though, that her eyes sparkled disconcertingly.

"Well, I need to return to my room for a bit. Thanks for...everything." Selverine started up the path toward the manor at a faster pace.

"Yeah, and thanks for your help getting the recipe."

She waved, then jogged until she disappeared inside.

Starstinger grinned, her eyebrows raised as if she was amused.

"What?"

"I wonder what she would've said, if you *had* asked her?"

"She'd say *no way*, obviously. I'd never ask someone like her out. She'd never say yes."

"Acres, *she* asked if you were asking her out. She didn't say she'd say no if you were."

"What?"

"If you had actually asked right then, she might've said yes."

"Wha—oh skunks." My stomach plummeted to my toes. "Do you think she *wanted* me to ask her out? No, there's no way—it would be ridiculous to think she'd actually say yes." I eyed her. "But you think I *should've* asked?"

She smiled mischievously. "Well, Acres, it's like you say about your plant experiments: if you don't try, you'll never know."

It was an intriguing idea. But I also could save myself the embarrassment when she inevitably told me I was an idiot to think she'd consider me.

Though if I took a sip of perception potion right before a spar...maybe I'd hear her thoughts. I'd know everything I needed to know. Hopefully I had enough left to do both.

What am I thinking? I'm not my father. I don't use floramancy to take advantage of people. If it's not for information to help my friends, like with the guard, then I couldn't use it that way.

Besides. There's no chance she'd be thinking about me. And if she was, she didn't seem the kind of person who'd hide it.

Starstinger's obnoxious grin finally broke through my thoughts.

"What are you looking at?" I scowled, heading to the manor.

"Just watching your face as you mull it all over. Entertaining."

"Yeah. Well, sorry to disappoint, but that's the last entertainment you'll get out of me from that. I'm not wasting any more time on it."

She padded ahead to face me, leaving little pawprints in the sand as she walked backward, her grinning face cocked to one side. "We'll see."

Chapter 30
REENALYN

I wonder what Acres and Selverine are talking about?

I'd been staring out a front window worrying about Bennet and Whisper and wondering when Zaylan's castors would return when Acres and Selverine strolled into view, deep in conversation. I'd never seen them alone together before. If it was anything interesting, I'd hear it in their feelings later whether I wanted to or not.

Was Acres limping? He rubbed the back of his neck and winced as Selverine crossed her arms, raising an eyebrow at him.

Maybe not limping. Maybe making a fool of himself in front of a girl he had a crush on?

I grinned, wondering if love was in the air for the two of them.

Which reminded me...where was Zaylan? I hadn't seen him in a while. The one time I'd caught a glimpse of him, I hadn't sensed any romantic feelings.

He might've just been busy—romantic feelings weren't always on someone's mind. And he had a lot of responsibilities. But I still worried...what if they were gone for good?

Was it something wrong with me after all? I'd been accused of being too silly, too daydreamy, and the super confusing *too much,* many times before. Maybe that was still my problem.

Rubbing my temples, I wondered how to fix whatever was wrong with me so I'd finally be worth someone's love. Was it possible?

More feelings tickled my senses. Some were from people I didn't know—a guard or maid or manor cook, maybe. I couldn't pick up on Selverine or Acres yet. Beldon was around near the garden door, pining over Trinka. I hoped my advice to him hadn't been too interfering.

What was that other feeling? It was a pleasant spark. And from someone I'd met recently but didn't know well. And there was a feeling for...wait...*me?*

I leaped to my feet, upsetting the chair and squeezing my eyes shut to focus.

Was it Zaylan? *It must be Zaylan!*

I froze for a couple of beats, hope rising in my chest. It came from just below me and a little under the kitchens.

I beamed. It *must* be Zaylan. He still felt something!

I had to tell Mella...well, maybe that's what I would've done first if she hadn't been a skunk lately. What I needed to do was tell Cupid. He'd taken a nap earlier. Where was my spear? Did I leave it upstairs in my bedroom?

I swept across the entryway and up the spiral staircase. Then almost ran right into Zaylan himself.

"Oh!" I squeaked, bumping my head on the staircase ceiling again.

Pain roared through my head.

Come on! Did I have to do that in front of him, at this moment, when his feelings needed to be fanned into a flame rather than snuffed out?

I hesitated to meet his eyes, wincing. "Sorry, I didn't realize you were there. I must've been a little distracted." *Wishing I could go five seconds around you without embarrassing myself!*

He smiled, and my heart soared. "Not to worry, Reenalyn. What a pleasant surprise running into you. I'm afraid I'll have to ask you to excuse me though. I have a pressing matter to attend to."

With a nod, he stepped around me and ascended the rest of the stairs, then strode toward his study in the opposite wing from our guest rooms.

I wished I could've talked to him longer, but hitting my stupid head on the ceiling again right in front of him had stolen what little confidence I had. Checking for his feelings, I couldn't feel them.

But they'd just been there!

Was he masking them somehow? Maybe that was why they kept coming in and out.

Bumping my head was dumb for sure, but not enough to make him *completely* lose interest, surely.

Thinking back to the feelings I'd sensed from his direction, I marveled at how similar to Dane's they were. He...*admired* me. What had I done to make him feel that way? He barely knew me.

But he *admired* me.

Stifling a giggle, I ducked, skipped up the rest of the stairs, and strode down the hall to find Cupid.

As I closed my bedroom door and spotted my spear on the plush duvet, I wondered how Zaylan had reached the staircase so fast. He'd been one floor down and on the opposite side of the manor a few moments before. And then I was running into him.

He must be in incredibly good shape—two lengths of the manor and a flight of stairs didn't faze him.

I grinned and fell backward onto the bed, hugging myself and imagining the next time I'd see Zaylan. What would I sense from him?

I called Cupid from my spear to fill him in.

He yawned and stretched, then noticed my stupid grin. "Ooh, what's that look?"

"I just ran into Zaylan, and I sensed another feeling!"

His face lit up. "Well, of course you did. You're incredible, so it's only natural he'd notice and appreciate it."

I scratched the green spikes on his head. "Thanks, Cupid." My smile faded. "I am a little worried, though. I need your help."

"Of course." He nodded, eyes bright. "Anything."

"I know you don't think I'm *too much*, which I appreciate, but some people do."

He cocked his head, his tall spikes leaning to one side.

"I'm afraid if I can't reel in the too muchness, Zaylan might change his mind about me. So could you help me figure out how?"

"Uh, I'm not sure I follow."

"It's okay, Cupid. You don't have to pretend nothing's a little off with me. I already know. And I need help fixing it so Zaylan doesn't change his mind."

Cupid frowned. "Who's been telling you something's wrong with you?"

"I mean, no one's said that *exactly*. But, just, different people have said things over time that add up to that." I smiled. "No one to beat up for me, though. Sorry."

"What do you think is wrong with you?"

I rolled my eyes. "Come on, Cupid, that's sweet of you, but you don't have to pretend you haven't noticed. I'm a little *too much* sometimes." I shrugged. "I won't be upset at you for agreeing. But I will be upset if you keep pretending you don't know, because I need your help to fix it."

Squinting, he scratched his chin with one clawed hand. "Reenalyn, I genuinely don't know what you're talking about. Nothing's wrong with you. If someone stops having feelings for you, that's on them. Not you. It might be disappointing, but nothing you need to change yourself to prevent. How could you be happy with someone you had to become a different person for?"

"Cupid, that's sweet. But you're missing the point. This is the *one chance* I've ever had, and probably will ever have, to find love." Sitting up, I put my hands on my hips. "I'm going to do whatever I must not to miss out on it. And I'd like your help. As my castling and closest friend."

"First, let me ask you this: Do you respect him?"

"Of course—I mean, I think so. He's the only person who's ever had feelings for me! How could I not?"

Laying his clawed hand gently on my knee, he said, "Is that a good reason to fall in love?"

I frowned. "I thought you'd be more excited for me."

"I *am* excited for you, Reenalyn! Here's what I think. You and Zaylan need to go on a date. A regular old date. Alone. No castlings, no other people. And talk. Get to know each other. Find out what there is to respect and love about each other. Then both your feelings will have a solid foundation."

Scrambling off the bed, I skidded to a halt in front of the vanity mirror. "Cupid, you're a genius!" I swiped the brush off the vanity and dragged it through my hair. "I'll ask him right now."

Striding toward the door, I pulled it open, then leaned back in and pointed at Cupid. "But this conversation's not over. You're still going to help me fix myself later."

Twirling out the door, I headed for Zaylan's study.

And the confidence filling me a moment ago disappeared.

I slowed on the balcony, suddenly unsure. What was I thinking, asking the *regent of Morrenfayre* out on a date with *me*, a girl from the poorest part of a neighboring kingdom?

I considered turning back.

But I didn't feel like squeezing more help from Cupid just yet.

A door opened in the hall on the far side of the balcony.

Zaylan walked out of his study, jotting in a little book.

My heart stopped.

All words left my head.

He looked up, his dreamy eyes meeting mine. "Oh, hi, Reenalyn. What a treat to run into you twice in one afternoon."

Smiling warmly, he tucked the pen and book in his trouser pocket.

Speechlessness still filled my head as my heart lifted at his words. "Um..."

His eyebrows rose. "Can I help you with something?"

"Yes, actually." Realizing I was fiddling with my tunic between my thumbs and forefingers, I forced my hands to my sides and my eyes to meet his. "Would...would you like to have dinner with me?"

Time slowed and my cheeks burned as I waited breathlessly for his response.

"Tomorrow night?" he asked with a grin.

I blinked. That...that was a yes, wasn't it? "Um, yes. Tomorrow night is perfect!"

Don't squeal! Keep it together! Don't be too much!

"Amazing. Morrenfayre is pretty short on taverns, but I could have the cook make something special for us. And we could dine alone in my study, if you like." He grinned sheepishly. "I know that's not very romantic, but with my duties and the search for your friends—"

"No! No, that sounds absolutely lovely. Thank you." He wanted it to be *romantic*!

Reaching for my hand, he said, "The pleasure is mine, Reenalyn."

Gently taking my hand, he pulled me toward him and pressed his lips to my fingers, his eyes never leaving mine.

I completely melted. My heart soared, and I was probably hyperventilating, but I kept the rest of myself under control.

"I'll see you there," I said, positively beaming as I floated back to my room.

"Until then, beautiful," he called after me.

Don't freak out, don't freak out...

Slipping through my door, I closed and leaned against it, hardly believing what had just happened.

"And?" Cupid demanded, eyes wide.

"Eek!" I squealed, dancing around the room. "He said *yes*! And he called me *beautiful*, and we're going on a *date* tomorrow!"

Falling onto the bed, I yanked a pillow over my face and squealed again.

"Okay, okay." Cupid pushed the pillow away with a chuckle. "Breathe!"

Rolling to my side, I propped my head up and grinned. "Cupid, can you believe it? It's finally happening *to me!*"

CHAPTER 31

SELVERINE

Gripping the rail, I climbed the spiral staircase.

Had I just been *refused?* For the first time in my life?

I hadn't actually asked Acres out, true. But I'd given him an opening.

And he didn't take it. He directly said he wasn't hitting on me. Even though he'd also said the queen's decisions didn't have to define me, that I could choose who I wanted to be. He gave me something...hope, maybe? And something safe to eat. Without expecting anything in return.

Surely he'd expect something at some point.

Though he'd also bought potion ingredients for Mella and the others and even me with his own money. Had he been doing that all along? Surely his fellow cohort members chipped in. Not that it covered how much time he spent developing and perfecting potions. And experimenting on himself?

What did he get out of all this?

Nothing I could see.

And he'd still turned me down.

Well, good. I don't date Wrynfordians. Or people obsessed with boring stuff like fossils.

I didn't want to admit it, but the rejection stung. What didn't he like?

Not that I cared, of course. It just wasn't the usual reaction. It had been refreshing at the ball, before the punch. But now...

Planning to inspect my reflection as soon as I entered my room, I strode down the hall.

Were those voices coming from Willova's room next door? I paused. At least one man's voice. What the skunking muck was a *man* doing in Willova's room?

I twisted the knob and threw the door open, rushing in with my trident raised.

My jaw dropped.

Willova sat at the vanity, and Kaido skunking Felzane stood behind her with a pair of sharp blades aimed at her neck.

"What the mucking skunks!" I shrieked, launching across the bed and shoving Kaido into the wall. I crouched between them, aiming my trident at his mucking throat. Eyes wide, he dropped the blades and held up his hands.

The blades clanked against the floor. *Scissors?*

"She *asked* me to do it!" he wailed, pressed against the wall.

Do what? I glanced at Willova and was shocked to see her miles-long red hair hanging in choppy clumps around her shoulders.

"Oh, skunk off, Kaido!" I shouted, chasing him around the foot of the bed. "Get out!" I brandished my trident and drove him from the room. "And shut the skunking door!"

When the door slammed, I leaned over the bed, staring in shock at the crimson waves strewn around Willova's boots—some over a span long, others shorter than a pinky nail.

Sliding back over the bed more slowly this time, I raised my eyebrows at Willova in the mirror. "You don't *look* traumatized, but I know better than to believe your face. What the skunking muck happened?"

Willova faced me, her temporary cutlass on the vanity table. It was an odd combination—the cutlass where someone would usually get ready for the day in less ridiculous circumstances.

"Earlier today, I ran into Kaido looking miserable. He asked if I would spar with him, and I needed to practice, so I said I would. After a bit he asked if he could try his hand at my cutlass, and offered to let me use his whip. So we switched."

"You *handed* that *idiot* the only weapon you know how to use and took one you have no experience with? What if he'd attacked you?"

"He was sad. But not angry. I didn't think I was in danger."

"Uh-huh. Willova, we need to work on your self-preservation skills. And beyond self-preservation, you don't have to do everything anyone asks you just because they asked."

She hung her head, staring at her lap. "He's not like Drazdan," she whispered.

"Maybe not, but he's still a mucky person. I'd avoid him, if I were you."

Her green eyes met mine in the mirror again. "So I shouldn't do whatever anyone asks me to do, unless it's you? Is that it?"

Scowling, I spat, "I'm not *commanding* you to do anything. I'm offering friendly advice. Forget about it. What happened to your hair?"

She hung her head. "I accidentally caught his sword arm with the whip and couldn't let it go, so we tripped over each other, and the cutlass slashed through it. And I tore my dress trying to untangle the whole mess."

I blinked. That actually happened? "And somehow your head is still attached to your shoulders."

"I tried cutting my hair myself to even it out, but I didn't get it straight. Kaido offered to help because he felt bad and because he'd cut his sister's hair plenty of times. I said he could because perfectly straight will go over better when I return home to get Faultless back."

I sighed, running my fingers through my own hair and leaving my head in my hand. "That explains the different lengths on the floor." I met her eyes, trepidation looming in my gut. "We'll have to plan better this time. We've got to rescue Faultless without another confrontation with Drazdan."

"He'll be so furious." She sighed. "He won't believe me that it was an accident. But he didn't want me to tie it up to spar. And honestly, Selverine, it feels so good." She grinned one of her rare grins, transforming her plain face into something beautiful. "And look at this." She stood and twirled in a circle, showing off leggings and a green tunic.

My jaw dropped. "Willova, you're wearing *pants*!"

Her smile crinkled her eyes. "Yeah. And they're *so* comfortable. I can't wait to spar in them. They feel a bit too loose in the waist, though. It could just be how used to dresses I am, but if I can track down a needle and thread, I might take the waist in a bit. I can't risk them falling off during a spar."

Her cheeks reddened at the idea.

"They look great on you. And way better for sparring for sure. Where'd you get them?"

"Kaido borrowed them from Mella for me. Since the death of my dress was his fault."

"Oh. That was helpful of him." Was it just me, or was he being *too* helpful? "How does it feel to have the normal clothes?"

She beamed at the mirror. "*So* good." Her smile faded. "But it would make Drazdan so angry. I'll need to find another dress to wear when we get Faultless..."

No, you don't! "Willova, he doesn't have the right to—"

"But he will anyway, Selverine, and getting Faultless away from him is the most important thing."

Setting the trident on the bed, I crossed my arms. "Okay. So what are you going to do once you've found her?"

"Leave Terrenthyrs, probably."

My arms dropped to my sides, surprised and relieved she'd finally decided to get away from him. "Good! It's about time."

She faced me. "I've felt so free here. If I weren't missing Faultless, this would be the perfect life. Free of Drazdan." She hugged herself, rotating in little half-circles. "I don't want to be trapped again."

"Good. You don't deserve to be."

"Selverine, I'm sorry for trying to hook you up with Drazdan. I didn't know what a nice person you were then. I wanted to avoid the beatings by doing as instructed, and I dreamed of freedom from Drazdan by passing him off to someone else. But even if things hadn't worked out the way they did, I still wouldn't have let you go through with it. I would've stopped it before he could hurt you. I'm sorry I didn't make that decision sooner."

Two people thinking I'm a nice person in one day. *What is this?*

"It's fine, Willova. Don't worry about it. I would've bumped him off on someone else, too, in your shoes."

Sliding off the bed, I leaned my trident against the wall. "Now how about you let me try my hand at cleaning up the absolute mess Kaido made of your hair?"

***

"You don't have to slog through this with me, you know," I told Willova as she brushed a few decades' worth of dust off yet another book stack and flipped the top one open.

"I don't mind. Besides, I owe you for the help with my hair." She smiled, swishing her shoulder-length waves from side to side like she'd been doing for the last half hour.

"Why do you keep shaking your head like that?"

"Because my hair feels so light and free now. I didn't realize how heavy it was before. I hope the new look will keep me cooler, too. Maybe I'll sweat less. Oh, look at this one."

She held out the book, and I took it. It was a thin leather-bound volume with pages and pages of faded handwriting. "Great. More handwriting." I slapped it closed and handed it back. "Knock yourself out."

Willova swished her hair back and forth as she focused on the first page. "I think this was for keeping track of appointments."

She flipped the page, and I cracked another one, grateful to find printed words I could easily read.

"Selverine! This was Narellen's schedule!"

I threw my book down and darted around the table to look over Willova's shoulder. "Really? Are you sure?"

"Yes!" She pointed to a scribble. "Princess Narellen to see Prince Roxland of Larzanobyl, and a date."

Her finger dropped to the next line. "Princess Narellen to have new dresses fitted. Princess Narellen to attend a party. Princess Narellen to see Prince Roxland again."

"Maybe something a maid would've kept for her? Since she wouldn't have written about herself that way," I guessed. "What else does it say?"

"More of the same." She flipped pages faster, briefly glancing at each as she went. "Lots of parties and visiting with the prince. Oh!"

"What?"

"The maid's handwriting gets sloppier here." She skimmed the rest of the book. "And it stays like that for the next several pages...the rest are blank."

I frowned. "Why would the handwriting suddenly change? A different person?"

"Maybe."

"Or the writer could've had an injury. My grandmother could get harsh with servants she felt weren't doing a good job."

"Or she could've been stressed. She skips some words in these entries, like she was writing things down quickly. And...weird. No more prince."

"Really? So she stopped seeing the prince at the same time the handwriting got stressed. Maybe the prince dumped her, and she took out her disappointment on the maid?"

"I don't know, Selverine. It's like she became a totally different person. Not a single party, no more dresses. Meetings with the king and attending royal court and lessons from tutors."

"Huh. Maybe her father felt she was being too frivolous and forced her to take more responsibility."

Willova nodded. "Could be. Oh, this is interesting."

I leaned in. "What?"

"The last entry is an appointment with a doctor, but it's cut off partway through. And then no more appointments after that."

"So...she was sick? But she didn't die, so whatever the doctor did, it must've worked. But why did the entries stop?"

I remembered the lack of a husband's name next to my grandmother's in the genealogy book. "Or...she was pregnant. With no husband."

Willova raised a red eyebrow. "What makes you think that?"

"I found some genealogy stuff, and my grandmother and her son are named, but no father for him. Maybe no one knew who he was."

Closing the book, Willova set it down. "If you come back with me to get Faultless, you could ask her."

"What?" I blinked. "I'm never speaking to the queen again, Willova. She's a snake. And she's too good at using manipulative floramancy. If I visit her, I'd always wonder if I was under her influence without realizing it. It's bad enough I can't eat anything without dousing it in too much antiflora powder. I'm not doing that to myself, too."

Willova shrugged. "Then I guess we'll never know."

She opened another book, swishing her hair absently as her eyes moved over each line.

And I realized Willova Calentine, who I'd pitied this whole time as a weak coward, was braver than I was.

She might not do much to protect herself, or even me since she knew I could hold my own. But she'd do anything to keep Faultless safe, even face Drazdan with imperfect hair.

I, on the other hand, would do anything to protect *myself*, even miss out on potentially vital information in order to avoid being in the same room with my grandmother.

Mucking skunks! What am I going to do about that?

Chapter 32

Acres

Silvery moonbeams shimmered in the fountain water streaming overhead. I eyed the strange trumpet-shaped flowers growing on the trellis above the garden. With petals ranging from pale yellow to deep crimson, they were striking. What floramantic properties might they have?

More importantly, where were the thyka plants? The apothecary had mentioned the purple petals only opened at night and could be hard to see—looked like she was right.

A fluttering gold moth caught my eye. I followed it to the fountain. It rested on a crooked dry stem bent toward the ground.

More gold flickers opened and closed their wings nearby. Squinting, I could just make out the sharp point of a thorn on the nearest stem.

With great care, I clipped off a few thorns and placed them in a thick container in my bag.

Thank you, moonbeam moths.

Catching sight of pinkish berries growing on nearby shrubs, I stooped and broke off a delicate cluster. Those might come in useful.

The whole manor garden was undoubtedly an incredible feat. How the plants got enough water to thrive in the heart of this desert, I couldn't fathom. The number of unfamiliar plants here made for endless floramantic possibilities.

Even so, I recognized enough that between them and the apothecary's recipe, I could take the next step toward enhancing the soothing potion for Mella.

Fresh plant samples in hand, I climbed the stairs to the guest wing and headed for my room with a sigh. Because there was one thing the garden didn't contain: aged deecho fern. The last thing I needed to make more perception potion.

Only one small swig remained.

Should I use it *for* Selverine, or *on* Selverine?

How was I even asking this question? I couldn't do that to her. I'd be just as bad as the queen, not to mention my father. So I would use it *for* Selverine.

If even that. I *should* eliminate the side effect and then use it on Zaylan as soon as possible. But I had no idea how to do that. And if I didn't get the chance to use it on him, I should probably save it for an emergency rather than to learn about the apothecary. We were sure to need it for something more serious eventually.

But Starstinger's point about Selverine wanting me to ask her out...there was just no way. Even so, how could I not check?

No. I wouldn't. I'd save it.

If only there would've been enough left in my system to listen to the apothecary last time!

Striding down the hall, I passed the guard with the fossil in her sword hilt and nodded. She must be on guard duty tonight.

She nodded and waved. "Night."

I opened my door, slipped into my room, and closed it behind me. Starstinger jumped at the noise and landed on the bed, her ears back.

"Sorry." I laid the plant bits out by category of leaves, stems, roots, and flowers on the vanity acting as my desk during our stay. "I think I've figured the soothing potion out. A little ground cactus flower that acts like caffeine, to combat the drowsiness, and a little waxen root for soothing properties without drowsiness."

She tiptoed a few dainty circles on the bed, then reorganized herself into a compact huddle with her paws tucked under her chest. "And you'll be testing this on yourself, I imagine."

"Yes. This new combination should do the trick."

Starstinger fell sideways and covered her face with her paws. "Acr-rres," she moaned. "When will you ever take a break and do something fun for yourself?"

"Soon," I promised. "I need to get this potion figured out."

Rolling onto her back, she sighed dramatically. "Uh-huh. I'll believe it when I see it."

***

Hours after going to bed, I rolled over and rubbed my dry eyes.

I'd used too much caffeine.

The dulling effects of the additional soothing ingredient were good—my rickety knee had finally shut up.

But I'd been unable to fall asleep, despite closing my eyes and controlling my breathing.

My feet hit the cold wooden floor. Sliding from bed, I eyed my throwing stars on the nightstand and considered casting Starstinger.

But just because I couldn't sleep didn't mean she needed to be deprived, too. I elected to leave her alone for now.

Standing, I wavered, struggling to balance. Catching myself on one of the bed posts, I examined my knee. The pain in my leg was gone, which had been exciting, but the weakness was still there. If I didn't focus on it, I might step wrong and fall.

That was disappointing. So much for using this on myself as things progressed.

The caffeine had my mind racing, but no useful thoughts floated around. How long would this last? Maybe I should've waited to test it till my next turn on watch.

The early morning sky cast dim gray-blue light through the window.

That guard with the fossil tusk in her sword—Erisole? Did her castling manifest as an animal with tusks because there was a tusk in her castling weapon? She could still be in the hallway on duty.

I'd never be able to sleep or focus on my plant studies if I didn't ask. What if using fossils in a weapon could influence how the castling would manifest?

I had to know.

It was eating at me as much as the need for a better remedy for Mella and a cure for me, but it filled me with more excitement and curiosity.

I eased the door open and peeked out. The hallway was darker than my room, having fewer windows, so it took a moment of squinting to make out who was there.

And there she was. Erisole.

Along with Trinka and Mauler. Trinka fiddled with her spiked brass knuckles, while Mauler laid her head on her crossed paws on the floor, nodding off and then blinking fiercely.

I pulled the door wider. Erisole glanced at me when the hinges creaked and then away.

"Excuse me?" My voice was still hoarse.

She faced me. "Hey, Acres. What's up?"

I stepped across the hall to her and her boar castling.

"Hi. I was just wondering...what specific kind of animal is your castling?"

Better to ease into the questions rather than starting with the biggest one, right?

She placed a hand on the creature's head. "Tusker's a red river hog."

"Cool. What about the bone in your longsword? Is that why you named him Tusker?"

She nodded, running a finger over the hilt of her blade. "Yes.

"So it's a tusk?"

"I think so."

"Fascinating! Do you think that had anything to do with him manifesting as an animal with tusks?"

"Maybe." She shrugged, glanced at the floor, then met my eyes. "I like how it looks, and it has sentimental value. My dad gave it to me when I was little, and he told me it belonged to a woolly mammoth. He used to make up stories about the adventures it must've had before it died and became a fossil." Her smile faded. "So when he disappeared while I was designing my weapon, I decided to incorporate this treasure into it to remember him by."

"That's such a great way to remember someone special. He sounds like an amazing dad."

"He was." She nodded.

"I'm from a place where we don't have fossils everywhere, and I've always been fascinated by them. So I love the idea of incorporating a bone into a castling weapon. I wish I'd had the idea myself—not that one would've fit in mine. But it's an awesome feature."

She grinned and peered toward the balcony windows where dim purple light shone through. The morning was coming upon us finally.

"Are you that interested in fossils?" she asked.

"Yes! They're absolutely fascinating. I have a couple back home, but they're quite rare. I've found a few since arriving, but they seem to be rarer here than I'd been led to believe."

She smiled. "Actually, they truly are as common as rocks around here. Decades ago they interfered with crop growth and slowed progress, getting in the way of buildings and new roads. There's a whole dump site for them, actually."

"Dump site?" The horror of such valuable pieces of history being *dumped* mingled with the delight of how great a number of fossils free for the taking there could be.

"Would you like to see them?"

"Yes. Very much." *Most significant understatement of all time.*

She smiled. "Great. We'll take you if you like. I'll be off as soon as the morning-shift replacement shows up." She yawned. "Well, I guess I should get some sleep first. How about we meet in the garden this afternoon?"

Every fiber of my being trembled with excitement. This was too good to be true. "Great. Thanks. I'll...see you then."

I spun, heading toward my room. Might as well read if I was destined to stay awake.

Snatching a book from my growing stack, I dropped onto the bed, plants all but forgotten, and sighed. *Wait till Starstinger hears about this!*

Chapter 33

MELLA

S taring at my reflection in the mirror, I made a face at my bent leg and slumped. My underarms were already sore from practicing with the crutches Dane had found for me. I was *not* looking forward to stumbling around with them in front of everyone.

And I'd have to leave the practice scythe behind. There was no way to carry it while using the crutches. Sighing, I left it on the bed and had to admit how absolutely useless I'd be in a fight for Bennet and Whisper. Where were Zaylan's castors, anyway? Had they found them by now? What would we do if they hadn't?

I should've brought my new scythe. Waiting to cast before all of Terrenthyrs to prove a point was so incredibly stupid.

Hauling the crutches out, I leaned on them and swung my good leg forward. After a few sets of these, I reached my door. Squeezing one crutch between my arm and my side, I opened the door.

Relief washed over me at the empty hall. Trinka and Mauler must've stopped keeping watch when the sun rose.

Good. I need to get down two flights of stairs before anyone sees me.

Trudging on with the crutches, I winced at the scraping noise the wood made against the stone floor.

There was nothing for the spiral staircase but to tuck the crutches under one arm and scoot down one stair at a time on my backside. Wincing with every screech of the crutches against the iron, I couldn't believe my luck at not running into a single person. Odd that there weren't more guards. But this morning, I'd take it.

A face peered around the corner from the dining room. Reenalyn.

I bristled. "Well you caught me at a bad time. No boyfriend or castling to help. I must look pretty pitiful."

She frowned, rounding the corner with Cupid on her shoulder, his emerald tail wrapped around her other arm. "I was going to ask if you needed a hand."

Shoving to my one foot, I tucked the crutches into place and launched forward. Wobbling, I willed myself to get it together. "I'm fine, thanks. Looks like I can handle it on my own."

"What happened?" she asked, trailing me.

"I sprained my ankle sparring with Kaido."

"Oh." She fell into step with me. "At least let me get the door for you."

"Sure."

We crossed the main floor, reaching the door that led to the second set of stairs.

Reenalyn stepped around me to open it. Something looked different about her. Focusing on her face, I realized her hair wasn't a giant blonde tail behind her. It was done up in an elaborate arrangement of twists and braids.

My jaw dropped. "Reenalyn, your hair looks amazing. What's it so fancy for?"

She beamed. "I have a *date* tonight."

"You do? That's wonderful! With who?"

"With someone who might already be falling for me."

I gasped. "So you *can* sense when someone has feelings for you! Wow. It must be incredible to know exactly how he feels without having to ask."

"It is!" she squealed.

"Reenalyn, you've got to tell me who it is!"

Grinning, she rocked back on her heels. "Well...it's someone you know. But not someone from home. Someone from Morrenfayre."

"Holy muck! Who is it?"

Leaning toward me, she whispered, "Zaylan!"

"Oh, skunks." I hadn't considered him. But he was one of the few men I'd ever seen who was taller than Reenalyn. And he wasn't bad looking, either, if a bit older than us. "Congrats, Reenalyn! That's amazing!"

"Thank you! I wasn't sure if you'd be excited for me or not."

"Oh, well." I'd forgotten I was annoyed with her for taking her castling for granted and thinking my life was so much easier because I had a boyfriend. She was about to have both, while I still didn't have a castling. I shrugged. "I'm happy for you. But I do need to get going. I...have a meeting downstairs."

"A meeting?" she asked, opening the door wide for me to hobble through.

"Yep. Thanks for your help. Let me know how the date goes."

"I will!" She smiled hesitantly as the door swung shut.

I *was* happy for her. And her hair did look amazing. How many hours had she spent on it? But Zaylan? He struck me as...not good relationship material. I hoped I was wrong for her sake.

***

"Take that desk." Ariona shrugged toward the middle of the room, her blonde hair cascading over her shoulders. "Knock yourself out."

She spun back to the easel, the sides of her dusty, paint-splattered vest rippling with her movement.

"Thank you." I hobbled over and sank into the chair, setting the crutches on the stone floor.

"Parchment and drawing stuff are in the compartment under the desktop," she added, glancing over her shoulder at the frilled lizard castling perched there, apparently not a hybrid.

"Got it. Thanks." Lifting the desk's surface, I spotted whitish parchment as well as black, charcoal sticks, white chalk, and a broken pencil.

A lot of desks were empty. Only about half of them were occupied with people a little younger than me. The boy next to me was probably about twelve. Maybe thirteen. He rested his cheek on his palm, looking miserable. Was he missing his family?

"Hi." I introduced myself. "I'm Mella."

He glanced at me, then away. "Hey."

Then nothing else.

"What's your name?"

"Cairdon."

"That's a nice name." I smiled, trying to sound cheerful and friendly.

"Doesn't matter though, does it?"

I frowned. "What do you mean?"

"All right everyone, eyes up here!" Ariona called the room to order, her frilled lizard castling sitting primly on her shoulder with his forefeet laced together. He looked like he needed a pair of lizard-sized spectacles.

Cairdon started lazily drawing with white chalk on black parchment.

"Now, today we're going to practice the three-quarter view of the face." Ariona took her own chalk and drew a huge oval on the board. Then she started drawing horizontal lines through it. "Remember, the eyes go father down than you'd think. You have to leave room for the forehead. And here is where the lips will go," she said, pointing to the lines.

Peeking at Cairdon's parchment, I was surprised to see an animal forming quicky under his skilled hand. He wasn't following instructions.

It made me want to try drawing an animal. I wasn't technically in the class. She was letting me sit in for something to do while my ankle healed.

I immediately thought of the tiger I still had a chance to cast, and I liked how Cairdon's white-on-black sketch looked. So I decided to go for a black and white tiger.

I started with the face and messed up too bad to fix it.

Scribbling through that, I started again with the body. It still looked funky, but I kept on with the legs, tail, and finally the face.

"So that's how you do it. Good luck." Ariona dropped into a desk at the front of the room and bent over her own parchment.

Frowning at how childish my next attempt looked, I peeked over at Cairdon. He'd drawn a perfectly three-dimensional-looking skunk. A *skunk* of all things? And with wings? What an imagination.

I tried wings on my tiger, but they didn't help how silly the rest looked.

Flipping the parchment over, I tried once more, this time trying for the three-quarter's view of the face like the teacher was explaining. It helped because it didn't require me to make the features perfectly symmetrical, but it was still...off.

I tried wings again, but they were no help.

"Hello, gorgeous."

I rolled my eyes without looking up from the parchment. "Why, hello, *hideous*."

"Aw, come on. I know you're still into me."

"That's what we call being delusional. And get out. This is *my* art class, and you're not welcome."

Kaido smirked, slipping into the open desk on my other side. "You going to make me leave, with that ankle? Not skunking likely."

Cairdon made a little growl of annoyance and scowled at Kaido.

I wasn't about to explain myself to Kaido. "Look, Kaido, do us both a favor and *move on*. You moved on easily enough *in the middle* of our *relationship*." I made air quotes because really, it didn't count. "Why can't you do that again?"

He took a piece of chalk and slowly swept it over my parchment into a little hook, then started an intersecting line through it. I focused on my chalk instead.

"Because I'm in love with you, Mella." He presented his parchment. A fancy lettering of my name adorned it. "So much so that I'm going to get your name tattooed permanently right over my heart." He placed his hand over his chest. "Where it belongs."

"Okay, Felzane, you do that. But it's not going to change my mind."

"Wait until you see it."

"Sure."

"You'll love it."

"I'm trying to concentrate."

"Oh, am I distracting you with fantasies of my—"

"*No*, you're distracting me with fantasies about punching you in the face."

"You wound me." He grinned.

"I wish." Crumpling his parchment, I swept it to the floor.

I tried to ignore him. Unfortunately I could still see his smirk from the corner of my eye as I worked on getting the black-and-white tiger's tail right. It looked more limp than I was going for. I tried again in a blank spot on the page, trying to get it at the right angle to look like it was swooshing back and forth like Starstinger's did.

"You know, you don't have to secretly draw it all over your page from memory. I'll show it to you and let you practice drawing in person as looong as you'd like."

It took me a few seconds to realize what he was talking about, and I tried in vain not to react when I figured it out. But my chalk slipped, and my eyes rolled anyway.

From memory, my foot. Thank good fortune he's full of muck about that.

"Sorry, Kaido, I heard Acres say he left his microscope at home. So I guess you're out of luck."

"So," Ariona said, standing again and eyeing Kaido, "I forgot to mention, when you're drawing a three-quarter's view, you'll have to..."

"Ouch. Harsh, but clever. Nice one." Talking over her, he winked at me.

I didn't have to let him talk to me this way. It was well past time for this to stop. Snagging a crutch from beside the desk, I shoved it into his throat.

Coughing, Kaido fell out of his chair, skidding backward into the next desk.

The entire classroom went dead silent.

Pinning him by the throat with the crutch, I scowled. "Kaido, I've tolerated your ridiculousness long enough. This is your final warning. Say any more of this muck to me, and I'm going to stab you with my scythe."

"And now we can all continue drawing *in silence*." Ariona emphasized the last two words, eyeing us with concern now.

Frowning, he shoved the crutch away and got to his feet. "Whatever, Mella." Making a show of looking around my desk, he said, "I don't see any scythe. But you know what I do see?" He shoved his hand in his pocket and pulled out something metal. "This."

My breath caught as I stared at my missing key. The symbol of the one home I'd had where I was welcomed and loved. Pinched between his stupid ugly fingers.

"Been looking for this?"

I made a swipe for it, but with my limited mobility, I didn't have a chance.

"Not so fast. If you want it, you have to do something for me."

Fury roared through my veins. But there wasn't much I wouldn't do to get that key. *Muck it all!*

"I can see you're curious, yes?" He grinned.

I would *not* give him the satisfaction of an answer. I glowered, too pissed off for words.

"Don't worry, I'll give you options. You just have to do one of three things, and I'll return the key. One, you can—"

Something flashed across the room, knocking into Kaido's hand and sending the key flying.

The key clattered over the stone, followed by a sheathed knife.

A boy behind Kaido shoved his chair away from his desk and headed toward the key.

"Wait, how did you..." Kaido glared at him, then faced the front of the room where the knife had flown from.

Ariona stood one desk away with her arms crossed, an annoyed eyebrow raised at Kaido. "I was talking."

Scowling, he looked her up and down. "I don't skunking care, kid. Muck off."

The boy appeared behind Kaido, leaped onto his desk, and had the pointy edge of the key pressed to his throat in a flash. "Don't talk to her like that."

Kaido's eyes bugged, and he started to push away, but the boy dug the key in hard enough to draw blood. Kaido's hands flashed up. "Okay, okay."

"Apologize. Now."

"Sorry," Kaido spat, without a hint of penitence.

The boy yanked the key away and shoved Kaido from the desk. "Now get out."

Kaido faced the boy, his scowl growing darker as he realized how much smaller and younger the kid was than him.

Seething, he spun and stomped from the room.

"Uh, thank you." I nodded at the boy, then Ariona. "Nice aim."

The boy slid off the desk, wiping Kaido's blood from the key on his tunic and then handing it to me.

"No problem," Ariona said. "What a piece of muck."

"You have no idea." I rolled my eyes.

"That's Rayzor." She gestured to the boy.

"What's going on in here?" Famita, the guard with too many castlings, stood in the doorway, glowering. The winged monitor lizard who'd bitten Marken stood at her feet, the beaked possum stood on her shoulder with its pink tail wrapped under her arm, and the badger stood behind her, peering expectantly into the room.

Ariona tapped my desk with one finger. "And that's why you have to hold your chalk at a better angle, okay? Now." She clapped her hands, striding to the front of the room as Rayzor sank into the chair Kaido had vacated. "As I was saying—"

"No more art nonsense this morning," the guard shouted. "Outside for exercise. Now."

Chairs squealed against stone as they obeyed, gathering their parchments and heading for the door.

Famita held out her hands, and they each placed their stack of parchments over them.

A moment later the room was clear, and Famita eyed the parchment on my desk, then me.

"Oh, it's not an actual drawing. Just doodles. I don't know what I'm doing yet."

Sighing, she held her hand out for mine, too.

Dropping the key into my pocket, I gathered the crutches and got to my feet. With a wistful glance at my rough first attempt, I slid the parchment from the desk and hobbled to the door.

Famita took the parchment and held the door for me to hobble through.

"Thanks," I said, surprised by the kind gesture.

With a nod, she strode down the hall after the others, the stack of parchments under her arm and her castlings all around her.

Why did they collect the drawings? Wallen had said something about how no one was allowed to take anything with them from the room. Weird.

More importantly, when had Kaido swiped my key? The absolute skunk. And some art class kids had gotten it back for me.

Maybe there was more to these kids than I'd originally thought.

CHAPTER 34

SELVERINE

Tossing her crimson hair out of her face, Willova dodged another strike from my trident, met it with her borrowed cutlass, and shoved my attack back a step, her sunburned face impossibly expressionless.

Crossing my arms, I heaved a sigh. "What's wrong now?"

Willova straightened and sheathed her cutlass, taking a deep breath. "I can't get used to this blade."

"You're doing great. You've had it a handful of days and you've still beaten me time after time."

"I could've done better."

"Maybe. But what good does it do to focus on everything you didn't do well instead of everything you did do well?"

She met my eyes, her delicate scarlet brows coming together in confusion. "If I only think about what I did well, if anything, then I'll think I'm better than I am. I have to pay attention to my failures to learn from them. To achieve perfection worthy of the family Calentine."

I sighed. "Sure, evaluating failures can help you improve. But you're not only evaluating them. You're reliving them, drowning yourself in them. You don't have to do that."

"I don't know how not to."

"All right, fine. Change of subject. Imagine we finished rescuing Faultless, and you never have to see Drazdan again. Where would you go?" I asked.

"If I could bring Faultless, anywhere."

"And what would you do to support yourself?"

Willova sighed, her boots slogging through the sand. "I don't know. I can't do anything well enough..."

"But if you could, if skills and perfectionism and all that weren't a problem, what would you do?"

She considered. "I don't know. My best skill is fighting with a cutlass, I think, but I'm too small to be a bodyguard or a real soldier. I've cooked a bit. Maybe I could do that with more practice. I've also cleaned. Floors and fireplaces and things. Maybe that."

I raised an eyebrow. "Cooking and cleaning? Drazdan had you doing all that for him as well?"

"He had to let most of the staff go because of finances. I wasn't allowed to ask for details. But I had to help more after that."

"And let me guess. He didn't lift a finger?"

"No. Because it's my fault Mother died, and in turn, Father. If they were here, we'd have more money. I can't make up for the loss I caused, but I could help handle the consequences."

I frowned. "Right. And how has he figured those things were entirely your fault?"

"She died defending me. I was young—I don't remember it. But she defended me and died. And Father died of grief after."

"Oh. I'm sorry." I hadn't expected that. There was enough love in her family for someone to die for her? And someone else to die of grief at the loss? How had Drazdan come from two such people? "That still doesn't make it your fault."

"I wish that were true, but there's no explaining this one away, Selverine."

"Willova..." My voice trailed off as several other voices came alive on the wind. Glancing toward the manor, I spotted Famita, the guard with several hybrid castlings, leading the wards of the manor out past the garden. "I wonder what they're doing?"

My heart dropped as the petrified avian and hybrid castors loomed in my mind.

Was she about to do that to these kids?

Should I help try to intervene? Readying my trident, I stepped forward, then watched in astonishment as the beaked possum, winged monitor lizard, feathered badger, and black jaguar with ivory wing bones jutting from its shoulders leaped over the sand and each mowed down one of the kids.

My jaw dropped, and I took off running. How could she just sic her castlings on children like that?

The unmistakable sound of laughter brought me up short.

The tackled kids were laughing, each hugging one of the castlings.

Were...were the hybrids their original castlings? Had Famita been the one to hybridize them? But then why was she letting them interact now?

By the fierce look she sent my way, I gathered I wasn't supposed to see that.

Someone should be ashamed—twelve- and thirteen-year-olds casting? They hadn't had sufficient time to choose a weapon and hone their skills.

But Famita was...indulging them? Secretly. Perhaps at great risk to herself, if I knew anything about Zaylan.

"We should probably keep this to ourselves," Willova whispered. "So they don't get in trouble."

Nodding, I turned away. "I think you're right."

"Selverine—um, how are you doing? You know...with Horizon still missing?" I stiffened, and Willova backpedaled. "I'm sorry, you don't have to tell me. I shouldn't have—"

"Thank you for caring enough to ask, Willova. I'm not doing great." I faced her. "How about you?"

She wrung the cutlass handle. "Anxious to see her. Worried for her well-being."

"But Drazdan wants you, so he'll keep her in one piece to use as leverage. So she'll be okay while you're here letting your wound heal. How is that doing, by the way?"

Annoyed at myself, I realized I'd forgotten it. She'd been sparring so normally. How much was it costing her to act like it didn't hurt?

"It's much better."

"Good. You probably shouldn't strain it, though. Let's take a break."

As we returned to the manor, Acres strode from the garden, waving at the slender guard with dark hair in a pixie cut and a tusked hog at her heels.

Was *she* why he'd rejected me earlier?

Great. Just great.

CHAPTER 35
ACRES

It still felt weird that we were going to a *dumpsite* for *fossils*. I couldn't imagine fossils being so numerous that people needed a place to throw them out.

Please throw them all at me! I'll take every single one!

"So, Erisole, how far is it to this fossil dumpsite?"

Squinting ahead, she blew a short strand of black hair out of her face. "It's called Fossil Gulley, and it's just a few minutes away. You can almost see it from here already."

"Awesome."

Tusker's wide nose sniffed the air as Starstinger's whiskers twitched.

We started on the same road Selverine and I had taken to the apothecary's place yesterday, but after a few minutes, we turned off at a point with the same sand and rocks as everywhere else—I never would've found it by myself.

The sun glinted blindingly off the red sand. Many small rocks were scattered on either side of the road. Taller boulders rose well above the sand the farther from the manor we walked.

A subtle incline had me breathing heavily after too short a time, my leg twinging with each step. The botched potion had completely worn off, so I felt it. I hoped I wouldn't collapse this far from the manor. Good thing I had Starstinger with me.

Finally the incline stopped at an edge with lots of blue sky behind it and what looked like another cliff many dozen spans away.

"Is that a cliff?" I asked.

"It sure is." Erisole tousled Tusker's hair between his ears, smiling like she wasn't out of breath.

My chest suddenly hollowed out. Had they thrown the fossils over the cliff? They would all be broken!

"Here they are." She stepped to the edge and spread her arms wide.

With a gulp, terrified I was about to be unbelievably disappointed, I planted my feet next to hers.

First, relief. It was the edge of a cliff, yes, but the fossils were piled so high they nearly reached the cliff's edge. Nothing would fragment on impact—at least not because of height.

Second, overwhelming delight.

The canyon was stuffed to the brim with fossils. Thousands upon thousands of fossils. And one huge bone stuck out from the others in the middle of the expanse. The top was broken off, so I wasn't sure whether it was a humerus or tibia. What creature could have grown so big? Was the rest of its skeleton buried in this pile?

Finding an entire skeleton here would be about as challenging as finding a particular piece of fuzz on a lamb's ear plant, but if they'd found so many only to throw them away...there must be more undisturbed.

"So, Acres, what do you think?"

"I can't believe there are so many."

"Is it true that finding a rock with a fossil is more valuable than finding a pure rock with no fossil where you come from?"

I blinked at her. "Yes, of course."

"Wow."

Wow is right!

"So here it's better to find a plain old rock without a fossil in it?" I asked.

She laughed. "Of course."

"That's crazy," I said, returning to the pile. "So where did these come from?"

"People used to find them in the fields when they plowed in planting season. Sometimes they appear after rain erodes the ground."

"So you do get rain?"

"Yeah, there's a rainy season. But it doesn't last long."

"Incredible. Would it be okay if I took some home?"

She shrugged. "Does it look like anyone would miss them?"

"I guess not. Thanks."

"Sure thing. So you've seen this place. What are you going to do?"

I glanced at Starstinger to find her already watching me. "Well, I'd like to collect a few to take back with me, for starters."

Starstinger grinned a kitteny grin at me. It was still as cute as always, even though she was longer and leaner than back then.

"I'm in!" And she leaped off the edge and landed lightly on the pile without shuffling one piece of bone out of place.

"Be careful out there!" I called as I knelt and lowered myself to my stomach to peer over the edge. I could reach the top layer of fossils. Grasping at some kind of scapula, I caught it under the ridge and lifted it.

"This is a shoulder bone," I told Erisole as I set it next to me.

"Fascinating," she said with a smile.

I faced her. "I'm completely boring you, aren't I?"

"No, really, you're not. I'm amused by how interested you are in these things."

"Well I'm fascinated by the fact that you're not."

"I didn't say I wasn't. Just that I've never met anyone else who was. Remember my sword?"

"That's right! I wonder if there are any woolly mammoth bones in here?" I started looking.

"No idea. But if you find one, definitely let me know."

Starstinger emerged from the eye socket of a giant skull with a large clavicle in her mouth.

"Wow! What a collarbone! Whatever this belonged to was about"—I estimated how many of my collarbones would fit inside this one—"nine or ten times as big as an average human."

Erisole and Tusker raised their eyebrows. "All I can say is I'm glad I'm alive now and not when these things were," she said.

"Practically, I understand the sentiment," I agreed, reaching for what looked like a fibula as Starstinger took another dive into the pile, "but honestly, I wish I could meet one. Or all of them, really."

"You're a little crazy, Acres."

"And you're pretty cool, Erisole."

I regretted it as soon as I'd said it. I didn't mean to sound...weird. Erisole *was* cool for sure, but...emerald earrings flickering through long hair and an intelligent smirk flashed through my mind.

Maybe it didn't sound weird. It was merely an honest compliment.

"Thanks," she said with a smile, brushing Tusker's ear tuft out of his face.

I breathed a sigh of relief.

"How many fossils do you think you'll be able to lug back to Terrenthyrs?"

I paused with the tips of my fingers brushing an enormous femur. Could I tell her I was staying? Did I still want to stay at this point? This place wasn't what I'd expected. Until seeing these fossils, I'd been leaning less toward spending the rest of my days here.

But I could hardly tell a stranger before the other Wrynford castors. They deserved to hear the news first, and I hadn't decided on what the news would be, if there was any.

"Whoa," she said. "Am I sensing inner turmoil? What about that question bothers you so much? If it's about deciding which ones to bring, I'm sure you could rent a wagon or something to help you transport as much as you want."

"True." I nodded vaguely, focused on the femur. "That's a great question. I'll have to think about it." Glancing across the infinite pile of bones, I had another question. "Speaking of questions, where does this gully lead?"

She sat next to me, shading her eyes with one hand. "It goes by the manor, a few hundred spans behind it. But there aren't many fossils in that section. It's steeper there, and besides, it's on royal property. So people haven't been tossing their rubble back there for decades like they have here. If any are there, it'll be little ones water has washed in from this pile."

"Water?"

She nodded. "Water flows under all this." She gestured to the tangled pile of fossils. That's why the manor is built where it is and how the garden and well stay watered."

"Oh! Fascinating." It was interesting, but the femur I couldn't dig out was more so.

A moment later there was a noise at my side, and she laid on her stomach next to me, peering over the edge at the bones. She faced me and grinned. "Well if your goal is to have so many that you're stressed out about which ones to bring, you're going to need help getting to them." And she reached down and gripped a vertebra about the size of Starstinger's head. "How about this one?" She held it up for me.

"That one's awesome. Thank you."

"Sure thing." Smiling, she reached down for another.

Smiling to myself, I did the same. Erisole was pretty cool.

Chapter 36

MELLA

Shoving the lid of my desk up, I snatched another piece of parchment and slammed it closed. Maybe drawing was too frustrating to be a good distraction while I waited with my useless ankle for Zaylan's castors to return with news of Whisper and Bennet.

Brushing what must've been the twentieth mucky drawing I'd done so far to the floor, I brandished my chalk over the clean sheet.

Now, hold it at an angle like Ariona showed me. Yes. And don't press too hard. Right. And...

Ugh! Once again, the line was wrong. I couldn't make the chalk do what I wanted. Why was this so hard?

Father had declared my artistic abilities worthless when I was seven, since they didn't make money or improve the family's social standing. So I hadn't drawn another thing since.

Instead, when I'd needed to express myself, I'd taken up illegal musical instruments.

But now that I'd spent a few hours in this art class while the others sparred outside and my useless ankle healed, I wished I'd spent more time honing those skills.

I tried everything from a simple snake—after Kaido got bored and left. I didn't need any more stupid innuendos from him—to Whisper. I'd even tried drawing Dane. But I couldn't get anything to look quite right.

Another attempt at the black-and-white tiger grimaced from the parchment.

The shoulders turned out a little more realistic than my first attempt, but it was nothing like Cairdon's. He made sketch after sketch of lifelike animals.

"And that's how you do more realistic shading," Ariona said. "She'll be back any second to make us leave, so you probably want to finish up."

Mine wasn't going to get any better. Leaning back in my seat, I scrubbed my hands over my eyes. If only failing at drawing was my biggest problem. I couldn't find Zaylan to ask about the castors he'd sent to look for Bennet and Whisper, they'd been gone for so many days now, and the ceremony was two days away. It was now completely official I wouldn't make it back in time.

And I couldn't draw, either.

Those who were working on projects leaned over their desks, their wrists flying over the page.

Poor Cairdon seemed absolutely miserable, even though he was churning out gorgeous works of art in no time.

"Hey, Cairdon, why are you so sad?"

He lifted his eyes to mine—dark eyes under dark scruffy bangs. "If you don't already know, then I'm not allowed to tell you."

He dropped his eyes to his drawing of a zebra running through a grassy field, adding several wavy strokes of chalk to accent the zebra's flying mane.

Huh. That sounded kind of disturbing.

"Why's that?" I asked.

He slid another piece of parchment out of his desk and started on the outline of another animal. "That answer would also fall under the list of things I'm not allowed to tell anyone who doesn't already know."

"Okay." *Snarky.* "Who said you have to keep these secrets?"

Ignoring me, he added a long tail and forelegs—bent as if preparing to jump—and hind legs to the already longish body.

A squirrel? No, the tail wasn't poofy enough.

"What will happen if you tell me?"

"I'll get in trouble," he mumbled, glancing at me, then the parchment, where he hastily scribbled in two pointy ears and a pointy nose.

"What does that mean?"

Cairdon worked furiously to fill in fur, and a little white weasel took shape under his skilled hand, the black parchment only showing through two beady eyes and the tip of the nose.

"Something pretty bad." He struck a slanting line over the top of each eye and pulled down the edge of the mouth, giving the creature an angry scowl.

I glanced around the room at the other kids. They all still looked sad. A few had trembling lower lips.

"Why are you all here?" I asked. "The village looked pretty desolate when we came through. Just old people and really young—"

"Shh!" he hissed without taking his eyes off his work. "You can't talk about that. I'm not talking to you about it."

At last, Cairdon looked right into my eyes with a desperation I didn't expect to see. What was I missing?

The door slammed against the wall as someone threw it open.

All heads whipped to face the door, Ariona's frilled lizard castling skittering off her shoulder to cling to the back of her shirt.

"Let me go!" a girl screamed from the doorway.

The guard with the feathered lion castling dragged in a young girl by the arm. He threw her into the room with a scowl, then pointed at her.

"Get used to her. She's one of you now," he growled.

His feathered lion castling gazed sadly past me. I found Rayzor returning his sad expression.

Then the door slammed behind the man and the lion, and everyone's gaze fell on the girl, lying in a heap of tears and scraped knees.

Ariona strode between the desks and kneeled at her side. "Lishia?"

The girl sniffled and met Ariona's gaze. "Ari?"

Ariona sighed. "I hoped they'd be able to keep you hidden. They'd managed for so long. I'm sorry."

Lishia swiped her tears away, glancing around the room, recognition and surprise lighting her eyes. "This is where everyone's been all this time?"

Ariona shoved to her feet and nodded, holding out a hand.

Lishia took it, and Ariona pulled her up. "Come on. Pick a desk. We should have a few more minutes."

"For what?"

"Art class. They let us draw because..." Her eyes fell on me, and she paused. "Well, I'll fill you in later."

Annoyed, I glanced at Cairdon. His gaze stayed on Lishia, his usual dreary boredom gone. His wide eyes fell on his drawing, and he scowled, squeezing his chalk enough to whiten his knuckles.

He suddenly faced me, determination shadowed with fear in his face.

I raised my eyebrows.

The door flew open again, and Famita leaned in. "Scribbling time is over. Now."

Quick as a flash, he scrawled something on the page, then scooped up all his drawings except that one. He tapped its eyes twice, then stood with the others without another glance at me.

Standing to my one foot, I hauled the crutches into place. Gathering my drawings, I planned to throw most away. Holding them as best I could in one hand as I leaned on the crutches, I swiped his weasel drawing, folded it up, and slid it into my pocket. I'd look at it later and see if I could figure out what he was trying to say.

As I fell in line with the rest, I watched as they each handed their drawings to the guard before leaving the room.

I fumbled with the crutches as the last kid handed in her drawings and left the room. The guard raised an eyebrow, tapping her foot impatiently.

"Here." I laid my parchment over the stack.

"And the one in your pocket," she spat.

Skunks. With a scowl, I handed that one in, too. What had Cairdon been trying to say?

REENALYN

Everything was coming together for my date with Zaylan. All that remained was to find the perfect flower for my hair. Maybe I'd bring in flowers for a centerpiece, too.

Strolling through the garden, I considered the flowers growing on cactus. They were beautiful, with multiple layers of fuchsia petals, and unique to Morrenfayre as far as I knew. But they didn't have a stem to pin into my hair or set behind my ear.

But the reddish-orange trumpet-shaped flowers growing on vines—one of those should work.

I tilted my head to inspect the vines, all of which were quite high, growing over lattices and archways and the tops of the tallest garden plants. Even I would struggle to reach them.

Surely a stemmed flower was somewhere within my reach.

Standing on my tiptoes, I strained my arm as far as it would go. My fingers brushed the edges of a deep-red flower's petals. With a startling *pop*, shreds of petals flew every direction, leaving a little brown husk in the flower's place.

I dropped back down. Had the flower just exploded?

Did the orange ones do the same thing?

Shifting a few spans to the side, I reached for a trumpet-shaped flower with tangerine petals.

The moment my fingers touched it, the petals ripped themselves off and shot in every direction with a louder, longer *boom* sound.

Did Acres know about this? Why were they like that? Though I understood why they were so high now, why have them in the garden? Maybe they were a pest deterrent. They'd certainly surprised me.

Leaving the strange flowers alone, I strolled down the stone path in search of a less explosive decoration.

Some nice pale pink flowers bloomed beside the fountain, stretching toward the sky on long stems. *Perfect!* I gathered several of these and laid them in my basket.

Rounding the water fountain, voices sounded through the light mist. I peered through the leaves of a tall bush.

Was that Acres with one of the Morrenfayre guards? Instead of Selverine? Maybe it was a coincidence, or maybe I'd been wrong about Acres and Selverine. I had been distracted by Zaylan and his feelings.

Acres and the guard slowed to a stop and faced each other, deep in conversation. Acres clearly felt a little awkward—his gaze kept skipping around from one random thing to another before landing on the guard's dark eyes again.

Hmm...I wonder...

I picked up the basket of flowers I'd been collecting and strolled over to them. "Hi, Acres!" I called with a wave.

He waved. "Hey, Reenalyn." Once I reached them, he added, "Reenalyn, this is Erisole, a manor guard. Erisole, this is Reenalyn. She came with me from Terrenthyrs, and we were in the same cohort together last year."

I held out a hand. "It's lovely to meet you, Erisole."

She shook my hand with a smile. "Same."

"Well, thanks for today, Erisole. I'm sorry to leave just when you joined us, Reenalyn, but I have to work on the remedy for Mella. There's an ingredient that must be added exactly seven hours after the initial mixture is combined."

Starstinger, draped over his shoulders, rolled her eyes dramatically.

"See you later." I stepped to the side to give him and Starstinger a clear path to the manor. "Good luck!" I called. Then, to Erisole I said, "Your castling is cool."

"Thank you." She met my gaze with eyes so dark, I couldn't see the difference between the pupil and the iris.

Her romantic aura was...hard to find? If she was into Acres, it should have been at its loudest and brightest with him so near, but I sensed nothing. Not an inverted thing like Trinka's. Like she wasn't trying not to have feelings, she just automatically didn't. Or maybe she was masking them somehow, like Zaylan seemed to do.

Her brows furrowed a little, breaking my stare. "Sense anything interesting, Reenalyn?"

Blinking twice, I backed up and focused on her whole face once more. "What?"

She crossed her arms with a sly grin. "What are you trying to find out about me?"

"Huh?" I stuttered, unsure how to respond. How could she have known what I was doing? We were simply having a conversation. "Sorry, I didn't mean to bother you..."

The only explanation was someone had told her about my ability. Acres? Did he know? I'd never noticed this particular guard speaking to any others from Wrynford. I must've missed something.

"Ah, sorry," I said sheepishly. "I didn't expect anyone to know about that." That must be how she knew to hide them from me. But how did she know how to do that? "I couldn't pick up on anything. Were you hiding it intentionally?"

Now she was the one to look confused. She arched a dark brow. "Hiding what?"

"Romantic feelings you have for Acres, or anyone, I guess. Weren't you just masking them? You had to be. I couldn't sense them."

"Romantic feelings?" She laughed. "Sorry, I'm not much of a romantic. I wasn't hiding anything. You know, you can hang out with someone without being in love with them. He told me about his interest in fossils, and I knew where to find them. So I took him to see them and then brought him back. Nothing romantic about that."

"Oh. Okay." No romantic thoughts about anyone ever? I seriously doubted that. But if that's what she wanted me to think, I'd let her think I believed her.

"Holy skunks." Her eyes widened. "Your sixth sense is…what, exactly? Sensing romance?"

"Wait, sixth sense? Yes, I can sense romantic feelings, but…are you saying you've heard of this kind of thing before?"

She nodded. "I can sense inner turmoil, I guess. Like when someone is struggling with a decision. I could sense it with you a few minutes ago. Something to do with me, I think?"

"I…um…yes. I was curious whether you and Acres were interested in each other, but I couldn't sense anything from you. So I wondered why that was." *And the inner debate was over whether I was rooting for Acres and Erisole or Acres and Selverine.*

She smirked. "Snooping on peoples' romantic feelings? That's pretty personal."

I fisted my hands on my hips. "I didn't *mean* to, but it's impossible not to pick up on emotions if I'm near enough to hear them. I didn't sense much from Acres, probably because he was so focused on his potion task. But with you, I found a total lack of romantic feelings. Which makes no sense. Why's that?"

She laughed. "Ha! Why should I explain anything so personal to you?"

I rolled my eyes and gave up. "You have a point. But hey!" I pointed at her. "You snooped on my inner turmoil. So you don't get to frown on me for noticing something personal about you. Inner turmoil is just as private as romantic feelings."

She nodded, dropping to sit cross-legged on the sand. "You're right about that. So how much do you know about sixers?"

"Sixers?" I sat across from her, Cupid shifting to keep his balance as I knelt and sat. "Nothing."

Erisole's hog laid its head in her lap and closed its eyes.

"Haven't you heard the lullaby about Wexel and the others?"

I frowned. "You mean:

Ask Wexel for the truth,
You can trust his word,
Brellna will be the first
To guard your secrets in this world.

To Karmell you can take
Your very greatest fear,
To tell how great you'll be,
Thornyn is always there?"

I'd sung that lullaby to my younger siblings more times than I could count, but I'd never guessed it could have anything to do with me.

"Yep, that's the one," Erisole said. "They're all sixers. People who had a sixth sense. There used to be a lot of them around, but these days there aren't many."

"Why?" I asked.

"Why do you think? If you brag about your abilities, people will flock to you to help them fix their problems. While being a sixer was prestigious once, it became a negative thing. Either you were well-known and had no life because you were fixing other peoples' problems all the time, or you were well-known and hated for keeping to yourself and selfishly not helping everyone who needed something from you."

She patted Tusker's head. "So sixers became less well-known for survival. Now we don't talk about our gifts. We keep them secret."

"Then why are you telling me about yours?"

She shrugged. "Inner turmoil isn't super useful. I can't tell what decision someone will make, which would be the better choice, or what they're thinking after they make a decision. I can't sense their motivation. So it's not a very useful skill."

"Wow," I said. "I can't imagine having to hear people's inner struggles all the time. That must be exhausting."

Erisole smirked. "Maybe, if you couldn't turn it off. But I can, so it's not so bad. I mean, inner turmoil can be a doozy sometimes, sure. But I don't have to listen to it if I don't want to, you know?"

I stared at her, jaw dropping. "Uh, no, I *don't* know. What are you talking about? There's a way to turn it off?" Crossing my arms, I leaned excitedly toward Erisole. "How?"

"Easy." She pushed me out of her space, and I tried to sit still while I waited a hundred years for her to tell me already. "You decide not to listen. Think about something else."

Deflated, I frowned. "You think I've never tried drowning all that out with other thoughts? That doesn't actually work, Erisole. At least not for me. Even if it starts to work, as soon as I realize it's working, my focus goes right back to everything I don't want to think about."

"Then focus on something so interesting you're too distracted to realize you're distracted."

I raised an eyebrow at her.

"Come on, Reenalyn. You're not going to tell me the ability to eavesdrop on other peoples' romances is the most interesting thing about you, surely."

Ashamed, I realized it had become exactly that recently. But it hadn't always been, had it? "I have Cupid, my castling, and he's a big part of my life. As are my family. And my cohort."

"Sure, but isn't there anything about *you* specifically? Anything you care about that's special to *you?* Besides other people."

"I'm a violinist. I haven't played in a while—not since we came here. I left the violin at home because I didn't want it to get damaged. Maybe I should've brought it with me."

"I'm sure we could find one around here for you. But you don't have to actually play. Just think about it. Think about the part it plays in your identity. How you're proud of yourself and always enjoy playing—stuff like that. And as you think about it and who you are, you'll stop needing to soak up who everyone else is to feel purpose in your life."

I blinked. I didn't need to soak up who everyone else is to feel purpose...did I? I didn't think so. I squirmed away from the thought.

"Hit a soft spot, did I?"

Glowering, I crossed my arms. "Are you snooping again? That's hypocritical at this point."

"Nope, I'm not." She shifted to stretch her legs out and lean on her arms behind her, looking as carefree as they came. "I turned it off."

I raised an eyebrow. "And it didn't automatically turn on when you thought about it again?"

"Nope."

"That's what I don't get."

She leaned forward. "Maybe you don't have to. Maybe you won't until you practice more."

"Fine. I'll try."

Arms crossed, I closed my eyes and pictured my violin. Pulling it from its felted case. The shine on smooth Emberlyn wood. The smell of wood and oil. The sound when I touched bow to strings—

"Hey!" The shout echoed against the manor, startling my eyes open. It was Xerrome and his enormous rhino castling.

Rumble's gray leathery shoulders rose several specks above Xerrome's dark hair. The rhino had one long horn at the edge of his nose, and a shorter one between that and his eyes. The long one must've been longer than my arm. The huge castling shook the ground with each step as it approached.

Xerrome stared past us as he walked by, his wooden scabbard slapping his thigh with each step. "You two need to vacate the premises." His eyes landed on my elaborate hair, which made me even taller, for a moment before flicking away. "Zaylan needs this area clear."

He probably thinks my hair looks ridiculous. But ooh! Zaylan? Is he coming out right now? I looked around for him. *Surely he'll like my hair. It won't make me too tall next to him.*

Erisole strode toward the manor. I followed, glancing behind me at the enormous castling. It must be the biggest castling I'd ever seen. Bigger than Mauler and Brawler for sure—even bigger than King Jorros's polar bear castling.

And no Zaylan anywhere.

Nearly tripping over Erisole's castling, I steadied myself and faced her. "What? Why'd you stop?"

She wore a sly grin and a raised eyebrow. "The question is, have you?"

I frowned, then remembered the exercise of a moment ago, before I was distracted by Xerrome's rhinoceros. "Oh! Um..." My mind roamed around for the familiar annoyance of Dane and Mella's loud emotions, but I couldn't sense them. No way had I actually turned it off that fast. The first time I'd tried?

"Well...I don't hear anything..." Suddenly everything came crashing back in a whirl of colorful emotions. My head ached at the depth of it all. I didn't want to take it all in at once. It was usually a more gradual thing. "Ow."

"Oh yeah. I forgot to mention that part. The longer you turn it off, the more…overloaded you'll feel when you turn it back on. It doesn't last long, but it's definitely a headache. It gets easier. But I've never left it off for more than a few days. You've got to give it a break often enough not to hurt yourself."

"So I actually did it? Wow."

She grinned. "Yeah. For about a minute. And you feel that headache now, yeah?"

Wincing, I nodded slowly.

"Well, remember that and practice in small intervals, okay? The longer you go, the more of an adjustment it will be for you. Don't hurt yourself."

"Got it."

***

My reflection smiled, not a hair out of place. If only I would've brought my ballgown from the Grand Castors' Ball! The cleanest tunic and pants from my pack would have to be enough.

At least my hair was exquisite. Exactly how I wished I would've worn it at the ball. The fuchsia flower tucked behind my ear added a nice splash of color. Zaylan was sure to like it.

I hoped I'd get the chance to ask him what made him start caring about me. It had happened so fast. But I wasn't complaining.

Someone knocked on my door. Had he come to pick me up?

Heart racing, I straightened my tunic and strode for the door.

I pulled it open, and there he was, dressed much more finely than me. He wore a formal suit, eyes shining above his smile as he bowed. "Reenalyn, you look lovely."

I held in a squeal and curtsied in return. "Thank you. You look fantastic. I'm sorry I didn't have anything more formal to wear."

"Not to worry. It will just be us tonight, dining in my study. No one will notice." With a grin, he held out his arm.

Beaming, I took his elbow and strolled with him down the hall. The sounds of sparring pulled my gaze to the window. The others were training outside. *I should join them tomorrow.*

Zaylan's feelings grew stronger as we crossed the balcony and approached the study door, erasing all other thoughts.

My heart raced as he reached for the doorknob and swept the door open, pulling me in after him.

Beautiful purple flowers decorated the bookshelves and stood in vases on the desk and side tables. A white tablecloth covered the desk, and two chairs were pulled up to the front and the side, the closest two chairs could be without being placed right next to each other. The way taverns arranged chairs so couples could gaze into each other's eyes as they enjoyed each other's company.

"What do you think?" he asked. "I had it decorated just for you."

"I love it! Thank you, Zaylan." I searched his eyes, wondering if this was the right moment for our first kiss.

A sliding door slammed in the wall next to the desk, and I jumped, reaching for the spear I'd left in my room.

But it was only Xerrome, scowling more angrily than I'd ever seen. He stepped from the side room, pulled the sliding doors closed, then approached us. "My apologies, Zaylan," he said with a bow, not acknowledging me. "I'll leave you now."

He disappeared, letting the door fall mostly closed behind him.

"Sorry about him." Zaylan winced, pulling my attention back to his beautiful eyes. "Shall we sit?"

"Yes, that would be great." I smiled, wishing we hadn't been interrupted.

Zaylan held out the chair in front of the desk and gestured for me to sit.

Grinning and barely holding in another squeal, I sat as he pushed the chair in. No one had ever held out a chair for me before. Was this really happening?

Stepping around me, he took the other seat and laced his fingers over the table. "Thank you for dining with me tonight."

"Of course! Thank you for saying yes to my super-awkward invitation."

He grinned. "The food will be here any moment. While we wait, tell me about your family."

It was so kind of him to start by asking me about myself! "Well, I'm the oldest of five, with two younger sisters and two younger brothers. My parents own a cello-crafting business, and I've worked in it since I was little."

Realizing his feelings had faded, I wondered whether he was masking them or if the reminder of my humble origins had dampened them. "Um, I guess you probably don't want to hear about my working life, though."

"Hmm? Oh, no, I don't mind. Tell me about it."

"Oh, um, okay." Smiling, I stilled my twisting fingers and focused on how to present my work in the best light. "We made cellos, but that wasn't my favorite. It was all right, but we also repaired damaged string instruments. I enjoyed the repairs. Replacing old strings, polishing scratches, tuning. I got pretty good at it."

I'd leave out the house cleaning I did on the side.

"And what's your favorite part of the job?" he asked, gazing intently at me.

I realized with relief that his feelings were blooming again. He must've found my job more interesting than I'd thought he would. Another good sign!

Before I could answer, the door opened and Xerrome returned, a tray loaded with silver platter covers on one shoulder. With his arm held up, his armor sleeve slid down, revealing surprisingly impressive arm muscles.

Glaring as usual, and avoiding my eyes, Xerrome placed the platter on a side table and brought one dish after another to the desk, eyes down.

"I've talked too much about myself. Zaylan, tell me about your family."

Folding my hands, I rested my chin on them and watched him, anxiously awaiting his response.

"Well, my father was regent before me. He sadly passed away a few years ago, and I had to take over in his absence."

"Oh, Zaylan." I reached across the table and touched his hand. "I'm so sorry. I shouldn't have brought it up. I didn't know."

"Not to worry," he said, smiling and shifting his hand to grasp mine.

Xerrome returned with another dish and coughed violently, splashing a bit of brown sauce on my arm before Zaylan's hand reached mine.

"Apologies." Xerrome retrieved a napkin from the tray and handed it to me without meeting my eyes.

"It's fine." I frowned, wiping the steamy liquid from my arm.

"Be more careful, please, Xerrome." Zaylan raised an eyebrow, a look of surprised interest on his face rather than the annoyance I expected to see.

"Apologies," Xerrome repeated, retrieving the tray and marching from the room.

"I'm sorry about him," Zaylan said, reaching across the table.

With a thrill, I reached toward him. Our hands touched, and he held mine, brushing his thumb over the back of my hand.

"He's always in a bad mood. Where were we?" he said.

"Oh, um, your family?"

"Yes, that's right."

As his feelings faded again, I regretted missing the opportunity to change the subject. He must miss his father terribly.

"I have a younger sister," he began, pulling the lid from one of the platters. As he told me about his family, he lifted a plate and placed a generous serving from each platter on it.

With a grin, he handed it to me.

"Oh, thank you." I accepted the full plate from him. So nice of him to serve me, when he's the royal one!

"Of course. Feel free to get more whenever you want." He served himself a plate and the conversation returned to his father's regency.

"Did you want to be regent?" I asked.

He nodded. "Yes, definitely. I always wanted the position my father had. I was happy to accept it in his stead."

Nodding, I chewed a bite of meat I couldn't identify and wracked my brain for what had brought his feelings back earlier. We were talking about my job. Was he so sad about losing his father that the topic dulled his feelings? Of course that made sense. What could I ask him to change the topic?

"Zaylan, there's something I've been wanting to ask you."

He leaned in, smiling over his plate. "What's that?"

"I'm curious"—I couldn't meet his eyes or stop my fingers from twisting my tunic—"what attracted you to me, at first? It seemed like you started, well, having feelings for me really quickly, which is wonderful. I'm curious what brought them on."

I finally met his gaze, anxious for his answer to be super sweet and romantic and maybe bring us back to that almost-kiss moment.

Smiling, he nodded. "It was the first time I saw you spar. You're good with your spear. It's impressive."

Staring at him, I waited for him to realize the mistake. Because it hadn't been the first time he'd seen me spar. That must've been a day or two later. But the first time I'd sensed his feelings was when we first approached the manor.

But he just smiled.

"Oh, um...thank you?" What was I supposed to say? I couldn't bear to ruin the moment, but I couldn't pretend not to be surprised or confused by his answer.

Sliding his chair back, he pulled it toward mine. "What about you?"

Leaning forward, he spun my chair to face his, making my heart flutter. Without taking his eyes from mine, he returned to his seat.

"It was when we first arrived," I said. "You looked out the window as your guards brought us in, then you met us at the door. And as you led us inside, I felt it for the first time."

He leaned forward, his knees pressing against mine.

"Zaylan, it's only been a few days. Do you worry we haven't had enough time to be sure about our feelings?"

There. I'd said it. Wincing, I met his eyes.

"No, I don't think so. I'm not one to waste time once I'm sure about something. If we're both attracted to each other, why pretend otherwise? How long we've had so far doesn't matter. What matters is how we choose to spend the rest of the time we have together."

Okay, that was incredibly flattering and sweet.

Smiling warmly, he drew closer.

"As I got to know you, my feelings for you grew," he whispered, "because of your beauty, as well as your skill with a spear. It didn't take weeks or months for those to make an impression."

I gulped. Okay, so I was still confused about his initial feelings, but what made them grow into more...I tried to shove Cupid's words from yesterday out of my head.

Beauty and skill with a weapon are excellent reasons for feelings to grow!

He leaned closer, taking hold of the armrests.

He was definitely going to kiss me.

I wanted to be kissed so much!

He was absolutely gorgeous, from his amazing hair to his tan and his beautiful eyes and smile. And my height didn't bother him because he was taller than me.

That was what had initially attracted me to him. His appearance. Which was *fine*! It was perfectly normal to first notice someone because they're attractive. What mattered was the reasons the feelings grew.

Cupid's stupid words intruded again as I realized the only thing I had to go on was sensing his feelings for me.

That was all that had made mine grow.

He was about to kiss me. My first kiss—finally!

But what did it mean? If all I liked about him was his appearance and the fact he liked me...that wasn't much to go on.

Pausing, he backed away. "I'm sorry, Reenalyn, I must have misread. I thought you wanted this. But the look on your face says otherwise."

I covered my face with my hands, mortally embarrassed. "I'm so sorry, Zaylan. I do want this...I don't know what's wrong with me."

"Not to worry, Reenalyn. Maybe we need to slow down. How about we call it a night and have lunch tomorrow?"

I beamed, relieved at the idea of space to think and appreciative of the second chance. "That sounds perfect. Thank you, Zaylan."

As he gently took my hand and kissed it, the mask over his feelings slipped, and I basked in their warmth.

He had welcomed me and my friends, foreigners, into his home.

He'd fed us. Multiple times. Delicious food.

He'd given us comfortable, safe, and richly furnished rooms.

He'd even sent his best people out to help us find Whisper and Bennet.

Hadn't those good things influenced my feelings as well?

Standing, he pulled me up, walked me to the door, and gave a little bow. "Goodnight, Reenalyn. I hope you sleep well, and I look forward to seeing you tomorrow."

He kissed my hand, never taking his eyes from mine, as Xerrome appeared, scowling, apparently to remove dishes.

I stepped out of the doorway to let him in, my hand slipping from Zaylan's. With a smile and a bow, he backed into the study, addressing Xerrome, his words too low for me to hear.

Why hadn't I thought of those things before? Of course my feelings were based on more! I was overthinking Cupid's words. And it had cost me my first kiss.

Stomping over the balcony, I ran into Beldon and the red-haired guard, Wallen, laughing as they made their way up the spiral staircase.

"Reenalyn!" Beldon exclaimed. "We missed you for training tonight. You okay?"

Forcing a smile, I nodded. "Yes, I was, um, talking to Zaylan."

Dropping into a chair, Beldon raised an eyebrow. "Oh-ho!" He grinned. "How interesting." Eyeing my hair, he gave me a knowing look. "I see why you missed sparring then."

Giddy and a little embarrassed, I reached my door and threw it open, darting inside. "Yes, well, goodnight, Beldon!"

His chuckle danced through the door as I closed it.

Disappointment with tonight and hope for lunch tomorrow warred in my head, unsettling me. I needed sleep. Then I could return to this with a fresh mind.

Eyeing my spear, annoyance at Cupid for getting in my head at the wrong time filled my mind. I'd update him tomorrow.

Searching for something other than Zaylan to help me fall asleep, my mind landed on Xerrome. He'd been decent in the desert yesterday. Why was he so scowly again today?

CHAPTER 38

ACRES

The *swish swish* of Starstinger's tail on the bed increased tempo.

"Uh-oh. Here comes a lecture," I said, crumbling a dried leaf into a potion on the vanity.

"Well, you clearly need one. Acres, we came here in the first place for you to get a break from floramancy and spend time studying fossils like you've always wanted to." She rolled onto her back and stretched her limbs, sharp claws extending. "But all you've done so far is study floramancy harder than ever." Rolling onto her belly, she folded her front paws under her chest and wrapped her tail around herself. "And that's left you with no time to do what you came here for."

Glancing her way from the handful of leaves, I held up one finger. "Actually, I discovered Fossil Gulley yesterday, you may remember."

"Yes, an entire two hours between the walk there, gathering a few fossils, and walking back. It's been seventeen hours since we returned, and you haven't looked at them since."

She had me there. "Hey now, four of those hours were sleep."

Her eyes flashed. "Acres Parrianther, you told me you would get seven!"

I winced. "Yes, well, I *planned* to go to bed right after you fell asleep. But I was on a roll with this potion. And I can't not help someone who needs help. Isn't another person's health more important than a hobby?

Besides, this isn't just for Mella. This could be super useful for loads of other people for generations to come."

She blinked slowly, like she was taking time to decide how to phrase something I wouldn't like to hear. "There's *your* health to consider, too. That's what's important to me."

I shrugged. "Maybe the potion could help me, too."

She scowled. "Acres!"

I sighed, facing my makeshift desk to crumble another leaf. "You're right, Starstinger. We should take a day off soon."

"How about now?"

"Now? But I'm right in the middle of something."

"Which is your excuse *every time* I try to get you to leave. So why not now?"

I glanced at the green bits on the desk, honestly curious about the effect they'd have on the pain-relief potion. How much they might improve it.

"Never mind. I'm deciding." She stood and lightly leaped off the bed, landing with a barely audible thump. "We're going now."

"Literally right now?"

She raised a brow, her ears laying slightly back. "Listen to yourself, Acres. I shouldn't have to convince you to go hunting for fossils. Seriously. Haven't you been dying to return to Fossil Gulley? Think of what else we could find!"

A grin spread over my face despite myself, and I stood and stretched. "You have a point, as always." Swiping my water flask from the vanity-turned-desk, I headed for the door. "Let's go."

***

There, in my hand, was a perfectly intact skull of a Dilophosaurus, complete with two crests on top and most of its teeth intact. I could hardly believe it. Who were these people to throw away incredible stuff like this?

I added it to my growing pile of favorite finds and leaned over the cliff to reach for more treasures, grateful the rocky edge wasn't the crumbling type.

Movement caught my eye—Starstinger scampering through the piles of fossils with something dangling from her mouth. It caught the sunlight too much to be a bone.

"What did you find?" I asked, pushing myself to a sitting position.

She leaped to the edge and curled up next to me, dropping the item on the sand by my leg. "Metal jewelry, I think."

A piece of tarnished metal curved into an incomplete circle. At one end, a filigreed *M* stood out among several little holes. Had precious stones been there once? An intricate flower was etched on the other end with what looked like spines peeking out from underneath. It reminded me of the purple flowers that grew on the thyka thorns, or the pink ones that grew on cactus.

I examined it closer. "I think it's a bracelet. Wow, I mean, I sure do prefer fossils to any jewelry myself, but since I'm obviously alone in that sentiment here, how'd this piece of finery end up in the trash pile?"

"What do you think the *M* is for?" Starstinger asked.

"Merrandil? If it's something from the royal family."

Standing, she shrugged. "Could be." With a flick of her black-tipped tail, she soared back over the cliff and disappeared in the pile of bones.

Would Selverine like this? Something that may have belonged to her family? It wouldn't hurt to keep it on hand, just in case. Even though it wasn't a fossil.

I added the bracelet to my favorites pile and returned to the cliff's edge.

***

By the time we decided to call it a day, the pile was way too big for me to carry to the manor. So I grabbed the complete skull, dropped the bracelet into my pocket, and hoped the pile would still be there when I returned.

Brushing dust off my pants, I glanced down at Starstinger. "You know, we're already partway to the apothecary's place."

My leg gave out a little, but I thought I hid it well enough that Starstinger missed it.

She rolled her eyes but smiled, her too-big ears standing straight. "You don't have to run an errand for the day to be considered a success, Acres. But if you insist."

Falling into step with her, I strolled to the apothecary's hut to get the aged deecho fern to make more perception potion.

This time, the musty scent and lack of light didn't bother me. I approached the counter—thankfully already knowing where it was—and rang the bell.

The apothecary appeared a few moments later.

"You again, I see." She slid behind the counter. "How goes the experimentation? Do we have a new soothing potion to benefit all of Morrenfayre?"

"Not quite yet, though I'm making progress." I set the skull on the counter. "I'm here for another ingredient."

"And what would that be?"

"Do you have any aged deecho fern?"

Her eyebrows rose. "For the soothing potion?"

I shook my head. "No, another project." I was pretty sure I had enough other ingredients to make more perception potion. But I hadn't brought any deecho fern, which was a key ingredient. I'd thought I had enough pre-made potion not to need any deecho fern. I would have if I hadn't smashed them all like a complete idiot.

She crossed her arms. "Don't see that often. It doesn't grow around here. Sorry."

Skunks. So no chance to make more of the perception potion.

"Then I'll take another measure of powdered spiny mushroom, please." I laid a coin on the counter. It thudded dully against the worn wooden surface.

She reached for the coin, her sleeve pulling back to expose her wrist. That shiny bracelet Selverine had noticed the first time we'd come here glimmered in the dim glow of the candle.

A flower and an *M* decorated one side—identical to the one in my pocket.

It disappeared as she pocketed the coin. "I'll be back in a moment."

Surely not. That would be too much of a coincidence. Probably most people around here wore them as some kind of local fashion. Thinking back over everyone I'd seen, though, I couldn't remember seeing a single bracelet.

Erisole definitely hadn't worn one. The few villagers I'd seen looked like they would've traded theirs for food long ago. I hadn't met any nobles other than Zaylan, and I was pretty sure he didn't wear jewelry.

Still. What are the odds I'd find a bracelet in Fossil Gulley and then find its twin on the apothecary's wrist?

"Starstinger, did you see that?" I whispered.

Draped around my shoulders, she was close enough to whisper to without being overheard, even if the apothecary's castling lurked nearby.

"Yes."

"Should we risk asking about it?"

"She's clearly not trying to hide it. How upset could she be by a question?"

"Good point."

The apothecary returned with a small jar and set it on the counter, rested her hands a few specks behind it, and eyed me. "Will there be anything else?"

"Just a question, if you don't mind, ma'am."

She stared, one eyebrow rising slightly.

"I noticed the bracelet on your wrist."

Her hands slid off the counter, covering her wrist as if to hide the bracelet. *Interesting.*

"I was wondering...what does the *M* mean?"

"Why? What do you think it means?"

"Maybe they stand for your last name?

Her eyes grew intense and her voice sharper. "They? Have you seen another bracelet like this one?"

Muck. "Um..."

"You have! I see it on your face. Where is it?" she demanded.

Starstinger stood on my shoulders and hissed a warning.

The apothecary took a deep breath without taking her eyes off me. "I've been missing it for a long time and would appreciate having it back."

"I think I might've seen it at Fossil Gulley. Why is it so important?"

"It was a gift."

"Someone gave you two identical bracelets?" I asked skeptically.

Her eyes sparked. "No. If you don't need any other ingredients, please leave."

I hesitated, then retrieved the skull and backed away. Opening the door, I let myself and Starstinger out and blinked in the midday brightness.

"She's hiding something, but how important is that to us?" Starstinger asked as she slid from my shoulders and alighted on the bleached wood porch.

I shrugged. "Yeah. I'm curious, but it's not going to help us find Bennet and Whisper or improve the soothing potion."

"Why didn't you just show it to her?"

"Because...I thought Selverine might like it," I admitted.

Starstinger beamed. "There's an idea."

CHAPTER 39
REENALYN

After spending too long listening for Zaylan's feelings and not managing to locate him, I finally dragged myself from my room and to the balcony. I took a seat in one of the chairs and smiled at the garden.

Dane and Mella strolled down one of the stone pathways, his hand on her shoulder as she hobbled with the crutches. Their mutual affection didn't irk me as much today now that I had some of my own at last. But it wouldn't hurt to try Erisole's trick.

I struggled to block it by mentally practicing a song on my violin—thoughts of Zaylan's eyes kept interrupting. So I thought about him instead.

It worked, and I realized I would have a few moments of blissful, emotionless silence before the headache would crash down on me again.

I wanted to tell Mella about it, but I realized I couldn't tell where she was without the tenor of her emotions to point to her location.

A little inconvenient, but worth it.

But I could tell Cupid. Where had I left my spear?

Remembering it was in my bedroom, I stood and headed for the hallway as a crash sounded from the other direction.

Zaylan's study.

Was he okay?

Sprinting across the landing, I reached the door to Zaylan's study, caught the edge of the doorway, and slung myself in, assuming a defensive stance.

His study was normal—no tablecloth or flowers now. Just the desk at the far end and the books on the shelves in the walls. And on one side of the desk, Zaylan was slamming the set of doors closed.

He faced me, his blond hair askew, his face red with anger.

"Oh. Zaylan?"

He froze, eyes wide. An instant later he relaxed to his usual smiling self, running his fingers through his disheveled hair. "Reenalyn, hello. You caught me by surprise. What can I do for you?"

"I heard a crash, so I came to see what happened." I took another step into his study. We were alone. We had plans to have lunch together in a bit, but...would he finally kiss me now? "Are you okay?"

"Yes, yes, fine, fine." He faced the desk and waved a hand as if to dismiss my concern. Reaching the desk, he turned to me with a smile and leaned against the front of it. "Fine now that you're here, that is."

I beamed, my heart soaring. "Oh, well."

I stopped myself from glancing at the floor like an embarrassed child. I felt my mind reach for his emotions, longing for the reassurance of the feelings I'd sensed last night. It seemed an easy *yes* considering what he'd just said.

But I sensed nothing. Was my sense still turned off? I hadn't felt the headache, so they must've been. And they were still off because I'd been distracted by the crash.

That's right. The crash.

"Zaylan, what happened? Did something break?"

"Yes, I'm afraid so. I tripped and dropped an armload of books in the other room. Knocked over a side table—glass, of course, with a vase on it, naturally." He shook his head and rolled his eyes.

"Oh, okay. Well, I'm glad you're all right."

"That's kind of you, Reenalyn." His eyes crinkled with a little smile when he said my name, and a thrill of emotion rolled through me. But it was my own.

I missed the feelings I'd reveled in last night. Why had I picked this moment to practice turning off my sixth sense?

Suddenly impatient with this whole turning-it-off thing, I slapped the heel of my palm against my head and listened hard for Mella and Dane, trying to figure out how I'd turned it back on before.

"Reenalyn? Are you okay?"

"Yes, just, a headache." And there it was. A giant migraine twice as strong as yesterday's, shooting pain through my eyes and twisting my stomach. I hadn't turned it off for twice as long, had I? I was sure I hadn't. That wasn't fair!

Mella and Dane's annoying regard for each other colored my senses more than any of the others, which made it more irritating. Why couldn't I sort out Zaylan's from the noise? That was all I wanted. Maybe because I didn't know him as well enough yet. Because his emotions were newer to me.

"Reenalyn?"

"Ah, sorry. I think I should lay down for a minute. I'm sure it will pass soon." I shoved away from the doorframe, reeling from the emotions of Mella, Dane, Beldon...

Why could I hear *them* and not Zaylan? I was most familiar with the essence of their feelings, sure, but I'd spoken with Zaylan, spent time with him. Felt his feelings up close. His should be just as apparent as theirs.

Could he mask his feelings like Erisole?

That must be it.

Unless he didn't feel that way anymore?

"Just a moment, before you go." Zaylan crossed the room toward me.

Would he finally kiss me? His beautiful bright eyes held mine, and I searched them for something, anything..."Yes?"

"That friend you're looking for—Bennet..."

"Mm-hmm?" I closed my eyes and rubbed my forehead with two fingers, trying to focus on his words.

"He cast her with a weapon the first time, and an instrument the second, right? Or was it the other way around?"

"Um, no, that's right. But Mella cast the second time, not Bennet. Bennet used the weapon, then Mella used the instrument. How will that help you find them?" Another jolt of pain shot through my head, and I stumbled away from Zaylan and his beautiful eyes. "I'm so sorry, Zaylan. I need a minute."

"Of course," he said, stepping to the side. "May I escort you to your room?"

My heart thrilled. He *did* still care! "Yes, I'd like that. Thank you."

He held out an elbow, and I took it, fantasizing that I might faint, and he would have to carry me.

"Tell me, Reenalyn, what's your least favorite instrument?" he asked.

"My least favorite?"

"I know how much you love the violin. Is there one you particularly dislike?"

He was making small talk about my interests to distract me from my headache. How sweet!

"Oh, yes. I like most instruments, though the violin is by far my favorite. Hmm...I don't love the harpika. It's a little piece of wood with several strings down the front. That's probably my least favorite."

"Really? And why's that?"

I considered. "Because you hold it in both hands and play it with your thumbs. Way different than the string instruments I usually play with a bow. It's too tricky for me." I stuttered and winced as my headache pulsed.

"How interesting," he said vaguely as we reached my bedroom door.

"Sorry, am I boring you? I should've asked what your least favorite instrument is." I smiled through the throbbing headache, waiting for his response.

"Actually, Reenalyn, it's the violin. And unfortunately, nothing you could say would interest me. Not even asking me a question about myself."

I stopped in my tracks. I must have misheard... "Wait, what?"

Facing me, he went on. "I was attracted to you at first. You are a pretty girl. But after our date last night...I'm afraid it isn't meant to be. Don't get me wrong, you're a wonderful person. You're just...a little too much for me. You and that weird hairstyle."

My ears rang.

I swayed, catching the doorframe for support.

No. No!

Pain seized my head as my heart imploded.

He wasn't falling in love with me.

He'd started to—I'd felt that.

But I'd ruined it.

My one chance.

"Oh."

I had nothing else to say. Stepping into my room, I met his eyes for a terrible vulnerable moment.

He glanced around the room, then nodded and strode away.

Closing and locking the door, I sank against it and covered my face. His words boomed in my head, mocking me over and over. *You're too much, you're too much, you're too much...*

I shouldn't have talked so much about my family. I shouldn't have gone on and on about the violin. I should've reined in how proud I was of Cupid. Which thing had made me too much? If only I had left it out!

The sobs finally came. And they didn't stop.

CHAPTER 40

ACRES

Trudging back to the manor, I admired the complete Dilophosaurus skull I'd dug out of the gulley and tried not to think about my one remaining dose of the perception potion.

But it kept stealing my focus.

The clear answer was that I should save it for an emergency, and in the meantime, try to fix that side effect that gave it away every time. Starstinger was brilliant, but she was most certainly wrong about Selverine being interested in me.

There was no way.

I might give her the bracelet if an opportunity presented itself, but...I certainly couldn't expect her to fall in love with me over it.

So no reason to waste the last of the potion on sneaking a listen to her feelings. Plus, if she ever found out, she'd think of me just as she thinks of the queen. Wincing, I realized the loss of whatever respect she had for me would sting. Deeply.

Helping her learn about her family would be nice, even if it was just as friends.

But could I place the value of that knowledge for her above the safety of everyone else here? What if we needed some intelligence and that was the only way to get it? Selverine wasn't in the Wrynford cohort.

Something nagged at me—a deeper feeling of empathy for Selverine's desire to understand who her family was. But if they were anything like mine...she'd be better off not knowing.

As far as I knew, she didn't know her mom or any siblings. Her grandmother misused potions on a larger scale than my father, but they did share a weakness for the power and control it gave them.

But what if they were better than that? It would be a shame for her to spend her whole life feeling ashamed of them when they were actually people to be proud of.

The fact was, I couldn't decide for her whether to investigate her family.

That was her choice. Which was a relief.

But it still left the question of how to use the last swig.

No, there was no question. I should save it unless I could fix it and use it on Zaylan. Obviously. That was the most logical choice.

Nearly dropping the skull, I wiped away the sweat on my forehead with my wrist. Floramancy complicated things so much. And this desert sun was no joke. It was a bad day to have span-long locs refusing to stay tied in place. I took the last swig from the water flask, wishing there were more left.

"Hey, Acres!"

Shading my eyes, I squinted toward the garden for the voice. It sounded like...

Selverine stood there, waving, her loose sparring clothes rustling in the light breeze. With her long hair rippling behind her and her tan skin against the rusty desert sand...

"She's a mucking desert goddess."

"She sure is!" Starstinger agreed, grinning.

"Holy skunks. Did I say that out loud?"

"Oh, yes. With the breeze floating her way, she probably heard you, too."

I rolled my eyes. "No, she didn't. Don't be ridiculous."

"I'm not the one staring at her instead of answering."

Oh skunks. She had just called out to me. Shooting my hand into the air, I waved. "Hi, Selverine!"

"Did you mean to wave the hand with the skull?" Starstinger slinked around my ankles.

"Muck!" Dropping the skull, I looked at my hand, then bent to retrieve the skull, tripping over Starstinger. "What the muck, Starstinger?"

"How was I supposed to know you were about to dance a jig instead of responding to her?"

The skull was miraculously still intact. With a wince at Selverine, I tucked it under one arm and marched on toward the manor's front entrance.

Next, I need to find a potion to make me invisible when I do stupid muck like this.

"Aren't you going to talk to her?" Starstinger huffed, racing to keep up with me.

"She doesn't want to talk to me. She just waved to be polite."

"Then why is she coming this way?"

"What?" I squeaked.

"Hey, Acres! Wait up!"

Sure as skunks, there she was. Striding toward me across the sand. If only I could take that last swallow of perception potion before she got to me—

"What's the hurry?" She crossed her arms, standing right in front of me.

"Uh, Mella. Mella's potion." I shook my head. What happened to my brain? "The soothing potion for Mella, I mean. I picked up another ingredient from the apothecary."

Her eyes brightened. "She say anything interesting while you were there?"

Why hadn't I used the stupid potion to read the apothecary's mind? I would've had a useful answer!

Instead, I shook my head. "No, sorry."

Should I give her the bracelet? Or wait for a better time?

She shrugged, her hazel eyes sparkling in the sunlight. "Do you have time for a spar first?"

I blinked. Selverine Merrandil wanted to spar. With me?

I'd probably do something so stupid I'd have to spend the rest of my life in hiding. But Starstinger would murder me if I skipped this for potion research.

"Oh, sure. Yeah, I have time."

"Great. Come on." She flicked her eyes toward the garden, then headed that way, her arms swinging.

"You gonna stare at her all afternoon?"

I jumped at Starstinger's voice. "Would you cut that out?"

She grinned her most mischievous kitteny grin.

Hurrying after Selverine, I patted my weapon pocket, assuring myself the throwing stars were there. They clinked reassuringly.

But holy skunks, Selverine fought with a *trident*.

I'd never sparred against a trident before.

I'd probably spent less time sparring over the last year than Selverine had in the past month.

Why hadn't I listened to Starstinger all those hundreds of times she'd encouraged me to practice more?

If I embarrassed myself in front of Selverine—

Taking a deep breath, I reminded myself Starstinger had to be wrong. No romance was at stake here.

Selverine had asked me to spar. Simple training. It wasn't like she expected me to kiss her or something.

CHAPTER 41

SELVERINE

Acres dodged my stab with the trident and pivoted, then threw a star into the protective leather vest tied around my chest. "Oof."

The impact would definitely bruise, but the leather had done its job. As it had many other times since I left Willova, Beldon, Trinka, Kaido, and Dane to spar with Acres.

"Sorry." Acres reached toward me. "Are you—"

With a battle cry, I lunged at him and slashed at his exposed shoulder, the longest spike finding purchase. "Gotcha!" I grinned.

"Ah." Acres winced, wiping sweat off his forehead and slinging it away.

He stumbled forward, and I reached out to steady him.

His hand touched my arm for an instant before he yanked it away like I'd burned him. "Muck. Sorry."

"You okay?"

"Yeah." Acres laughed, bouncing on his toes. "I guess I should've stretched more before getting started."

I shrugged. "Water break?" I asked as I glanced at the knot of Wrynfordians several spans over to check on Willova.

Beldon swung his mace at her, and she blocked with the temporary cutlass, bracing for the impact. I breathed a sigh of relief. Better Beldon than Kaido or Trinka. They'd eat her alive.

"Sure, water sounds good."

We fell into step and strolled toward the water fountain. Beldon gestured as if he were explaining something to Willova, then pointed toward the fountain.

"I meant to tell you," Acres panted. "I found something interesting at the Fossil Gulley this morning."

"Let me guess. Another fossil?" I hoped he wasn't about to launch into a lecture about fossil types and extinct species. I was surprised it had taken him this long to mention the skull he'd carried over with him. It had horns or something all around the top. Mildly interesting.

"No, actually. A bracelet identical to the one the apothecary wears. And it has an M on it."

That perked my interest, though I was probably getting my hopes up for nothing. "Really? Huh. I wonder why there was another one just like it. Where is it?"

He pulled the metal circle from his pocket and held it out to me. The silver was tarnished, but parts of it still caught the light and glimmered.

I took it, running my thumb over the ornate M as Willova and Beldon reached the well.

"Selverine," Willova asked, "is that the bracelet from the ledger we found?"

"What?" I examined it again. "Yes, it does seem to match the description."

"Wasn't there something about the king commissioning one for his daughter, and then commissioning another identical one?" Willova fanned her sweaty face, the underarms of her borrowed tunic darkened with sweat.

"So it could've been Narellen's—the Narellen from Terrenthyrs?" Acres asked. "But then why does the apothecary have the other one? And why did this one get thrown out? It looks too expensive and fancy for even a spoiled princess to throw away."

"Maybe my grandmother stole one when she stole the apothecary's name? If that's what happened," I speculated.

"You know, the word 'daughter' had been distorted a little—like someone tried to erase and rewrite it." Willova swished her hair around her shoulders. "Or like there was an S on the end. Could Queen Narellen have had a sister?"

I met Acres's wide eyes over the bracelet.

"Half-sister, maybe? But I think Narellen murdered all her siblings," I said.

Acres put his hands in his pockets. "What if one got away?"

It still wouldn't explain the name, but what if the apothecary was actually my great aunt?

"Maybe she also knows why the schedule book ended so abruptly with a half-entered doctor's visit," Willova added.

I bit my lip. "I wish! Ugh, the unanswered questions are killing me!"

I drove the points of my trident into the ground, and it wobbled before steadying. Had she known my parents? What if she knew why my grandmother killed them?

"But I don't know how we'd ever get it out of her." Hands on my hips, I paced in frustration. "Acres!" Pointing at him, I paused.

"Yeah?"

"You don't have any, like, interrogation potions, do you?"

"Uh, not exactly. Not...strictly speaking."

Why's he wincing? Never mind. Solutions...

"Torture is always an option..."

Willova's and Acres's eyes widened.

"No, no, never mind." Embarrassed, I waved away my words at their expressions. "I'm not like Drazdan, and I'm not like Grandmother. That leaves telling her who I am. But that could either make her want to tell me information, or want to kill me. For revenge on my grandmother or who knows what. Without knowing more about her, I don't love that option." Sighing, I started pacing again. "But it might be all we've got."

Would she also have answers about the house full of petrified hybrid and avian castors?

"I mean..." Acres stuffed a couple of loose locs back into the knot on his head. "Is there really a hurry? We have time to strategize and consider other options, right? No reason to consider risking your life...right?"

"Actually Willova needs to return to Terrenthyrs to get Faultless from her evil brother," I explained, gesturing to her. "I need to go with her to stop said evil brother from imprisoning them both. Or worse. And I'm not leaving the country of my heritage without answers."

Pausing, I met Acres's eyes. "So yes, there is a hurry. A big one."

He stared at me a moment longer than normal, then seemed to make a decision.

"My castor has a pretty mind," Starstinger had said. What was going on in that mind now?

"Right. Well, I need to work on the soothing potion, so..." He slid his stars into his belt bag and stooped to retrieve the bones. "I'll see you both later. Thanks for sparring, Selverine."

He scooped up his fossils and disappeared down the garden path toward the manor.

"Well, I guess it's not his problem," I grouched.

Why had I thought for a moment that he was working on a solution, too? Stupid idea, letting myself get my hopes up.

All he'd said about making my own identity regardless of what bad decisions my family may have made—that didn't mean he actually cared. He was just stating facts I should've been smart enough to realize on my own.

Why did I keep thinking he might care a bit more? Just now, it had seemed...But I was wrong about him. Again. Instead, he'd just ran off.

The disappointment stung more than it should have.

"Selverine?" Willova asked.

"What?"

"Are you okay?"

I forced my gaze from his retreating form to Willova's green eyes. "Of course. Why?"

Her eyebrows drew together. "You look sad."

"Well, I'm not," I spat. "I thought...But I shouldn't have assumed. He's still Wrynford, and I'm still royal—sort of. I can't expect him to understand."

"Understand what?"

"Nothing. Think Beldon would be up for another spar? You two against me?" I needed a distraction.

Chapter 42

REENALYN

When the headache finally faded, it left me drained. I didn't even have the heart to cast Cupid. I wanted to be alone. And that wasn't like me.

So I found myself in the garden again, in the same place I'd been earlier with Erisole, learning about sixers. If only I wasn't a sixer. What good had it ever done me? Not a bit. I was destined to have a deeper insight into literally everyone else's love life, while completely unable to have one of my own.

I sat on a stone bench surrounded by plants and pulled my knees up to my face. Resting my heels on the bench's edge, I hugged my legs and wept.

"Reenalyn?"

I jumped, setting my boots on the ground. The cool stone chilled my legs. "Who's there?" I called, ashamed of how scratchy my stupid voice sounded. Wiping frantically at my teary face, I squinted between the leaves to see who was there.

I sensed Dane's feelings about Mella before I caught a glimpse of his face.

"Reenalyn, what happened? Are you all right?" Dane and his pale hair and soft eyes—reminding me with another stab to the heart of Zaylan—ducked under a trellis.

I broke down again, pulling my legs back up and dropping my face to my knees. "I'm..." I gasped a few hoarse, pitiful breaths. "I'm fah-ine. Just ba...being ridiculous."

I couldn't get the sixth sense to turn off. Was it worth having Dane's obnoxiously wonderful feelings for Mella right under my nose to have someone to talk to?

He sat gently on the other end of my bench. "Reenalyn, if you're hurting, crying isn't ridiculous."

I considered his words but held my silence, shaking slightly with heaving breaths.

"Can you tell me what happened?"

The thought of what happened, and then the thought of explaining what an idiot I'd been, overwhelmed me with emotion, and my sobs increased.

"It's me," I whispered as more tears forced themselves out.

"What's you?"

"The problem." I sniffled. "I'm too much. Too tall."

"Why do you feel like you're too much and too tall?"

"Zaylan." I held my breath for a minute, trying to calm down.

"What did Zaylan do?"

Staring at the ground, I sighed and resigned myself to telling him. "Sometimes I've wondered if maybe my ability to sense romantic feelings in people was limited when it came to myself. Like maybe I couldn't sense anyone having feelings for me because it would give me too much of an advantage, and so that's why I never sensed it. Because surely people noticed me like they noticed everyone else."

I swiped tears away and then spread my palms on the bench behind me, planting my boots on the ground. "But now I think it must be because no one ever actually has had feelings for me."

"Why do you think that?"

"When we first got here, Zaylan...he was attracted to me. I actually felt it—his emotions. He thought something about me was pretty. I felt it plain as I feel anyone else's romantic feelings. It was the nicest feeling, Dane, to sense admiration from someone for *me*, rather than for literally anyone else. It's never happened before. Almost every time I've seen him since we got here, he's been radiating those feelings...*about me*. And he's been so kind to me, so sweet. Showing me he liked me. And he's as skunking *tall* as me!"

My voice broke on a high note, and I had to take several deep breaths to get control.

Dane's eyebrows rose, probably because he'd never heard me cuss before.

"But today"—I sighed, my shoulders slumping—"today, the feelings were completely gone. Not a hint left. And then he told me...I'm too much. That he doesn't—*can't*—love me."

I dropped my face into my hands and dissolved into sobs once more.

Dane reached over and awkwardly patted my back. "Reenalyn, can I tell you about my mom?"

I blinked. His mom? What did that have to do with anything? "Okay." I sniffed.

"My mom was the tallest woman in our...hometown, by far. She towered over most of the men, too, especially my dad."

Now my eyebrows rose. "Your mom's taller than your dad?"

"Yeah." He smiled. "But there was never a man so much in love with and in awe of a woman as my dad with my mom. Sure, they got plenty of stares. And sometimes people treated them badly because they looked different. But they've been together for decades, and they're perfectly matched. Their strengths fill in the spaces between each other's weaknesses, and they're so happy."

"Really?"

"Yep."

Mella and I had once wondered questions like these to each other, back when she spent more time with me than him. "Dane, if you were so happy with your parents, why'd you move so far from them?"

He swallowed. "They wanted the best for me, and it was safer for me in Terrenthyrs. I'd like to return and help them someday, though. Maybe bring them back with me."

Vague as ever, but I didn't have the energy to ask for details. "They sound nice. I'd like to meet them." I tried to smile to thank him for the encouragement.

"I'd like for you to meet them, too."

"What are their names?"

"Jeretha and Bokirk."

I let out a deep breath and brushed off my knees for no reason. "So I need to find myself a Bokirk, then."

He smiled. "No, you don't *need* to."

I frowned, confused.

"Look," he went on, "you don't need someone else to make you complete or prove you have value or something. But if you *want* to find someone and you're worried about being too tall to do that, don't be. My mom—who is much taller than you, I might add—found someone who didn't need her to shrink to someone else's idea of the right size. Her height didn't bother or intimidate him. He wouldn't change anything about her."

Taking another deep breath, I slid off the bench. "Thanks, Dane."

He stood, shoving his hands into his pockets. "You're welcome. I'll see you later. Let me know if there's anything I can do to help."

I smiled and nodded.

He waved and headed down the stone path.

Slowly striding to the manor, I tried to imagine Dane's mom—a woman taller than me!—but it was hard. I'd forgotten to ask Dane what she looked like besides being tall. Judging by how fair Dane's skin and hair were, I guessed hers were probably similarly colored. So that would make her kind of a blonde, like me.

My boots crunched over the stone path through the garden.

When did I let my worth be decided by some guy I barely knew?

Frowning, I chided myself like Cupid would.

I was worth more than Zaylan's opinion of me. More than anyone's opinion of my body.

There was more to me.

Pulling open the garden door, I strode into the manor, my steps echoing on stone.

If Zaylan had no respect for that...well, it would be a lie to say I didn't care. But probably with some time, it would be true. I'd be able to say it was his loss, and I was better off without him, and mean it.

I did mean it a little. Maybe with time I could mean it all the way.

I grasped the railing and stepped onto the spiral staircase.

What had happened to the fierce joy Mella had once admired in me? I'd lost it, distracted by the one thing I couldn't have that I forgot to enjoy all the good things. If changing myself to please Zaylan had worked, I would've had to stay different for the rest of forever. That would've been a bad thing. I wasn't perfect, but there were a lot of things to be proud of.

Like the beautiful spear I'd created and the wonderful castling that had come from it—exactly the castling I needed.

And the good food I could make. And the emotions I could coax from a violin. And my wonderful brothers and sisters and parents. And friends.

Stepping onto the second floor, I straightened my shoulders and held my head high.

Cupid was right. My value wasn't based on Zaylan's attention, or anyone else's.

I strode for my room as the epiphany settled over me. Cupid needed to know. He wasn't the I-told-you-so type. And he'd like the story about Dane's parents. He'd believed in a Bokirk for me all along, though he wouldn't have known to call it that.

It was too bad Zaylan missed his chance.

Too bad for him.

Pushing open my door, I headed for the tall window where I'd left my spear leaning against the wall. But it wasn't there.

With a frown, I brushed the curtains aside—maybe it had fallen behind them.

Nothing.

I pivoted, searching the room.

"Cupid? Where did I put you?"

The floor creaked, and I spun toward it.

A guard with their face covered loomed in the doorway, their hands reaching for me.

Fear spiked in my chest. Where was my spear? Who was this?

Stumbling back, I dropped into a crouch and drew out my boot dagger.

Eyeing the guard's sword grimly, I pivoted again and sliced the curtains from the wall, flinging them into the guard's face.

He cursed and his head covering slipped, revealing red hair as I flipped over the bed and pelted out the door.

Into the arms of three other guards and their growling castlings. Someone knocked the dagger from my hand as another tied a gag over my mouth.

Far too late, I tried to scream for help.

But none came.

They dragged me down the spiral stairs, my heart hammering and my head aching from getting bumped into the low ceiling over and over. Then across the main floor and down to the basement.

Finally, we crossed a hallway, and one of the guards knocked on a wooden door.

It opened, revealing...*Zaylan?*

He smiled, his feelings still completely blank.

"Ah, Reenalyn. You're just in time. Please, come in." He beckoned, and I yanked my elbows from the guards' grips and walked through the door, glaring at him.

Silver shards glittered on the floor.

They crunched beneath Zaylan's boots as he crossed the room.

He faced me. "Ah, yes, that." He gestured toward the glittering shards. "You won't be needing that old thing anymore."

My heart seized.

Those glittering shards were what remained of my shattered spear.

A scream tore through me, loud and taut and unbearable. Not even the gag could muffle my shriek as I fell to my knees over the remains of my shattered casting spear.

"No!"

CHAPTER 43

ACRES

I paced the garden sitting room, the last drop of perception potion in a vial in my pocket, determined to go to the apothecary and use it *for* Selverine. Muck saving it for an emergency. If I didn't use it soon, I'd never be able to resist the temptation to use it *on* Selverine.

And I'd never come back from that in her eyes.

Starstinger sat in the doorway, watching me, her tail flicking.

But if we had a real, actual emergency, I would regret not saving it. Was my will so weak?

I paused before Starstinger.

Why did it have to be so hard to decide?

The vial of perception potion burned in my pocket.

Where was Selverine? If I happened to run into her on the way to the apothecary's...no. No. I would not become that person.

Would I?

"Ugh!"

Turning, I spotted Trinka perched on one of the chairs. She nodded when our eyes met.

Embarrassment warmed my face. I must look like a complete idiot with the pacing and whining.

I dropped into one of the other chairs, and Starstinger leaped into my lap. After a few circles she settled down, tucking her paws under her chest and wrapping her tail around her. I stroked her soft yellow fur.

Shifting my leg to get more comfortable, I jolted when something sharp poked it. Starstinger shot up, ears back and hissing.

"It's all right, Starstinger. There's something in the cushion..." I carefully slid my hand under the seat cushion until I found—a corner of something...wooden, maybe? I got ahold of it and pulled it out.

It was a little book, about the size of my hand. One of the corners had jabbed my leg.

I flipped it open. Handwriting covered the first few pages, but the rest were blank. I skimmed the last written page and paused when I recognized a name.

Starstinger, reading over my shoulder, found it at the same time. "Does that say...?"

"Trinka, your name's here," I said. My eyes slid to the notes under her name when the book suddenly disappeared. "Hey!"

Trinka examined the book behind me. "What's this?" she growled.

"I have no idea. I just found it under the chair and was taking a look when you swiped it."

"Why's my name here?" she asked as she flipped back a page. "All our names are."

"What?" I stood and rounded the chair. "Let me see."

She shot me a death glare, stopping me in my tracks.

Frowning at the book, she carefully tore off the bottom of one of the pages.

"What're you doing?" I snatched at the book, hating the sight of a page being mutilated.

Shoving the piece of parchment in a pocket, she tossed the book at me.

I barely caught it before it hit me in the face.

"It looks like a list of notes about us. Stuff we each want. I don't know how someone could know so much. Not even any one of us."

I opened the book and scowled at the ruined page. She'd ripped out the note about her.

"Why'd you tear yours out?"

She nodded toward the book. "Read yours. You want anyone reading personal stuff like that about you?"

I flipped through the pages. Finding my name, I read the note beneath it.

Note: Wants to live longer so he can spend more time studying fossils.

I frowned. "Anyone could've guessed this. I haven't exactly tried to hide it. Why would I care if anyone saw this?"

The *live longer* part pulled my attention. Did it mean *live longer* like anyone would want to spend more time doing something they enjoy, or did it have a deeper meaning specific to me? It couldn't. No one else knew. Did they?

She held my gaze, then glanced away. "Maybe mine's worse than yours." Meeting my eyes, she said, "More importantly, isn't it a little disturbing that someone here has *notes* about our *wants*? I doubt they're planning to make our birthdays special."

I took a seat, shocked. Would we ever escape this kind of manipulation? Trinka may be the most suspicious and paranoid of any of us, but she was right about this. Strange.

I flipped back a few pages, Wallen's name standing out. *Note: Wants to complete a task assigned to him by the queen in order to achieve higher social status.*

What the muck?

Trinka stepped toward me and snatched the book again, flipping it open and sitting on the sofa behind her. She scanned the pages slowly.

"Snooping on everyone else's wants?" I accused.

She ignored me.

Beldon entered the room, and Trinka's head shot up. She immediately closed the book and ignored him. But her face wasn't as perfectly blank as usual. Now she frowned a little, and her eyebrows drew together.

Was she reading about Beldon? I was about to tell on her, when she suddenly pitched the book at my face and strode from the room.

Selverine appeared, a stack of books in her hands.

"Selverine!" I shouted, without the slightest idea what I planned to say as I fumbled to catch the book.

She halted, glowering. "What?" Fire sparked in her eyes.

Nope. Too fierce and gorgeous. She's one thousand percent not into me and never going to be.

"Sorry, never mind," I stammered.

She rolled her eyes, marching toward the dining room.

I scowled at Starstinger. What had she been thinking? There was definitely no way. And if I could learn anything useful for her from the apothecary, I'd have to talk to her again to tell her about it.

That settled it. I would save the drop for an emergency. That was the right thing to do.

Something brushed against my hand.

I glanced down to find Starstinger tapping on my thumb with her paw. The thumb I held the book with.

The book of *everyone's greatest desires*.

I should definitely not.

Opening the cover, I flipped past Mella and Reenalyn and found her. Selverine.

Note: Wants to know who her family was so she can understand who she is.

Muck.

Snapping the book closed, I shoved it in my pocket and strode for the door. The apothecary better still be open.

***

Racing back up the road toward the apothecary, I hoped I'd make it before she closed.

I was using the last sip for Selverine. The greater good be skunked.

Judging by the satisfied smile on Starstinger's face, she agreed.

Maybe all the castors would need it at some point and not have it. But they would have the improved soothing potion, which they wouldn't have had without me. That was my contribution.

I knew what it felt like to have memories stolen. It was different for Selverine. Narellen had denied her stories and facts—memories she'd never gotten to make—rather than real memories removed without her permission.

Even so. Providing facts was within my power.

And I was going to do it.

Breathlessly, I jogged up the stairs and finally slowed, heaving for breath. Taking the vial from my pocket, I downed the last drop and twisted the handle.

"Hello?" I called as I entered the apothecary's shop for the second time that day. My eyes slowly adjusted to the dimness as the door closed behind Starstinger and me.

"You have no business here. Get out!" the apothecary spat.

"Actually—"

"I said, *get out*!" she repeated.

Was the potion in effect yet? I couldn't tell. I usually had more time before using it. I'd only get one chance. How could I distract her without getting thrown out?

"Do you know of the wasting disease?"

Silence for a moment, then the sound of shuffling feet. "Why?" she hissed, close behind me.

I faced her. "I have it. It's killing me now." I'd never said that out loud before. Not even when I explained it to Starstinger. "And my symptoms are worsening quickly. I can't find anything about a treatment, much less a cure, in any book here or in Terrenthyrs. Do you know anything that might save me?"

I couldn't meet her eyes as I let out this horrifying confession. If she didn't know anything, what else was there for me to do?

Shoving my panic down, I stepped closer. I had to touch her.

She crossed her arms, her angry expression replaced with grim blankness. "There is no cure—none that I've heard of."

I closed my eyes and let the misery seep in. It was over. There was no hope.

"But..." Her voice trailed off as my eyes flashed back up to her.

"But what?"

"But I may know where to find out about a treatment. Leave me in peace and let me look for it. Come back tomorrow, and if I can find it, it's yours."

The rush of relief and hope was almost more than I could handle. "Thank you."

She nodded, gesturing toward the door.

But I still had to touch her.

But now if I did, and she felt the effect of the potion, she might be angry and take back her offer to help.

I couldn't abandon my chance for a treatment.

But I couldn't leave Selverine in the dark, either.

At least I know now a treatment might exist. I'll have to find it myself.

"Thank you for looking for the treatment for me. I appreciate it." I held out my hand, hoping she'd shake it.

Eyes still wary, she took my hand.

The shop vanished as she looked down through my eyes at her decades-younger wrist, admiring the polished bracelet shining against her smooth brown skin. The bracelet's twin sat in her other palm.

Her elaborate purple dress swished and joy filled her as she approached another girl, one with pale skin and light hair, wearing plain clothes and carrying a feather duster.

"I made him get another one. Just for you!" she said, presenting the bracelet to the other girl.

The plainly clothed girl lit up, her eyes dancing as she accepted the gift. "Thank you!"

She slid it over her wrist and held it out to admire it, her eyes sparkling...

Shelves and potions crashed around me as I slid to the floor, heart racing.

"What did you do to me?" the apothecary screamed. "I felt something leave me. What was it!"

I stumbled to my feet. "I didn't take anything from you! I only shook your hand."

This stupid potion!

Her eyes narrowed. "What are you? A sixer? No, sixers don't have to touch to get in your head. Whatever you are, get out!" she shouted, pushing me toward the door.

"I'm sorry! Thanks for the help—"

She scowled in the doorway, the daylight illuminating her pale face. "I wouldn't think you'd have to have extra abilities to tell I'm pissed. Don't come back!" she shouted, slamming the door.

Well there went my treatment. What did sixers have to do with anything? An enhanced ability to sense anger wouldn't be very useful since that one's easy to read.

But sensing peoples' wants, their greatest desires...that would be a useful sixer ability.

Whose book did I have in my pocket? Tapping my pocket, I found it empty.

Spinning around, I searched the porch for it. Then the sand in front of the shop.

Hopefully it had fallen out on the road, because I'd never get it back from the apothecary now.

Heading down the road with my eyes peeled for the book, I pondered her memory.

If the apothecary was pale skinned, why had I seen the memory from the point of view of the girl with skin like mine?

Chapter 44

MELLA

My stomach growled as I stuffed the crutches under my sore arms and hobbled from the art class.

Thankfully it was almost dinnertime. The scent of roasted meat and peppered turnips wafted down the stairs, and my stomach growled again.

Wincing at the pain in my underarms, I leaned on the crutches to take the first step up the basement stairs.

"Need a hand?" Dane's smiling ocean eyes peered around the doorway of the main floor.

"Yes, please! Skunks, am I glad to see you."

Jogging down the stairs, he asked, "Where is all the artwork you've been working on? I'd like to see it."

I rolled my eyes. "They take everything from us before we leave the room. No one's allowed to take any parchment out."

He frowned. "I wonder why?"

I shrugged. "Look, I'm starving. Are you gonna give me a hand getting up the stairs or what?"

"Yes, after I give you this." Pulling something from his pocket, he held his fist in front of me and opened his hand, revealing a silver necklace. "So the key doesn't get lost again."

"Oh, Dane," I said, leaning on the crutches and pulling the key from my pocket.

He took it and slid the chain through, then stepped behind me.

Bearing my weight on my good ankle, I pulled my hair out of the way as he fastened the necklace.

Facing me, he smiled, then met my eyes. "Beautiful."

"Dane, thank you. This is perfect."

Pecking my cheek, he whisked one of the crutches away and wrapped an arm around me, careful not to touch my tender underarms.

"How are the armpits today?" he asked seriously.

I laughed. "Classy. Still sore from the crutches. Though those are a definite improvement on having Kaido's help."

"Acres said he's making progress. Hopefully he'll be able to share the improved soothing potion soon."

"Thanks, Dane." I leaned up and kissed his jaw. "How's your shoulder?"

"Better." He frowned.

"What's wrong?"

"Are you and Reenalyn okay?"

"I'm not exactly sure, honestly. Why?"

"I saw her a few minutes ago, and apparently Zaylan hurt her feelings, and she's taking it pretty hard. I tried to encourage her, but I'm not good at that kind of thing. I'm sure it would help if you talked to her."

Nodding, I wondered what had gone wrong with Zaylan. Things were perfect between them yesterday.

"Yeah, of course. Thank you." My stomach growled again. "Um, do you know where she is?"

"Maybe in her room?"

Thinking of another set of stairs—which I'd have to scale and then climb down—between me and dinner, I made a face.

"Why don't you eat first, then I'll help you get up the stairs to talk to her?"

"That sounds like a great plan. Thanks, Dane. I'll eat fast."

Dane guided me toward the dining room, leaned my crutches against the wall, and pulled a chair out.

"Thanks," I whispered as I took the seat.

"You're welcome." He sprinkled a pinch of powder over our plates and goblets, then forked a piece of quail meat into his mouth and washed it down with a swig of water.

Muscles in his neck and face flexed as he chewed and swallowed. His biceps and forearms moved and flexed as he stabbed a bite of prickly pear. His eyebrow rose as he found me staring at him.

I grinned and returned to my plate.

How had he pulled that muscle in his shoulder? I snuck another glance at him. His tunic stretched over his shoulders more than it used to.

He'd said he'd been hanging out with Beldon more...was he doing extra workouts?

A pressure on my toes—was he playing footsie with me?

I tried to rein in my stupid grin as I tapped the top of his boot.

He hooked his boot around my intact ankle. Lightly stroking my boot with his, he took another sip like nothing was happening.

I glanced across the table at a solemn Willova, a scowling Selverine and Trinka, a lost-looking Beldon, and a sullen Kaido. They stared at their plates. Acres was staring at piles of leaves and stems and a piece of parchment laid out where his plate should've been.

Everyone but Reenalyn.

Warmth smoothed over my knee.

Dane's hand!

Sparking chills raced through my skin from his touch.

He glanced at me curiously out of the corner of his eye.

I slid my hand over his and entwined our fingers.

His eyes closed, and he swallowed.

Suddenly I was much less hungry for food than I'd been a few moments ago.

Guilt washed over me. Here I was flirting with Dane while Reenalyn was sobbing her broken heart out alone upstairs.

Stuffing the last few bites in my mouth, I shoved my chair from the table.

Dane seemed to understand and took a long drink of water while stabbing the last bite with the other hand. "Hang on, I'm right behind you," he said.

"Where are you two off to in such a hurry?" Kaido grouched.

"None of your business," I tried to say through my mouthful.

Kaido's eyes bugged. "Going to have se—"

"I said none of your business!" I shouted, nearly spitting my food at him. I got my crutches under my arms and took a shaky step.

All eyes on me, my face heated as I struggled to get around the table with the crutches.

Folding his arms behind his head, Kaido crossed his boots on the table and leaned his chair back on two legs. "If you say so, girl."

Dane strode around the other side, passing behind him.

Kaido smirked. "Just remember, when you finally wake up, I'll be right here, ready to take your breath away as soon as you—"

His boots lurched into the air as Dane yanked his chair back. With a splintering crash, Kaido's chair slammed against the stone floor.

Kaido's eyes bugged as he rolled clumsily out of the chair, pausing on his hands and knees, struggling to breathe.

"Oh, my bad," Dane said. "Did I take *your* breath away?"

I laughed out loud as Dane wrapped an arm around me, helping me toward the spiral staircase.

Kaido coughed shallowly.

"Well," Selverine said, "you *did* have that coming."

With an incoherent shout, Kaido launched himself after us.

"Hang on, Mella," Dane said as he laid my hand on the stair rail and stepped between me and Kaido. Hefting a crutch, he shoved it into Kaido's gut just as he reached him.

Kaido hit the crutch at full speed, then whimpered and sank to the floor.

"Kaido, there aren't words to describe what a piece of muck you are." Dane pressed the crutch into Kaido's chest. "You *had* a chance with Mella, and you skunked it up. You no longer have a chance. So please, for all our sakes, pick someone else to pursue and leave us alone."

Scowling, Kaido shoved to his feet, still breathing roughly. "I might take your advice if you were more of a man, instead of a skinny albino child, but since you are what you are"—Kaido gestured at Dane's whole body—"I don't think I have anything to worry about. She'll realize soon how much better she could have it."

I leaned against the rail and crossed my arms, bearing my weight on one ankle. "Right. I'd be so much better off with you, someone who dumped me and let me find out by seeing you at the ball with another girl on your arm, than with Dane, who's brilliant and reliable and supportive and kind, everything you aren't."

Kaido met my eyes and seemed to make a decision. Closing the distance between us, he leaned in like he was going to kiss me.

The piece of muck! Ducking out of the way, I shoved the other crutch into his crotch with all the strength I could muster, just as Dane threw a punch at his face hard enough to knock him backward.

"Monkey's teeth, Felzane! Get it through your head already!"

Kaido landed on his back, the breath knocked out of him once more as he wheezed, and covered his crotch with his hands, his face contorted in rage and pain.

"If you ever get that close to me again, Kaido, you'll get worse," I hissed.

Dane knelt on one knee next to him. "Touch her again, and a few punches to the face and groin will be the least of your worries, Felzane. We're done tolerating your muck."

Heart racing, I watched Dane straighten and step over Kaido. Angry and fierce and defending me. *Wow. He looks so good.*

Wrapping his arm around me, he led me up the stairs.

I grinned. "You know, Dane, throwing punches and declaring dark threats looks good on you."

He let out a harsh laugh. "I know you can take care of yourself, like you just did." Dane gestured back down to the stairs. "But if he ever does that again, I'm putting a stop to him. Permanently."

"It's a deal." I held tight to him as he helped me up the stairs.

Once we were around the first spiral and out of sight, I stopped and faced Dane.

"I think we both deserve a kiss for fighting him off," I whispered.

Dane grinned, the look in his blue eyes making my heart fly even faster. Throwing the crutches to the landing above us, he wrapped his other arm around my waist and kissed me. Leaning closer, he pressed me against the wall, one hand protecting my head from the stone.

I wrapped my arms around him and slowly slid my hands up to his bare neck, lacing my fingers over his skin.

He had definitely been doing extra workouts.

I pulled back just long enough to say, "Muck him. You were amazing."

"So were you." His voice came out breathy.

He leaned back to meet my gaze, looking at me like I was too good to be true.

More sparking shivers.

I hoped he'd never stop looking at me like that.

He kissed me again, pressing me even closer.

I pulled him to me, but a scarlet smear on the ceiling caught my attention.

Dane felt the change in my posture and pulled back again to look at me. "Mella? What is it?"

I pointed. "Is that blood on the ceiling?"

He reached up and slid his finger through it. He frowned, sniffed it.

"Reenalyn's bumped her head on the ceiling a few times. Do you think she could be hurt?" I whispered, concern icing over the warm feelings I'd just basked in.

The spark in his eyes dimmed, replaced by concern for Reenalyn. "Let's go check on her."

He helped me up the stairs, then handed me the crutches, and strode with me to Reenalyn's room.

"Reenalyn?" I knocked softly on the door, but no answer. Twisting the knob, I leaned in.

The curtains were torn from the hangings and strewn on the floor, along with the bedclothes. And red blotches dotted them and the stone.

I gasped, throwing the door wide open. "Dane? What happened?"

He darted into the room. "I don't know. You don't think she could've hurt herself...?"

I shook my head. "Not likely. Even as upset as she must have been if Zaylan dumped her. Someone else did this. We have to find her *now!*"

CHAPTER 45

SELVERINE

I had to hand it to Dane. That was ballsier than I expected from him. And skunks did Kaido deserve it.

Chuckling, I slid back into my seat to finish my dinner. I'd sprinkled it with a generous amount of antiflora powder—not enough to turn it invisible—and I wasn't going to waste the potion or my meal.

Spearing another bite, I winced at the soreness from sparring with Acres. I'd misjudged him before for his choice of weapon. The razor-sharp stars and his skill with them were effective and impressive. Not the wimpy little things I'd taken them for at the Castling Ceremony a year ago.

"Selverine?"

The man himself. "Yeah?"

"I wanted to tell you something."

I waited. "Okay, sure. What?" I stabbed another bite and popped it in my mouth.

He cleared his throat. "Could we step into the other room?"

I chewed slowly, surprised by the butterflies suddenly fluttering in my stomach. Had he decided to ask me out after all? Why else would he ask to speak to me alone?

Swallowing, I stood and stepped around my chair. "Sure."

I followed him to the sitting room by the garden.

Voices from the entryway caught my attention. Zaylan speaking with a man I'd never seen before, and I woman I thought I recognized from the tavern. A huge brown lizard with a feathered tail licked the air from the far side of the man, while a feathered fox with an avian beak protruding next to its muzzle prowled by the woman's boots. Zaylan's castors, finally returned? Did they have news of Bennet and Whisper?

I'd find out in a minute. I was *not* missing this.

Acres sat in a chair and gestured toward the settee in front of him.

Holy muck. He was about to ask me. My heart raced as I breathed slowly, butterflies going crazy.

"Selverine," he met my eyes for a moment, then looked away.

"Yes?" I smiled, taking a seat. There was something so refreshing and sweet about how nervous he clearly was.

Ask me!

His eyes met mine again and he let out a deep breath. "I accidentally discovered a potion that lets me read someone else's thoughts."

My smile faded, the butterflies vanishing. Holy muck. Was he using potions like Grandmother had? Did he already know how much his rejection had stung? How much I'd thought about him since? What if he'd read my every thought the last few days and was nervous because he was trying to let me down easy?

Squirming, I glared. "Yeah, and?"

"It only works if I'm in contact with someone. Physically. I mean, I have to touch their skin to read their thoughts, and I have to have taken a sip of the potion recently."

Okay. That was a relief. Had he ever touched me? Only once, when we sparred yesterday, and he'd stumbled. But *I'd* reached for *him*. And he'd pulled away like I'd burned him. Had he seen something then? At least…it seemed like he hadn't been trying. Had he accidentally read my thoughts?

Still though. "Okay. What are you getting at?"

If he disappointed me by being like Grandmother with her manipulative floramancy, that would be even worse than when he'd disappointed me at the Grand Castors' Ball last year. There'd be no coming back from that.

"I had one sip left, and I decided to use it on the apothecary to find out how she's related to your family."

I blinked, surprise and confusion piercing the breath I'd held.

So he wasn't confessing to using it on me. He'd used it...*for* me?

I crossed my arms. "And? What did you learn?"

"I'm not sure. I saw a memory from the perspective of someone who must've been the apothecary. But she was dressed in a royal purple gown and had brown skin, like you and me and Narellen. She approached someone dressed in maid's clothes, who had blond hair and pale skin, like the apothecary does now."

"But hang on. That means you must've seen it from someone else's—maybe Narellen's—perspective, doesn't it?"

He shook his head. "I don't think so. It happened when I touched the apothecary's hand. So it had to be from her point of view. I just don't understand the switched stations and skin tones. But whoever's perspective it was, she never looked in the mirror, so I couldn't see her face."

"Huh."

"But the memory was of the bracelets. Someone had given the point-of-view girl one, and she 'made' him make another for the maid. So they were friends, maybe?"

"Maybe. But are you sure it had to be from the perspective of whoever you were touching? What if Narellen somehow gave the memory to the apothecary?"

Acres shrugged. "All the other times I've used that potion, it's been from the perspective of who I had contact with in the moment. I don't know why that would be different now, or why Narellen would have given the memory to the apothecary. But the apothecary made it clear I'm not welcome back, so I probably won't be able to ask her. But if you wanted to try, you could. Up to you. I wanted you to know what I discovered. I'm sorry it's not much. But you can do with it whatever you think best."

His gaze skipped away from mine again too quickly as he stood, a loose loc falling into his face.

This guy handed me a fascinating bit of intel with no strings attached, just so I could be better informed as I made my own decisions?

Acres Parrianther was a rare kind of person.

He hesitated. Would he offer his hand to help me up? Just how recently did he have to have sipped that mind-reading potion for a touch to reveal private thoughts?

I had a feeling he wouldn't snoop on me like that. But how could I be sure? I stood quickly before he could offer, just in case.

He met my eyes for a long moment, setting butterflies loose again.

I should say something.

He opened his mouth to speak.

Someone barged into the room, and I jumped. "Mella? What the muck are you doing here? I thought you...had better things to do."

She leaned toward me and whispered, "We're all in danger here. We need to get our weapons and find Reenalyn and make a run for it."

I frowned. "Where's Reenalyn? What makes you think we're in danger?"

"Reenalyn's *missing*, which is why I said we needed to *find* her." She rolled her eyes. "And there's blood on the ceiling of the staircase, like someone dragged her down it against her will."

Dane leaned in around the doorway. "Sprinter's weapon is gone," he hissed, his face drawn as everyone from the dining room crowded in. "I hope you have your weapons with you, because they're not in your rooms."

Beldon's eyes widened as Acres reached into the pouch on his belt and pulled his castling stars out to examine. "I've still got mine."

"Mine was in my room," Beldon said.

Kaido scowled. "Mine, too."

My heart dropped. I'd left my trident on my bed. Had the last chance of seeing Horizon again vanished?

Trinka slid her spiked knuckles over her fingers. It didn't mean she or Acres loved their castlings more. Just that their weapons were smaller and lighter and easier to carry.

Kaido leaned forward. "Where should we look?"

"They were taking her down the stairs by the look of it, not up. And there's not much on this level, but a lot of doors in the basement." Mella answered his question while eyeing the rest of us. "We could start there."

We left the room in a cluster, heading past the garden door toward the basement staircase.

A hulking castor with a king cobra castling ducked out of the spiral staircase, eyeing us. Who was that? I did a doubletake, noticing the feathers sprouting from the snake's hood and the row of talon-like spikes running down its long back.

Not only was I without a castling—so was almost everyone else on my side.

Another castor, the one with the two-faced fox, strode through the entryway and followed us with a dark look.

Were these the castors Zaylan had supposedly sent searching for Bennet and Whisper? Should I shout ahead to run? Maybe if I didn't let on they made me nervous, they'd stay far enough behind for me to lock the door to the basement stairs behind us. If it even had a lock...

Those in front filed through the door and down the stairs. Mella and her crutches slowed the rest of us down.

The door swung closed behind me and I checked for a lock. Thank good fortune there was one. I flipped the lock and hurried down the stairs after the others.

They stopped a few spans down the hall. Wallen stood, blocking a doorway, his arms crossed.

Frowning, I shoved through the others. Wallen was the one decent guard, and he and Beldon were friends. There was a small chance he might not be against us. "Wallen, have you seen our friend Reenalyn?"

He blinked and nodded, his face straight.

"Okay, well, where is she?"

He stepped out of the doorway and gestured us inside. "She's in there."

So he was in on it too?

Of course he'd been putting on an act. And I'd fallen for it.

Would I ever learn I couldn't trust anyone?

If we wouldn't be happy to find her...did that mean they'd petrified her like the Avian Army and hybrid castors?

Would they petrify us too?

"Um, guys, maybe we shouldn't—"

"Of course we are, Selverine, muck off!" Mella pushed past me and hobbled for the door as fast as she could with crutches.

The door at the top of the stairs crashed open—probably kicked in by one of the new hybrid castors.

There was no going back that way, and I had to get Horizon's weapon back. If there was any chance I'd see her again, it could only happen with her weapon. We poured into the room after Mella.

Reenalyn knelt in a pile of metal shards, facing the floor with tears running down her stricken face.

She had a gag tied around her mouth, and she didn't look up when we entered.

Mella hobbled forward. "Reenalyn, where's Cupid?"

Her lips trembled. And she looked pointedly at the shards of metal she sat in.

My heart throbbed with new terror.

"Reenalyn," Mella whispered. "That isn't..."

Reenalyn's face contorted with grief.

Dane's jaw dropped. "No."

Even Kaido's usually joking expression was shocked and grim.

More hybrid castor guards burst through the door. Between them and Wallen and their castlings, they outnumbered us and could easily restrain us weaponless castors in a handful of seconds.

They had shattered Reenalyn's castling weapon. How could they? And where was mine?

A derisive chuckle came from the other side of the room, and Zaylan walked in. "Thanks for bringing yourselves down. How obliging." He leered, eyeing us one at a time.

"Now that I know the true whereabouts of the queen, we can proceed. Selverine, you're a terrible liar. You said Queen Narellen had received my letters and would reply as soon as she could, but I didn't send any letters. And she won't be receiving any letters for a long time, locked away as she is."

I glowered at him, my stomach dropping. What a stupid mistake!

He rubbed his hands together, surveying us. "Now, we have nearly all your weapons in our possession."

Pointing at Trinka, he said, "Someone get the little one's spiked brass knuckles."

Two guards descended on Trinka, grasping her arms and struggling to take the weapons from her. She fought back, throwing kicks and spiked blows, drawing blood.

Beldon tore one of them off her and wound up to punch another's face.

Zaylan shouted, interrupting him. "Stop now or I'll destroy your castling weapon next, Beldon."

Beldon paused.

With a shout and a grunt, Trinka knocked them both away again, slicing one down the leg with the spikes.

"Really, how many of you must it take to restrain one person?" Zaylan rolled his eyes, gesturing for more guards to help. "Trinka, the same goes for you. Beldon's weapon destroyed if you don't submit."

She stilled, scowling fiercely. The castors wrestled the knuckles from her and forced her to her knees.

Zaylan gestured to Acres next. "His weapons as well."

I glanced at Acres. The taloned badger fixed its jaws around his knee, drawing a pained grunt from him, while its castor restrained his wrists and pulled his stars from their pouch.

No!

I stepped toward him, and someone grabbed me by my wrists, shoving my arms up uncomfortably behind me. Acres's eyes met mine, mirroring my fears.

Zaylan grinned. "And *now*, we have all your weapons. It's the ultimate leverage, you know. What wouldn't any of you do for the other half of your soul?"

CHAPTER 46

MELLA

They shattered Cupid.

I squeezed the handles of my crutches, rage, terror, and grief twisting in my chest at the sight of Reenalyn kneeling in silver shards.

They shattered him. Are they trying to make him a hybrid?

How did we let this happen? How could we have gotten so comfortable that we left our castling weapons alone and unguarded like this?

I could've throttled myself.

But one thing was certain. Zaylan was a dead man.

And I had to do it before he shattered any more castlings.

One of the new hybrid castors pulled a sheet from a table, revealing most of our weapons laid out. She set Acres's throwing stars and Trinka's brass knuckles on the table.

Which meant I better get started, because whatever was standing under the other sheet next to the table was surely bad news for us.

Reenalyn sniffled.

I winced, staring at Cupid's shards.

Tears welled in my eyes. It was too horrible. Cupid, gone.

A dark emptiness loomed before me as I remembered how it felt when I thought I'd lost Whisper. How it would feel if we never found her or Bennet. Willova and I were lucky not to have our castling weapons with us now.

I pushed the hopeless doom away. I had to keep fighting as long as I could to have any chance of preventing it, of helping Reenalyn.

Our fight seemed so childish now. Jealous of each other when we both had our own good things we shouldn't have taken for granted. Would Reenalyn ever be the same?

I took a deep breath and let it out through my nose, focusing on Zaylan.

"Gomund, restrain them next. Starting with her." Zaylan pointed at me.

Dane stepped between us. "You're not going to touch her."

"I thought we might encounter something like this," Zaylan said. "Let's see…" He lifted Dane's tent peg casting weapon from the table. "Is this yours?"

Dane scowled.

"Very good. Now then, you, step away. Mella, sit down on the ground. Gomund, take her crutches, then tie her wrists."

How would I walk with my hands tied and no crutches?

Gomund reached toward me, and Dane blocked his arm.

Zaylan nodded at Gomund, who then feinted to the side, punched Dane in the face, forced him around, and shoved him to his knees, facing Zaylan.

"Dane!"

He shook his head, blinking. How hard had that blow hit? He looked dazed. Then he fell forward, caught himself with his hands at the last moment, and kicked out behind him. He would've swiped Gomund's feet out from under him if Gomund hadn't just stepped back.

Dane was on his feet again, shielding me from both of them.

More castor guards approached, brandishing their weapons with their castlings showing their teeth at their sides.

Zaylan tsked. "Ah, see. I've been hospitable, but no longer. This is what happens when you hesitate to follow my orders."

Still gripping Dane's castling weapon in one hand, he threw the sheet off the thing by the table. It was something like an axe sharpener. But with two stone wheels instead of one.

Zaylan pressed a pedal, and the wheels spun toward each other with a small space between. In a flash, Zaylan shoved the tent peg between them, and an earsplitting screech rang as they filed a thin layer off the point.

"No!" I shrieked, throwing down the crutches. I sank awkwardly to the floor and held my wrists together before me. "There. You can tie them. Dane, it's okay." I scowled at Zaylan as he lifted the castling weapon from the machine. "See, he's standing down. Okay?"

Face twisted in anguish, Dane stepped aside as Gomund approached, pushing him to his knees again.

"Very good." Zaylan nodded. He pointed with the tent peg at Xerrome. "Bind the others."

Nodding, Xerrome snatched lengths of rope from the floor.

Starting with Beldon, he tied his hands together as Gomund moved from Dane to me, then the others.

Dane's sky-blue eyes met mine, full of concern. He inched closer, still facing Zaylan.

Xerrome bound Willova and Selverine, then hesitated behind Reenalyn.

"Not her yet," Zaylan commanded. "But take off the gag."

I glared at him from the ground as Xerrome followed his order.

"Now, let's get back to the experiment. Reenalyn?"

Her gaze lifted to his, bleary from the shock and grief.

Zaylan faced the table again and reached for a squarish object wrapped in a cloth. "I have something for you. A certain instrument. Inlaid with the point of your spear."

Reenalyn gasped, covering her mouth. "You mean, he might not be dead?"

Zaylan nodded. "Bring him back as a hybrid, and he'll be fine. If you can pull it off."

Reenalyn stared at the object with wide eyes.

Tossing the corners of the cloth aside, he revealed a book-sized stringed wooden instrument.

Her jaw dropped, then she glowered at him. "A harpika? Really? How can you be so petty and so cruel?"

Did he know she doesn't like two-handed harps? Not her style. And he chose it on purpose? What a skunk!

Holding the harpika in one hand, Zaylan spread his arms in an exaggerated shrug. "I'm giving you a chance to get your castling back. Nothing petty or cruel about that."

"What do I have to do?" she hissed.

He handed the harpika to her, and she accepted it gently, cradling it against her.

"Just say your castling call as strongly as you can while playing this. And we'll see what happens."

Reenalyn shifted the harpika and held it with both hands in her lap, her thumbs resting over the strings. Taking a deep breath, she strummed them once, winced, and strummed again more lightly.

"Join me, my Cupid,
Brave and true...

Her voice cracked and she paused, then started over.

"Join me, my Cupid,
Brave and true,
Surefooted and witty,
I already love you!"

She eked out the last word, then sobbed over the harpika. "It's not working."

Zaylan gritted his teeth. "Because you're a slobbering mess! Pull yourself together and try harder!"

Reenalyn shrank back from him, holding her breath to stop the sobs.

I leaned toward her, wishing I could do anything to comfort her. And I could've sworn I saw a flash of fury in Xerrome's eyes behind her.

"Again!" Zaylan gestured impatiently at Reenalyn.

She took a few measured breaths, then strummed the harp and struggled through her castling call.

No Cupid.

Fresh tears streamed down her face, splashing over her lap.

Oh, no! Please, no! My heart broke for her.

Why was Xerrome clenching his fists? What did he care?

Zaylan crouched and tore the harpika from Reenalyn's lap. "Shame. Another dud." He tossed it at Wallen, who—thank good fortune—had the decency to catch it.

"Store that with the other failures waiting to be destroyed," Zaylan said.

Wallen nodded and let himself out.

Zaylan eyed Xerrome. "What's gotten into you?"

Xerrome straightened, clearing his expression. "Nothing, sir."

Zaylan nodded impatiently at Reenalyn.

Stepping around her, Xerrome crouched. "Reenalyn, I have to tie your wrists, okay?" I'd never heard him speak so softly before.

Reenalyn stared silently at the floor as if she hadn't heard.

Xerrome gently pulled her arms in front, careful not to slice her knuckles over the sharp pieces on the floor, and bound Reenalyn's wrists.

"Take them to the dungeon." Zaylan inspected one of Trinka's spiked knuckles, then laid them back on the table and picked up one of Acres's throwing stars.

Xerrome hefted Reenalyn in his arms as Gomund crossed the room and opened a door on the opposite wall. Scowling again, Xerrome ordered us through it.

Skunks.

Dane leaned down, trying to get his arm under mine enough to haul me up.

"Uh-uh!" Zaylan sang, wagging a finger. "I've got a surprise for Mella upstairs. She's coming with me."

"Not a chance!" Dane launched himself at Zaylan. "If you think you're taking her out of my sight, you've got another—"

Zaylan punched Dane in the stomach, knocking the air out of him, and followed it up with a kick to one knee and a jab to the kidney.

Dane hit the ground.

"No!" I crawled toward him, but Zaylan blocked me.

"Gomund." Zaylan gestured to Dane, and Gomund hauled him up and dragged him, still fighting, through the door after the others.

"Mella!" Dane bellowed as the door slammed shut, leaving me alone with Zaylan.

"Come, Mella." He held out a hand. "Oh, I forgot. That won't work."

Wrapping an arm around my shoulders, he slid the other behind my knees and lifted me.

Cringing away from him, I watched his pine marten castling climb his shoulders. It fixed me with a beady-eyed stare, and my eyes narrowed.

I finally realized what Cairdon from my drawing class had tried to tell me. It wasn't a white weasel he'd drawn. It was Zaylan's pine marten. It was only chalk-colored because that was the color he'd had.

Had he been warning me about Zaylan?

Taking a deep breath, I leaned as far away from Zaylan as I could, dreading whatever was to come.

CHAPTER 47

REENALYN

I let the numbness overtake me. I couldn't handle the pain.

My castling. My Cupid.

Dead. I couldn't even bring him back as a hybrid.

Without Cupid, I didn't have anyone to see the world with me and understand. I'd never have someone sit on my shoulder and curl his tail around my arm, to mumble his dry humor in my ear.

It was too much.

Someone lifted me, carrying me away from Cupid's remains. I wasn't ready to leave. But no resistance was left in me.

When I felt that false feeling—the emotions of appreciation and tenderness and admiration—trying to break through my thoughts, I shoved it away, struggling to turn it off like Erisole had taught me.

So I was in Zaylan's arms. Skunk him. Hadn't he done enough? Couldn't he leave me alone? I'd never know how he managed to confuse my sixth sense, sometimes with fake emotions and sometimes with none. I'd been a fool to let myself listen.

Cupid was the only one who understood, who didn't think I was too much.

And now he was gone.

I tried to keep being numb as Zaylan's false feelings of esteem glowed brighter. If only he'd put me down.

Barred doors filled my periphery. The dungeon. He'd have to put me down soon and leave me alone.

But on he strode, leading the others behind us, past every cell.

He paused, shifting me in his arms. Then the sound of a key turning in a lock echoed in the room. He opened a door in the wall, wrapped his arm around me, and stepped through.

I eyed the key still in his hand.

No seam in the middle, so not the one I'd helped Marken hide in the tavern. What had happened to that one?

If only I'd stayed out of it. Maybe Cupid would still be alive.

When he finally set me down, the raw feelings roiling from him pricked my numbness. How was he doing it? How did he make me see such infatuation and caring and concern, and even rage on my behalf, when he clearly wanted only to harm me?

As my eyes adjusted, walls of bars appeared.

A cell. Of course.

"Hey, hey! Is it finally time?" someone asked from the wall of cells.

I blinked in the dimness and rubbed my eyes.

Hinges squealed, and a man strode from a cell, stretching his arms over his head.

"Marken?" someone asked from behind me.

The man squinted at me. "Reenalyn, right? Is that you?"

Why was Zaylan letting Marken out and not locking us up?

Zaylan clapped his hands once. "Okay, people."

Wait, that isn't Zaylan's voice. I blinked up at him. It was the wrong body, too. Much shorter and broader.

"Castors of Wrynford, listen up." A tan muscled arm slapped Marken's shoulder. "There's a way we can steal your castling weapons back. And Reenalyn." He faced me, and I squinted at him. "Don't give up on Cupid yet."

"Xerrome?" But where was Zaylan? He'd just been here... My eyes widened as I realized what he said. "What do you mean? I saw my weapon shattered, and I couldn't call him from the instrument."

Xerrome was the scowler, not someone on our side. He couldn't possibly say these things in front of Zaylan. But I still felt Zaylan's false emotions.

He must be standing right next to Xerrome.

I blinked, trying to focus through my grief without giving into false hope that would only break me all over again.

"Where's Zaylan?" I asked.

"He's in the manor. It's safe here. And Cupid still has a chance."

"What do you mean?" Trinka hissed while I peered around stupidly for Zaylan.

Xerrome nodded to her. "We have a mutiny to get underway and a lot of castlings to rescue. I've been trying to put a stop to Zaylan and his hybrid experiments and abuse for months. Now's our chance. While he's distracted."

"Distracted doing what?" Dane demanded, shaking off his ropes and marching toward Xerrome.

"He took Mella to his study. I understand how you'll feel about that, so you can go straight there and get her back. But I need everyone else's help." He produced an armful of empty grey sacks like the one he'd had when I'd run into him in the desert and met Trissa, and started tossing them to each of us.

Dane raised his pale eyebrows in surprise, then nodded.

My mind reeled. "Why are you suddenly on our side?"

"I've been on your side the whole time," he said, crouching and placing one of the bags in my hands. "I just couldn't tell you. I'm so sorry." He stared hard into my eyes.

As I decided to believe him, I realized something else.

It was in his eyes.

What I'd never seen in Zaylan's eyes.

The familiar, enticing, confusing, beautiful emotions toward me were coming from Xerrome.

Chapter 48

MELLA

Zaylan's fingers dug into my elbow as he hauled me up the basement stairs, across the manor, and up the spiral staircase. His footsteps echoed on stone and iron. "I can't fathom how some girl from the middle of nowhere in Terrenthyrs managed to cast a hybrid a thousand times more viable than any I've made, but you're going to tell me!"

I struggled to tear his fingers away. "I didn't do it on purpose!"

His grip tightened. "That only makes it *more* frustrating."

"I don't know how I did it. How am I supposed to figure out what I did by accident?"

"With proper motivation."

My skin crawled. That sounded bad.

He unlocked his study door and hauled me through.

Passing the chairs, he headed for the desk. Was he going to throw me on it? Or in the desk chair?

Turning, he wrenched open a set of sliding doors in the wall and dumped me on the carpeted floor.

Wincing, I searched this second sitting room for torture devices. But there were only more chairs and a large table in the center of the room. Something you might put a big map on for strategizing a war.

"Guess who?" Zaylan sang.

Movement in the table's shadow caught my eye. Was something moving under it?

Familiar kind eyes and grey hair leaned into the light.

"Bennet?" Gasping, I crawled to him, taking in his torn clothes, dirty face, black eye, and missing tooth. "Oh, Bennet! What happened? Are you okay?"

Slouching in a heap, Bennet cradled my mandolin against his chest. His eyes were wide with alarm. "Mella?"

"Yes, it's me! Where's Whisper? Did she really lose her mind? She didn't do this to you, did she?"

"What? No," he wheezed, laying a hand on my shoulder. "You shouldn't be here!"

"We came to rescue you."

Zaylan slammed the sliding doors closed and regarded us. "Now, Bennet. While I graciously chose not to harm Whisper before, circumstances have changed."

He eyed me, and Bennet tightened his grip on my shoulder, his mouth going grim.

"Whisper's fine, Mella," Bennet said, his eyes shooting daggers at Zaylan. "She didn't do this to me. He did."

Dropping into a plush armchair, Zaylan made a show of getting comfortable and crossing his boots over an ottoman. "Yes, now, Bennet. Where were we? Right. Cast the hybrid, or Mella bleeds."

Bennet gripped my shoulder tighter as he hugged the mandolin fiercely.

Zaylan leaned forward, his low voice menacing. "I won't ask again."

My heart broke once more. I didn't know what Zaylan would do to Whisper, but Bennet had obviously suffered for days trying to prevent him from doing it. And now he had to choose between us.

I gripped his withered fingers encircling my mandolin. "It's okay, Bennet. I understand. Whatever Zaylan has in mind, I can take it."

Bennet sighed. And began Whisper's casting call.

"Whisper, my only friend,
a secret till—"

Throwing a hand over his mouth, I cut him off. "Bennet, no! You can't—"

Zaylan grabbed my sprained ankle and wrenched it hard, dragging me away from Bennet.

I cried out, kicking at Zaylan with my other leg and missing.

Bennet started the call again.

"Whisper, my only friend,
a secret till the journey's end…"

With a scream of pain, I kicked Zaylan off my bad ankle and crawled toward Bennet. "No! Stop!"

Too late. Flecks of cotton, soot, and chocolate swirled together and settled into Whisper's hybrid eagle form.

What would Zaylan do to her? My heart wrenched as I stared, horrified, at Bennet. "You shouldn't have done that!"

Whisper stood hunched on Bennet's lap, ducking under the table and careful not to prick his thin skin with her raptor talons.

She regarded me, then swung her head around to scowl at Zaylan with that special brand of severity only eagles possessed. "It's all right, Mella," she said, backing off Bennet to stand on her own. "Bennet and I knew you'd try to rescue us, and we agreed to do anything necessary to save you."

Tears pricked my eyes. The tenderness in Bennet's brief smile squeezed my heart.

Zaylan clapped slowly. "Whisper, how lovely to finally meet you. You're just as breathtaking as I remember."

"You've met her before?" I asked.

"Oh yes. Seen her, at least. You may have noticed Morrenfayre is…running a bit low on good test subjects. I visit Terrenthyrs from time to time to add to our ranks. On one such trip, I saw your little display at the Grand Castors' Tournament. A hybrid actually flying! Few enough of the Avian Army can fly, and none of my hybrids have managed. My hybrids either have avian traits so small or deformed that they're useless, or the castling is unviable altogether."

Zaylan gestured toward Whisper. "Naturally I had to study her, but I couldn't reveal my absence from Morrenfayre or my interest in hybrids to the queen."

"So you sent other people to kidnap Whisper and Bennet for you, and burn the evidence," I said. "The fire wasn't Whisper's fault. Do hybrids actually lose their minds after a year, or was that a pile of muck?"

Zaylan grinned. "Some are less mentally sound than others. But you are quite gullible, Mella."

Fury stirred in my gut. "Why'd you let us relax for four days? Why didn't you start by throwing me up here and using us three against each other?"

He shrugged. "Torture is easy, but once it's done, you can't try a lighter touch. I wanted to learn what I could by observation first. And I needed to determine whether the queen was still safely locked away. If she were free, as Selverine implied, she might've heard what happened and suspected me. It would be a terribly unfortunate time for a visit from her just now. It took my castors a few days to return with confirmation that she is, in fact, in a dungeon cell and out of my way. Which they did this morning."

So that was why he sent people out. They *did* go back to Terrenthyrs, just not to look for Bennet and Whisper. And if they came back this morning... "Was that why you picked today to be so cruel to Reenalyn?"

He grinned. "She was even more gullible than you."

"You're even deader than you were a few minutes ago."

He chuckled. "Which brings us to what you're going to do for me."

I glared at him.

"All my hybrids to date have been the result of an avian castling transfigured into a hybrid through casting via a weapon. Instrument first, then weapon. Beginning with a pure avian, and adding another battle animal. Because it makes sense to run into battle with an assortment of weapons rather than an assortment of instruments."

An assortment? He plans to have more people like Famita with multiple hybrid castlings?

"However, many of these animals are not equipped with good enough wings to fly. It seems too much of the avian gets removed during the hybridization."

I interrupted him. "Is that why you haven't made Erisole or Xerrome's castlings into hybrids? Because they're too valuable to risk ruining with a botched hybridization?"

Zaylan dipped his head. "That's right."

"And that's why you've been experimenting on kids? Because their castlings are less of a loss when they don't work out?"

"Right again. Unfortunately, it seems casting too early, or losing your castling, can cause a mental weakness. I'm keeping them around for now for potential future experiments, of course. That's why they have regimented exercises and tasks like the art classes you've taken part in, Mella. It's all part of refining the process. Finding the best age to begin experimentation. I'll be culling more soon."

Rage filled my chest. I thought of Cairdon. "You forced those kids to cast early, and all for nothing?"

"It is a shame they couldn't do better. So naturally, when I went to Terrenthyrs to grab more subjects and check on Narellen, and I saw Whisper, I was intrigued. When I heard the story from Reenalyn, that she started as a battle animal and was transformed with the avian being the second part, I made the connection I'm sure you already know."

He leered at us, but I frowned, unsure what he meant.

"It's the *second* animal added to the hybridization that takes the most dominance in the hybrid's appearance and functionality!" He leaped from his chair, arms raised with a mad gleam in his eye.

Striking a thinking pose with his arms and chin, he paced before the sliding doors. "I hoped to prove this with Reenalyn's iguana, but alas. Something's still missing."

Fury boiled inside me. "What gives you the right to abuse people and their castlings this way? And for what? Just to satisfy your curiosity?"

Whisper met my gaze, her eyes questioning and full of sorrow. I shook my head. I'd explain later.

He ignored me, talking to himself. "So close, but still not viable."

I scowled.

He glanced between Bennet and me. "So tell me, one of you, why didn't it work? What went wrong?"

Then he grabbed my wrist and yanked, binding me against him with one arm over my chest and his jeweled castling dagger held to my neck. Struggling to balance on one foot, I cringed away from the sharp point already piercing the first layer of skin.

"No! Stop!" Bennet shouted, holding one hand out as if he could force Zaylan to listen to him.

Whisper flared her wings and straightened, her crown feathers standing on end and rage in her eagle eyes.

"What's it to be, Bennet? Hmm? She claims ignorance. So will you tell me what I'm missing, or must I prove I'll stab her first?"

Bennet's bewildered expression flicked between my eyes and Zaylan's. He had no idea what Zaylan wanted to know.

But I *did*. The only difference Zaylan hadn't identified yet was in the castling calls. Whisper had two different ones—the one Bennet gave her when she was first cast, and the one I accidentally gave her from my mandolin. Zaylan must've been reusing the originals even with the second castling object.

I could tell him—maybe save myself with that information. But how many more people and castlings—kids, even—would suffer for it? I couldn't give it to him. But could I die to protect it? Could I let him kill Whisper or Bennet?

"If you insist!" Zaylan shouted as he flipped the dagger and caught the handle backward so the blade pointed down toward my heart. Still struggling against his iron grip, I braced myself.

Zaylan hesitated another moment, giving Bennet a last chance to answer, then brought the knife down.

Something slammed against my chest, knocking the breath out of me and shoving Zaylan back a step.

The smallest tip of the blade sliced over a rib.

That was all the pain I felt.

I looked down, confused, and it was much worse than I'd feared.

Whisper had thrown herself between the knife and me.

Thick scarlet spread over the beautiful velvety grey plumage of her back.

"No!" Bennet screamed, reaching toward us.

Zaylan yanked the dagger from Whisper, and her body slid.

I dropped to catch her, supporting her weight as best I could, and shoving to the side, away from Zaylan.

"Well, that's a shame." He flicked her blood from the blade, then wiped the rest on her outstretched wing.

"Stop!" I screamed, shocked and horrified.

"This proves his ignorance. He would've told me to spare his castling, if not you." Zaylan pointed the dagger at me. "Which means you must know."

I ducked as a vase flew our way, crashing into Zaylan's face. Bennet followed, tackling him with a shout and knocking the dagger from his grip.

Whisper's head lolled to the side with her neck bent the wrong way. Her crown feathers—always standing on edge with her strong opinions—lay tamely against her head as it flopped over my arm. Was she still breathing? Her feathers made it hard to tell.

Tears blurring my vision, I glanced up to see Zaylan throw Bennet off him and grasp the dagger again.

I scooted us further away from the fight, torn between helping Bennet and comforting Whisper. "Whisper?" I croaked as I held her against my chest and pressed my hands over her wound. It was too late to stop the bleeding, but I tried anyway, wishing there was something I could actually do to help. To save her, to at least relieve her pain!

"Mella?" she wheezed.

"Whisper! Yes! I'm here," I whimpered, leaning my head closer to hers to hear her better.

Zaylan loomed over Bennet now, but Bennet blocked blow after blow.

I glared at Zaylan, my ear bent toward Whisper's beak, willing myself to hear her over them.

With a kick to the face, Zaylan finally bested Bennet. Stepping over him, he hauled him up to his knees to face me. "I see it in your face, Mella!" Zaylan grabbed a fistful of Bennet's hair. Shoving the dagger against his throat, he hissed, "You *do* know, even if this buffoon doesn't. So tell me now, or he dies, too!"

"Save him." The words drifted weakly from the bloody feathers in my arms.

The mandolin string I'd made from Bennet's bow snapped with a loud *pop* as Whisper went limp.

"No!" Bennet and I wailed.

"Now!" Zaylan screamed, pressing the knife against Bennet's throat hard enough to draw blood.

I'd have to tell him. Muck the consequences. I'd honor Whisper's last request and save her castor if I could.

"Last chance, Mella!"

"It's the castling calls!" I cried, tears thick in my voice. "You use the same castling call with the initial castling instrument and the second castling object." I choked on a sob and cleared my throat, still holding Whisper's body to me. "But Whisper had one castling call from Bennet, and another one I accidentally gave her when I cast her from the mandolin. Two castling calls, not one."

The room went still except for my quiet sobs over Whisper. Bennet stared, indescribable grief and pain pooling in his soft eyes.

"That could be it," Zaylan whispered, dropping Bennet's hair. "Yes, that *must* be it."

With a dazed look in his eyes, he dragged Bennet with him toward the doors.

"How did I never think of it before?" Yanking them open, he stepped through. "If you'll excuse me, I must test this theory right away."

Pulling the doors together, he faced us with a gleam in his eye. "If you're right, you'll be rewarded. But if you're wrong"—he made a disappointed face and kicked Bennet back into the room—"well, I'm sure you can imagine."

CHAPTER 49

REENALYN

I stumbled in Xerrome's wake, his hand grasping mine, pulling me forward. I strained to keep pace with him, hoping against hope he might be right about Cupid but hardly daring to believe it.

We darted up the basement stairs, and Xerrome led the way to the garden door. Most of the other Wrynford castors followed us, but Dane sprinted for the spiral staircase in search of Mella. I hesitated. What if he needed help getting her away from Zaylan? I couldn't let that skunk harm another of my friends.

"Reenalyn?" Xerrome had paused with me.

Right. This was my chance to get Cupid back. I had to try. *Dane, you can do this. You've got to.*

Xerrome's hand was warm and firm and gripped mine with gentle strength as he raced with me into the blinding sunlight, through the garden, and...around the back of manor? This had to be on the far side of the library.

We stopped at a door I hadn't noticed before, and Xerrome said, "Zaylan was bluffing earlier—trying to get you to make casting work by ordering the harpika destroyed. But he never outright destroys something that still holds mysteries." Xerrome fumbled with another key and wrenched the door open, all without releasing my hand. "This is where he keeps all the castling objects."

He pulled me into a room lined with shelves. Even the huge windows had shelves stretched over them. And the shelves were covered in wooden and metal weapons and instruments. At least, some of them were. Many others were empty, though with dust patterns as if they'd been covered in items in the past.

Xerrome gestured to one side and shouted, "Those that haven't been hybridized are over there, arranged by order of your last name, then first. Load as much as you can into the sacks while you search for yours."

Had the sack he'd carried that day been full of castling objects from this room?

Selverine, Acres, Beldon, Trinka, and Kaido bolted for that area, frantically searching for their weapons. Willova hung back, her gaze roaming the shelves as she kept her distance.

"Reenalyn." Xerrome looked up at me. "Cupid's over here."

He crossed the room, waving me over.

A sunbeam illuminated a beautiful mahogany violin with feathers etched on its face. But there was no piece of Cupid.

Next to it, under a label with my name, sat the harpika.

My least favorite instrument. Which Zaylan chose on purpose. He was pure cruelty.

But the silver point of my spear flashed from the wood beneath the strings. I stared at it, instinctively sensing some part of my Cupid inside. I nearly lost my breath in relief.

I could never dislike anything about Cupid. *Joke's on Zaylan. This is my new favorite instrument now.*

"Why didn't anyone invite us to this party?"

Xerrome stepped between me and the door as Zaylan appeared in the doorway. He strode inside, followed by two men and two women and their hybrid castlings.

A king cobra with feathers all around its hood and a row of single talon-like spikes down its spine slithered in, holding its head several spans high. A scowling chimpanzee with black feather-tufted ears knuckled its way inside, followed by a black-and-orange lizard with a wide head and winged forelegs who hissed, flicking the air with its dark purple forked tongue. A brown lizard many times larger than the other with hawk talons for feet and a feathered bird tail strode in alongside a feathered red fox with an avian beak sprouting next to its muzzle.

A spike of feeling slammed against my senses. Glancing ahead at Xerrome, I zeroed in on the precise angle. Zaylan stood in front of me and a little to the left, Xerrome mostly in line with him but slightly to the right.

And the emotions came from the right.

No way. Could it really have been Xerrome all along? But no, that didn't line up...

"Don't let the black-and-orange one near you," Xerrome hissed at me. "She's venomous. The cobra, too."

Zaylan crossed his arms, his eyebrows raised. "Come now, Xerrome. As the regent, I have a right to be informed of these events."

Behind me, metal scraped against wood as Beldon pulled his mace down from a high shelf with a grunt. Trinka stepped next to me, sliding her spiked knuckles into place. Selverine brandished her trident, and Acres aimed a throwing star as Kaido wound up his whip.

I grabbed a lance from a shelf below Cupid and faced Zaylan.

Xerrome threw up his hands. "Wait! No!"

"Ah, yes. I thought it might come to this." Zaylan rested a hand on the dagger handle in his belt. "One thing you should know before you attempt to strike—the walls of this room are tied to my life. If I die, they crumble. Shattering and burying every castling instrument and weapon within."

The walls are tied to his life? How? We'll have to knock him out, then...

"How?" Selverine asked.

"I acquired a spell."

A spell?

I focused on Xerrome again and found his eyes already on me, his expression grim. "He's telling the truth."

"Then how the muck did you think we'd pull off a mutiny!" Selverine shouted.

"A mutiny?" Zaylan's eyebrows rose. "Tsk, tsk, tsk. I'm disappointed. I'd hoped it wasn't you, Xerrome. But please, do go ahead and answer Selverine's question. I'm highly interested in your response."

"I expected you'd be distracted long enough for us to empty the room first," Xerrome said, his armor clinking as he shifted, angling himself between Zaylan and me once more.

Zaylan's eyebrows rose higher. "Ah! And you were planning to assassinate me yourself once the room was empty, were you? So you *do* know, and you thought a little change of heart would be enough to sneak you past my defenses." He shook his head. "Well you're about to be nearly as disappointed as I am in you, because that's not how it works."

How could a change of heart sneak someone past someone else's defenses? And by change of heart, did he mean...feelings for me? But it didn't add up...how could a change of heart do that?

A change someone couldn't know unless they sensed someone's thoughts or feelings after it happened.

Could Zaylan be a sixer? Could he sense...plans? Strategies? And Xerrome had made up his mind about a new plan after leaving Zaylan to take me and the others to Marken?

"So you can all set your castling weapons down—don't try to stuff it in your pocket, Acres, I see you—and come outside."

"You'd destroy all these castlings? And everything you've learned experimenting on them?" I asked, unwilling to lay down the harpika.

Zaylan shrugged. "The research in this room is my life's work. I've put in all the time and effort. Why share the benefits with anyone else if I'm not enjoying them?" His glare daring another protest, Zaylan surveyed us with raised eyebrows.

I set the harpika back where I'd found it. Xerrome took my hand again, startling me. But his warmth was comforting. *Did* he have another plan?

"So what's with the petrified people and castlings in that building deep in the desert, huh?" Selverine spat. "Is that another spell? Something you do to everyone who doesn't grovel at your feet?"

"That's something I do to people who bore me. Not a spell, though. Simply a failsafe the queen didn't hide very well."

What?

Selverine had no response.

"Reenalyn, I'm curious," Zaylan drawled. "Pick your new harpika back up and come here. I have need of you and Cupid again."

Heart sinking, I gritted my teeth and gripped the lance. I wanted to pitch it through his chest, but I couldn't risk striking a lethal blow.

Cinnamon and pepper flecks whirled in the corner of my eye.

Trinka's extra set of spiked knuckles! Just like when Queen Narellen sent us to the dungeon before the tournament. Brilliant!

Zaylan's four hybrid castors tensed, brandishing weapons, but they weren't fast enough.

Mauler took form next to Trinka and together they hurled themselves at Zaylan. The king cobra darted past the others, slithering into their path and wrapping around Trinka. Mauler dodged it and the others and tackled Zaylan through the door to the sand outside.

The other hybrid castors raced after them, castlings in their wake.

Beldon zoomed past me, grabbing hold of the cobra's head and fighting to unwind it from Trinka. It hissed and flailed at him.

"Quick, cast your castlings—" Xerrome said, some already partway through their castling calls.

"Not so fast." The palest largest soldier, who was apparently the cobra's castor, returned and trained an arrow on Xerrome, then shifted it to Beldon, silencing everyone before any other castlings took form. Beldon had ripped the snake off Trinka and seemed about to crush its head in his hands.

"You," the man said, "let go."

Beldon kept hold of the snake's body, Trinka breathing heavily next to him.

The man aimed at Trinka instead, and Beldon grudgingly loosened his fingers.

The snake dropped to the floor and hissed, eyeing Trinka again as it slithered back a few spans.

"You." The man trained an arrow on Xerrome. "Out. All of you. Now! And if you still have a castling weapon in your hands when you pass me, I'll shoot you and shatter it."

Furious and terrified, I laid Cupid's harpika on the shelf again, hoping now that Zaylan wasn't about to die. *Yet.*

The others laid their instruments down on the ground and filed out past him, Xerrome bringing up the rear behind me.

"I'll have the key from you. Traitor," the man hissed.

Xerrome scowled.

The man aimed the arrow at me without breaking Xerrome's gaze.

Xerrome pulled the key from his pants pocket and slammed it over the man's open palm, the seam in the key's middle catching the light. That *was* the key I'd snuck back to Marken.

Xerrome stepped forward between the arrow and me. Placing a hand on my back, he guided me outside.

I squinted in the blinding sunlight, taking in the sight of Trinka leaning on her toes toward the chimp holding Mauler down, Beldon's hand on her shoulder holding her back. "Wait, Trinka, please. You'll get shot," he whispered.

Another of the hybrid castors aimed a crossbow at the rest of us, the remaining hybrid castlings eyeing us with venomous stares.

Zaylan brushed sand from his clothes, straightening his tunic. Mauler had improved it with a set of claw tears through the fabric and a dark tinge spreading over the middle. Not a deathblow, but a small amount of well-deserved pain.

Wallen stood with the new hybrid castors, his arms crossed, taking it all in.

"What are you waiting for, Wallen?" Zaylan said. "Kill the two whose castling weapons don't work. We can't use them."

"Wallen?" Selverine shrieked, stepping forward. "Seriously? You were such a convincingly decent person."

Wallen shrugged with a sheepish grin. "I am. But I have a goal, too, and I can't accomplish it if one of you kills Zaylan and buries his research. So I'm afraid we'll have to put a stop to you first."

His hybrid kangaroo castling with taloned forepaws jumped in front of Selverine, then leaned back on its tail and aimed a kick at her with its powerful legs.

"You. Fellow ginger." Wallen pointed at Willova and closed the distance between them. "I'm sorry about this."

A throwing star zinged by, lodging in the kangaroo's skull and throwing off its aim. It missed Selverine and thudded on the ground, blood pooling in the sand.

Willova stood still, eyes on Wallen, her face expressionless but her fists clenched.

Raising his falchion, he aimed at her throat, swinging the blade around in an arc.

"Willova, no!" Selverine screamed, launching toward her. But she was too far away. Then a blur slammed into Wallen as Willova ducked under the blow.

Was that Kaido, wrestling the falchion away from Wallen?

It was. Had he just done something selfless for someone else?

Chaos erupted as castors and castlings fell on each other, hissing, snapping, striking. Trinka launched at Mauler and Beldon swung a kick up knocking the crossbow into the air.

Something hit me from the side, and I fell, skidding on the sand. I spun onto my back without missing a beat, kicking at whatever it was.

The enormous brown lizard with a feathered tail and razor-sharp teeth hissed and launched, its open jaws barely missing my knee as I scrambled away.

Suddenly Xerrome was there, swinging his wavy sword into the lizard's chest.

It hit the ground, spasmed, and stilled. Someone screamed, "No!" from the middle of the fray—its castor, now castlingless.

Swiping his thick forearm over his face, Xerrome smeared away blood and faced me. He tossed his sword into his bloody hand and offered me the clean one.

Emotions radiated from him. I grasped his hand, and as he hauled me up, I actually felt a spark zing from his hand through mine and up my arm. Standing, I looked down at him, captivated by the depth of his feelings.

Most times I'd felt what I thought was coming from Zaylan, Xerrome had been standing somewhere near him, as his righthand man.

All the times I'd felt nothing from Zaylan and thought he was masking his feelings—those were times Xerrome wasn't around.

But when I'd seen Xerrome yesterday in the garden, I hadn't felt anything.

Because Erisole had just taught me how to turn it off!

It *had* been Xerrome all along. But...why? I thought he was annoyed at all of us from Terrenthyrs, and now here he was placing himself between me and danger for the third or fourth time today. What changed his mind?

And the first feeling had been when we entered the manor—something must still be wrong with my senses. Nothing had happened to spark interest from Xerrome at that point.

The feather-tufted chimp appeared behind him, raising a muscular arm to strike.

I grabbed Xerrome's sword, plunged it through the creature, kicked it over, and tossed the sword back to Xerrome.

Xerrome's eyes widened as his feelings grew even more. I was so tall that he had to look up to meet my eyes, but his were only full of wonder. Not embarrassment or resentfulness. Not judgement. Just mysterious warmth.

With a sudden deafening roar, the battle came back into focus. Xerrome squeezed my hand and nodded. I returned both gestures, not entirely sure what they meant, and watched him trade sword blows with one of the new hybrid castors.

I fell backward as someone yanked my hair.

"Thought you'd get away with that, did you?" Zaylan hissed in my ear as I struggled against him. "Not a chance. You're a useful piece of leverage, now. Let me introduce you to the dungeons. Where you should've already been."

CHAPTER 50

MELLA

Whisper's blood cooled.

Chills rose on my arm as the bright red blood darkened and dried.

I couldn't believe she was gone.

How could this have happened? They'd been here all along? *And when I finally find them, Zaylan...does this.*

Grief overpowered my fury and left me cold and sad and paralyzed.

Bennet's face was a mask of shock and pain. He stared at Whisper from a few spans away, his arms outstretched as if he wanted to go to her but realized it was already too late.

I couldn't handle his expression. My heart ached and my hands shook—and I'd only known her for a little over a year. I couldn't imagine what it was doing to Bennet, who'd known her for a decade before she was taken from him, spent many more decades missing her, and then had only so brief a reunion with her before she was cruelly snatched away again.

"Mella!" A muffled cry came from a few rooms over.

"Dane?" I cried, my voice choking on tears. "I'm in here! Zaylan's study!"

Bennet's disbelieving eyes never left Whisper.

"Mella?" Dane's voice was reassuringly close as he hauled the doors apart and burst in.

Catching sight of Whisper, he knelt beside me. "Oh no, Mella. Is she...?"

I nodded, another tear falling to splash on her feathers. "She sacrificed herself to save me."

Dane glanced at Whisper's body, then at Bennet. "We need to get you two out of here before he comes back. Come on."

My legs were stiff. Dane helped me up, wrapping an arm around me. I stumbled to my feet, doing my best to cradle Whisper's body gently and lean on Dane as little as possible so he could help Bennet, too.

Dane paused next to me as if to make sure I was steady and then spoke softly to Bennet before hauling him up, too. "Come on."

With an arm at the small of my back and a hand on Bennet's shoulder, Dane guided us from the sitting room and through Zaylan's study.

I struggled to hold Whisper's body while limping, nearly dropping her once.

Dane stooped and swung me up into his arms, cradling me and Whisper both.

"Dane, your shoulder—"

"It's better now."

"Selverine! Selverine?" someone called from the stairs. A voice I didn't recognize. A moment later, an older lady with greying blonde hair heaved herself onto the balcony and wheezed, "Where are Selverine and Acres?"

Dane paused, scowling at this stranger. "I have no idea—"

Shouting and clanging sounded from the balcony window facing the garden.

Dane glanced toward the window. "Sounds like it's getting messy out there. You should get out while you can."

The old woman panted, holding up a little brown book. "Do you recognize this?"

"Look," Dane spat, "there's a battle happening outside. We've got to move—"

"Have you ever seen Zaylan, the regent, with it? Or someone else?"

Dane shuffled us forward. "I think I have seen Zaylan with it, actually. Why?"

She darted back down the stairs. "I know how to stop him! I may be the only person who can do it!" she shouted. The garden door slammed behind her, sending an echo through the room.

CHAPTER 51

SELVERINE

Furious and terrified that the walls would collapse and take away any chance of getting Horizon back if Zaylan got what he deserved, I fought my way through the hybrid castors to retrieve my trident. Diving out of the way of a strike from the feathered king cobra, I reached the door and yanked the handle.

Mucking locked? Seriously?

I was pretty sure it was this room that the rubble in the library staircase blocked off. Was there a chance I could get in through there? It hadn't looked like something you could dig through quickly, but maybe it was worth a shot.

Turning back, I glimpsed Zaylan dragging Reenalyn roughly toward the manor. He couldn't see Xerrome sprinting up behind him. But Wallen also raced after them.

With a shout, Wallen leaped at Xerrome, tackling him to the ground.

Could I risk my trident to help Reenalyn? I'd at least shoved the empty sacks around it and the others' weapons as I'd followed everyone out a few minutes ago. It wouldn't be enough padding to stop a heavy stone, but smaller debris, maybe. Even so, it had been months. She was probably never coming back to me. And Reenalyn was still alive and needing help to stay that way.

I pelted toward them, pissed at Wallen for fooling me into thinking he was a decent person and then trying to kill me and Willova. I'd help Reenalyn get free, then try the library.

Xerrome bellowed at Wallen, but Wallen pinned Xerrome's arms to the ground. I had no weapons, but I reached them and kicked Wallen squarely in the face. A satisfying crack distracted him long enough for Xerrome to get free and charge after Zaylan and Reenalyn.

"You're a piece of skunk muck," I informed Wallen.

He chuckled, sitting and gingerly feeling his nose. Blood streamed from one nostril. "And you haven't scratched the surface of what a brutal person Queen Narellen can be."

"What?" Caught off guard by his unexpected comment, I wavered before throwing another punch.

He shoved up from the sand and darted after Xerrome.

"What do you mean?" I shouted, racing after them.

"I mean you'd better help me keep Zaylan alive, or it'll be both our heads."

"You tried to kill me!"

"Yeah, because then it would've just been your head."

"What the muck are you talking about?"

Wallen dove for Xerrome again, who dodged him and sped on toward Zaylan.

But as Xerrome leaped at Zaylan brandishing his wavy sword, Zaylan pivoted, dropped Reenalyn, and threw his dagger into Xerrome's shoulder.

Reenalyn screamed, "Xerrome!"

Xerrome fell back as Zaylan laughed. "I thought you said you'd figured it out," Zaylan spat. "Apparently not, or you would've known I can see every threat coming from hundreds of spans away."

An old lady darted through the garden as Zaylan railed at Xerrome. A silver bracelet glinted on her forearm. I squinted. Was it the apothecary?

She hurried toward us, the wind blowing her greying hair around her face.

I took in her facial features and body type for the first time in broad daylight. She looked nothing like me. Shorter and fuller-figured, she also had wispy blonde hair mixed with the grey, and fair skin.

My hopes that we were related evaporated under the desert sun.

Drawing a knife from her belt, she aimed at Zaylan's middle and threw all her weight into the stab.

The knife lodged itself in his side.

Zaylan arched away from her, his eyes bugging.

She yanked the knife out and brandished it, her teeth bared.

Blood poured from the wound, and Zaylan spun and stumbled back, staring at the apothecary in total shock.

How had she managed to do that when no one else could?

"No!" Wallen shouted, catching Zaylan and easing him to the ground.

"How"—Zaylan wheezed—"did you manage to sneak up on me?"

The apothecary approached and stood over Zaylan, clutching the bloody knife. "It all goes back to greatest desires, doesn't it?"

Blinking, Zaylan glared. "How...?"

"I figured you out," the apothecary said, pointing a finger at him. "How you always knew exactly what to say. How your manipulations are so subtle you can successfully coerce anyone into giving you what you want. You're a sixer. And your sixth sense is for greatest desires."

"How were you able to hit him without him sensing you?" Xerrome asked.

"You've never been able to because your greatest desire in that moment was to end him, right?" she asked. "So he always sensed you coming from a mile away. But he couldn't sense *my* intentions because my greatest desire has nothing to do with him. Ending his tyrannical rule was merely a stop on the way."

Wide-eyed astonishment on his face, Zaylan tried to speak, but coughed up blood instead. Blood leaked into the sand. She must've struck a vital organ.

Which meant the room with the castling weapons would crumble soon.

Reenalyn stared in horror, then shot up and raced for the manor.

"It's locked!" I yelled, about to run with her for my trident. Maybe there was enough time to get in through the library still...

"Reenalyn, don't!" Xerrome shouted, pelting after her.

I turned to follow him when a horrible *thunk* drew my attention back to the apothecary. The handle of a knife stuck out from her side.

"No!" I screamed.

Zaylan smiled, his throwing hand dropping to the sand next to Wallen's now-empty knife holster. "I can't fathom," he wheezed, "why speaking to this castlingless descendant of the queen who abandoned your country for another would be your greatest desire. But whatever the reason, you won't get it now."

Castlingless descendant of the queen? That was me.

He fell back against Wallen, his breaths shallow and wet.

Glancing at the apothecary, I found her eyes on mine. Why would speaking to me be her greatest desire?

"Selverine," she said, hunching over the wound. "Would you help me to the garden for some potion ingredients? Seems I'll need to get there rather quickly."

I stepped toward her, offering my arm. "Okay…" But did I have time? The ground shook, and I turned to see the manor trembling as well.

I was too far away, even if I dumped the apothecary to bleed out in the sand and raced back. I'd never make it in time now. I should've run when I had the chance!

She gripped my arm with surprising strength. "Also, you should know, I think I'm your real grandmother. Sort of."

What the muck?

Chapter 52

REENALYN

"Cupid!" I screamed, tearing over the sand toward the room of castling objects. I had to get him out before Zaylan died and the stone walls collapsed and crushed the castlings inside.

"Reenalyn, wait!" Xerrome called from behind me. He shouldn't be running with that wound.

But I couldn't stop. There wasn't time.

I slammed against the door and turned the handle as the ground rumbled.

Only seconds left.

The door wouldn't budge.

"Come on!" I shouted.

Falling debris echoed behind the door.

Zaylan must be dead, or nearly there.

I clawed at the door handle, then stepped back and kicked at it.

I might not make it.

But I had to try.

A huge stone fell from the wall to my side, throwing sand all around.

Just like the enormous boulder used for shattering castling weapons in the coliseum.

"No!"

Something yanked me around the middle.

I fought against it, reaching for the door.

But Xerrome's hands were too strong. They pulled me back from the manor, dragging me over the sand as the walls imploded, burying my Cupid beneath layers of stone.

"No! Cupid!" Shoving to my feet, I whirled on Xerrome. "How could you do that?"

Sweat slid down the side of his face, his chest heaving. "I'm so sorry, Reenalyn. But I barely got you away in time. You would've died, too."

"You can help me dig him out, then!"

"Of course." He started toward the pile of stones with a nod, surprising me.

I marched after him, realizing he could've died, too. If it would've collapsed a moment earlier, it would've killed us both.

Who was this guy to risk his life for me?

Swiping away tears, I knelt in the rubble of the south wing. How would I ever find Cupid's new tiny castling object in all this? Had it been made well enough to withstand a building collapse? My spear had been, but whatever Zaylan had done...I had to hope. It depended on how the wreckage landed. There was a chance.

With a shudder, I scooted a little farther and shuffled through more wood and stone.

Xerrome knelt a few spans away, lifted a broken door that must've weighed as much as Mauler, and hauled it several spans out of the way. Then he returned and started sorting through the debris underneath.

Xerrome pulled something from under a piece of wood and brushed it off. My heart leaped thinking it might be Cupid, and then sank back to my toes when I realized it wasn't. It was a silver longsword, and it was in one piece.

Holding the sword out in both hands, Xerrome got to his feet. "This is Marken's. I'll be right back."

"Okay."

My gaze fell to the place he'd been kneeling as something caught the light. Several silvery glimmers. Crawling over to it, I squinted against the shine. Gently, I pulled it from the pile and held my breath.

It was the harpika. Inlaid with Cupid's spear point.

Tears welled—tears of relief. I wasn't sure I'd ever see him again, but here he was, different, but in one piece.

CHAPTER 53

MELLA

Reenalyn knelt in the rubble, something small clutched to her chest.

Oh, no. Had Cupid's new instrument been shattered?

"Reenalyn!" I called across the rubble. I couldn't navigate the mess on the crutches.

She looked up, meeting my gaze, and got to her feet.

"Reenalyn, are you okay?" I asked as she got closer, relieved to see her in one piece.

She climbed over the broken stone and debris and reached me, throwing an arm out to hug me. "I'm in one piece, and so is the harpika. What happened to you? Are you okay?" She eyed the blood covering my front.

"No. But I'll tell you in a minute. Have you tried casting Cupid again?"

"Not yet. I just found him, and I'm afraid to try after it didn't work before."

"I think I know how to fix that."

Her eyes widened. "You do?"

"I think that when the castling object changes, something else has to change with it. Either a new castor, or a new castling call."

Understanding lit her eyes. "That's how you cast Whisper, and how Zaylan made the hybrid castors cast their hybrids."

I nodded. "And it hasn't worked for you because you're the same castor using the same castling call. I think what you need is a new call."

She held the harpika out in front of her, her eyebrows drawing together as she chose the words.

"Return now, my Cupid,
The old and the new,
Whoever you are now,
No matter what's changed in you."

The same emerald-green shimmery powder that had always flowed from her spear tip before poured from the harpika. A sprinkle of crimson spiraled into the mix on an invisible wind.

Slowly, a smaller, brighter avian-winged body with Cupid's face and tail appeared before me.

The same long green scaly tail curled out from behind like before, but scarlet and emerald feather tufts sprouted all over. They matched the feather pattern covering his avian body, and the huge wings folded on either side.

Finally, his eyelids parted, and Reenalyn waited for his reaction.

He turned his bright green head to face her, considering her for several seconds as she held her breath.

"Reenalyn?" he croaked.

"Yes!" She smiled through tears. His voice was the same. "It's me. Cupid, just breathe, okay? Some stuff happened, and you look a little different than you used to, but it's going to be okay. What do you remember?"

She glanced at me, beaming joy and relief. I smiled and nodded, swiping away bittersweet tears. Dane wrapped an arm around my waist.

Cupid blinked slowly, taking in the destruction around us. "I feel strange."

Reenalyn reached out and stroked his head spikes. "That's understandable," she whispered.

"What happened?" he wheezed.

"Do you remember how you said in Terrenthyrs that you'd kill anyone who tried to change me? And how I said I'd do the same for you?"

"Mm-hmm." His eyebrow ridges angled in confusion.

"Well, I guess I have someone to kill now. Or at least I *did*, but someone else already took care of it."

"Zaylan's dead?" I asked.

Reenalyn nodded. "Finally. That's why part of the manor imploded—I'll explain in a minute."

Cupid looked himself over. His eyebrow ridges rose as his eyes roved over his altered body down to his feather-tipped tail.

"How did *this* happen?"

"I was an idiot about Zaylan. He used me, made me think I needed to change. Then used us for an experiment and forced horrible changes on you. He was a sixer, like me. But he could sense people's greatest desires. So he sensed how much I wanted to be loved, and took advantage of that to get information from me, and wound up hurting you, too. I'm so sorry."

Cupid rested a consoling feathery foot on Reenalyn's leg, just like he used to do with his scaly one.

"It's amazing that the harpika wasn't harmed in the collapse," I said.

"Harpika!" Cupid exclaimed. "That skunk deliberately used your least favorite instrument?"

Reenalyn nodded. "He did. But since you're okay, it's on its way to becoming my new favorite."

The intact strings reminded me of the now-broken one on my mandolin.

I was not okay, but I needed to say something to Reenalyn before telling her about that. Something I feared I'd never get to say when I'd seen the blood on the stairwell ceiling.

"Reenalyn, I'm so sorry for being jealous of you and your castling and for being a total skunk. I shouldn't have treated you like that."

She met my gaze. "I'm sorry too, Mella. I was jealous and resentful and giving in to that didn't do any good. I won't be that way anymore."

"Me either. Our friendship is more important than any of that."

She nodded with a smile. "Yes, it is."

I swallowed. "But I've got to tell you some bad news."

Her smile faded. "What?"

"We found Bennet and Whisper, but Whisper is...she's dead."

Reenalyn clutched Cupid to her with one hand as the other flew to her mouth, and tears pooled in her eyes. "Oh no. Mella, I'm so sorry." She reached out and touched my arm.

"I should've done a better job of protecting her." I looked for a place to sit, heavy with guilt as I finally put it into words. "He had them in the manor the whole time, questioning and threatening them. All the *help* he offered was just to waste our time."

Dane took one of the crutches and held my hand, helping me to the ground. Taking the other, he laid them both at my feet and sat next to me.

"Did you say Whisper and Bennet have been here the whole time?" Beldon joined us, followed by Kaido. Trinka spotted us gathering and walked over, both sets of spiked knuckles in place again.

"Yes. Zaylan had them in his study."

Kaido crossed his arms. "Why?"

I swiped another tear away. "Because he's the one behind the hybrid experiments, not Marken, and he wanted to find out why Whisper turned out better than all of his experiments."

Beldon eyed the rubble. "Did he?"

"He killed Whisper and threatened to kill Bennet if I couldn't tell him why. I guessed it could be because she had two different castling calls—the one Bennet gave her and the one I gave her later—while he always used the same one twice."

My voice stuck in my throat on the last words. I stared at the sand, unable to meet their eyes.

Dane squeezed my hand, the others silent.

"How's Bennet?" Beldon asked.

I shoved a tear away. "Not good. He's inside."

Dane put an arm around me. "Mella's not doing so good either, so how about we give her space?"

His words were a relief. The exhaustion and strain I'd been fighting finally washed over me, and I knew time alone or alone with Dane would help me process what had happened. I needed to cry, and I didn't want an audience.

Everyone nodded, and a few patted my shoulder, giving condolences. Then Dane helped me up and led me slowly toward the manor. Bits of debris littered the sand. I knew I should help dig for castling weapons—I would after I had a few minutes to grieve.

We entered the manor, and there sat Bennet on the stairs, right where we'd left him, still cradling Whisper and sobbing over her, the mandolin at his side. My gaze caught on the broken string. The one I'd replaced with Bennet's bowstring over a year ago. The one that had started all of this.

The bowstring—

Holy muck.

The one on the mandolin wasn't the only one.

I had more back in Wrynford.

Maybe, if we could replace the broken string with a new strand...

What if it could bring her back?

I had to try. For Bennet.

Sitting on his other side, I handed Dane a crutch and wrapped my arm around Bennet.

I shouldn't get his hopes up just yet.

But hope beat in my chest like an avian testing new wings.

CHAPTER 54

SELVERINE

"I'm sorry—what did you say?" I asked the apothecary as she stumbled beside me, struggling over the sand toward the garden. She gripped my arm in one hand and steadied Zaylan's knife with the other, leaving it in to slow the bleeding.

How was she able to walk at all in that condition?

"I believe you are actually *my* granddaughter, not the granddaughter of the person you know as Narellen," she said, taking a deep breath.

"What makes you think that?"

She pressed her hand to the wound. "This will sound impossible, but please hear me out."

I glanced back at the ruins of the manor. I needed to find my trident. Find out whether I'd lost any chance at all of getting Horizon back. But I had to hear her out. "Okay. I'll listen."

She closed her eyes, took a deep breath, and focused on me. "Several decades ago, *I* was the real Princess Narellen."

My eyes flicked to hers. "So what, this fake kidnapped me? Or my father as a child?"

"In a manner of speaking, you could say so, yes."

I waited for her explanation with a raised eyebrow, bearing more of her weight as we neared the garden.

She took another deep breath. "The person you know as Narellen was my lady's maid when I was about the age you are now. She and I were friends, at least I thought. But then she did something to me."

The apothecary trailed off, and I impatiently brought her back to the point. "Did what?"

"Are you aware of a certain type of magic called...soul shifting?"

I frowned. "No. What is it?"

"It's not a well-known thing—thank good fortune. Or more people might be transposed like I was. All that time Luma had spent asking me questions about myself...she hadn't been getting to know me because she wanted to be friends. She'd been learning how to impersonate me. So she stole my body and took over my throne."

"She...stole your body?"

The apothecary nodded. "Yes. I don't know how she did it. If it was a potion, I've never come across it, though I've certainly tried. I woke up in her body one day and found her living in mine."

My skin crawled. I didn't want such a thing to be real, but the memory Acres found...this explanation was the only one that fit with it being from the point of view of the princess. "Didn't you try to reclaim it?"

Blissful relief from the sweltering sun covered us as we stepped into the shadows of the foliage. There was a bench somewhere around here...

The apothecary nodded. "Of course. But no one believed me when I was in Luma's body speaking with her voice. The one time I managed to get my father's attention with something only the princess could've known, Luma put on an outstanding performance and convinced him her maid had been eavesdropping, which got me removed from the manor."

We reached a stone bench, and I eased her down to it.

She winced, leaning on the trellis next to her. "Quick, Selverine, would you please pick some of those weeds by the fountain? And one of those purple flowers growing around the thorns? It will look like a green bud this time of day."

Nodding, I hurried to get what she needed while she tore off a piece of vine from the trellis and sliced it open with a fingernail.

Her story sounded pretty unbelievable. But that memory...

I brought the leaves and buds to the bench. The apothecary placed a few of the petals on her tongue, then laid the rest and the weeds over the two halves of the vine on the bench and shoved her palm into them, smooshing them together.

"Luma had grown up in a family of floramancers, so without any money or any relatives who would believe me, I went to her home. Her relatives quickly grew impatient with me, as I hadn't taken the trouble to learn as much about Luma and seemed to have forgotten everything they'd painstakingly taught her. Finally, I took what I'd learned and relocated to another part of the city to use it for good, like healing, rather than selling poisons or false feelings of pleasure. I found satisfaction in healing people, so that became my life."

"And then you had a kid that Narellen—Luma—kidnapped?"

The apothecary sighed, swiping a tear from her cheek. "Sort of. When Luma stole my body, I was already pregnant. I didn't know it yet, but when I caught glimpses of Luma a few months after and how much she was showing, I put it together with the dizziness and nausea I'd experienced in the weeks before."

I barely kept my jaw from dropping. "Skunking muck! She stole your *pregnant* body?"

"Yes." The apothecary nodded gravely. "She stole things from me I didn't even know I had until after I'd lost them."

She scraped up the mush, pulled out the knife, and pressed the mixture over the wound with a hiss.

"Who was the father?"

The apothecary smiled for the first time since I'd known her. "Your grandfather was a wonderful man. I loved him more than anything, and he loved me. he commissioned this garden for me, too. It was my favorite place my last few months in the manor." She laid a hand lovingly over the trellis and smiled sadly.

"How do you commission a garden?"

Shaking her head, she met my eyes. "I still don't know. But he managed it somehow."

She sighed, her smile fading. "We were engaged—he would've been a wonderful father. It grieved me to see the pain in his eyes when Luma rejected him, and he thought it was me. I tried speaking to him on more than one occasion, but the one time I reached him he didn't believe me.

It broke my heart, especially for our son. I tried to kidnap the baby once, but I was captured and imprisoned until after Luma fled the country. Your father—only a few months old at the time—got injured when they caught me with him and took him away. So for his sake, I chose not to try again."

My mind reeled. Could all this be true?

She peered at the mush over the wound, which had apparently stopped the bleeding. "I know it must be a lot to take in. But for what it's worth, I would like to know you. If you would care to let me."

I crossed my arms. "I have a question."

Her eyebrows rose. "Of course."

"Why use the name Narellen Merrandil? Wouldn't people think it was strange for you to be calling yourself the queen's name?"

"At first I used her name, Luma, but after her family rejected me and time passed, I had no reason to continue using hers. I wanted to use my real name again, to own some part of my original self, but it would've been odd, like you say. After Zaylan's family took power, most people were conscripted into the Avian Army, and a few more decades went by, hardly anyone was left who remembered we once had a princess called Narellen. So I took the name back."

She breathed deeply, then chuckled with her eyes closed. "I certainly didn't expect a few teenagers to recognize the name."

Her eyes flashed open. "Where's Acres? Is he okay?"

I automatically glanced back toward the collapsed wing. I thought I saw him kneeling near it, probably digging for his stars. I narrowed my eyes. "Why are you so concerned with Acres? I thought you were pissed at him."

She eyed me. "I made a promise to him I intend to keep. But I need more time."

Cryptic much? Why was she promising Acres things?

"Why don't you go check on him? I just need to give this a few more minutes. It normally works faster than this. Must've done more damage hobbling over here."

Seizing the chance to check on Acres and look for my trident, I nodded. "Okay. I'll be right back."

Chapter 55

REENALYN

I strode back to the rubble where I'd found Cupid to look for other castling weapons, my heart heavy for Whisper, and still full of questions for a certain rhino castor who was supposed to meet me back there.

Watching Dane help Mella inside had reminded me... "Cupid!"

His eyes flicked up to me full of curiosity.

"You'll never believe this—"

"Reenalyn! You found him!" Xerrome jogged back to me—to *us*—beaming like he was as relieved as I was.

The red stain on his shoulder caught my attention as he approached. "Your shoulder! Are you okay?"

Standing before me, he glanced down at it. "It's not deep. It'll heal. More importantly, Cupid's safe."

"Yes—thanks to you, actually," I told him. "You knocked something loose with your boot when you stood, and his harpika was under it."

Xerrome smiled warmly. "I'm glad I was able to help."

I'd never noticed how striking his smile was—had I ever seen him smile? Just the time he'd walked out of the house in the desert and not known I was right outside.

"Reenalyn?"

"Oh, yes?"

"Um, what are you staring at?" He chuckled.

Definitely the first time I'd heard him laugh. It touched something inside me in a way I'd never felt before.

My face heated as I realized I'd been staring at him. "Sorry, it's just..." But how could I explain without sounding insane?

"Just what?"

I struggled for the right words, then decided that was ridiculous. No more fluttering around making guesses and daydreaming when I could just get it all straight with a conversation.

I took a deep breath, and said, "You know how Zaylan was a sixer?"

Xerrome's eyebrows drew together. "Uh, yes. I'd suspected it for a while, and I heard the apothecary's explanation."

"Right. Well, I'm a sixer, too."

His eyebrows rose, and I winced.

"But I can't sense anyone's greatest desire. I sense...erm...*feelings*, I guess." I was totally messing this up. How'd I explain it to Mella?

"Oh." Was his face heating too?

"So the thing is, I'm sensing you have...*feelings*. For me. If I'm not mistaken..."

Glancing away sheepishly, he chuckled. "Well, yeah. You're not mistaken. You caught me."

My heart fluttered. "Oh." For some reason, I didn't expect him to admit it so easily. Could I trust him? It still didn't make sense that he'd felt it so early on...

"Well, thank you. But, um, *my* feelings are a little...confused? We've barely spoken. I've only ever seen you scowl at me and my friends until today. So I guess what I'm asking is, why? You don't know me, but you seem to care about me as if you knew me much more." Like, *a lot* more. "Does that make any sense?"

Chuckling again, he ran a hand through his dark hair, his eyes on the rubble. "I see what you're saying. Remember when I found you and your friends in the tavern before you all came to the manor?"

What did that have to do with anything? "Yes, I remember..."

"And Marken dropped the key like a bloody idiot?"

I nodded.

"Right, well, he's my best friend. Since childhood. So he's a pretty important guy to me, and if Wallen or the castor with the feathered fox would've seen the key, I would've had to let them take it and ask some uncomfortable questions, or blow my cover and risk my sister's safety and the lives of everyone working against Zaylan. You somehow made the key disappear and returned it to Marken without any of the other guards catching on. Which was pure genius, and I still haven't figured out how you did it."

"Oh. Trissa—she's your sister?"

He nodded.

"And why was the key so important?"

He nodded. "I'd sent him to a blacksmith to have it repaired. It's an old key, and the only spare Zaylan didn't know about that could open the old reading room—where he stored the castling objects. The plan was to get them all out before killing him so no more castlings would be at risk. Which we were supposed to do that day, until you all showed up." He clenched his fists. "We got a lot of them out, but not all of them. We're going to find some shattered ones in all this."

"The empty shelves—you'd already gotten those castling objects to safety? In the house further out in the desert?"

He nodded. "Gomund, Erisole, Famita, and I have been sneaking them out a little at a time since the key breaking ruined our original plan."

I frowned. "Why'd Marken risk going into the tavern with something so important? When people were waiting for him?"

"Zaylan had sensed the threat and sent several of us out as a precaution. He wasn't sure who he could trust. Marken let himself get seen by Wallen, one of the guards loyal to Zaylan, and tried to hide in the tavern. Which obviously went wrong."

Sighing, he met my eyes. "If Zaylan had gotten the key, he would've known someone knew about the spell. He might've caught us moving the weapons and instruments to another location. It would've ruined any chance we had of saving the Avian Army. What you did—you saved a lot of people. People I care about. And my castling. And you did it without anyone realizing it. You were being kind—which seems to be something you do often."

I met his gaze. "So...you care about me because I helped your friend, which unknowingly also saved some other people?"

He nodded. "That's how it started. Since then, you've surprised me again and again by being such a kind person. Especially finding my sister in the desert and comforting her. It's something I appreciate about you. I mean, not to mention..."

He trailed off, making a face like I was supposed to get what he was saying. But I didn't.

"Not to mention what?"

He gestured to all of me, heaving a huge sigh. "You're just...gorgeous. Of course I'm attracted to you. Especially how you did your hair last night. The truth is, I wished you had done all that work for me, rather than Zaylan."

"You *liked* my hair?" I asked, stunned.

He grinned. "It was incredible. How many hours did it take you to do the braids and twists? It was a masterpiece."

He couldn't be real. There was no way.

"But...I'm already taller than you, and that made me even taller. Didn't it bother you?"

"Ah. Well, the height difference isn't exactly ideal. We'd probably get a few looks. But!" He held up one finger. "I *am* taller than you if I'm sitting on Rumble. So there's that. And being short isn't the same as being weak, you know. I did carry you down a flight of stairs and through a long tunnel earlier without breaking a sweat."

"So hang on. You're worried *I* have a problem with *your* height?" I asked.

He raised a dark eyebrow. "Isn't that what you just said?"

"No." I laughed. "It's not."

"Oh." His brows drew together. "Then what exactly are we talking about?"

"You...I..." I laughed, speechless and unable to believe what I was hearing. This guy thought my height made me *more* attractive and feared I'd reject *him* because he was shorter?

"All right." He took a deep breath, his face so open and warm, if a bit hesitant. "I'm baring my soul here. I don't expect you to feel the same way about a lowly manor guard you've only known as someone who scowls all the time. But would you mind explaining what you meant when you said your feelings are confused?"

"It means..." What did it mean?

Part of me was already falling for him. He'd liked my hair! But as in love as I was with the idea of being in love, I couldn't trust feelings I'd only had for a day. That hadn't worked well last time. I'd need more time to be sure.

But I *did* have a good feeling about this.

"It means I like what I know about you so far, and I want to learn more. And find out if my curiosity will grow into something more."

"Really?" His eyebrows shot up like he was actually surprised. "Wow. Yeah. I'm in. How do we do that?"

"I guess we need to spend time together. Find out if we feel the same way the more we learn about each other."

He grinned. "I like the sound of that."

"It's a date, then." I beamed, my heart full of relief for Cupid and hope for Xerrome.

"Do you think..." he trailed off, glancing away with a shy smile.

"What?"

"Don't worry about it if it's too much trouble, but it would be cool if you did your hair like you did last night." He met my gaze sheepishly, like he was asking a lot.

I beamed. "Exactly like I did it last night? Braids and twists and extra height and all?"

"Exactly like that. I wouldn't change a thing."

CHAPTER 56

ACRES

Flinging stones and wood scraps out of my way, I dug through the rubble for my throwing stars. One had been inside, and the other was still lodged in the kangaroo castling's skull, as far as I knew. I'd been forced into hand-to-hand combat after that—thank good fortune for Beldon, Trinka, and Mauler. And then the whole wing had crashed down over where the kangaroo had fallen.

Metal gleamed, and I shoved debris away.

But it wasn't mine.

It was something longer. Clearing away the rubble, I uncovered it. A trident. Selverine's castling weapon. Relief washed over me. There were a few scratches, but no real damage.

Thank good fortune hers was safe.

I pulled it out and laid it to the side where it wouldn't get lost under the wreckage I'd have to dig out to get to Starstinger.

After uncovering a sword, a harmonica, and a few other weapons and instruments, another gleam caught my eye. Carefully retrieving the throwing star, I blew off the dust and admired it.

It was safe and whole.

I could finally breathe.

Even if I never found the other, I'd still be able to cast Starstinger from this one. And odds were good if I'd managed to find this one loose on its own, I'd find the other one stuck in the kangaroo. I opened my mouth to say my castling call, and my gaze fell on Selverine striding toward me over the sand.

It would be inconsiderate to return her trident with my castling by my side while she still couldn't get hers to emerge.

Standing, I slid my throwing star into its pouch and brushed sand off my pants, then grasped Selverine's trident. I picked my way over the rubble to meet her.

Her eyes met mine as I neared, and my face heated from more than the midday sun. When hers lit up and she actually smiled, I stopped in my tracks.

She really was a mucking desert goddess.

Jogging now, she raced toward me. Or rather, toward her weapon in my hand.

She'd never run like that just to get to me.

"Acres! You found it!" She stopped in front of me, her boots throwing some sand onto mine. "Wow. Thank you."

Reaching for it, she accidentally brushed my hand with her fingers as she took it from me.

"You're welcome." I watched her eyes sparkle as she examined the trident for damage.

"I was so afraid it would break under the debris, since it's so long and thin," she said.

"Fortunately not. You forged it well."

Her eyes met mine. Shifting the trident to one hand, she stepped toward me. And then her other arm wrapped around me, and her cheek brushed mine as she...hugged me?

"Thank you, Acres." A moment later she stepped back, her eyes on mine.

What was she thinking? Why look at me for so long? *Should I say something?*

"Did you find Starstinger?" she asked.

"Yes, I did." Pulling my throwing star from my pocket, I held it up. "Only one star so far, but yes."

"Right. You cast from two weapons. How'd you manage that?"

"Well, I—"

"Acres!" Erisole cut me off, running over and kicking up sand in her wake.

Selverine glared at her. Very darkly. Why? I'd never seen them talk before.

"I'm so glad you're okay," Erisole continued. "And you found your weapon. Good! Listen, who finally pulled off killing Zaylan?"

Selverine held her trident in both hands. "The apothecary, actually."

Erisole wasn't listening. She gazed at the distant desertscape beyond the battlefield. What was she looking for? "They'll be free at last," she said.

I frowned. "Who will be free?"

"The rest of the Avian Army. Zaylan's kept them away for years. My father's in there. I can finally speak to him again."

I grinned. "Erisole, that's wonderful! Where are they?"

"In an abandoned building way out there." She pointed to the wilderness. "Xerrome and I have been trying to take Zaylan out for ages, but he always sees the threat coming from a mile away."

"That's because he's a sixer who can sense peoples' greatest desires." Selverine inspected her nails like it was no big deal.

"What?" Erisole's jaw dropped. "I wondered! But how did you know?"

"The apothecary said so after she killed him."

"Really? Wow. How'd she get around it, then?"

Selverine met her eyes for the first time, then looked away. "She had a different greatest desire. So since killing him wasn't it, he didn't hear her coming."

"Brilliant! I wonder what her greatest desire is?"

Selverine shrugged. "I guess you'll have to ask her yourself."

Someone called Erisole from the other side of the rubble.

"Better go see what she needs. Glad you're both okay." And she jogged away, Selverine glaring after her as if she'd said something rude.

"Acres...the apothecary told me some pretty crazy stuff." Selverine's eyes met mine again. "I'll tell you about it later. But first, if you only had one dose of the perception potion left, why'd you use it on the apothecary? Why not on Zaylan or one of the guards?" Selverine whispered, her scowl replaced with an unusually open expression.

"Because..." Could I tell her the truth? "Because I wanted you to know the truth about your family. I don't know whether it will bring you relief or disappointment or how difficult it will be to handle. But if you want to know the truth, then you should be able to."

She regarded me in silence, her eyes flicking between mine as the wind brushed her hair to one side and the sun brought out the gold sparkles in her eyes. "Why do you care?"

"I care because," I cleared my throat, "I know how it feels to have questions about your family. How frustrating missing details are. And I know not knowing is worse than knowing the worst, because then at least you can accept it and choose to move on." *I also care about you, but I'm not brave enough to admit that.*

She nodded. "Thank you, Acres. For giving me the choice. I appreciate it more than you know."

With a nod, she walked away.

Leaving me with a racing pulse, a spinning head, and a disturbing realization. I had absolutely fallen in every way for Selverine Merrandil.

CHAPTER 57

SELVERINE

Jealous of Erisole now, too? Just great.

The dust from the south wing was literally still settling all around us, and I was over here fretting about a stupid crush that would surely fade any time now.

Please.

Erisole could have him. He'd already said he wasn't interested in me. So what?

I had bigger problems.

Like actually being royalty. Finding out that Queen Narellen was actually a queen by blood and not just marriage to Jorros had been one thing. But finding out that someone—who was actually a decent person, as far as I could tell—was the reason added a different weight to it. It was easy to shirk any responsibility imposed by Queen Narellen. But the apothecary...something about that was different.

At least I had a few years to figure it out. With Narellen in prison and Zaylan dead, the apothecary could take back the throne. Get the Avian Army and the hybrid castors back to their families and homes.

I considered the apothecary's words about wanting to know me. I decided I would like to learn more about this history and the apothecary. So long as I didn't have to rule anything.

My boots clapped over the stone path as I entered the garden, stomping Acres and his stupid face from my mind.

I stopped short.

The apothecary was still. Too still.

She slumped against the trellis, her hand fallen from her wound. Her face pointed toward the south wing. Like she'd been watching for me.

But she was gone.

And all my answers with her.

My chance at respecting and liking someone in my family.

Gone.

Tears rolled down my cheeks as I stared. What was I supposed to do? Tell someone?

Acres.

No, not Acres! He's busy. But I've got to tell someone. She'll need to be buried...

A pattern stood out on the bench. Something I hadn't noticed before.

I peered at it, stepping closer.

Lines scraped away from the remains of the mushed-up potion she'd made using the bench and her hand as a makeshift mortar and pestle.

Letters? A message?

I couldn't make it out.

But Willova could read anything.

I turned back toward the south wing to call for her, my glance lingering on the wound. The skin had gone a sickly purple color under the blood, and the veins stood out even darker.

Poison? Had Wallen been carrying a poisoned blade?

And the apothecary hadn't realized. She stopped the bleeding, but not the poison.

Ugh. Muck Wallen!

Stepping to the edge of the garden, I searched the crowd of heads bent over rubble and arms digging through it for Willova's red hair.

Acres's loc bun caught my attention first. I rolled my eyes and shoved him from my mind.

Except...the apothecary had promised to help him with something, and she'd been worried enough about him that she wanted me to check on him.

But however much time she'd needed to help him...she didn't have any now.

Was that what she left a note about?

"Willova!" I shouted, my voice shaking. "Willova, where are you? I need your help *now*!"

ACKNOWLEDGEMENTS

First of all, I thank God for the joy He gives me through writing, and for the many wonderful people He's blessed my life and writing career with.

I couldn't have started writing in the first place if not for my wonderful mom, Jenny Glass, who persevered through teaching me how to read and write despite many vehement protests, and for my grandmothers, Brenda Glass and Ollie Jo Tompson, who passed their ambition, sticktoitiveness, and work ethic on to me. I'm so blessed to have such amazing women in my family!

I couldn't have written consistently over the last nine years if not for my amazing writer friends from Dream Big Writers, Writers Business Mastermind, Snack Pack, Scribblers, NaNoWriMo, and Instagram, especially Kristin Ardis, Teresa Beasley, Holly Davis, Renee Dugan, Alicia Grumley, Michele Harper, Cam Steiman, Annie Sullivan, and Brittany Wang. I deeply treasure your manuscript critique, constant encouragement, and mutual delight in the craft of writing, and I couldn't imagine my life without you!

I couldn't have published another book so quickly after the last if not for my incredibly supportive husband, Ben; mother-in-law, Missy; and grandmother-in-law, Grandma Smith; who have given me the gift of time to write and helped make the story spotless. There's nothing like having a conversation with real people about the people you made up!

I wouldn't have managed to promote the series without my amazing ARC and Cover Reveal teams! I can't begin to thank you all enough for your help promoting *Whisper of Weapons* and laying the foundation for *House of Hybrids* to enter the world! To Adela Bec, Adreanna King, Alex,

@alexbetweenpages, Ally Lopez, Amanda, Anais, Anny Peters, Antonia C., Asmae, The Bookaholic Writer, Brittany Ford, Claudia Mirea, Deidra, Delia Balas, Elma, Georgie, Hannah, Hannah Delano, Holly Davis, Jacques de Villiers, Jaylin, Joana Almeida, Kat, Katie Prokop, Kriti, Leslie Kmetz, Lindsey Adams, Lori, Madeeha, Mandi Oyster, MariahsCosyCorner, Melanie, Mitra, Nisa, Nivi, Olivia Renner, @opened_books, @over.on.my.bookshelf, Paige Lobianco, @patienceandpagesRifah, Sabie, Samantha Parisi, Sarah Foil, Shayla Morgansen, Sharon, Sheriece, @spiritedbookishbabe, Stephanie Meredith, and Vânia—thank you so much for posting on Cover Reveal Day, squealing about the characters with me behind the scenes, and leaving reviews! I appreciate you so much and am so honored to have you on my team!

And to my lovely fellow authors, Annie Sullivan, Cassidy Clarke, Chelsea Bobulski, Holly Davis, J.M. Hackman, Julia Simpson, Kim Chance, Renee Dugan, and Shayla Morgansen, who read an early copy and wrote an amazing endorsement blurb for one or both books, thank you for your time and your beautiful words!

SAVANNAH J. GOINS is the author of multiple sweet, swoony, and spice-free YA romantic fantasy novels. While working at an exotic animal clinic, she came in contact with both tiger and dragon blood more than once. Whether she has magical abilities as a result is yet to be determined. When not writing, she hangs out with her family, draws zentangles, and helps homeless dragons find forever homes in the real world by volunteering with an exotic animal rescue.